Boundless Ambition

Tim Tigner

This novel is dedicated to the memory of Dr. Edwin Joules Delattre. A man who made a crucial difference to me and my family. A teacher, mentor, friend and force I will never forget. Bless you, Ed.

ISBN: 9781653947478

For more information on this novel or Tim Tigner's other thrillers, please visit timtigner.com

People can be absolutely, astonishingly amazing—some for their capabilities, others for their character. If an action, event or behavior in this novel strikes you as unrealistic, kindly do a quick Google search or consider the author's biography.

Please note: You'll find links to the events that inspired this story, and to other research, at the end of the novel.

ACKNOWLEDGMENTS

Writing novels full of twists and turns is relatively easy. Doing so logically and coherently while maintaining a rapid pace is much tougher. Surprising readers without confusing them is the real art.

I draw on generous fans for guidance in achieving those goals, and for assistance in fighting my natural inclination toward typos. These are my friends, and I'm grateful to them all.

Editors: Suzanne S. Barnhill, Andrea Kerr, Judy Marksteiner and Peter Mathon.

Technical Consultant: Author and commercial pilot Ward Larson. Private pilot Michael Leibowitz.

Beta Readers: Errol Adler, Martin Baggs, Dave Berkowitz, Edward Bettigole, Doug Branscombe, Kay Brooks, Anna Bruns, Diane Bryant, Pat Carella, John Chaplin, Dianne Chiappari, Lars de Kock, Robert Enzenauer, Hugo Ernst, Rae Fellenberg, Geof Ferrell, Mike Galvin, Rob Gunn, Emily Hagman, Cliff Jordan, Robert Lawrence, Michael Leibowitz, Kerry Lohrman, Margaret Lovett, Debbie Malina, Michael Martin, Joe McKinely, Michael Picco, Lee Proost, Robert Rubinstayn, Chris Seelbach, Gwen Tigner, Robert Tigner, Steve Tigner, Wendy Trommer, Elizabeth Utley, Alan Vickery, Sandy Wallace, and Mike Wunderli.

Prologue

THE HELICOPTER ROTORS beat the humid air like the wings of angry dragons as Lucille Ferro descended toward the hunting lodge. Or perhaps that was just her imagination. The freshly minted CEO projecting her frustrated mood.

Luci had been battling for status her entire career, and was sick of the subtle slights and standard assumptions. While every sister knew her struggle to some extent, Luci had been hit particularly hard. The industry sectors she'd selected and ascended were bastions of brotherhood. The military. The airline industry. And now energy. Yet even as chief executive of the biggest blue-chip in the baddest industry, she still got snubbed by the boys.

The revenues generated by KAKO Energy dwarfed those of the other two Texas companies in the cozy little alliance they called the C3. But rather than wave her ace, Luci had gracefully agreed to accommodate the group's established rules. Tradition was important, deep in the heart of Texas—but that wasn't what drove her decision.

Luci had pulled on jeans and boots, and agreed to fly up from Houston for a weekend on their turf because she wouldn't allow ego to interfere with her agenda. Not given the stakes, or the audacity of the proposal she'd be putting forward. Her plan would make them all unbelievably rich—if they screwed their courage to the sticking place.

Three men in cowboy hats watched her approach from the edge of the helipad. Two CEOs, easily discernible by their pompous stature despite the twilight hour, and a lone ranch hand who ran forward while the rotors were still spinning. Hat in hand, he opened her door and held it politely as she disembarked.

Once Luci had both feet on the ground, the young man extracted her roller bag from the luggage compartment. Then, to her surprise, he extended the handle and leaned it in her direction while bowing his head. A handoff gesture.

Apparently, he wasn't planning to carry it.

Luci accepted her bag without comment.

The ranch hand proceeded to shock her a second time by climbing into the seat she'd just vacated and shutting the helicopter door.

Perplexed but unperturbed, Luci wheeled her bag toward the C3's other two members without a backward glance. No sooner had she cleared the rotor area than the engine accelerated and the helicopter began to ascend.

"Welcome to Lonestar Lodge. Pardon the unconventional greeting," the host and senior member of the trio said, touching the brim of his hat before extending his hand. "I find these meetings work best when there's nobody else around."

The handshake revealed rough skin. That shouldn't have surprised her, but it did. William Zacharia Bubb, founding CEO of Steel Shield, was a former UT Longhorn quarterback turned Marine, turned defense contractor. His appearance reflected that rugged history. Big and broad, with a face well-suited for delivering both steely stares and *Aw, shucks, ma'am*—as evidenced in the video clips she'd studied.

"Nobody else?" she asked, glancing around.

"It will just be the three of us this weekend. Hank was the last of the help to leave. Trust me, by the time Sunday morning rolls around, you'll be a convert. After a week in a big-city boardroom, there's no work setting more refreshing." He turned and gestured toward the roof that was visible up the flagstone path.

"I'm sure you're right. Thank you for the invitation, William Zacharia."

Despite the remote setting and their informal dress, Luci knew from her research to address her host only with his full first and middle names—or the initials WZ. She understood what motivated the apparent eccentricity. She related to it. The obvious Billy Bubb contraction would cripple a climb up the corporate ladder. A less-than-respectful nickname could hold a person back in business almost as much as having female genitalia.

"I believe you already know Benjamin Lial, CEO of Grausam Favlos," William Zacharia continued, gesturing to his left.

"I do indeed," Luci said, accepting the hand of the construction magnate from Fort Worth who always reminded her of Dustin Hoffman. "We met when I was president of Apex Aviation and you were bidding to build Istanbul's new mega airport. Good to see you again, Ben."

"Likewise."

William Zacharia grabbed the handle of Luci's bag while she shook hands with Ben. "I suggest we push the property tour to morning. This time of year, the rattlers get rambunctious at night."

C C C

Benjamin Lial studied the new arrival as William Zacharia poured three glasses of Blue Label Ghost whisky. Luci fit the requisite image of an inspiring CEO—to the extent that any woman ever could. Tall and athletic, with hypnotic blue eyes and a cultured deep voice, she came across as both fresh and familiar. Part mother, part father, all business.

Ben had been less surprised than most when KAKO Energy brought in Lucille Ferro to become its new CEO two months earlier. He'd worked with her a few years back, or rather in parallel, when they were both jockeying for favorable slices of the pie on a major overseas project.

Observing Luci in action, whether behind the scenes or on center stage, was like watching Simone Biles on the balance beam. She had the strategic mind and tactical instincts required to succeed in industries that required short-term shrewd maneuvers and long-term gutsy gambles—industries like defense, construction and energy. Industries well-positioned to help one another. In short, he considered her an ideal addition to their little club.

William Zacharia raised his crystal tumbler as they sank into the soft leather seats he had arranged around his indoor campfire. A custom fire pit that he claimed to have designed with the C3 meetings in mind.

Ben knew there was a large evacuation vent and fire-suppression system some eighteen feet above them, but he couldn't see it in the flickering light. In fact, little was visible in the cavernous room besides the fire itself and the three figures surrounding it. No doubt that was exactly what the architect had planned.

"To our shared success," the host said.

"To our shared success," Ben and Luci repeated before savoring the precious first sip.

"Fifteen years ago, our predecessors began these meetings with the realization that our organizations share similar business models and face the same daunting challenge: gargantuan growth. While most CEOs spend their careers aspiring to one day reach a billion dollars in revenue, we are expected to grow by at least that amount every year. Year after year."

Ben found himself nodding along, despite having heard the ego-stroking compliment several times before.

"Annual growth of a billion dollars," William Zacharia repeated, "is way beyond what most people can fathom, let alone achieve. It takes relentless drive, ruthless determination and boundless ambition. Experience demonstrates that it also requires *cooperation, coordination,* and *cunning.* Those are the tenets of the C3 alliance—"

"And our reason for gathering here this weekend," Luci interjected, "enjoying your fine hospitality."

Neither of them noted the real reason the three CEOs gave up one weekend every quarter to collude, Ben observed. Not that it would be difficult to deduce were anyone to learn of their meetings.

As CEOs, all three had their compensation linked directly to their company's stock performance. Obscene payouts were possible, but corporate boards didn't offer their chief executives those nine-figure pay packages out of the goodness of their hearts. And they weren't just buying big brains with key connections either. The board members were counting on their CEOs to do whatever it took to keep the share price climbing ever higher. They needed chief executives willing to outwit, outplay and outmaneuver the competition. To go above, beyond and around the law using cutting-edge tactics and clever tricks that could never be detected, much less proven in court.

"The helicopter is scheduled to return for us Sunday morning," WZ said, setting down his glass. "But I propose that we agree not to leave until we've reached accord on the single most important decision of the next few years." He paused there for effect, even though both guests knew what was coming. "Deciding who will become our country's next president."

"And what tactics will give us the greatest influence over him— or her," Ben clarified.

"Agreed," Luci said, with a smile in her eyes.

"Good. I'd like to kick off the discussion with an observation."

Two nods prompted him on.

"Elections are traditionally unpredictable and early polls considered worthless, but this time around the numbers have been remarkably steady, with Hughes constantly hovering at thirty-five percent, Ames around twenty-five, Saxon near twenty, and the rest of the pack in mid-to-low single digits.

"Effectively, we have a three-horse race. Agreed?"

More nods.

"All three leading candidates are business-friendly, pro-military and sufficiently hawkish. Hughes, with Caterpillar in her backyard, will probably be best for Ben. Saxon, as an oil man, clearly works well for Luci. And Ames, as a decorated veteran and self-declared hawk, is my first choice. But all three are acceptable. Agreed?"

"I'm with you," Luci said as Ben signaled his approval.

"Given that, I say there's no need to fight the tide. We make like Alabama and roll with it."

"Meaning what, exactly?" Ben asked.

"Politicians remember their early donors. The ones who made a difference when the odds were still high and the faith was still low. Sure, they smile and shake your hand whenever you write a check, and if the amount is big enough, the door to the Oval Office will then open whenever you knock. But…" WZ raised his whisky glass with extended index finger, "the connection candidates make with late donors is less visceral."

He took a sip. "What we want is a president who both *knows* that he owes us and *feels* that he owes us—and governs accordingly. Therefore, what I'm proposing is that we give big to the Super PACs supporting all three. Nine figures big. A hundred million dollars to each.

"I'm also proposing that we do it now. Now, before Iowa and New Hampshire. Now, when it will feel like a gift from God rather than just one more log on an already blazing fire. This tactic will triple our spend, but it will also virtually guarantee the desired result."

Ben cleared his throat as William Zacharia set down his glass. "I want to talk more about tactics for presenting our donation checks, but I'm onboard with the basic strategy."

Both men turned to Luci.

The newcomer held their gazes, first one, then the other, building tension, creating doubt. "Essentially, your plan is to pay three hundred million dollars to ensure that the next president feels a one-hundred million-dollar debt of gratitude."

"Deeply feels," WZ clarified.

"Deeply feels," Luci repeated. She pressed her lips together for a few seconds, then said, "I'm not interested."

Her words sucked so much oxygen from the room that Ben thought the fire might extinguish. The bonhomie evaporated like alcohol on a hot barbecue.

"Why not?" WZ asked, slow and low. "Your predecessors always supported our political projects. Dollar-for-dollar, they've proven to be the best investment around."

Ben believed he could read Luci's thoughts at that moment. *Go there, I dare you. Tell me I need to fall in line like a good little boy.* But she didn't take that route. Instead, she said, "As we all know, feelings are fickle. And the further the calendar flips from the day of our gift, the more the president's sense of obligation will fade."

William Zacharia again raised his drink-holding index finger. "That would be true if politicians only looked backward. But they don't. Trust me, they're always thinking about the next election. Always craving the next big check, the one that will save them from spending too much time sucking up to housewives over rubber-chicken dinners, and shaking thousands of snotty hands."

"Quid pro quo is programmed into every politician's code," Ben added, hoping for a quick and amicable resolution. "It's their default operating system."

When Luci replied, her voice projected a tantalizing lilt. "Perhaps. But only until the president feels that he's delivered his half of the implied bargain."

Ben suddenly understood where she was going, and immediately became intrigued. "You think we can do better. Better than the system that's driven our elections for generations. I'd love to hear how."

C C C

William Zacharia was quickly coming to the conclusion that he didn't care for Luci very much. But he was a practical man. He didn't have to like someone to work with her. "What, specifically, is your problem with my proposal?"

Luci stood up and walked to stand behind her chair, leaving only her face and hands visible in the flickering firelight. "Your proposal simply isn't good enough, William Zacharia. I don't want POTUS beholden to us out of gratitude for prior donations, or courting us for the next big check. Both situations are fragile. They break the instant a better offer comes along. No, my new friends, I want the president of the United States *owned* by us. And not just the man, the office."

I want to pitch a no-hitter and quarterback the Super Bowl, WZ thought, biting his tongue.

"Sounds good to me. How do we arrange that?" Ben said, making his reply sound only mildly sarcastic.

Luci answered his question with one of her own. "Who's the most likely nominee?"

"Hughes."

"And when will she lock-in her frontrunner status?"

"After New Hampshire, assuming she places first there and in Iowa."

Luci turned to WZ and waited silently for his opinion.

"Agreed. So long as South Carolina's not a surprising disaster."

As if propelled by those words, the C3's first female member began to walk the perimeter of their circle. She stopped in the space between her male colleagues' chairs. Rather than look at either of them, she spoke directly to the crackling fire. "I know something about Joy Hughes. Something her campaign manager doesn't. Something her husband doesn't. Something that, if exposed, would make her un-electable."

The two senior members both turned toward the new initiate with wide eyes and sinful smiles.

She did not return either gaze, but added, "We were sorority sisters, and roommates."

"Blackmail. I like it," WZ said. He was dying to ask exactly what she had on the candidate, but knew that would be fruitless, not to mention bad form.

Luci offered nothing more.

"When do you intend to spring the trap?" Ben asked.

Luci continued staring silently into the flames.

William Zacharia found himself squirming on the hook before she finally let out a little line. "We can do better than blackmail."

"What's better than blackmail?" he blurted.

Luci walked back toward her chair, this time taking the inside track. She didn't sit, but rather turned around before it. "Blackmail is a high-risk endeavor. Extreme and unpredictable. It's good for a one-off demand. For forcing a single action. But it's not realistic to expect a person to function long-term while writhing in a vise. Certainly not a person who's also dealing with the pressures of the Oval Office."

WZ had no idea where this was going. Glancing at Ben, he observed a similarly confused expression.

"Here's what I'd like to suggest we do," Luci continued. "We go to Preston Saxon, the number-three contender, and we offer him two things. We offer him three-hundred-million dollars, and we offer to put Joy Hughes on *his* ticket."

"What do you mean?" Ben asked.

"I mean, Hughes endorses Saxon, and runs as his vice president."

"Well knock me over with a feather," William Zacharia said. "So first you dash Hughes's dreams. Then, when she's despondent, when her golden road becomes a brick wall and she's staring at you with tears in her eyes, you offer her second fiddle. That's a beautiful scene."

"But how will she explain it?" Ben asked.

"She's bowing to Saxon's experience. He's got twenty years on her. She'll look selfless, magnanimous and wise."

Ben flashed a conspiratorial smile. "She still gets a federal mansion, a jet, and a place in the history books as the first female VP. Plus perfect positioning to ascend to the Oval."

"She gets up to sixteen years in one of the federal government's top two slots," WZ said.

"All the while knowing that we can bring her down," Luci added.

WZ raised his glass. "Meanwhile, Saxon knows without any doubt that he owes his presidency to us."

Ben also raised his drink in salute, but Luci left her tumbler on the end table. "I'm just getting started. Shall I continue?"

William Zacharia was suitably impressed with Luci's initial idea and duly intrigued by her tease, but he knew where this was going. Same place things always went when newcomers tried too hard to prove themselves. He settled back and braced for disappointment.

C C C

Luci was pleased with her debut performance. She had them hooked—and they hadn't even heard the big news yet.

"By all means, do continue," Ben said with wonder and admiration in his voice.

"I'm not about to offer Saxon this windfall with nothing but an implied quid pro quo in mind. Remember, it's Ames who's placing second in the polls. He's the obvious alternative. The easier alternative. Saxon's third-place status means he'll be much more eager than Ames. Much more malleable than Ames. So after dangling the golden carrot before Saxon, I'm going to make three demands—then throw in a kicker."

Luci let the tension build before elaborating. She could see they were both brimming with enthusiasm. She doubted either had been this excited since their last bonus discussion. "In exchange for our support and Hughes' unprecedented endorsement, Saxon must agree to let us pick his Secretary of Defense, Secretary of Energy, and Secretary of Homeland Security."

"Giving us significant influence over policies and purse strings," Ben said with a smile that nearly split his face.

"In the areas that matter most," WZ added. "What's the kicker?"

At last, Luci sat. "As you're well aware, Cabinet members control their own kingdoms. I want to ensure that we reign on Pennsylvania Avenue as well. Once Saxon has swallowed the bitter pill of allowing us to pick three Cabinet positions, I'm going to insist that he permit us one more key appointment."

"Which is?"

"White House Chief of Staff."

The two men turned to meet each other's eyes. After a moment of silent mind-melding, they turned back toward her and WZ spoke. "I get the feeling you're not just positioning us for general success. You have a specific end in mind, don't you? Some grand plan for using this unprecedented influence?"

"Indeed I do," Luci said, raising her glass at last. "Tell me something, William Zacharia. What's the biggest score ever orchestrated by an American company in your industry?"

"What do you mean by orchestrated?"

"She's referring to the marketing two-step," Ben said, beginning to nod along. "First you create a need, then you fulfill it."

"Precisely," Luci said.

WZ grew a wry smile as he too caught on. "That would have to be Iraqi WMD. Halliburton scored about $40 billion off that contract."

"Indeed they did. A substantial score and yet just a slim slice of the trillions   Uncle Sam has doled out funding recent foreign crusades."

"You have our attention," WZ said. "What are you going to do with it?"

Luci took a sip of whisky, then set her glass aside and said, "If you gentlemen will indulge me, I'd like to tell you about a plan I've code-named Operation 51."

PART I

One Year Later

Chapter 1

The Letter

PRESTON SAXON closed the thick white door, cutting off the clamor so completely that it was like God had flipped a switch. He stood still for a second with his hand still on the knob. As he surveyed the empty office just redecorated to his design, he felt his face stretching to accommodate a smile. *How many times had he fantasized about this moment? Ten thousand? Twenty?* Today would undoubtedly rank as the pinnacle of his life—but would this high prove to be a peak, or the start of a new plateau?

Saxon wasn't sure.

As his smile faded, he walked to the Bronco Buster sculpture and ran a sweaty hand over the cool bronze. In his heart, Saxon knew he shouldn't be there. Wouldn't be there—if three Texas CEOs had knocked on another door that cold night in New Hampshire.

But they had selected him over Ames and the others.

And then they'd delivered.

Now it was his turn.

He took a deep breath and stepped behind the desk. *The* desk. Pressing his knuckles atop the recycled English oak planks, he mused that it was undoubtedly the world's most expensive piece of rental furniture.

At the moment, it displayed just three objects: a large black telephone, a shiny silver letter opener, and an embossed white envelope with his name and new title. Handwritten by the previous renter. As was the custom.

Saxon picked up the envelope and read the proud words aloud, "President Preston Saxon."

His smile returned.

Everyone had to address him with deference now. Even his predecessors. Even his enemies. He was no longer a mere man. He was an office. An institution. An administration.

President Preston Saxon settled into his new chair and stroked the rich leather with his fingertips. *This would do. This would definitely do.*

He slit the thick envelope and extracted two folded sheets of matching stationery. The letter was written with the same hand that had penned the envelope.

Saxon tested his new chair's rollers and recline ability, then put his feet up on the Resolute Desk.

Dear President Saxon,

Before you know it, you will be writing your own version of this very letter. As you put pen to paper, you will find yourself reflecting on the most important years of your life. You will be cursing your foes, congratulating your friends, and contemplating your legacy.

Losing power forces one to look back at opportunities lost. Something that you and I will inevitably do for the rest of our lives. Given that, I want to take this opportunity to share with you a few thoughts on minimizing your regrets.

As I reflect, I wish that I'd done more to embrace the first half of our name. We are the United States. Unity is what drives our success and our power. Red is made stronger by Blue, and vice versa. All too often, I lost sight of that bigger picture.

I should have acted more as the office and less as a person. As veterans of this lofty office, we will never have another serious want or need. We are set for life. The country, however, has countless crucial but contentious concerns that can only be served by selfless executive attention. In other words, taking will gain you nothing; giving will bring you peace.

That sentiment leads to the final observation I hope to impress upon you. I wish I'd ignored everyone lobbying for self-serving reasons. The whole lot. The ninety-nine percent. It was the one percent pushing agendas that benefited others who proved to be the people worth heeding. They initiated the actions that now make me comfortable confronting history's mirror.

My prayers are with you,
President William Silver

Saxon shuffled to the second page.

P.S.: Get to know Chef Cristeta. She has a knack for brightening the darkest of days with small insightful acts of culinary kindness. Think of your Secret Service agents as angels. That mental trick makes them feel much less intrusive. And finally, when you find yourself needing something important done discreetly, call Kyle Achilles.

Saxon looked up from the letter toward the bust of Abraham Lincoln and then the portrait of Andrew Jackson before glancing back at his predecessor's closing words. "What an ass. Good riddance, Bill." He crumpled the two sheets and tossed them into the trash.

As the President headed for the Oval Office door and the jubilant chaos waiting on the other side, he remembered the policy on preserving paperwork. One of the many inconveniences to which he'd swiftly have to become accustomed. He pulled the first sheet of Silver's letter from the basket, ironed it with his hands, and slid it back into the envelope for posterity.

Six Months Later

Chapter 2

The Knock

KYLE ACHILLES slid the *Lonely Planet* travel guide into the outer pocket of his bag and zipped it shut without stretch or strain. His strict carry-on-only policy could be challenging when visiting colder climates, but packing for tropical Fiji was easy.

He was excited about the trip. The cageless shark diving in Fiji was reputed to be the best in the world, and the cliff diving was supposed to be spectacular. Achilles had learned to cliff dive as a safety precaution, given all the sea cliffs he climbed without the aid of ropes—and the very real potential for falls.

The shark diving just struck him as really cool.

He looked over at his wife. Katya had covered the bed with half the contents of her closet. Knowing better than to comment on the scene, he simply said, "I've got extra room if you need it."

She remained focused on her folding. "I'll figure it out."

As Achilles unzipped his bag, intent on leaving it at Katya's feet, someone knocked on their front door. The unexpected visitor hadn't rung the bell, and he wasn't using a polite *tat tat tat*. The unexpected visitor was pounding with an authoritative *thunk thunk thunk thunk thunk*.

"Someone's trying to exude authority KGB-style," Katya said.

Achilles checked the bedside security monitor while grabbing the Glock 19 from his nightstand. The screen showed two large men in dark suits at their door and a black Chevy Suburban in their driveway. "It's not a neighbor looking for his lost dog."

Katya followed him downstairs as the knocking continued. Glock in hand, he cracked the door with the chain still in place and his foot bracing it for further support. "Can I help you?"

"Pardon the intrusion, Mr. Achilles. Mrs. Achilles. We just drove down from Sacramento to ask the two of you a few questions. I'm Special Agent Richardson, and this is Special Agent Reed. May we come in?"

"May I see your credentials?"

The special agents took turns holding their credential wallets up to the gap in the door. Both looked perfect. "You can come in, but you'll need to leave your sidearms in the car."

"That's against FBI policy."

"My policy is not to allow armed strangers into my home. But that's okay, we can talk through the door crack."

Richardson shook his head, disappointed but defeated.

Reed said, "If it's just the two of you home, we could leave our weapons by the door—assuming you'll do the same."

"It's just us." Achilles opened the door and gestured to the entryway table. "Guns go there."

After they'd disarmed, Achilles added his Glock to the collection, then followed his wife and the special agents to the kitchen table. As everyone took their seats, Achilles asked, "How long have you guys been with the FBI?"

The men glanced at each other before answering. "Ten years for me," Richardson said.

"Five for me," Reed said. "But this really isn't about us."

"Who is it about?" Katya asked.

Richardson and Reed kept their eyes on Achilles. "You've done some work for former President Silver."

"I used to work for the government, if that's what you mean."

"I'm not referring to your years with the CIA. I'm talking about some off-the-books work you did specifically for Silver."

"I'm afraid you have me confused with somebody else. I resigned in 2015 and returned to rock climbing. I'm a competitive free-solo climber. Hardly the kind of guy who hangs out with former presidents."

"Rumor has it you saved Silver's life in Russia a few years back."

"Rumor has it you guys have aliens locked up in Nevada."

"Are you denying it?"

"I'm telling you that to the best of my knowledge, I didn't save the president's life." That was true. The attack from which he'd saved Silver was intended to be crippling, not life-threatening. "Not the kind of thing a person would forget," Achilles added.

"It's a crime to lie to federal agents, Mr. Achilles. You could go to jail for up to five years."

"I have no concerns regarding my compliance with Title 18 of the United States Code, Section 1001. But I don't take kindly to being threatened, so now I'm asking you to leave my home."

"We also understand that he's called on you a few times since, for assistance on special projects."

Achilles shook his head as he rose to his feet. "Thirty-two, fifty-three. I'm sorry you guys wasted a trip based on bad information."

"Thirty-two what?"

"Thirty-two, fifty-three," he repeated, his eyes on his wife. "It's another U.S.C. regulation. Look it up when you're back in the office."

The attack the agents launched as they rose was a slick and seamless effort, unfolding without covert signals or coordinating glances. One second they appeared to be gracefully accepting a temporary defeat, the next Reed had Katya in a chokehold and Richardson was flying toward Achilles.

Chapter 3

The Caller

KATYA WAS SURPRISED to hear her husband ask the FBI agents to leave their sidearms by the door. He'd never done that before. It was the first sign that he didn't believe they were who they claimed to be. Then he slipped in a confirming question about how long they'd been with the Bureau. An innocuous and typical icebreaker among people establishing a common connection, but another incongruity with her husband's normal behavior.

For a moment, she wondered why he'd let them in, but quickly figured that out. He wanted to learn what they were after. If the pair were serious about achieving their objective—a safe assumption given the penalty for impersonating federal officers— rebuffing them would amount to inviting more aggressive action.

Achilles pushed the charade as far as he could, then flashed her a covert warning when the physical attack became imminent. 'Thirty-two fifty-three" wasn't a U.S.C. regulation. Or if it was, that was coincidental. It was a code coming from a game they played. A mental exercise that was kind of a modern mathematician's version of Scrabble. One that was good for a few laughs. She and Achilles would convert words to numbers using a telephone keypad. Fifty eighty-three was 5-0-8-3 which was LOVE, not to be confused with 5-0-5-3, which translated to JOKE. Fifty-one seventy-seven was KISS, not to be confused with seventy-one, seventy-seven, which translated to PISS.

This was not the first time she'd heard Achilles say thirty-two fifty-three. He'd recently evoked an eye roll after using it while a woman jogged past them in a bikini on the beach at Half Moon Bay. Code 3-2-5-3 stood for FAKE.

Today, the cipher represented the same word, but it conveyed an entirely different meaning.

Katya had gotten the message, but she had not managed to prepare herself to defend against the fake agents in time. She hadn't completed the choreography in her head. The preemptive ballet of action and reaction that would result in Reed doubled over clutching his crotch or clamping both hands over a wounded eye. She'd been a split-second too slow, and that shortcoming was all the gap the closest imposter had needed.

But not Achilles.

He'd done the proverbial homework. He'd prepared his muscles and rehearsed his moves. By the time Richardson began cocking his arm, Achilles was already in a defensive stance. When Richardson launched his assault, Achilles was primed to turn it against him.

The men were similarly sized, both a bit north of six feet and 200 pounds. Both appeared to be rugged and fit. But Katya knew that her husband was much more than he seemed. He had the conditioning and cardiovascular system of an Olympic athlete, a biathlete to be precise. Atop that hardy pump and sturdy frame, he'd packed thousands of cliff-climbing hours, toning himself to the point where he could hang using individual fingers and toes. He was a rock. Unshakable in body and spirit.

The clash happened so quickly that Katya probably couldn't have followed the moves even if she hadn't been in the midst of her own assault. But she was, so she completely missed their brief battle. By the time Reed finished executing the quick sequence that ended with his left arm wrapped around her neck, Achilles had Richardson doubled over in an armlock that teed his nose up for a knockout knee strike.

"If you don't release my wife within the next three seconds, you and your partner are going to experience a world of hurt."

Katya prepared to do her part, knowing that her husband's growled warning was no bluff. After he counted two, she'd stomp her clog down hard on top of Reed's right foot, then bring her right arm back, aiming her elbow at his solar plexus and then her fist at his crotch. She doubted that the combination would completely disable her much-larger opponent, but she'd do her darnedest.

"That's enough! Stand down!" The commanding voice wasn't that of Richardson or Reed. It didn't come from anyone in the room. By the time Katya identified the source as a phone in Richardson's suit coat pocket, Reed had released her.

"Put the phone on the table and go wait in the backyard," the third party barked.

"Sit by the fountain where we can see you," Achilles added, as Reed relinquished the phone.

Once Katya's assailant was outside, Achilles released Richardson, allowing him to follow.

As the second fake agent departed, Katya pulled a Ruger slim subcompact from beneath the kitchen pencil drawer. Then she flipped the phone over so they could read the screen. It said BLOCKED and indicated that the call had been in process for twenty-one minutes.

Achilles closed and locked the sliding door before asking, "Who is this?"

"If you'll log onto Wi-Fi, you can enable FaceTime and see for yourself. The phone's passcode is THEFBI."

"Eighty-four, thirty-three, twenty-four," Katya said reflexively.

Achilles unlocked the phone, connected it to their guest network, then activated the app that turned voice calls into video calls.

It took Katya a few seconds to place the face of the man with the blocked phone number. His hair looked Photoshopped from a fashion magazine and he was dressed in a tailored navy suit with a precisely positioned purple tie. When recognition struck, she almost gasped. The man who had sent two thugs to their home was the White House Chief of Staff.

Chapter 4

The Invitation

ACHILLES WAS AT ONCE SHOCKED and not the least bit surprised. He was shocked because he thought his White House involvement had ended with President William Silver's second term. And yet he was not surprised because politicians were often the source of devious schemes.

As he waited for White House Chief of Staff Rex Rowe to explain why two brutes were in his backyard under false pretenses, Achilles was surprised to find himself more excited than upset. He didn't need Katya to tell him why. He missed the big game. The excitement of high-stakes missions. Especially the kind that President Silver had used him for. Small-scale, off-the-books operations with minimal bureaucracy, maximal impact and unlimited adrenaline.

After leaving office, the former President had used a kind thank-you note to imply that Saxon might also want to make use of his special skills and situation, but up until that moment, Achilles had not dared to believe it.

"Thank you for speaking with me," Rex Rowe began. "Let me begin by apologizing for the aggressive behavior and explaining why you have two of my men in your backyard. I sent them there on a mission, an important mission, and believe it or not, they were successful."

Achilles respected public offices even when he didn't care for the people who occupied them, so he restricted his reply to a simple, "How so?"

"They completed all three objectives in quick order with minimal fuss."

The phrasing effected a paradigm shift in Achilles' mind, and he immediately understood everything.

Katya was less familiar with covert ops—and she probably had a headache from the hair grab—so Achilles wasn't surprised when she pushed back. In fact, he found himself smiling as she did. "Minimal fuss? If you'd waited two more seconds, your men would be stretched out in an ambulance rather than seated in my backyard."

"Point taken, however my men were willing to accept those lumps—because of what I needed to know."

"It was a test," Achilles said, meeting his wife's eye.

"What did you need to know?" Katya asked, catching on.

"Given that your husband has been out of action for a while, and that I'm relying on a recommendation rather than direct experience, I asked them to determine three things. Your husband's loyalty, his mental acuity, and his physical capability.

"He didn't betray his work for President Silver. He did figure out that Richardson and Reed weren't actually FBI agents." Rex paused there to glance at Achilles. "How did you do that, by the way?"

"Their credentials look brand new. The wallets clearly haven't spent years going in and out of pockets. And both men are big and young. It's usually the senior guys who get assigned to Washington. While those could be considered circumstantial evidence, I confirmed my suspicion beyond a reasonable doubt when both men fumbled before answering how long they'd been with the Bureau."

"Right." Rex turned back to Katya. "Mental acuity confirmed. The third thing I needed to verify was your husband's physical prowess. It's now obvious that he hasn't been rusting away on the shelf. So mission accomplished."

"How can I help you, Mr. Rowe," Achilles said, cutting to the chase.

"Please, call me Rex. And you can help your president by hopping on an airplane about three hours from now. Alaska Airlines has a direct flight to Dulles departing San Francisco at 3:45."

Achilles recalled the suitcases waiting upstairs. The ones they'd been packing when Richardson and Reed began pounding on the door. "When can Katya expect me home?"

"You'll be back by noon tomorrow, leaving you plenty of time to catch the overnight flight to Fiji—should you still choose to take that trip."

C C C

The dashboard clock displayed 12:44 a.m. when an Uber dropped Achilles at the front entrance of the Hay Adams Hotel. After politely waving off the doorman and waiting for his ride from the airport to depart, Achilles walked south on 16th Street. He cut through Lafayette Square and crossed Pennsylvania Avenue to the White House's Northwest Appointment Gate.

As instructed, Achilles said nothing to the Secret Service officer standing at the window. He had half expected it to be either Richardson or Reed, but neither he nor the officer behind him looked familiar. Rex hadn't divulged who actually employed the two men who visited his house, but Achilles figured the Secret Service was a good guess. It went with keeping the circle small, something this evening's setup indicated to be a primary concern—as it had been with all his prior White House assignments.

The attending officer remained silent while his eyes darted back and forth between Achilles and the screens that undoubtedly displayed his picture and the results of various ongoing scans. After a few seconds, he nodded, exited the booth and began walking toward the West Wing.

Achilles followed, through the dimly lit lobby and to the right, then left past several dark offices, then left again past a few more until they were standing in a corridor with the Roosevelt Room on one side and a door set in a curved wall on the other.

The Secret Service agent gestured toward a decorative niche. "Leave your iPhone out here. Just don't forget it when you leave." Achilles did as he was told, impressed that the scan had correctly identified his cell phone brand.

Turning toward the door, he considered knocking but thought better of it. Soundproofing might prevent him from hearing a reply, and in any case, his arrival was clearly choreographed. He would not be surprising President Saxon.

The thick door swung soundlessly on heavy hinges to reveal a room only slightly brighter than the hall. As the lock latched behind him with a slight but solid click, Achilles found himself standing on the far left side of the Oval as viewed from the desk.

Above him, dimly lit by recessed lights, was the domed ceiling with its raised Presidential Seal. Across from him, currently covered by curtains, was the exit to the West Colonnade and the Rose Garden—a tidbit he drew from the memory of a daytime visit. To his left, the famous fireplace with two yellow chairs poised for photo ops. To his right, past the bookcases and couches, was the more-famous desk.

Leaning against that historic antique was a now-familiar male in his mid-fifties whose dark eyes retained their spark despite the hour. While clearly a man of power and poise, he was not the official owner of the Oval Office. He was not the President of the United States.

"Good evening, Achilles. Thank you for coming."

Chapter 5

The Mission

AFTER THEIR FACETIME CHAT some ten hours earlier, Achilles read up on the distinguished politician now standing before him. The White House Chief of Staff graduated from both Harvard Law and Harvard Business School, where legend had it he bonded with each and every one of his fifteen hundred peers.

After graduation, Rex parlayed his classmate connections and uncanny charisma into what quickly became one of the most influential lobbying firms in Washington. Rumor had it that over the years, he'd been offered the chairmanship of both major political parties and a few Cabinet positions, but he'd declined all overtures—until Saxon made him one of the most powerful backstage operatives in the world and certainly the most dominant in D.C.

"Again, my apologies for the crude introduction earlier. I trust you understand why it was a prudent move on my part."

"I do. Happy to be of service," Achilles said, trying not to show his disappointment over President Saxon's absence.

They shook hands, then sat facing one another across a carpet displaying the Presidential Seal. Although the sofas were soft, both men sat forward in engaging postures, with hands clasped and elbows on knees.

Rex opened with a question. "Are you familiar with DelMos Technologies?"

"The name rings a bell, but little more. It's a joint-venture, right? Delhi and Moscow?"

"That's right. DelMos makes missiles. The DelMos I is a hypersonic cruise missile compatible with ship, submarine, aircraft and land-based mobile launchers. It's as good as anything we have. The forthcoming DelMos II is rumored to fly considerably further and faster."

"Rumored? You don't know?"

Rex shook his head. "We know the size and weight, but not the speed, range or other more-sophisticated indications of what we're up against. The Russians are masters at misinformation campaigns, and the Indians aren't bad either. DelMos Technologies is known to falsify internal reports and documentation in order to keep even their own people unaware of the current state of affairs."

"Rendering both humint and sigint suspect," Achilles clarified, referencing human and electronic intelligence-gathering techniques.

Rex straightened up. "President Silver was right; your mind moves as fast as a fencing foil."

Achilles ignored the flattery. After reading about Rex's ability to bond, he was expecting something of the sort. No doubt the chief of staff had an arsenal of colorful compliments locked, loaded and ready to fire as required.

"Since we can't use indirect methods of ascertaining and replicating the threat, we're forced to use the direct one."

"You need to inspect a prototype," Achilles guessed.

"Precisely! Although *need* is an understatement. It's imperative that we learn exactly what we're up against as soon as possible. I can't disclose the specific reason why, but the fact that you're getting this assignment at a midnight meeting in the Oval Office —"

Achilles saw another compliment move from the magazine into the chamber as Rex trailed off, but the chief of staff didn't pull the trigger. His people-reading instincts were stellar.

Rex changed directions. "Stealing a top-secret military prototype is *casus belli*. That wouldn't necessarily be a prohibitive risk if the target were a third-world dictatorship, but India is both an ally and the world's fourth-ranking military power—after the U.S., Russia and China. And Russia, well, you understand the ramifications of poking the bear better than I do."

Achilles did understand. He spoke Russian, had extensive covert experience in Russia, and was married to a Russian—a Stanford mathematics professor whose PhD was from Moscow State University. "The risks outweigh the rewards."

"They do. Bottom line: the United States government can't be caught stealing the DelMos II."

Realization struck Achilles like an icy river—one that quickly gushed from his brain to his gut. "Emphasis on *the United States government.*"

Rex flashed a candid smile. "I've got to admit, I was skeptical. When President Silver recommended you, I thought it was a common courtesy. A throwaway offer meant to make both parties feel good in the moment. A 'look me up if you ever come to town' kind of thing." He made air quotes as he spoke.

Achilles found himself feeling friendly. Rex's charisma was working its magic despite the forewarning. The man really did have a gift for guessing and pressing buttons. "What convinced your boss otherwise?"

"We did a discreet background check, of course, and what we found was plenty impressive, but it was the context of the recommendation that did it. Silver put your name in the traditional presidential letter to his successor."

"Really?" Achilles asked, surprised.

"Yeah. He did it in a postscript on a separate page, presumably so that it could be omitted from the official record. Along with some other personnel tips. Saxon figured there was no reason for Silver to bother if he wasn't sincere."

Rex reached into his breast pocket and extracted a manila envelope too thick to be a copy of the letter. "Here's a printout of the information we have on the DelMos II. Read it, then shred it. The envelope also contains passports and a flash drive. The flash drive has biometric security. It opens when pressed top and bottom with your right thumb and index finger."

"What's on it?"

Rex tapped the envelope against his own open palm with a gleam in his eye. "Access to a bank account with a seven-figure balance, and the number of an extraordinary procurement officer."

"A procurement officer?"

"An extraordinary one. Your own personal genie. Someone you can text for anything you need to complete the mission."

"Anything?"

Rex shot Achilles a sideways smile. "From blueprints of the Kremlin to a chartered submarine."

Achilles was liking Rex more and more. "Sounds intriguing. Anything else on the drive?"

"Do you need more? Don't millions of dollars and Aladdin's lamp strike you as enough?"

"Perhaps a plan?"

"I understood that those were your forte."

One had to admire the masterful way Rex manipulated emotions using wonder, gifts and flattery. Had Achilles not been primed, he might have been misdirected. "Meaning you want to be able to raise your right hand and swear that you knew nothing about the plan—if it fails."

Rex stood and turned toward the door. "I'll give you a ride back to the hotel."

Achilles didn't follow his host's lead. "I haven't said yes."

Rex stopped and turned but didn't backtrack. "Saxon is convinced that Silver wouldn't recommend a man who says no. Come on, car's this way," he gestured.

Achilles felt both honored and aghast. Was he that predictable? That manipulable? Was everyone putty in this man's hands?

Achilles collected his phone and followed Rex to his personal vehicle. The Executive Parking Lot was actually just a blocked-off section of the road that separated the West Wing from the neighboring Eisenhower Executive Office Building.

Not surprisingly, Rex unlocked the closest car. His black Cadillac CTS looked new, but the headlights marked it as an older model. Achilles found the implied frugality and modesty to be both surprising and endearing. Perhaps there was more to Rex than a golden mind and a silver tongue.

He'd likely never know.

They would probably never meet again.

That was the nature of covert ops. Of puppets and their masters.

"You don't use a driver?"

"They offered me one, but I declined. I come in early and leave late, so traffic's not an issue, and this fifteen-minute commute is about the only alone time I get. I find it relaxing. Cars are much easier to control than governments."

The Cadillac's ignition brought a wired cell phone to life, its screen displaying a short stack of text messages. For a second, Achilles found Rex's behavior odd. Why would someone keep his phone in the car rather than take it into the office? But of course, the answer depended on the office. The White House had protocols regarding recordkeeping and the use of personal electronics, plus a prohibition against conducting private business in federal offices. Rex undoubtedly had confidential legacy engagements he couldn't commingle with his official new ones.

What a life these guys lived. Achilles was happy to play his part, but grateful that he got to do so from the outside.

The drive to the Hay Adams took about sixty seconds. Neither man spoke. It was late and both had a lot on their minds.

Rex put his car in Park, then turned in his seat to offer the manila envelope.

Achilles accepted it.

He immediately noted that the contents didn't feel right. The envelope had more heft than he'd anticipated.

Rex picked up on this and gave a go-ahead nod.

Achilles pried open the metal clasp and peered inside. "Four passports?"

"American and Russian—for you and Katya. It wasn't just you we were testing."

Chapter 6

The Recording

AS HER HUSBAND walked through the front door, Katya sensed that he had the weight of the world on his shoulders. Given the time zone difference and the fact that he'd been in the air for longer than he'd been on the ground, they hadn't spoken since his White House meeting.

She kissed him and they retreated to the kitchen where she had mugs waiting for her tea and his coffee. While Katya poured, Achilles turned on a workout playlist and increased the volume. Then he put an arm around her shoulder and guided her to the bench in the backyard beside the gurgling Spanish fountain.

Katya understood the implications. He was worried about being overheard. Not a good sign. "What did the President ask you to do?" she whispered.

"He wants me to acquire a prototype missile. Steal it and sneak it back into the United States without anyone knowing who really took it or where it went."

"Steal it from where?"

"Either India or Russia. It's being produced by an Indian-Russian joint venture called DelMos, although most of the work is done in Delhi."

At least it wasn't North Korea, Katya mused. A swarm of questions began buzzing around her brain, but rather than spit them straight out, she took a second to think.

Achilles complicated the situation before she completed her initial analysis. He set down his coffee mug and pulled a half-size manila envelope from his pocket. He slid out four passports and presented them to her, covers closed. Two were dark blue, two were burgundy.

She opened the first, a dark blue one from the United States. It displayed Achilles' picture, but the name was Kyle Adams. The second, also American, was even more surprising. "Kate Adams?"

"Rex suggested that you accompany me for safety reasons. He thinks I'll attract less attention traveling as a tourist with my wife. Turns out he wasn't just testing me yesterday. While he's obviously right about you and your capabilities, he's wrong in his assessment of the mission—as non-operatives often are. Taking you doubles the risk."

Again, Katya bit back an impulsive response. She didn't want Achilles to dig in. Instead she selected the second of the passports with the familiar burgundy color, and flipped it open to the data page. As anticipated, it was Russian. Also as expected, it displayed her photo. The name beside it was Katya Akulova. "Let me guess," she said, pointing to the cover of the last passport. "Konstantine Akulov?"

"Kiril."

"Isn't it bad tradecraft to use aliases resembling real names?"

He half smiled. "It's worse tradecraft to forget your name, or misspeak."

Despite knowing next to nothing about the specifics, Katya suddenly found herself afraid—not of going, but of being left behind. Of spending days or weeks alone in a big empty house, worrying. She had to get her husband to agree to include her in his plans—as Rex Rowe had suggested. But how?

Katya stood and started circling the fountain to buy a few seconds. Given the stubborn streak that Achilles occasionally displayed, she decided to proceed tangentially, to work her way onto the team without directly addressing the issue.

Sitting back down, she asked, "Can the op wait? Or do we need to cancel Fiji?"

"I'm afraid we have to postpone Fiji."

"We'll lose the plane tickets and hotel deposit."

Achilles pulled a red flash drive from the envelope and held it up. "We'll come out of this all right."

"Cryptocurrency?"

"A slush fund. And Aladdin." He spoke the last word playfully.

"Aladdin?"

"Contact information for a person Rex refers to as *an extraordinary procurement officer.*"

Katya had a few ops under her belt, all beside Achilles. None of them had involved significant outside support. Quite to the contrary, all had isolated them. "Interesting. That's one claim I look forward to testing. But back to the missile. How big is it?"

"You and your numbers," he said with a smile. "It's thirty feet long with a two-foot diameter." As her eyes widened, he added, "It likely weighs in at over six thousand pounds."

"So we won't be slipping it under your coat. How does Saxon suggest we steal it?"

It was Achilles' turn to rise. "I didn't actually meet with Saxon."

"What?!"

"My midnight rendezvous was in the Oval Office, but the chief of staff was the only other person in the room. Rex didn't suggest a plan either."

"Seriously? He just said fetch?"

Achilles wetted both palms in the fountain and then wiped the cool water on his face. "Knowing nothing about the plan bolsters his deniability if things go south. It effectively leaves the president in the clear. Which is why you should stay home. I'll need you on the outside to help spring me if I get caught—because they're clearly not going to."

Katya had not considered that angle in her rudimentary analysis. She bought another few seconds to think. "That's hardly fair."

"The world's not a fair place. But they're giving me a choice—and unlimited covert assistance." He waggled the red flash drive. "That makes this about as fair as it gets in government work."

Katya needed nuance. Detail. "What, exactly, did Rex say?"

Achilles delighted her with a surprise move. He pulled his AirPods from his pocket and handed her one.

"You recorded the meeting?"

"Not my first dance with politicians. And these days, recording conversations couldn't be easier. A single tap on the watch face is all it takes."

After they'd each popped in an AirPod, he raised his Apple watch and tapped the red circle in the lower right corner. A few seconds later, she heard the White House Chief of Staff say, "Good evening, Achilles. Thank you for coming."

They listened to the whole meeting, which Katya found surprisingly short, given the size and complexity of the mission. Nonetheless, it was long enough to lead her to a clear conclusion. No way was she going to sit home, blindly hoping that her husband would eventually return. Her nervous system was wired for action. Like a shark—the translation of her new Russian alias—Katya was compelled to keep moving. "I'm surprised Rex let you record the meeting."

"It never came up," Achilles said with a wink. "The Secret Service agent had me leave my phone outside the Oval Office, but no one said anything about my watch or recording. Security didn't even ask my name when I showed up. The whole meeting was clearly arranged to be off the record, and that resulted in circumventing some of the usual bureaucratic procedures. It also put me on alert."

Katya often marveled at her husband's prescience and preparation. It was what made him such an exceptional operative—when duty called him back to service.

Eager to keep the collaborative discussion rolling along, she returned to the key question. "How do we steal something sized like a bundle of telephone poles and twice as heavy?"

Achilles flashed a smile. He knew what she was doing. "There are two general tactics worth considering: *stealth* and *deception*. I gave some thought to both while trying to sleep on the plane."

"Stealth and deception are different?" Katya asked, reeling him in.

"Fundamentally so. A stealthy approach would be like your stereotypical art museum heist. We sneak in during the dead of night using sophisticated gadgetry to defeat the security systems. Or we slip in during the day as visitors or employees and hide until all's quiet. Or we conceal ourselves in a delivery crate and emerge at midnight, Trojan Horse style. The issue with all of those is that they only get us halfway to victory. They give us possession of the missile but they don't get us out with it."

"And deception does? I guess I'm not sure exactly what you mean."

"Deception means we walk in the front door and then get them to give us the missile."

"That would be a neat trick," Katya said, thrilled by both the idea and her husband's use of *we*. Whether the word was intentional or subconscious, she had changed his mind. *She was in!* "Do you have a specific act of magic in mind? Or are you still brainstorming?"

"The key to a successful deception is to insert it into a known scenario, an ordinary activity." He paused there, as was his habit when discussing an area of expertise, giving her time to process.

She didn't need long. "In order to avoid raising red flags?"

"Exactly."

"So what *ordinary* activity has them holding the door open while we walk out with a treasure the size of a small submarine?"

Achilles tossed a pebble in the fountain. "I have no idea."

Chapter 7

The Invisible Man

KATYA WATCHED ACHILLES pop the flash drive into a cheap computer he'd just purchased. A machine that was not, and never had been, connected to the internet. "Air-gapped is the technical term," he explained.

They were back inside at the kitchen table, after acquiring equipment and sweeping for bugs. They'd found no listening devices, but he had jazz streaming through a nearby speaker just in case.

The flash drive reacted to his fingerprints as promised, opening to display two text files, one titled *Funds*, the other *Procurement*.

The Funds file contained the login information for an account in the Seychelles. Achilles typed the details into a fresh burner phone, and they found themselves looking at a two-million-dollar balance.

"Now that's what I call verification," Katya said, her voice filled with verve.

"Maybe yes, maybe no. Let's find out." While Katya conducted other research, Achilles spent an hour transferring the entire balance to a new account at a bank in Singapore—one that claimed to specialize in international private banking and wealth management services.

Once that transaction was successful, he turned back to his wife. "*Now* it's confirmed. And you're right, it's a very good sign."

"Why did they give us two million dollars?" Katya asked. "That seems an odd amount."

"It feels right to me. Once we get the missile out the front or back door at DelMos, we'll need to transport it out of the country and then secretly into the United States. Given the size and weight of the thing, we'll have to fund either an expensive charter or a hefty bribe or both. That single expense is inevitable, and it will probably suck up a million dollars or more. They foresaw it and removed the speed bump that a smaller transfer would have created."

"I see your point. Never had to budget an undercover op before." She put a hand on his shoulder. "Shall we test Aladdin?"

Achilles opened the Procurement file and read the simple message: "Text your request." A ten-digit number followed.

He stored the number on the burner phone as "Aladdin" then texted, "I need a hacker par excellence."

They stared at the screen for what felt like minutes but was probably just seconds, waiting for a sign of life to emerge from the void. When no immediate reaction ensued, Katya asked, "What now?"

"We keep brainstorming."

Their last brainstorming session, a long back-and-forth fueled by caffeine and fruit salad, had led them to conclude that the best way to identify and exploit "usual activity" at DelMos was to hack into the joint venture's email server and study what employees were saying.

"Do you think we should target their Moscow operation, or the one in Delhi?" Achilles asked with a leading lilt in his voice.

"Moscow, of course," Katya said, knowing intuitively that she was mistaken the moment the words crossed her lips. Achilles wouldn't have used his Socratic tone if the answer were obvious. Still, it felt right. "We know the territory. We know the language. We'll blend into the population. In Delhi, by contrast, we'd be salt in the pepper shaker."

"That may be the deciding factor—if we select a *stealth* scenario," Achilles concurred. "We'd definitely draw much less attention in Moscow. If we go with *deception*, however, blending-in ceases to be the driving variable."

"What replaces it?" Katya asked, enjoying the pedagogical discourse.

"Credibility. Where are we likely to appear more credible? To fool the locals? In Delhi, posing as Russians, or in Moscow, posing as Russians?"

The burner phone beeped before Katya could voice the obvious answer.

Achilles studied the screen. "The message is an email address: vapor+blue_horseshoe@JackGriff.in."

"That's an odd email, in several ways," Katya said. "What's with the plus sign?"

Achilles didn't reply immediately. He appeared to be trolling his memory. After a few seconds, he smiled and nodded. "Plus signs can be added to some email addresses. The part after the plus doesn't impact routing, but it does allow you to turn one email into an infinite number."

"Why would you want to do that?"

"The feature serves several functions," Achilles said, nodding to himself. "For one, it lets you use the same email for multiple accounts. Like our frequent flyer accounts. You can register using our Gmail with +Katya and I can register using it with +Kyle, keeping things simple. Or, the + feature can be used for sorting purposes, which is what I'm sure The Invisible Man is doing. He's given us the code name *blue_horseshoe* and has all our correspondence funneled to a dedicated folder."

"The Invisible Man? Is that what you're calling the hacker?"

"His choice, not mine."

"I don't follow."

"Jack Griffin was the name of The Invisible Man in the famous movie of the same name. Took me a minute to make the connection. The other movie reference helped."

Katya shot him a quizzical look. "Other movie reference? What other movie reference? All you have is one email address."

"Blue Horseshoe was the code name Gordon Gekko used in the movie *Wall Street.*"

"The things you know."

"They're both classics," Achilles said, flashing his eyebrows. "I have a classical education."

Katya couldn't help but smile. She appreciated the moment of levity—and Achilles' ability to inject humor into trying times. "I can't fault your logic, but I do find it disturbing. And I'm quite certain that it wouldn't earn you a Stanford diploma."

"Maybe not, but I bet you a back rub that more Stanford students could identify Gordon Gekko than Carl Gauss—or any other mathematician for that matter."

Katya knew better than to take that bet. The most popular professors on campus often tied key lessons to characters or scenes from popular shows.

Achilles typed a text to vapor+blue_horseshoe@JackGriff.in. "Need access to all DelMos Technologies email. Ability to read and write."

This time, the text reply was almost immediate. "24 hrs."

Chapter 8

The Promise

ACHILLES FELT THE BURNER PHONE BUZZ and checked the screen. The second text from The Invisible Man showed him to be true to the letter if not the spirit of his promise. It came twenty-four hours after the first, and read: "+24 hrs."

Disappointed by the delay but not discouraged, Achilles set down the phone and turned to his wife. "Want to do the Dish?"

The Stanford "Dish" was a 150-foot diameter radio telescope perched in the rolling hills above the university campus. The large open space surrounding it was ringed with trails that were favored by both students and locals. There was something about exercising on those sun-drenched slopes that made Achilles' spirit soar, although whether it was the proximity to the venerated intellectual hub or the view all the way to the East Bay that did the trick, he wasn't sure.

"I'm game," Katya replied.

They drove to the Alpine Gate, which set them up for a 5.8-mile run with an 800-foot elevation gain. The longest and toughest Dish option.

"Have you had any ideas?" he asked as they began jogging. The question didn't require clarification. Figuring out how to finesse a top-secret thirty-foot missile out the front door of a foreign corporation was not the kind of challenge that slipped one's mind.

Katya was not a clandestine operative by training, but she had proved to be an excellent one in practice—thanks to her adventurous personality and sharp analytical skills. "Plenty of ideas, but no breakthroughs. You?"

"I thought I was onto something earlier when a parallel situation occurred to me. It was fiction, but with all the scientific breakthroughs these days the line between fiction and fact is so blurred as to be indecipherable. Anyway, I dismissed it."

"What was the situation?"

"In Tom Clancy's classic novel, *The Hunt for Red October*, the task was stealing a submarine. The CIA ultimately tricked the sailors into thinking that the nuclear reactor was compromised, making them want to abandon ship to avoid radiation poisoning."

"I like it. Keep talking."

Achilles jumped over a small black snake. "That tactic won't help us because DelMos missiles don't get equipped with warheads at the factory. Those get added later. DelMos is only developing the transportation system. The missile."

"Oh," Katya said, obviously deflating.

"The operational upside for us is that security at DelMos will be much more lax than it would be if nuclear material were present. They're essentially a machine shop. No more magical than an automotive plant."

Stanford's Hoover Tower came into sight as the couple jogged over a rise. It was distant, but still an inspiration. At that moment, it made Achilles think of a missile silo. The DelMos missiles didn't require silos. They were designed to be launched from a platform, making them much more versatile and thus more dangerous. You could park one almost anywhere.

"The closest our countries ever came to war," Achilles said, referencing his native United States and her Russia, "was the Cuban Missile Crisis. Although those missiles could fly two-to-four times farther than the DelMos, thousands of miles instead of hundreds, they used 1960s technology. Compared to them, the DelMos is smaller, faster and significantly easier to conceal."

"A scary thought."

"I'm not trying to scare you, but I do think it's important that we enter into this operation with the stakes in mind. This could be a very big deal. It's also an extremely risky one. That's why President Saxon took the extraordinary step of recruiting an outsider—someone with known allegiance and capabilities, who can easily be disavowed if things go sideways."

Katya sprinted a few steps ahead, then turned and jogged backwards so she could face him. "It's also why you should bring me along. I can help, both tactically and with your cover. You owe it to your president and country to maximize your odds of success. Rex implied as much when he gave you two sets of passports."

Achilles knew that participating in the mission was important to Katya, and he wanted both her assistance and her company. She would undoubtedly be an operational asset. But he wouldn't be able to forgive himself if anything happened to her. And heaven forbid there came a time when he would have to choose between sacrificing either her or the mission. "Let's wait to make that call until we have a plan."

Katya's expression hardened. "Okay. But promise me you'll be impartial."

"I can't do that. I love you too much."

"I know. But you also love our country. Promise me you'll keep that in mind."

"I promise."

They made no further breakthroughs on the run, but a text from The Invisible Man was waiting when they returned. It consisted of just one word, technically speaking. A website address.

"Click it," Katya prompted.

"Let's grab a shower first. Whatever we find, it's likely going to lead us down a deep rabbit hole. I'd rather go in feeling fresh."

Katya followed his gaze to her sweat-soaked shirt. "Judging by the look in your eyes, I'd say you're feeling plenty fresh already."

Chapter 9

The Opportunity

THE WEB ADDRESS supplied by The Invisible Man took them to a posting on a chat board dedicated to World War I. It was at the bottom of a thread that appeared to have otherwise been dormant for years.

The information you requested can be accessed <u>HERE</u>. *Bookmark it, as this post will be deleted shortly.*

Achilles clicked the hyperlink. The screen that popped up was clearly a back office page, monotone with basic fonts and lines.

"Look at that," Katya said, her voice elevated by enthusiasm.

Achilles took a few seconds longer than his wife to make sense of the spreadsheet before them. "He tapped into a service DelMos is using to translate all their emails into English from Russian and Hindi. This is as good as gold."

"Platinum, I think." As Katya spoke, the column labeled *Hindi;W=50>English* added a new entry on top, pushing the bottommost off the screen. "It's live."

They watched the screen for more movement. When nothing happened, Katya pointed to the last column, which had just one entry and an odd header. "What's BH?"

"BH is us. Blue Horseshoe."

She opened the single BH email and found the instructions they needed.

Compose here to write emails to any address, from any address. Replies to messages sent from this overlay will come to this gating mailbox, from which they can be processed forward to the actual named recipient, or deleted before being seen.

Achilles was now thoroughly impressed—with Rex, Aladdin, and The Invisible Man. "This guy is first class. I suppose setting up a parallel overlay like this is fairly rudimentary to professional hackers, something they could describe to their peers in a single tweet, but it's miraculous to me."

"Was it always like this? Working for the CIA?" Katya asked.

"It was never like this."

"Really?"

Achilles shook his head. "Outsiders think the CIA is a magical place due to the sexy missions and all the secrecy, but I think novelist and former agent Barry Eisler got it right when he said, 'Think of the CIA as a post office with spies.'"

"Wow, that's depressing."

"Only until you add context. While ours may not be ideal, we've still got the best postal system in the world."

They brewed hot beverages and got to work reading, with Achilles tackling the English emails and Katya the Russian. They found the DelMos emails to be pretty much what anyone who has worked in a corporate environment would expect. Lots of talk about tasks, targets and timelines, heavily seasoned with side discussions ranging from lunch plans to commute times to sports scores.

They were just twenty minutes into their reading when Katya said, "I found something exciting. In fact, it's exactly the kind of normal operational opportunity we blindly speculated about."

Achilles wheeled his chair over to where he could view his wife's screen.

Katya pointed with a French-manicured finger. "They're planning to transfer one of the prototypes from Delhi to Moscow for stress testing, whatever that means."

"When?"

"A week from today."

Achilles exhaled, long and slow. "The transfer operation presents a perfect opportunity, but a tight timeline."

The excitement on Katya's face began to morph toward fear before Achilles' eyes.

He knew what was happening.

He'd seen it happen dozens of times on fellow operatives.

Fear strikes the moment an operation switches from being a theoretical exercise to becoming an actual plan, complete with a countdown clock. It's the physical manifestation of an ancient proverb in action: *Be careful what you wish for.*

"Do you really think we can hijack a plane in this day and age? With any reasonable probability of success?" Katya asked.

"No."

"And not just any plane. A military transport plane, with a top-secret missile aboard?

"No."

"I don't see how.... Did you say *No?*"

"I did."

"But you also said 'the transfer operation presents a perfect opportunity.'"

"It's as perfect an opportunity as we could reasonably hope for. But I don't think hijacking an airplane is the way to exploit it"

"I see." Katya's expression transitioned back toward excited as their discussion returned to theoretical territory and her analytical brain reengaged.

Achilles waited quietly, knowing his wife rarely needed guidance when analysis was involved.

"Are we going to hijack the transport truck, either on the way to or from the airport?"

"Do you think that would be less risky?"

"A little bit," she said, scrunching her face.

"You may be right. Depends on their security procedures. But either way, that's not the tactic I'd propose we take."

Katya averted her gaze and her fingers began tapping her forearms. One, two, three, four. One, two, three, four. When she finally looked up, Achilles knew that she had it. "We impersonate the Russians. We modify the transfer plan using email, then show up on a plane from Moscow. If we get it right, then they'll hand over the missile." She stopped there as the second half of the thought lodged in her throat, the if-then scenario that began with them getting it wrong.

Chapter 10

The Risk

KATYA FOUND HERSELF SURVEYING her house with fresh eyes as she prepared to fly east to India rather than west to Fiji. She'd always known their home was special. If Kyle hadn't inherited it, they could never have afforded it. Not in that prestigious ZIP code with its explosive price inflation. But it wasn't the location or architecture that were stimulating her sense of gratitude that afternoon. It was the little luxuries common to most American houses. The private bathroom with its hot running water and tub. The kitchen with its miraculous assortment of food storage and preparation appliances. The air conditioning, heating, and security systems. Then there were the furnishings: the comfy chairs, convenient tables, and soft beds.

While pulling the bathing suits from her carry-on bag and replacing them with more practical clothes, Katya kept glancing over at their bed, with its thick mattress and soft white duvet. Heaven on Earth one might say—particularly if that person normally slept on the ground or a floor.

Katya was coming to grips with the idea that she could be spending the coming decades without a single one of the luxuries that now surrounded her. If they blew the mission, her life would consist of cold, hungry, tired, bored, sick and scared. Or *hot*, hungry, tired, bored, sick and scared—depending on whether they were imprisoned in Russia or India.

Nonetheless, she wasn't second-guessing her decision. Both math and morality made the correct decision obvious. Risking two lives to potentially save thousands, if not millions, was clearly the right choice. But when it was *your* life, your *everything* on the line, the calculation was considerably more prickly.

Still, she would do it.

She knew she would.

She would do it because she didn't want to be the kind of person who surrendered to fear. And because she believed in her husband. Deeply. Till death do they part.

"I just heard back from Aladdin," Achilles said, walking into the kitchen and snapping her back into the moment. "The plane has been chartered, the SUV rented, and the soldiers hired. He assures me that everything will be precisely as specified."

The last clause struck Katya as anomalous. "Has he gotten any more verbose with familiarity?"

"No, he—or she—continues to communicate with the clipped tone of a World War II telegraph operator. And frankly, that's fine with me. Brevity requires precision, and I want our lifeline thinking precisely."

Katya couldn't argue with that, but the whole scenario felt so unfamiliar that she was a bit off balance. She found an anonymous, omnipotent, robotic benefactor assisting from cyberspace to be disconcerting. Achilles seemed quite comfortable with the arrangement, however, and this was his world, so she resisted the arrogant urge to second-guess him—as he often did with her.

"How about the uniforms and documents?" she asked.

"They'll be waiting when we arrive at the staging ground in Kazakhstan."

Katya was impressed with the span and reach of their genie's powers. "How do you think Aladdin does it?"

Achilles shrugged. "Doing what he does takes only two things: money and connections."

"I get that, in theory at least. I guess I'm asking who you think he really is?"

"For all we know, he's an organization. But my best guess is that he's a former intelligence operative, like me, but one who served longer, rose higher, and then either jumped into the C-suite of a security or defense contractor, or founded his own company. In any case, you can be sure that he's among the best in the business."

"Why's that?"

"Because presidents get to pick who they want, and they have the means to identify the best."

The look in her husband's eye gave Katya the boost she needed. She stepped closer and took both his hands in hers. When their eyes met, she said, "Do you think we'll be back home soon?"

He squeezed her hands. "I have no doubt."

His decisiveness surprised her. He was neither a sugar-coating kind of guy nor the least bit naive. "Why's that?"

"Because to have any other thought would decrease our odds of success."

It sounded like a throwaway line, but she saw that her husband was serious. "Says the guy who climbs cliffs without a rope."

"And yet still lives."

He kissed her. "But seriously, surviving risky situations is like riding a bike. When things get shaky, the smart move is to relax and concentrate on the road ahead. Focusing on hazards tends to steer you toward them."

Katya appreciated the analogy but wasn't completely convinced. "What about when things aren't shaky?"

"Remain alert, retain composure, and just keep pedaling."

"Or flying," she said, looking over at her repacked bag.

Achilles' gaze followed hers. "India, here we come."

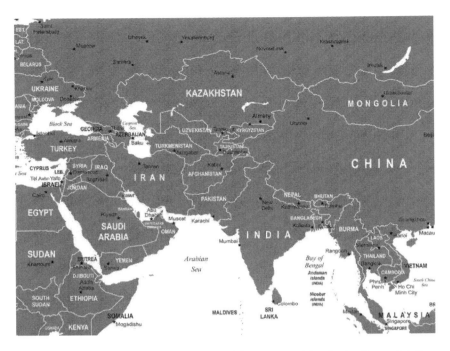

Moscow to Singapore, with Kazakhstan and India in the middle.

Chapter 11

The Debt

ALTHOUGH THE OPPORTUNITY Achilles and Katya had identified in India had them working against a very tight timeline, they did not fly straight to Delhi. First, they had to pick up the Russian plane and the Russian soldiers their charade required. The former Soviet Republic of Kazakhstan was the perfect place to procure those, but they didn't fly directly there, either.

One didn't pay moonlighting pilots—particularly those who were willing to borrow their government's plane—using anything but cold hard cash. Bricks of hundred-dollar bills, to be precise, packed into locking metal briefcases.

Achilles and Katya stopped in Singapore to withdraw a million dollars in the specified format. The sophisticated island city-state was more than a major international business hub. It had recently replaced Las Vegas as the second busiest gambling center in the world—following Macau. Given the environment, the service sector was primed to delight wealthy clientele, and it had no shortage of hundred-dollar bills.

The business backdrop didn't guarantee that every local bank would have millions sitting around in prepackaged bundles, but it meant large cash requests would not be unusual enough to raise red flags.

To avoid the risk of losing even a few critical hours in Singapore, Achilles had called ahead to inform his new bank of their requirements and schedule. Mr. Lee Lim, Relationship Manager, informed him that the funds would be ready at the requested time. He added that if they would be so kind as to provide their flight details, a town car would meet their incoming flight and then transport them back to the airport at their convenience. Perhaps with a bit of sightseeing along the way?

Even though Singapore's severe penal code and complete ban on guns made it one of the safest cities in the world, Achilles figured that grabbing a cab while toting a million in cash might not be the wisest move. He passed on the sightseeing, but accepted the ride, noting that they'd be coming in commercial and flying out private.

The first stage of their journey went precisely as planned. Not more than an hour after their overnight flight from San Francisco touched down, Lee handed Achilles a large gold-plated pen emblazoned with the bank's regal logo and pointed to the paperwork before them on his weighty oak desk. "Just sign here and here, Mr. Adams."

Achilles scribed large As and jagged squiggles, an autograph befitting a man who could move millions around the globe with a few flicks of his wrist. His action drained the two million dollar account of half its funds and transformed the debited digital currency into cash.

After flashing a satisfied smile, the banker removed two aluminum briefcases from a locked credenza behind his desk. He laid the matched set atop his big desk and opened each lid with a ceremonial flourish reminiscent of food service at a Michelin-starred restaurant. *Voilà!*

The count was easy. Five bricks of cellophane-wrapped bills filled each case. A total of ten thousand pieces of paper worth one hundred dollars each. Achilles split open a random bundle and pulled out a single bill. He gave it a thorough inspection before signing beside *Received*.

As Achilles handed back the pen, the banker said, "Please, keep it with my compliments."

Achilles stood and extended his hand. "You've been most kind."

"My pleasure, to be sure. If there's nothing else I can do for you, then I'll escort you out. Your driver is waiting at the side door."

C C C

Lee Lim looked to the heavens as his brother drove the Adamses in the direction of Seletar Airport. After a full minute of staring up into the haze that was the Singapore sky, he returned to his opulent office and poured a cognac from the bar.

There were reasons wealth management bankers were paid far more than was necessary for the relatively easy tasks they performed. There was image: the wealthy wanted to work with people who looked the part. There was comfort: the wealthy didn't want to discuss their millions and billions with people who didn't also live relatively lavish lives. And there was security: the banks didn't want employees who would be tempted to steal.

Lee Lim had the right university pedigree, and it shined. He earned a solid six-figure income, and it showed. Lee was also honest by nature, so the conclusion of the human resources screeners had been spot-on.

Except not really.

HR had failed to account for Lee's brother.

Tan Lim had a problem. An addiction. A fatal flaw. He was a gambler—and not a very good one. He played well above the reasonable limits for a man with a limo driver's income.

While that would create a bad situation in any location, it was particularly unfortunate in Singapore—given the caliber of the city-state's mafia. Since overt acts of thuggery garnered a swift, harsh and decisive response from the government, Singaporean crime bosses had adapted to become much more subtle and sophisticated than the knuckle breakers who terrorized other gambling centers.

Scheming was just the first step of their slick system. They also innovated, orchestrated and insulated, ensuring that their fingerprints would be nowhere near the scenes of their clever crimes.

When Tan Lim's debt hit half a million dollars, they didn't threaten to break his legs. They didn't dangle him off a balcony. Such tactics were much more likely to result in suicide or a botched crime than to put that half a million in their pockets. Instead, the enforcer assigned to his case schemed and researched. He then organized a meeting with Tan's male family members, including his brother and their three cousins.

In the crematory room of a funeral parlor, the enforcer explained exactly what the five Lims were going to do, and he handed out assignments. Lee was the lynchpin.

While the furnace blazed beside them, the mobster told Lee exactly what to look for and what to do when he saw it. He told Tan and their cousins—an aircraft mechanic, a fisherman and a personal trainer—precisely what had to happen when Lee called. Then he showed the five of them pictures of what would happen to Tan if they didn't perform, pictures that would make a billy goat puke. He ended by giving the family sixty days.

Despite knowing that his brother's life was on the line, Lee had let the first two opportunities slip past. Both times he'd been too nervous to make the call. Then copies of the photos showed up on his office chair the morning of day thirty-one.

Four days later, lightning struck in the form of a call from Kyle Adams. A foreigner passing through with his wife. To be honest, Lee didn't feel terribly bad about separating the couple from their million in cash. People with private jets obviously had money to burn. It was the enforcer's insistence that the couple be fed to the fish that weighed on his soul. That and the fact that Singapore's draconian no-guns law would leave his cousins armed with nothing but knives and baseball bats.

Chapter 12

The Diversion

ACHILLES WOULD NOT NORMALLY have been looking forward to getting back on a plane having just gotten off a flight that lasted eighteen hours, but at that moment he found the prospect appealing. To avoid luggage screening going out of Singapore, and to ease customs clearance going into Kazakhstan, they were flying private. That meant a bed, which was just what his jet-lagged body wanted.

"Private out of Seletar Airport, correct?" the driver reconfirmed, given that they'd flown into Changi.

"That's right."

"I'll have you there in about thirty minutes."

Singapore's highway system uses separated, elevated roads and tunnels to create exceptionally efficient traffic flow. It also benefits from the low congestion levels created by an automotive tax and fee structure that increases the cost of car ownership fivefold. As a result, the commute from the city center to the airports on the outskirts is worlds different from what one experiences in San Francisco and New York.

There was very little stop-and-go movement before the Seletar Airport signs appeared. Achilles was pleased—until they shot past the exit for the Business Aviation Centre. "Wasn't that our turnoff?"

"Seletar is different from Changi, sir. They allow people flying private to go straight to their plane. Management is trying to steal business from their bigger rival, and it's working."

Indeed, they were heading toward a string of hangars. The door to one began opening when the limo approached, as if responding to a remote control. Instead of rolling up like an enormous home garage door, the twenty-foot panel split in the middle, folding outward as it rose, creating a ten-foot awning.

The growing opening revealed an assortment of wheeled tool trollies and work tables along with a white seafood delivery van—but no jet. The discrepancy rocketed Achilles' radar to full alert, slowing time and heightening his senses. When the door reversed course and began closing after they entered, he lost all doubt.

Wise men have long professed that he who hesitates is lost. While that ancient proverb applies to countless situations, it is never more true than in combat, whether the battlefield is a Middle Eastern desert, a gladiatorial arena, or the backseat of a town car. Achilles did not hesitate. He didn't wait to see what weapons might appear. He didn't attempt to elicit an explanation or offer a bribe—not with a million dollars in cash right there for the taking. What he did do was grab the metallic bank pen from his breast pocket and clench it in his left hand like a dagger.

The human trachea is a very robust piece of anatomy. Framed by bands of hyaline cartilage and controlled by smooth muscle, it is simultaneously flexible and rigid. Tasked with keeping the airway open, and evolved over millions of years, it is surprisingly difficult to slit and challenging to crush. While punctures are easier to inflict, they are not inherently fatal. They do, however, deliver a severe shock to the system and create an extreme distraction during combat situations.

Achilles opened two holes in the driver's windpipe at jackhammer speed, then buried the golden instrument deep enough in his side to puncture a lung. This multi-organ attack proved too much for the recipient's brain to process. He went limp like a bounce house whose blower had blown a fuse.

But he remained buckled into the right-side driver's seat, and the car continued rolling toward the white delivery van.

Achilles responded by worming himself halfway over the driver's seat and making three more moves in rapid succession. He shoved the gear selector into neutral, pressed the driver's seatbelt release, and turned the wheel left as far as it would go. He held on with a white knuckled grip as the town car swung around 180 degrees, crashing into tables and scattering tools. The flying instruments weren't what drew Achilles' eyes as the limo came to a halt facing backwards. They were locked on the men exiting the white van.

Three assailants emerged, all wearing white industrial coveralls. Two were wielding baseball bats, the third a pair of butcher knives. Despite the uniforms and what was clearly a common intent, they didn't strike Achilles as either professionals or a team. Their faces expressed too much emotion and their bodies revealed too much hesitation.

A quick glance gave Achilles all he needed to complete his threat assessment. Numbers. Positions. Weapons. While that information fed secondary calculations, he switched back into threat-neutralization mode. First he hit the automatic door lock, then he grabbed the disabled driver by his belt and heaved his limp body toward the passenger seat. Even though the man was relatively slight, repositioning him required a series of very awkward moves. By the time Achilles managed to muscle him aside, the three assailants were just a few feet away.

Chapter 13

The Downfall

ACHILLES STOLE A GLANCE over his shoulder to evaluate his opponents as they closed in, sizing them up for psychology, capability and hierarchy. The most muscular of the three was swinging his bat around in circles, psyching himself up. The smallest one was rigidly holding his bat up with both hands as if he hoped it was magic. The third guy marched with his knives held down at his side, like a robot programmed never to stop.

"They're almost here," Katya said, her voice so calm it made him proud. Their circumstances had changed from peacetime to war in the blink of an eye, but she'd remained as cool and focused as a veteran weapons officer during a dogfight.

The amateur assailants had undoubtedly been expecting easy pickings. An unsuspecting couple who could be yanked from the car and culled as easily as cows.

Determined to deny them any part of that scenario, Achilles dove the rest of the way into the front seat and wriggled into driving position.

The first whack bounced off the driver's window, sending the bat back toward the man wielding it. Unfortunately, it didn't crack him in the head. Achilles wasn't that lucky.

The wielder was by far the beefiest of the trio. A gym rat to be sure. But he wasn't the one causing Achilles the most concern. That honor went to the hard man holding the two large knives. Unlike the others, he had calloused hands and cold eyes.

Achilles switched the transmission into Drive as the weaponized Kentucky ash smashed against his window glass for the second time, shattering it into a thousand pieces and peppering him with hundreds of them. He ignored the flying debris along with the man now aiming an uninhibited swing.

The hangar that held them was about 120 feet wide and 100 feet deep. With the door down, it was effectively a self-contained combat arena. One with plenty of room to maneuver—and little place to hide.

Achilles slammed the accelerator.

The men sprinted after them in pursuit.

"I don't think this will punch through the door," Katya said, her voice growing louder as they approached the hangar's edge.

"I don't either. But that's not my intent. Hold on."

Achilles pumped the parking brake on and off as he whipped the steering wheel around, causing the car to turn much tighter than it had the last time. Then he took aim. "These guys are going to get a killer lesson in learning to think a few moves ahead."

Comprehension dawned on all three faces as the car reversed course.

Achilles targeted the psychopath first.

The butcher tossed his blades and tried diving out of the way, but his shoulders telegraphed his move in time for Achilles to react. The front bumper clipped the back half of the would-be killer's body, sending him sailing with an audible crack.

He landed in a limp pile.

Achilles wasn't aiming to terminate the three assassins, despite their obvious intention to turn him and his wife into shark chum. So he wouldn't be backing up for a double-tap with the tires. This was not personal. But Achilles wouldn't be pulling punches to save lives either. Putting their mission back on track was goal one, two and three.

"He's out of it," Katya reported as Achilles turned the car toward the next closest man. That assailant was running toward the hangar's only pedestrian door. Achilles didn't particularly care if the man got away, but he didn't know whether escape was the smaller man's primary intent, and he wasn't about to risk one of the less-favorable alternatives. Not for a man who'd kill innocents for money.

A decisive thud left the second assailant moaning on the hangar floor.

The remaining running man had nearly reached the white van by the time Achilles had the limo pointed in his direction. That forced a choice between one of two dangerous moves, and gave Achilles little time to make it.

He went with the option that posed the least risk to Katya. "Hold on!"

Rather than ram the van, Achilles turned the wheel hard a few yards early while locking the brakes. This slammed the middle of the town car into the van's front left corner and brought it to a halt with a conclusive crunch.

Satisfied that he'd penned the van in, Achilles shifted into Park. "Lock the doors behind me."

"Should I call the police?" Katya asked.

"Absolutely not. Around here they'll cane you on a public square for chewing gum. I'm going to wrap this up, then we're going to fly out of Singapore without looking back."

He stepped out, then leaned back in to drag the driver after him. Achilles didn't need to check to see if the man was alive because he'd been listening to his gurgled, wheezing breathing for the past few minutes. The others he'd dealt with would also make it, but neither would be playing hopscotch anytime soon.

Louisville Slugger was staring wide-eyed from behind the wheel. He seemed paralyzed.

Speaking over the top of the town car, Achilles said, "If you want to fight, get out of the van. If you want to talk, slide into the passenger seat and roll down the window."

The man blinked a few times, then slid over and lowered his window a few inches.

"What was this about?" Achilles asked.

"A gambling debt."

"Whose? The banker's?"

"No, his brother's," Louisville nodded toward the driver. "He owes half a million."

That cleared everything up. The motive. The means. The risky behavior and amateur execution. "Who are you?"

"His cousin. We're all cousins."

Achilles believed it. "You'll all live to see tomorrow. But I'd strongly suggest that you start over elsewhere if you want to see next week. Meanwhile, you and I have a problem."

"I'm sorry, man. So very, very sorry. It wasn't personal."

"My wife's with me. It doesn't get more personal. But that's not the problem I'm talking about. We need an hour to get out of here."

The man's face dropped. He understood. He had to be silenced with more than a promise. Achilles saw him searching for a minimally invasive solution. Surprisingly, he found one. "You can lock me in the back of the van. You just gotta turn the refrigerator off so I don't freeze."

Achilles gave him an A for effort but an F for content. The man might suffocate if they followed his plan. Either he wasn't particularly bright, or he had something sneaky in mind. "All right. Let's do it. Pass me the bat," Achilles said, extending an open hand.

The man did.

Achilles positioned himself in the wedge between their cars where the driver would be exiting.

The background humming he'd been hearing ceased, indicating that the refrigerator had been switched off. Then the man got out, hands held high.

"Show me," Achilles said. "Slowly."

As the man took hold of the rear door handles, Achilles whacked him on the back of the head.

Chapter 14

The Portrait

KATYA BURST OUT of the car as the last of their four assailants slumped to the ground. She needed to move, to burn off nervous energy. After scanning the scene of the ambush for signs of danger, she ran to hug her husband in a full body embrace.

Achilles obliged, but only momentarily. "Let me check on something."

Bat in hand, he began running toward the first man they'd hit with the car. The one with the psychopathic stride who'd been wielding knives. She understood why. He looked like the kind of monster who'd bounce back in a movie. But Achilles reversed course after closing just half the gap.

"He's not faking it. And he couldn't do anything if he were. His right knee's bent the wrong way."

Katya shivered. "Let's agree to never walk around with a million dollars in cash again."

"No argument here."

Achilles surveyed the hangar. "I've got some cleanup to do. Please check our location on your phone's map app. Determine exactly where we are in relation to the private aviation terminal, then figure out the best way to get there—either on foot or by taxi."

"Okay."

"I worry that if we don't leave Singapore within the hour, we may be stuck here for years."

"On it."

She went to work with the map, glancing up at Achilles while her screen paused to load. He began by wiping down the town car's smooth surfaces, eliminating their fingerprints. He finished up about the same time she did.

"What did you learn?" he asked.

"It's too far to walk without being conspicuous. There's a flying school next door. We can call a cab to meet us there."

"Please do."

She did, while he moved on to less pleasant business.

Achilles began staging the scene by pulling the pen from the unconscious driver's side and placing it in the hand of the last man who'd been standing. He continued by hauling the stabbed man back into the driver's seat, then pressing his palms and fingers against the wheel. He finished by popping the trunk and closing the car door.

After removing their bags, Achilles looked at her, smiled and asked, "How long?"

"Dispatcher said five minutes."

"Good." He gave her appearance a close examination. "You look fine. How about me?"

"You've got blood on your shirt and tie. Probably best to ditch the jacket too."

"I've got a windbreaker in my bag."

"That will look funny."

"Will it look felonious?"

"Good point."

"Rich people are supposed to be eccentric, right?"

Katya couldn't argue with that. "Put it on. Cab's probably already next door."

They put the packed aluminum briefcases atop their roller bags and exited onto the concrete runway apron.

She was eager to ask her husband how he thought things would play out, but forced her focus to their current circumstances. Fortunately, those proved uneventful.

The cab ride was just a cab ride, short but well tipped.

The formal procedures for their private international charter proved to be more like registering at a fancy hotel than checking into a commercial airline. The staff were polite and attentive, the wait minimal, and the furnishings a few notches above normal. The business aviation center even had house music playing to give the place a relaxing mood.

A black Lexus shuttled them from the executive terminal to the Falcon 7X that would be theirs for the next eleven hours or so. It appeared to be a fine choice from the outside. The inside didn't disappoint either.

"It's so big," Katya said, looking around as they sank into two of the twelve cream-colored leather recliners.

"Almaty is 3,400 miles from Singapore. Can't fly that far with anything but a large jet, not direct anyway."

"Can I bring you anything to eat or drink before takeoff?" their flight attendant asked.

"Thanks, but we're going to try to get some sleep," Katya said.

"I'll dim the lights and bring bedding. There's a button on the wall that will turn your loungers into a bed, but I'll ask you to wait on that until after takeoff. There's also a button you can use to call me at any time. My name's Charlotte."

"Thank you, Charlotte."

Katya had visions of red and blue lights racing toward them across the runway, but what played out was completely routine. Other than the bedding service. They taxied, they waited, they took off.

When they were finally, gratefully airborne, Katya turned to her husband and asked, "Why didn't they have guns? I kept waiting for the bullets to start flying."

"Using a gun in a crime gets you the death penalty in Singapore. Possession alone gets you fourteen years and a public flogging. That's why I wasn't particularly concerned about our airport ride. Lesson learned."

Katya wanted to explore that topic further, but she had a more practical concern at the moment. "How do you think things will play out in the hangar?"

Achilles' thoughtful nod told her he'd been asking himself the same question. "I believe the banker will be the decision maker. My guess is that he's been panicking for the last fifteen minutes or so. Soon, he'll start calling his brother and cousins, if he hasn't already. Maybe he'll rouse one from oblivion. Maybe he'll freak out when nobody answers and will drive over. Either way, he's likely to be as concerned about keeping his job as about the health of his family members. He's going to want to avoid instigating a major police investigation while getting them medical attention."

"Do you think that's possible?"

"Not entirely. But if they all stick together on a story, the police will move on. With us gone, there are no third-party victims. If they all say the same thing, the police won't care."

"What kind of a story?"

"Presumably a crazy accident. I'm sure they'll get creative."

"What about the half-million-dollar debt?"

"The mafia won't be happy, but that's not our concern."

"Do you think they'll run?"

"They will if they're smart, but I doubt it. People prefer the devil they know to the unknown. That's one reason battered wives stick around."

"Well, I bet you cured the gambling problem that started it all."

"One can only hope."

They lay in silence for a long time as the Falcon streaked northwest across the sky. Long enough for future expectations to begin stealing mindshare from past events. As dangerous as the

Singapore fiasco had been, it counted as child's play compared to what lay ahead. Amateur thugs sent by a local mafia boss were one thing, the Russian and Indian militaries quite another.

Katya opened her eyes to see that Achilles was watching her from his bed. "This is it, isn't it?" she asked.

He requested clarification, even though she suspected he knew exactly what she meant. "What do you mean?"

Truth be told, she wasn't looking for an answer. She was seeking emotional release. "We're approaching the point of no return. Entering the danger zone. Diving into the deep end. When we get off this plane, we're effectively committing to an act that may well alter the course of our lives."

"And we've got pretty good lives," he said, sympathetically. "Lots to lose."

"Exactly. I can't help but question the wisdom of accepting this assignment."

"The human propensity to leave the tough stuff to other people is why the world faces so many problems in the first place. We tend to take like we're entitled, but don't give like we're obligated."

She couldn't argue with that.

"I'm not immune to those impulses," he continued, his voice soothing, his eyes full of affection. "Excuses are always easy to find, while solutions are often difficult to accept, so I force myself to stay focused on the big picture."

"And what picture is that?" Katya asked.

"The portrait of the person I want to be."

Katya knew what he meant, but it was her turn to ask anyway. "A person who can be counted on to step up when others back off, regardless of the risk or inconvenience?"

"Something like that."

She leaned across the aisle and kissed her husband.

Chapter 15

The Russians

THEY SLEPT until the pilot announced landing in Almaty, at which point Achilles cracked a window shade. He found a full moon illuminating Kazakhstan's largest metropolis.

"It's beautiful," Katya said, looking over his shoulder. "Between the twinkling lights and the mountains in the background."

Achilles agreed, although he hadn't come for the scenery. Three factors had led him to select Almaty for their staging operation. One, it was on the flight path from Moscow to Delhi, making their approach appear appropriate to Indian air traffic control. Two, it would be easier for them to work with than the other countries along that flight path—namely Kyrgyzstan, China, and Pakistan—since the people and customs were more familiar. And three, it was full of Russian equipment and soldiers, both of which could be rented under the table.

Once Achilles knew exactly what he wanted and where, he'd outsourced the procurement to the man who'd been provided for that purpose. True to his name, Aladdin had organized the plane, people, and other supplies, arranging to have everything delivered in one tidy package for a single fixed fee.

Now, just as their "procurement officer extraordinaire" had promised, an SUV was waiting at the bottom of their jet's airstair. It was a civilian vehicle, a black Mercedes of the style favored by Moscow's elite. By contrast, the two men standing at parade rest beside the open passenger door were not private citizens. They wore the duty fatigues of Russian Air Force sergeants. The one whose insignia marked him as a senior sergeant stepped forward as they descended. "General Antonov, Major Brusilova, welcome to Almaty," he said, using the names Achilles and Katya had assumed for the operation. "I'm Sergeant Belikov."

"Should we salute?" Katya whispered, softly enough to avoid being overheard on the noisy airfield.

"Not when out of uniform," Achilles replied, realizing that they had some last-minute cramming to do. "And the lower rank always initiates."

"Thank you, Sergeant."

"Sir, I believe you have something for us?"

Achilles motioned up the airstair. "You'll find two briefcases just inside the door, along with our luggage."

Sergeant Belikov motioned to his companion, who proceeded to retrieve all four bags from the Falcon in a single trip. While the bags disappeared into the trunk, Belikov motioned to the SUV's open rear door. "If you please."

The drive to the waiting Ilyushin Il-76 took only a few minutes. It was also in the executive aviation section of the airport, not the military, as one might have expected given the flat gray paint job and Russian Air Force markings. The sergeant did not take them to an airstair. None was present. Instead he drove toward the tail and then backed up the rear cargo ramp into the belly of the plane.

The cargo hold was about twice as wide as the Mercedes and five times as long, leaving room to open both doors—and transport a missile. The four exited and walked around to the front of the SUV, where six additional soldiers of various ranks and two pilots were standing at attention. The men all looked sufficiently impressive, with rugged faces, tough physiques and close-cropped hair. Achilles was pleased to see them acting like he really was a general, whether they believed it or not.

"At ease," Achilles said, in Russian.

Sergeant Belikov addressed them. "It is your choice, of course— sir, ma'am—but I would suggest that you spend the night on the plane. That way you'll avoid passport control and leave no footprints in Kazakhstan."

"Sleeping arrangements?" Achilles asked, implicitly agreeing to the plan.

"You and the major can have the SUV. We have bedrolls. Wheels-up at 0600 will get us to Delhi at 0800 India Standard Time."

"Did our luggage arrive?" Achilles was referencing their papers and uniforms. He had supplied Aladdin with their requirements and sizes.

"Yes, sir. Two bags are waiting on the plane."

Achilles looked over at his wife a little later when they were alone. "You're in the Air Force now, babe."

"It's *major*," Katya replied in a tone that told him she was prepared for the dangerous mission ahead.

Chapter 16

The Major and The General

ACHILLES FOUND the cold-water shave in the Soviet-era military aircraft's tiny restroom to be surprisingly bracing. Routine tasks often had that effect on him during stressful situations, but he didn't think familiarity was the driver this time. The discomfort reminded him that he'd often roughed it during his years in CIA operations, and those had all worked out.

At least as far as the missions themselves were concerned.

The politics hadn't always ended smoothly.

His shave complete, Achilles moved on to makeup—a less familiar act and a more stressful one to be sure. His goal was to add about fifteen years to his appearance, making it match the stereotypical image of a fast-track general.

He set about scrunching his face this way and that, then painting dark makeup into the wrinkles, contours and sags. Once satisfied that he'd found all his natural fault lines, he feathered each marking in the proper direction, using the technique he'd been taught by an Agency disguise artist. To strengthen the illusion of depth, Achilles added a line of light color to the unfeathered side of each dark line.

"Not bad," he mumbled into the mirror.

For the finishing touches, Achilles powdered his face all over with light concealer, then added gray to his hair around the temples. The completed picture was both satisfying and disconcerting. He looked a lot older. Ironically, if anyone picked up on the powder, they'd interpret it as a general's vain attempt to look younger. To better fit the ideal image of a vigorous warrior. Nobody used makeup to appear older.

Katya had transformed into Major Brusilova by the time Achilles returned to the SUV with her tea, his coffee, and their breakfast. Two white rolls and a brick of cheese. They'd practiced with the stage makeup at home, so his appearance didn't shock her. "Good job with the hair," he said, referring to her military bun. Given the circumstances, he figured that greeting was better than, "How'd you sleep?"

"Can't be that good. You didn't salute."

Achilles couldn't tell from her tone if she was serious. They were both a bit off. Morning lag plus jet lag. Caffeine and calories would help. "Junior rank salutes first. You know that, right?"

"I know."

"Missions get blown by the little things. When you're playing a role, it has to come fast and look natural. People are like dogs, they pick up on tension—just subconsciously and without the growl."

His last clause elicited a smile. "I grew up in Moscow. I know how authority figures behave. Their confident body language, assertive verbal tendencies and imperious facial expressions."

"You want to go over it again while we eat?"

"I'm good to go, General."

He met her eye and saw that she was. "Hoorah, Major. Eat up, and we'll make the call."

Rather than run the risk of getting caught rescheduling the prototype transfer, they decided to show up three hours early under the guise of a surprise inspection. Surprise inspections being a common occurrence when the Russian military was involved.

They figured thirty minutes was the right amount of advance notice to give DelMos that Air Force General Antonov would be accompanying the transfer team. They would call it *a visit* rather than *an inspection*, but the rank of the powerful officer made the two synonymous.

DelMos Technologies was headquartered at Safdarjung, which had once been the main airport for the region around Delhi but had ceased commercial operations in the late 1960s when its runway became outdated. The once grand facility now housed only DelMos and the Delhi Flying Club.

Using her Major Brusilova voice, Katya got the joint venture's Delhi program director on the line and alerted him to their early arrival time. "The general wanted to come a bit early to have a look around before picking up the prototype. I'm sure you understand."

Anyone who worked with the Russians understood that they liked to throw their weight around. That was what powerful brutes did, and it was best not to aggravate them.

"But of course. We're honored by the visit."

"I'm sure the general would appreciate it if you were there to meet the plane," Katya added.

The program director was a distinguished academic. With PhDs in both mechanical engineering and aeronautics from prestigious Indian universities, Dr. Mishra was the joint venture's ultimate authority on technical issues. But the military was not his bailiwick. In Achilles' experience, people who had never worn a uniform tended to be intimidated by those who did. Throw in the fact that this uniformed Russian was a general, and almost anyone would be deferential.

Almost anyone.

Achilles did not know Mishra. He couldn't be certain. He was playing the odds. That was what successful operatives did—they worked percentages—with conviction, intuition and courage.

"I'm afraid the timing is a bit problematic," Mishra replied.

"Well then I'm glad to be dealing with such a renowned problem-solver," Katya shot back.

Mishra hesitated a bit longer than Achilles would have liked, but his ultimate answer was satisfactory. "Please tell the general that I look forward to welcoming him shortly."

Chapter 17

The First Problem

KATYA WATCHED the cargo door open in Delhi like it was the gate to Hell. Given the accompanying blast of heat and blazing sun beyond, she figured the analogy might fit in more ways than one. Still, there was something hypnotizing about watching the jet's rear partition swing up out of the way while the floor angled down to form a ramp.

The air that billowed in with the light wasn't just furnace-like, it stank. The Indian capital city was known for having hazardous pollution levels during the summer months, and one whiff was enough to confirm as much. How did people without air-conditioned homes and offices cope? What was it like in prison?

Katya pushed the troubling questions aside. Once the soldiers had removed the straps used to secure the SUV during flight, she took her seat and assumed a military disposition.

The sergeant behind the wheel waited to start the engine until his men had marched down the ramp and formed a corridor. Three men on each side, spaced equally between the bottom of the ramp and the assembled welcome party.

If all went according to plan, that would be the soldiers' only duty. Window dressing. Uniformed mannequins. A general's entourage.

If someone screwed up, however, or fate somehow intervened, then the mannequins would spring to life. They would help the imposters fight their way to freedom. Fight *and* flight, Katya mused. No *or* about it.

While she mentally rehearsed potential responses to the disaster scenario—running, fighting or hiding—the driver keyed the ignition. The noise functioned like the starter's bell at the Kentucky Derby, sending the soldiers springing into action. They pivoted precisely ninety degrees and whipped off crisp salutes.

The race was on.

A battle of wits.

A grand deception with all their lives on the line and the safety of America at stake.

With two supporting actors seated up front, and the main characters settled in back, the SUV descended the ramp. It drove to the end of the human corridor and stopped. The sergeants stepped out, opened the rear doors and snapped off salutes. Russian Air Force General Antonov and his aide, Major Brusilova, stepped onto the hot tarmac.

Katya followed a half-step behind Achilles as they approached the small welcoming party. Every move for the next ninety minutes would involve critical calculations—beginning with this one. At that very moment, Achilles was playing a high-stakes game of chicken. He wanted Director Mishra to speak first, to set the tone, so Achilles could adapt his tactics accordingly. Read, then manipulate, in constant iteration—as Rex Rowe so masterfully did.

Tension began to build as the gap between the two parties narrowed without either breaking the ice. The silence did not reflect a hospitable disposition.

At the same time, Katya found that her husband's strange uniform, makeup and demeanor were making it much easier for her to play the part of a major and general's aide. His every glance, word and gesture reminded her of her own role. They put her in character.

When Achilles was nearly within handshake range, the man Katya recognized as Director Mishra stepped forward from the group of five and extended his hand. "General Antonov, thank you for coming. To what do we owe the pleasure?"

"Director Mishra. I've been wanting to visit for some time. A last-minute schedule change made this quick trip possible." Achilles shook his host's hand a bit longer than necessary. Katya knew this was purposeful. He wanted to make a deep, reinforcing impression. Rock climbing had given her husband calloused hands and a vise-like grip. Combined with his athletic physique and the intelligent gleam in his blue-gray eyes, they completed the image of a don't-mess-with-me military man.

"Our good fortune to be sure," Mishra replied. "Although I fear I haven't had the opportunity to prepare a tour or presentation."

"I'm not interested in how our joint venture presents on special occasions," Achilles said in a neutral tone. "I prefer to see everyday operations."

"Perhaps you're thinking of Potemkin's famous deception?"

"You know your Russian history."

"For the last four centuries, Russian history has been world history," Mishra said, sounding sage as he spoke with his hands clasped behind his back.

"Good point."

Achilles gestured to the open space beyond the welcoming party's two SUVs. "I can't help but notice that you don't have the missile with you."

"We weren't expecting the pickup for some hours. It's being prepared for transport as we speak."

"I have an appointment at the Kremlin this afternoon. I'm afraid that gives me a hard deadline. Wheels-up in ninety minutes."

"I'll let the team know."

Katya didn't like the sound of that. The deadline truly was as hard as they came—but not for the reason Achilles stated.

The real transport plane from Moscow was set to arrive in three hours. Given that Ghandi International managed all air traffic control in the region, Safdarjung would get no advance notice of its arrival. But that arrangement didn't give the imposters three hours on the ground. They needed to get the missile out of Indian airspace before their deception was exposed. The border was a ninety-minute flight away.

To streamline their ground game, Katya and Achilles had formulated tactics that would both reinforce the charade and limit their exposure to the bare minimum. No more than ninety minutes.

Achilles swiftly segued his discussion with Mishra in that direction. "In keeping to the objective of observing everyday operations, I'd prefer a one-on-one tour. Just the two of us. Major Brusilova will remain with the plane to supervise the loading—and see to some urgent paperwork that Moscow just requested."

"I'd like that very much," the Director said with convincing inflection. "But I'm afraid I can't be your guide this morning. I have an important breakfast meeting with the mayor. Rescheduling would be very bad for our business."

Achilles stayed silent, but Katya was certain his face was speaking.

"Fortunately, several of my department heads are available." Mishra turned and gestured to the other four members of his entourage. Each stepped forward to shake Achilles' hand when introduced. "Aarav Khatri, Systems Development. Sai Bakshi, Engineering. Vihaan Acharya, Manufacturing Operations. And Prisha Chabra, Human Resources."

The first title made Katya cringe. The second forced her to fight back panic. How could Achilles wriggle out of that net? Four intelligent adversaries, three of whom would have nothing to do but scrutinize Achilles' every word as the fourth engaged him in shop talk that was over his head?

Katya struggled to concoct an excuse, something that would stop the tour without blowing the mission. Nothing came to mind. Before she knew it, her husband was gone.

Chapter 18

The Other General

STEEL SHIELD had been bribing generals and lawmakers since day one. That was how lucrative contracts were won, and how genteel business was done. The people who carved up a pie got a slice.

Successful players understood the unspoken rules.

But of course, there were exceptions. Every once in a while, a person came along who took the backstage game to a new level. A visionary. A pioneer. A person so skilled you never saw her coming.

William Zacharia studied his C3 colleagues as they settled into their customary seats around his fire pit. He now viewed them very differently from the way he had eighteen months earlier at Luci's first meeting. Back then, the three CEOs had gathered as glorified lobbyists. Petitioners to a government they intended to influence. Three out of thousands of players competing in the time-honored dance of quid pro quo.

Now … now, to the extent that it mattered to them, the C3 *were* the government. The Executive Branch. And as titillating as that twist felt, remarkably enough, it was not the most exciting development since Luci had replaced her predecessor.

The C3 would soon extend their influence far beyond Washington. Before long, the whole country would enjoy the impact of their genius. The three CEOs seated around his fire would be legends in their boardrooms. Very wealthy legends. All, WZ had to admit, thanks to Luci's marvelous Machiavellian mind and brilliantly boundless ambition.

If no one intervened.

If no unforeseen obstacle arose.

If the pieces continued to coalesce as planned and Luci's predictions proved accurate.

"Welcome back," William Zacharia said, soberly nodding to both guests. "I want to begin by thanking you for coming. Clearly, Operation 51 has reached the stage where quarterly or even monthly meetings will no longer suffice. Given that this lodge has served us well as mission command, and we've initiated the equivalent of a moon launch, I believe the three of us should plan to spend every weekend here until our eagle has landed."

"Agreed," Luci said.

"Whatever it takes," Ben concurred.

"Good. Given the assortment of external impediments arrayed against us, I'm glad we're in accord. Now, before we begin, there's something I feel compelled to say."

The others instantly grew silent.

William Zacharia let the tension crescendo, then gave it a further bump by slowly turning to meet the fairest member's eye. "I want to be honest with you, Luci. When you said Saxon was the smart play, I thought you were shortsighted. When you said we could control him, I had serious doubts. When you laid out your ultimate plan, I thought you were batshit crazy. But now that I've seen your ambition in action, I'm ready to openly admit before Ben and my maker that you're a goddamn genius."

"Hear, hear," Ben said.

Luci successfully fought back a smile, but couldn't keep her face from flushing. "Thank you. Lest we waver in our resolve as the inevitable issues arise, I think it's important for us to recognize that boldness is our friend. In the coming weeks, when doubts pester and fears scratch, we'll need to bear in mind that our operation is simply too audacious for the average mind to comprehend. A fact that will work to our great advantage.

"Trust me when I tell you that with sophisticated operations like ours, all you ever have to do to lead public opinion by the nose is offer a simple alternative, preferably one that evokes fear and anger. You push those buttons using some viscerally-appealing explanation, then repeat, repeat, repeat. History has shown that it works every time."

"The tactic is obvious when you point it out," Ben said. "But nonetheless impossible to defend against. Lazy minds will always grasp for simple solutions. Add an element of outrage, and you make it irresistible."

"Exactly," Luci said.

William Zacharia concurred, but he had latched onto two other aspects of the plan. "I like that our fingerprints are nowhere to be found. That we can win, but can't lose. However, I do harbor one concern."

Luci raised her eyebrows. "Namely?"

"This is an all-or-nothing play."

"The big plans always are." Luci's tone relaxed as she replied, but her face remained tense. A second later, she revealed why. "I'm afraid my plan to acquire the warhead has fallen behind schedule. I've been assured that it's just a temporary setback, but beyond that, things get murky."

"Murky?" Ben repeated, as the first chink in Luci's armor appeared.

WZ was wondering when it would all start to fall apart. He sat upright and spoke calmly. "I think it's time for you to brief us on the details of your plan."

The three had divvied up the workload of Operation 51 based on who had what expertise, connections, and capabilities, with WZ procuring the missile, Luci obtaining the warhead, and Ben preparing the launch sites. Beyond that, they'd kept their discussions vague in order to create credible deniability if things went south. In the vernacular of clandestine operatives, they'd compartmentalized.

"I agree," Ben said. "If there's a problem that could put the whole program in jeopardy, let's put our heads together."

Luci stared at her own tented fingers for a few seconds before speaking. "My contact is General Gromov. Until last month, he was in command of the 42nd Rocket Division in Yekaterinburg, Russia. Now, he's the commander of the 31st in Orenburg. The 42nd reports to the 31st, so the warhead that General Gromov intends to steal remains under his command, but obtaining it is less convenient than it was a few weeks back."

"So the specific warhead you're pursuing is still on the Russian Army inventory? It's not one that fell off the books when the Soviet Union fell apart?" Ben asked.

"No, we need a new one. New missile, new warhead."

WZ jumped in. "How is he planning to steal an inventoried warhead without getting caught? The type we're targeting weighs about four hundred pounds, and they're much too big to be slipped into a briefcase."

"He's identified a group of ten warheads that are held in reserve, meaning they're not assigned to a specific delivery system, and as such are low profile. He's going to swap one of the ten out with a dummy. A lookalike that will pass the quick visual inspection of a daily count.

"The dummy will be made of a highly combustible material, and programmed to self-destruct before the next mechanical inspection, on a day when Gromov and his co-conspirators can arrange to be nowhere near the facility. The warhead will effectively vanish in a flash of bright light and dark smoke, leaving no trace beyond a pile of soot on the concrete floor beneath its storage rack. The conflagration that destroys it will trigger the fire suppression system."

"Washing away the soot," Ben concluded.

"And making it appear that the warhead disappeared during the ruckus. Brilliant," WZ said. "Since the plan comes from the former facility commander, we can safely assume that he knows how to bypass the bunker's security systems and evade other entanglements. Is the issue one of timing?"

"More like two of timing," Luci said with a straight face. "Obviously, he needs to pick a night when only his people are working. Guys he trusts. Soldiers who will play for pay. As commander, that was easy to arrange. Now, it's more challenging to orchestrate."

"And the second timing issue?" William Zacharia asked.

"It has to be a night when the general is able to visit. Sounds simple enough until you look at a map and give it some thought. It's a thousand kilometers from Yekaterinburg to Orenburg—so he can't just hop in a truck like he's going to the store. Obviously, flying is faster but much higher profile, and he'll have the dummy warhead with him. You get the picture."

"What's his prediction?"

"As I said, it's murky. Gromov has his eye on a beachfront retirement estate on Majorca and he's dreaming of the payout that will get him there. He can't wait. He talks about it all the time, about trading snow for sand and his sidearm for a fishing pole. But he can't force the schedule without risking detection. So all he'll commit to is 'soon.'"

William Zachariah felt his temples begin to throb. "Is 'soon' a week? A month? Longer?"

"We're exposed at the construction sites," Ben added. "Every day of delay is a roll of the dice."

William Zacharia knew the construction site exposure was actually between zero and next-to-nothing. The dice might be rolling, but they had a thousand sides, not six. He wouldn't have agreed to the plan otherwise.

"We'll know when he knows," Luci said. "Meanwhile, rest assured that it is the general's highest priority."

"Should we be seeking an alternative source?" Ben asked.

That was the important question, and William Zacharia knew the answer. "No. Not yet. Asking around about buying a nuke is the riskiest thing we could do. And frankly, I'm not worried about Gromov failing to deliver."

"Why not?" Ben asked.

"We have the world's most powerful force on our side."

"And what's that?"

"Greed."

Chapter 19

The Procurement Officer

LUCI USED A BREATH CONTROL TRICK to bring her blood pressure back to normal, inhaling on a three-count and exhaling on a six. In...two...three. Out...two...three...four...five...six. In... two...three. Out...two...three...four...five...six. Surely after all the obstacles the C3 had plowed past or pushed aside, her master plan wouldn't fall apart on account of a staffing change in the Ural Mountains. Surely, she would not prove to be the C3's weakest link.

"Let's move on to site construction," William Zacharia said, snapping Luci back into the moment.

Ben slid to the edge of his armchair, as was his habit when speaking. He liked to talk with his hands. "My pleasure. Both locations are progressing as planned. Fences are up, foundations are laid, and the superstructures are almost complete. I expect to begin equipment installation next week."

"No security issues to report?"

"None. As you know, we selected sites on government land in very sparsely populated areas. Nobody for many boring miles around. We also posted counterfeit government signs every fifty feet along the fence line detailing the severe consequences for trespassing."

"What about local law enforcement?" Luci asked, getting a long-held question off her chest.

"I had a couple of very official-looking men in suits pay them courtesy visits and leave them very legitimate-looking business cards with a hotline to call if any concerns arise. Odds are, they never will."

Luci frowned. "Aren't you worried that those fake cards will eventually become condemning evidence?"

"Just the opposite, actually. The cards contain actual names and titles—only the phone numbers were altered—so they're essentially real. Best of all, I used actors who looked like the men they were impersonating."

"So any witness testimony will work in our favor," Luci said, now nodding along.

"What about the construction contractors?" WZ prodded.

"Both companies are Grausam Favlos affiliates, of course. Distant enough that I can avoid the investigative spotlight, close enough that I can intervene if required. Both have a solid history of similar contracts with the purported employer, and are being supplied with everything from cooks to whores so they have no need to interact with the locals. Like the military encampments they're all used to.

"Both sites have foremen who are dedicated, disciplined and loyal. The laborers were hand-selected for their discretion. Each is intimately familiar with the security requirements of military projects. All appreciate the associated perks and fear the potential penalties. None suspect that things aren't as they seem."

Ben paused to let them dwell on the picture. It was a pretty one. In Luci's experience, people were easy to dupe when the proposed scenario conferred elite status and steady pay. Out there in the middle of nowhere, government contracts were probably the best deals around. Nobody would consider questioning a project's legitimacy. They'd just count their lucky stars and cash the checks.

Having placed that positive image in their minds, Ben passed the ball. "How's the missile procurement coming along, William Zacharia? Today's the day, right?"

Their host nodded. "So far, so good. Today is the day—in India. In fact, they should be leaving Indian airspace with the missile as we speak." He pulled a burner phone from his pocket and paused with his hand over the keypad.

Luci figured he was deciding how much to share. She watched him work it. First he assumed a distant stare, then he started nodding to himself. "Back at the beginning, I had Rex give Achilles the contact information for a 'Procurement Officer,' a text-only number he could use to request anything and everything he needs. It routes through TOR to my burner phone."

"You made yourself their primary resource?" Luci said, impressed.

"I did. That blindly provides them with all the resources and capabilities at my command, and it gives me both visibility into their operation and a crucial amount of control."

"How have they used this gift?" Ben asked.

"Primarily to request support services. Their first ask was a hacker, so I set them up with the best guy on the planet. More importantly—"

"Who's that?" Luci asked, cutting in.

"I don't know his real name, or even his location. Nobody does. He goes by Jack Griffin, The Invisible Man." WZ turned back to Ben. "More importantly, I got to select and hire the teams that are helping them pull off the heist."

WZ used a speed dial, then placed the phone on speaker.

The call was answered on the second ring. "Da."

"Are we happy?"

The Russian switched his language, but not his style. He spoke three words softly, then disconnected. "We'll know shortly."

Chapter 20

The Picture

KATYA'S STOMACH SANK as Sergeant Belikov pocketed his phone, broke from the pack at the foot of the ramp, and walked her way with a militant stride. She was sitting in the shade of the cargo bay, breathing through a scarf while pretending to type furiously on a laptop at Moscow's urgent request.

"We can't wait much longer," he said.

Achilles and his escorts had driven off an hour and fifteen minutes earlier. She hadn't heard from him since, and his phone was going straight to voicemail. "We can't leave without the general, or the missile."

The sergeant retained his granite expression. "Actually, we can."

He had a point. She couldn't stop an armed contingent of soldiers. Could she steal the keys? Did planes have keys? Probably not. "We have an agreement."

"We do. In by 0800, out by 0930."

"Out by 0930 with two passengers and a missile."

"I only have control over the plane and its pilots. The missile and passengers are your responsibility. Takeoff is in fifteen minutes."

Katya had a choice to make. Perhaps the most important split-second decision of her life. Should she try to delay the plane, or attempt to hurry Achilles?

She closed her eyes. Achilles would not have lost track of time. Either he was being detained, or he needed more time to complete his mission. Katya decided to assume the latter and help however she could. *Why wasn't he answering his phone?* "We'll pay five hundred thousand dollars for an additional ninety minutes."

Sergeant Belikov cocked his head. It was his turn to think, but not for long. "It's not a question of money. It's a question of safety. When the real plane shows up, these people will know they've been had. That a top-secret missile is being stolen. They're more likely to shoot us down than let us leave the country with it."

"Maybe yes, maybe no. But making that decision and implementing it will take time."

"Major, to get where we're going, we have to fly north. Do you know what countries border India to the north? I'll tell you. It's China and Pakistan. India's mortal enemies. You can bet your last breath that India can put fighter planes in that airspace faster than you can pack a parachute."

"But—"

"I'm not risking this plane and ten soldiers over one man and a missile," Belikov said, taking a half-step forward. "Konyets rasgovor." *End of conversation.*

"Then I'm taking the SUV," Katya said, standing firm before turning to run down the ramp while her mind did the math. The DelMos facilities were about a kilometer from the end of the runway where the plane was parked. Call that a minute. Two round trip. That left her ten slim minutes to find Achilles and get him in the Mercedes. A realistic timeline if the holdup was for a typical reason. A rambling host, an equipment snafu, or the late arrival of something or someone. But ten minutes probably wouldn't cut it if the holdup had a less innocent cause.

Why wasn't Achilles answering his phone?

The powerful German engine roared to life and Katya hit the gas. As she focused on the distant warehouse with the intensity of a diving falcon, a convoy emerged from it and turned in her direction. *Was the jig up? Were they coming to arrest the imposters?* She saw flashing lights, but they weren't red and blue. They were yellow. Hazard lights. The missile.

Was Achilles with the convoy? Surely he would be.

Katya reversed course and parked. By the time she stepped back onto the tarmac, the soldiers had regrouped in their split-column formation.

The missile—or rather the long gray tube containing it—was secured to a custom-built carrier. A low-profile, twelve-wheel vehicle resembling three golf carts that had been decapitated and linked like train cars. Clearly, the conveyer had been cobbled together for factory use rather than field deployment.

It was also moving painfully slowly.

Maybe ten miles an hour.

Achilles could run faster—and Katya wished he would. She wanted him to jump out of the lead jeep and run into her arms. But not really. That would blow the mission, and the mission was something they deeply believed in.

She watched and waited with the patience and discipline of an actual military major, calculating the subsequent steps against the clock. No doubt Sergeant Belikov was running the same numbers. Time required to drive the missile up the ramp. Additional minutes to strap it down. Then loading the SUV and locking the hatch. No chance they'd finish all that by 0930.

She glanced over at Sergeant Belikov. He did not appear happy. But bad as it was, he couldn't leave now.

The heat was stifling under the summer sun. Easily north of ninety and given teeth by the smog. How could people live there? Twenty million of them. She supposed the locals would say the same if they visited her hometown in winter. Now there was an idea. Katya pictured the Moscow River as seen from her university dorm. The image helped her cool down.

Her husband appeared.

The enlisted men snapped off salutes as their general stepped from the DelMos Range Rover. Achilles' face betrayed no emotion and his body language belied no tension. *How did he do that?* Probably exercising the same neural discipline that kept him calm on cliffs, Katya figured.

"Vce v poryadke, General?" Katya asked as her husband returned her salute. *Is everything okay?*

"Poleteli," he replied. *Let's fly.*

Alas, they couldn't do that. Not yet.

The two turned to watch the loading procedure. The Indian technicians parked the missile at the base of the ramp, between the flanking Russian soldiers, then went to work releasing the straps that secured the missile tube to the middle cart. Surely they didn't expect the soldiers to carry it onto the plane? They'd need twice as many men, at least.

The reason for that odd action became apparent when the Indian team continued driving the missile up the loading ramp. Releasing those particular restraints allowed all twelve wheels to remain grounded despite the sudden change in incline.

"How was the tour?" Katya mumbled in Russian, eyes still on the action.

"They took a team picture with me in the middle, then posted it on the DelMos home page."

"Oh, no."

"I put my hat on when the camera came out. Between that and the makeup I doubt anyone will be able to identify me. But if someone in Moscow sees it and decides to pick up a phone while we're still on the ground…"

"Or over Indian airspace," Katya added.

"What happened?" Sergeant Belikov asked, edging closer.

Achilles told him.

"That clinches it. We're in for a rough flight."

Chapter 21

The NOE

THE SECOND THE CARGO RAMP CLOSED, drawing the curtain on their charade, Sergeant Belikov shouted, "Get us in the air, now! Fastest possible takeoff."

The pilots reacted like the well-trained military veterans they undoubtedly were, slamming the Ilyushin into action and leaving the passengers scrambling to secure seats.

Achilles enjoyed a wave of relief when the wheels left the ground, but he knew the battle was miles from being won. About two hundred fifty of them, to be precise. The distance to the Pakistani border.

After the initial ascent, he unbuckled and bolted for the cockpit.

A straight flight path from Delhi to their destination in Turkey would take them over Pakistan, Afghanistan, Iran, Iraq and Syria. They'd planned to deviate from straight to avoid Iraq and Syria, keeping things simpler and less predictable. But present circumstances demanded that they rethink everything.

Sergeant Belikov was one step ahead of Achilles. "Change of plans. The minute we clear Delhi airspace, turn west, then keep us NOE on the shortest possible path to the Nepalese border. One that avoids urban areas. Maximum speed."

The pilot replied with the Russian version of, "Wilco, sergeant." Then added, "You better buckle up."

"What's NOE?" Katya asked over Achilles' shoulder.

He hadn't heard her approach over the roaring turbofans. "Grab a seat."

Ilyushin Il-76 aircraft differed from similarly sized Boeing and Airbus jets by more than just the rear loading ramp. The Russian planes had cockpits designed to accommodate five flight officers seated in an X pattern, and windows covering the floor of the nose. As Sergeant Belikov strapped into the middle chair where the navigation officer would be on a combat flight, Achilles and Katya grabbed the rear two seats.

"NOE is Nap-of-the-Earth. Flying low to the ground to avoid radar. The guys I flew with always called it hedgehopping, which kind of sums it up."

"How low are we talking?"

"No more than two hundred feet."

Katya paled. "Two hundred *feet*? The spire on my university was over two hundred *meters*. Nearly four times that high."

"I'm sure they'll attempt to avoid buildings," Achilles said in a futile attempt to calm her nerves.

Katya didn't dwell on altitude. Her analyzer was obviously still spinning. "Nepal is the wrong direction. The opposite direction."

"But the closest international border."

They lapsed into silence as their torsos lurched and their stomachs churned.

Achilles tried not to think about what might happen. He tried not to focus on the clock. Normally, avoiding distracting thoughts of doom was his forte. But he usually faced life-threatening situations alone. Accent on the solo part of free-solo climbing. He should have left Katya at home. Worrying was better than dying.

"I'm glad I came," Katya said, interrupting his thoughts as she read his mind.

"What?"

"We're in this together. Life, I mean. *Through good times and bad*, was our vow."

Achilles had the *till death do us part* portion on the top of his mind at that moment, but knew better than to say so. "I love you."

"I love you, too."

Sergeant Belikov broke the moment, issuing a further command to the pilots. "Once we've crossed the border, circle back to our planned course, avoiding Indian airspace."

"We don't have the fuel for that. Flying low guzzles gas. If the winds work in our favor, we may make it to Turkey, but only if we don't deviate around Syria and Iraq. Otherwise, we should plan to refuel in Iran."

Which was less risky? Achilles wondered. Transporting a stolen Indian missile on a Russian aircraft into Iran, or running out of fuel over Syrian airspace. Not an everyday calculation to be sure.

"Work the wind as best you can," the sergeant said. "Let's avoid tangling with Iran. Meanwhile, keep us below the radar until it will look like we took off from Lahore."

"Wilco."

Sergeant Belikov turned to look at Achilles over his shoulder. "How could you let them take your picture?"

"It would have been suspicious to object. They did it in the cafeteria, where similar photos with other visitors decorate the walls. The Russian president and Indian prime minister among them. Still, I would have found a way to wriggle out if I'd known the plan was to post it immediately."

"You should have anticipated. Your oversight has put all our lives at risk."

"You're right. You want a cookie?"

The sergeant chuffed but said no more before turning back around.

Achilles rose and left the cockpit with Katya close behind. He wanted to inspect their prize.

Inspect was an exaggeration, since the missile was packed in a pipe. Fondle was more like it.

The container was hot to the touch after sitting in the sun, but not finger-frying. It was constructed of an alloy that didn't absorb heat, painted battleship gray. Both sides had "DelMos II" stenciled in white, flanked by the Indian and Russian flags. That was the extent of the markings. The ends were capped with bolted steel plates. Achilles had not verified that the missile was actually inside, but since this was a friendly, intracompany transfer, he had no cause for doubt.

A speaker crackled as he stood there with the steel heating his palms and accomplishment warming his heart. Three sweet words followed, "We're in Nepal!"

Katya flashed him a big smile. "You did it!"

"*We* did it," he said. *Not yet, though.* They'd conquered the summit and were coasting, but plenty of crashes happened on the downhill side. No sense pointing that out, though. There was nothing he or Katya could do. Better to let her release some pent-up tension. He knew she'd been battling back images of growing old in an Indian prison.

"What a relief! Promise me you won't answer the next time Rex Rowe calls." She pulled back and he saw that there were tears in her eyes. The good kind.

"Not until after Fiji, anyway," he said with a wink.

Katya looked around the cargo bay. The soldiers were all focused on a game of cards. "What now?"

"I'm going to wash off this makeup. Then I suggest we take a nap. Let's aim to sleep through Pakistan, Afghanistan, Iran, Syria and Iraq." He omitted the phrase, "and hope we wake up."

Chapter 22

The Confession

TECHNICALLY, William Zacharia had not seen it all. But in his fifty-eight years, he'd come close. As an NCAA Division 1 quarterback, he had experienced the pressures of holding the hopes of thousands in his hands, and the carnal rewards that came to those who delivered. As a Marine who'd served in the muck, he knew the anguish of battles lost and the exhilaration of wars won. As a startup founder, he knew the tricks and tactics required to wriggle one's way up a greasy pole while others were trying to set it on fire. And as a blue-chip CEO, he knew the outlandish privileges that came with true power. The access, accommodations and connections that put one a mile above the masses and beyond the law.

Now he was close to completing a new conquest. Culminating a campaign that would bring him more wealth than the rest of his accomplishments combined. Hundreds of millions of dollars from what the history books would summarize as a single stroke. And in fact that's what it was. Or would be. If the cascade Luci had concocted continued as planned.

That was the question of the hour.

The question of a lifetime.

"He should have called by now," Ben said, rattling the ice cubes in his otherwise empty glass.

WZ saw with surprise that they'd already drained the first bottle of Blue Label Ghost whisky. He rose to grab another. "Relax. They got the missile. The hard part's over."

"They were supposed to be in Adana half an hour ago."

"If they flew direct. But they diverted to Nepal to escape Indian airspace as quickly as possible."

"I've factored that in."

"Are you sure? Ask Luci. She knows a bit about airplanes."

Both men turned to the retired Air Force pilot and former airline industry executive. She'd been unusually quiet that evening. Stewing over her own failure to deliver on schedule, he was sure. WZ admired the discipline Luci demonstrated by keeping it all corked up. He just hoped the setbacks got resolved before the pressure caused her to explode.

Luci gave Ben a matter-of-fact look. "Standard calculations go out the window when evasive flying is involved. Airspeed decreases at lower altitudes. Distances increase when you're forced to deviate around dangerous areas."

"And comms go quiet if a plane crashes, or is shot down," he countered.

WZ stepped between his two peers and began pouring from a fresh bottle. "Relax. Drink your whisky. We're about to put the operation's tallest hurdle behind us."

"Give your guy a call," Ben pressed.

"He's on an airplane. No cell service."

"Of course. Sorry. I hate being blind."

"You going to retire, once the big bonus comes in?" WZ asked Ben.

"Damn straight. No way I'll ever top this."

"Where will you go?"

The handsome construction magnate smirked. "Everywhere worth visiting. I'm going to buy a mega-yacht and sail around the world collecting properties. Every time I find a location I love, I'll buy the best home available and employ the most beautiful women I can find to look after it. Once I've tired of the oceangoing life, I'll spend my time visiting my collection."

WZ thought that sounded like a fine plan, but didn't comment, given the mixed company, "How about you, Luci?"

"I think I'll visit Ben's women as well. Leverage his groundwork."

William Zacharia felt his face flush.

"Just kidding. Those rumors aren't true."

WZ wasn't surprised by Luci's sexuality, but he was by her injection of humor. He was glad to see her opening up and venting a bit of tension.

"Seriously though, I haven't given any thought to retirement. I'm having too much fun," she added.

That was probably a lie, but WZ ignored it. His attention was suddenly elsewhere. His phone had begun to buzz.

Chapter 23

The Landing

AN ABRUPT CHANGE in engine pitch jolted Katya awake. She immediately checked her watch and found that they'd been flying for over six hours. A full hour more than expected. As that registered, she felt the plane shift into a steep descent.

Sitting up, Katya looked around. The Ilyushin had only a few small windows in the cargo bay. All were blocked by soldiers. "What's happening?"

Achilles looked over from the seat beside her. "I just woke up too. Let's go look out the front."

"I'm right behind you."

They carefully worked their way from the Mercedes to the cockpit, using stationary objects for support. The windshield revealed a varied landscape, one with both green and arid areas, hills and flatlands, and most strikingly, a body of water off to the left that extended beyond the horizon.

Sergeant Belikov was in the central seat. Achilles leaned toward him and asked, "What's going on?"

"A low-fuel landing."

Katya's stomach dropped. "Where?"

"Adana Sakirpasa Airport."

"We made it to Turkey?" she asked.

Sergeant Belikov turned to look her way. His face was serious but less strained than during their last encounter. "Barely. The pilots flew high and slow, minimizing drag and maximizing engine efficiency. The wind also worked in our favor."

"Well hallelujah!" Achilles exclaimed.

Katya glanced at the fuel gauges as they strapped into the rear cockpit seats. All four needles were dead-on zero. She decided not to focus on them, and redirected her attention to the place they'd be landing. Adana's airport became discernible before too long. It had a single runway and was set in the midst of a dense housing development.

The city of Adana, Turkey's fifth largest, is in the south-central part of the country, near the Syrian border. It stretches south from the Seyhan River for about five miles, after which farmland spans the remaining twenty-mile gap to the Mediterranean Sea. The airport straddles that rural-urban border.

Katya suspected that the Mediterranean was the next destination for the missile and perhaps them as well, but she and Achilles weren't certain. Aladdin had "arranged for them to be met on the tarmac" when he organized the flight. He'd also "made arrangements to get them and the missile home from there."

While she found that vagueness frustrating, Achilles said it was far from unusual. In fact, he said it was a standard operation-security practice. His job had been figuring out how to pull off the heist, then executing his plan. That kind of work was his specialty. He was happy to leave the heavy-duty logistical operations to specialists—given the size and sensitivity of their cargo.

Although Katya remained wary, Achilles didn't seem particularly concerned about the lack of transparency. He pointed out that they had experienced a similar situation in Kazakhstan when Aladdin arranged things—and that had worked out fine.

As Katya studied the surrounding geography, the plane suddenly became considerably quieter. It slowed and its nose angled skyward. The pilots immediately launched into action, adjusting levers and twisting knobs.

"What's going on?" she asked.

Sergeant Belikov replied without turning around. "Two engines just ran dry. The other two will shortly. When they go, so do the hydraulics that control everything."

"What do you mean by everything?"

"Everything that moves. Flaps. Ailerons. The nose wheel."

With that lovely revelation poisoning the air, and the runway looming large a good quarter-mile ahead, the plane went silent as a grave. The last two engines had died.

No shouts came from the cargo hold. Nobody spoke in the cockpit. The soldiers were disciplined and the pilots focused.

Achilles looked over with a reassuring smile. He kept his eyes on her for what felt like hours, while pictures of plane wrecks popped into her brain. Then the Ilyushin's rear wheels bounced down hard on dry Turkish grass. The front wheel quickly followed, but it hit the tarmac.

They were right of center, which was good, but the plane was angled toward the left, which most definitely was not. A busy road bordered the airport on that side—beyond which were densely packed houses.

The pilots' eyes remained riveted on the windshield while their hands sat frozen atop various controls. They did nothing as the Ilyushin raced toward the edge of the runway. Were they scared stiff and holding on for dear life? Or were they smart like snipers waiting for the ideal moment to strike?

The plane was going way too fast. It wouldn't be stopping anytime soon. Katya caught herself holding her breath.

She scanned the landscape. It was as flat as her kitchen countertop. She detected precious little that would diminish the plane's tremendous momentum before they hit the houses—other than the cars and trucks that happened to be passing at just the wrong moment. The airport fence might as well have been made of toothpicks for all the good it looked like it would do.

Her conclusion was not a happy one. The big Russian plane, along with its twelve passengers and one stolen missile, was about to enter city traffic.

Although they had exhausted the plane's fuel supply, with the way things had been going, Katya half expected a gas truck to be among the dozen vehicles they'd likely hit. Those were going in and out of airports all the time, right?

Even if the Ilyushin somehow avoided an incendiary explosion, she and Achilles would surely be consumed by a virtual one when the contents of the cargo hold were revealed.

This was not good. Not good at all.

When the speeding plane neared the tarmac's edge, the pilots began counting down. "Three, two, one." On "one" they simultaneously slammed controls, causing the plane to bank back toward the center of the tarmac. The Ilyushin course corrected, then Katya felt the tug of brakes. The mechanical resistance hit hard and fast, but it only lasted a few seconds.

"That was the last of the pressure left in the steering and brake lines," Sergeant Belikov commented without prompting.

The plane continued coasting toward the far end of the runway and then rolled into the grass, where the additional friction hastened its deceleration. They finally came to a stop within kissing distance of the far fence.

The pilot spoke, his voice calm and crisp. "Adana control, this is RA-8149G. We've suffered an engine failure and require a tow."

Katya couldn't hear the reply, and at that moment it wouldn't have held her interest if she could. A troop transport had just screeched to a halt near the nose of the plane and soldiers were tumbling out.

Chapter 24

The Container

KATYA WOULD NOT have thought it possible, but she found herself watching the tailgate lower with even more trepidation than the last time. Turkey was no safer for Americans than India, and this time they were in possession of a stolen missile.

The swarm of soldiers didn't help.

"They're American," Achilles said, tension draining from his voice.

"Are you sure?"

"The troop transport was ambiguous, but the uniforms aren't."

"That's good, right?"

"Very good."

What followed reminded Katya of Achilles' account of his White House reception. The formal actions of professionals all acting anonymously, all obeying the strict commands of a greater power who was not present.

Over the course of the next hour, she and Achilles were managed like luggage. They were loaded into the troop transport truck, which escorted the towed plane to a hangar at the far corner of the airport. Once everything was under cover and the door closed, the soldiers went to work transferring the missile into an ordinary forty-foot shipping container that was mounted on a waiting truck.

At that point, Katya and Achilles became spectators on their own mission. They watched events unfold from the comfort of folding chairs, their feet up on their roller bags, their eyes darting between the action in the hangar and that on their laptop computer screens. They had the DelMos email intercept open, and it was fascinating.

Messages had begun flying within minutes of the real transport plane landing. First there was confusion. *What caused Russia to send two planes? Was a power-play taking place between government agencies?* It took the better part of two hours to dispel that particular form of Russian paranoia. Once they realized that the missile had in fact been stolen, speculation and accusations began to fly. *Who had done it* and *who was to blame.* While that conjecture continued to rage, the most recent emails indicated that a cover-up was in the works.

"The Kremlin won't be embarrassed," Achilles said. "They won't let DelMos disclose the theft."

"Reminds me of the Kursk," Katya said, referencing a Russian submarine that had sunk during a training exercise. As no Russian who lived through it would ever forget, pride prevented President Putin from accepting rescue assistance for four days. All 118 sailors aboard died.

"Without any lives at stake," Achilles added.

They lapsed into quiet contemplation after that.

The first person to pay them any attention was the burly man who had exited the container truck's cab as the plane pulled in. While the Americans were finishing loading and lashing the stolen missile, the trucker made his move.

"I'm Calix," he said, extending a calloused hand to Achilles.

Katya pegged his accent as Greek. That fit the name and general location, she figured. His weathered-sailor look reinforced her appraisal—and seemed to foreshadow what was to come.

After shaking her hand in turn, Calix continued. "We're going to be spending quite a bit of time together in the coming days. But unfortunately, that doesn't include the first hour."

Achilles voiced her thoughts. "I'm not sure I follow."

"Aside from the obvious space constraint, we have security to consider." He gestured toward the open container door as the last of the Americans exited. "You're welcome to bring your chairs."

"You want us to ride in back with the—" Katya stopped herself in time. "cargo?"

"It's not so much what I want as what the situation requires. Please, we have a schedule to keep." He motioned again.

Achilles grabbed the backs of their folding chairs, then paused to ask, "How long will we be in there?"

"An hour, give or take. We've got an eighty-kilometer drive."

"To the port?"

Calix rocked his head side to side, then said, "Yeah."

The ambiguity concerned Katya, but her husband didn't seem worried. It was as though this unusual setup fit one of the scenarios he'd mapped out in his mind. His next question did surprise her though. "Do you have a gun in the cab?"

Calix narrowed his eyes, but after a second's pause he said, "Yes."

"Give it to me."

"Why?"

"I'll feel better. Wouldn't you?"

Both men turned to look into the long, dark container that now housed the stolen missile.

"I see your point," Calix said.

Two minutes later, the Greek swung the doors shut and slid the security bolts into place—with Katya and Achilles seated beside their luggage. Achilles was holding the semi-automatic he'd borrowed from Calix and a pair of bolt-cutters he'd taken from a departing American soldier. She held a bottle of cold water in each hand and worry in her heart.

Exercising control, Katya waited for the engine to come to life before speaking. "This isn't what I was expecting."

"Chaperoning the missile?" Achilles replied in a playful tone.

"You know what I mean."

"It makes operational sense. It keeps us with the missile while minimizing attention and people in the know."

"They could minimize it more by leaving us in the container until we croak. In this heat, that might not take long."

"We'd be making a racket before we died and a stink after. That would be a stupid way to get rid of us."

"Yet you grabbed a gun and bolt cutters."

"Crooks have been known to be stupid."

Katya chuckled. It felt good. "What you say makes sense, but I'm still nervous."

"Good. Remember the plan. Remain alert, retain composure, and keep pedaling."

"I'd rather pedal than sit here."

"It won't be long."

"So you believe what Calix said? That we're headed for a shipping port eighty kilometers away?"

"We are in a shipping container, and we're near Mersin, which is the largest port at this end of the Mediterranean."

"I suppose they could have shot us in the hangar if that was their intent."

"No, that would have been really stupid. Too many variables at an airport. They wouldn't risk it. Assassinated Americans draw a ton of attention. They'd have thrown us out of the tail gate over the deserts of northern Iraq. We'd have woken up in a plummeting SUV."

As Katya tried to repress that image, she remembered something she'd been meaning to discuss. "We've both been saying *they*. But I'm not sure who *they* are, and that has me worried. We're working for the White House, right?"

"Right. I think the president and his chief of staff have been anonymously keeping tabs on us from afar. Did you notice Calix's cell phone? He had it in his shirt pocket, with the camera pointing out."

"You think he was broadcasting?"

"More like recording for a private viewing later. Or for insurance against blame if something goes wrong. That would be a savvy move," Achilles added with a nod to his watch.

"You've been recording?"

"I've learned to be cautious."

"So why do I still have an uneasy feeling?"

"Your subconscious can't shake the fact that we're not here legitimately. That we have NOC status."

Achilles was right. If the operation hit a snag, they could be charged as spies and the government that hired them would disavow them. Giving them No Official Cover status was a blatant admission that secrecy was the president's preeminent concern. Katya found the implications unsettling, to put it mildly. "I also don't like that we're working for politicians."

"I hear you there."

A chilling insight struck Katya. "That Rex Rowe is one clever character."

"What are you referencing?"

"He managed something that seems impossible. He gave you the freedom to develop and execute your own plan, while simultaneously retaining control over everything you do, every step of the way, through Aladdin."

"Whose services would necessarily be central to any conceivable plan, given the complexity of the mission," Achilles added, his voice inflected with admiration. "You're absolutely right."

While they reflected on the broader situation, the truck slowed to a near stop, then turned. By Katya's calculation, they'd been off the highway for a few miles already. Surely they were nearing the end of the road? The container certainly felt like it had been heating up for an hour. It had basic ventilation vents that allowed it to adapt to pressure and temperature changes without deforming, but nothing more. The air would soon be stifling. She was glad they'd exchanged their military uniforms for t-shirts and jeans. "How close are we?"

Achilles pulled out his phone and looked at the map. He'd been keeping it in low-power mode to save battery. "We're there, and we aren't."

"I don't follow."

"We're very near the seashore on a small dead-end road, but about ten miles east of Mersin."

"What's there?"

He angled the screen so she could see it. "I'm checking, but the connection is slow."

Katya felt her anxiety increasing with every second the image failed to resolve. Once it finally filled in, her mood didn't improve.

Chapter 25

The Ship

KATYA STARED at the satellite image on Achilles' phone. The picture of their current location. "Why take a stolen missile to a seaside mansion? Do you think it's a secret military installation?"

Achilles panned the photo out to show the surroundings, then zoomed back in and pointed to the shoreline. "That's not a wooden dock. It's a concrete pier. Presumably for the owner's mega-yacht."

"You think their plan is to load the missile onto a yacht?"

"No. I think we're here for the isolated pier."

As he spoke, they felt the truck move through a parking maneuver that included backing up for quite some distance before coming to a complete stop. After the engine switched off, they heard both doors open and close, then footfalls. A few seconds later the container bolts retracted.

"I trust that wasn't too bad," Calix said, opening one door. He held nothing in his hands, but the driver standing beside him silently extended an open palm once they and their bags were on the ground.

"It's his Glock," Calix said by way of explanation.

Achilles returned the weapon. "Thank you."

The driver nodded.

While Calix closed and bolted the container door, the driver returned to his cab and immediately started the ignition.

"Thought you'd prefer to watch this part from the ground," the Greek sailor said. Once the truck backed past them on its way to the pier, they began following it at a leisurely pace.

The mansion to their left was an impressive white structure that appeared at once elegant and as solid as a military bunker. It also looked vacant, as if it had been sealed for the summer while the owner vacationed someplace more temperate. Perhaps aboard the mega-yacht for which he'd constructed the pier.

That pier was an extension of the driveway. Basically a concrete road extending into the sea. Very convenient for delivering cases of caviar, smuggled drugs, or a missile container. Once they were even with the shoreline, they stopped walking to watch what followed.

As Achilles had predicted, a container ship was moored where an enormous yacht obviously belonged. Or rather the forward portion of it. While the water was clearly deep enough to accommodate the cargo ship, the pier was undersized. Good enough for a smuggling operation though. And, come to think of it, probably exactly what the owner had in mind.

The colossal cargo vessel's living and working quarters were all aft, housed in a white steel structure that rose six stories above the deck. The remaining ninety percent of the ship was stacked high and wide with steel twenty- and forty-foot containers of assorted colors. There had to be many hundreds of them. Probably over two thousand including those below deck, Katya estimated. What a monster.

No sooner had the truck come to a halt than one of the ship's cranes went to work. It plucked their forty-footer from the truck with the ease of a child moving Legos and hoisted it into an empty slot at the front of the ship, making the missile a needle in a haystack. Then it grabbed a container that had been set aside, presumably from the same slot, and placed it on the truck.

"A switcheroo," Katya said, marveling at the plan's simplicity.

"One out of sight of the port authorities," Achilles added, as the truck began rumbling away. "I bet they've arranged a similar reverse operation on the other side."

"You'll get to see that as well," Calix said.

With all the excitement, Katya had practically forgotten that the Greek was there.

"Shall we go aboard?" Calix added with a gesture.

Container ships are about as far from luxury liners as submarines are from subways, but after an hour locked in a hot steel box, Katya wouldn't be complaining. She wondered if that very reaction had been part of Rex Rowe's plan. Given his extraordinary aptitude for manipulating people, she wouldn't be surprised.

"How big is this ship?" Achilles asked.

"It's nearly as wide as a football field and three times as long."

Calix led them up the steep gangway as Achilles still struggled beneath the mind-boggling math. Three football fields, controlled by a wheel and rudder. Unreal.

A couple of sailors began retracting the gangway the moment Achilles stepped off. He and Katya followed the Greek sailor all the way to the back of the ship, into the superstructure, up four levels and down a passageway to a compartment the size of a first-class train cabin. It had a small window that looked over the receding shoreline, which was starting to show a tinge of sunset-red. Narrow bunk beds lined the side walls, and a table folded down into the cramped central space like an apartment ironing board. The bottom starboard bunk had a book on the pillow and a small suitcase stored beneath.

"That's my bunk," Calix said, pointing. "You have your choice of the others. I'll be back in half an hour to show you around. Meanwhile, stay put unless you need to use the head. It's two doors further down."

He stepped out and shut the door.

Katya looked around. It didn't take long. The room was as spartan as a prison cell, and the furnishings matched that standard. Calix's paperback was in Greek. A thriller, judging by the cover.

That left the view—and the most important thing in the world: her husband. *Count your blessings, Katya.*

"How long do you think we'll be at sea?" she asked, unzipping her bag. Now that they were in the clear, with both the DelMos engineers and the Russian mercenaries disappearing in the rearview mirror of her life, she was eager to change out of her sweat soaked clothes.

"Let's see," Achilles said, pulling a fresh T-shirt from his roller bag. "Call it two thousand miles to the mouth of the Mediterranean, plus another three and a half to cross the Atlantic. That's five-and-a-half thousand divided by, say, five hundred fifty miles a day. Somewhere around ten days, I'd guess. Assuming we're going direct, which is probably safe. They'd want to minimize exposure."

"Ten days," she repeated, studying the room that suddenly looked even more like a prison cell. "You remember that you promised me Fiji, right?"

Achilles put his arm around her shoulder and guided her onto a bunk. The bottom mattress was low and the top high so even her six-foot two-inch husband could sit if he slouched a bit. "I'm sorry. I'll try to make it up to you."

"I'll be fine. I have everything I need, right here," she replied, giving him a squeeze. "But I sure hope there's a library on this ship."

"That's not all Greek," Achilles added. "Assuming so, a bit of time at sea reading books might turn out to be a blessing."

"There are worse pastimes," Katya agreed. "But what if there are no English or Russian books?"

"Then we call it a yoga retreat. Lots of meditation. Surely there's a sunny deck somewhere."

"And a detox," Katya added, getting into the game. "I'm guessing the food will be encouraging in that regard."

They laughed and hugged and kissed a bit before Calix tapped twice and opened the door. She immediately noted that his cellphone was no longer protruding from his shirt pocket. He held a polished wooden box the size of a small microwave under his left arm and had a cloth shopping bag dangling from his left hand. "Time to celebrate. Come with me."

Chapter 26

The Party

ACHILLES FOLLOWED HIS WIFE and their host up two levels to the bridge. He expected to stop there for introductions to the officers, but a curt half-nod from the captain quickly dispelled that impression. Apparently, their mission was an inconvenience to be tolerated rather than an adventure to be shared. Achilles could sympathize. They'd saddled the captain with delays on both ends, setbacks for which his superiors might grant him no slack.

Calix approached a ladder at the back of the bridge. On ships, all stairs are called ladders, but this one fit the traditional definition. "You mind?" he asked Achilles, simultaneously gesturing upwards while flaring his luggage-laden arm.

Achilles climbed and gave the hatch wheel a crank. The bolts slid smoothly aside, indicating recent if not frequent use. He flipped it open, exposing a rosy sky, then climbed through.

Technically, the white iron surface beneath his feet was called a deck, but the absence of guardrails and presence of antennae sure made it look like a roof. Achilles immediately spotted their destination. Beach chairs had been placed beside a capped protrusion near the aft edge, creating a coffee table arrangement with a seaside view. Someone had wrapped the tubular chair legs with rubber tape to make them stick, and weighted them down with large bean bags. Sturdy enough for a calm night like tonight, Achilles figured.

"Welcome to my office," Calix said. "It's particularly delightful at this time of day, when the sun has lost its bite and the sky is working God's magic."

He walked to the makeshift table and set down his load.

Achilles took the opportunity to admire the humidor. It looked like something you'd find in the Palace at Versailles. Handcrafted cedar, highly polished and finished with brass latches. It had two drawers on the bottom and the traditional hinged lid on top.

Calix, meanwhile, was focused on the contents of his shopping bag.

The sailor extracted a jar of black olives, an artisanal salami, a baton of bread and a rind of white cheese. Two paring knives and three small forks followed. Then came a thermos, three kanonakia glasses, and a bottle of Barbayanni ouzo. "This is my sunset ritual, whether on land or at sea. My religion, you might say."

He opened the thermos and shook a few ice cubes into each glass, then twisted the top off the liquor bottle. "Many make the mistake of refrigerating ouzo, and do themselves a great disservice." He poured the clear liquid, which became cloudy upon contact with the ice. "Another common mistake is to slam it like vodka." He shook his head. "Terrible. Ouzo must be sipped with food. Preferably in a location like this." He gestured around, then to the chairs. "Please, rest your souls and your feet."

They sat while Calix opened the olives, unwrapped the cheese, and sliced the salami. Once their host was satisfied with the arrangement, he picked up a glass. "*Na pane kato ta farmakia.* May the poisons go down."

The silky, licorice-flavored liquid burned Achilles' throat. He was parched after the ride and would have greatly preferred a big bottle of cold water. But he did not want to offend a man working so hard to be hospitable. The man with whom they'd be sharing a room for the next week or two.

"How did you get this job?" Achilles asked, spearing an olive and a slice of cheese.

Calix ripped the heel off the bread and took a bite, buying a minute to think. "I got a call from a powerful man. One I've worked for on prior occasions."

"Interesting. What did he tell you?"

"To meet a plane with a container truck. To escort two Americans and their cargo from the airport in Adana to this ship and onward to their final destination."

"That makes sense. When did he call you?"

"A few days ago."

"So this isn't your ship?" Katya asked.

"No. I boarded yesterday in Piraeus."

"What does the captain know?" Achilles asked.

"Funny you should ask. The captain repeated his instructions to me verbatim when I boarded. He wasn't very pleased with them, I assure you."

"What were they?" Katya prompted.

Calix switched to a deeper voice. "*You will be making two unscheduled detours during this trip. Heed the Greek's orders in that regard without question or comment.*"

"That's harsh," Katya said.

"Orders often are," Achilles said.

Calix raised his glass. "Cheers!"

They went to work demolishing the food, which was delicious. All obviously fresh from the farm. He and Katya both latched onto the idea of sucking the ice cubes once their glasses were drained. Calix kept refilling them, of course, but true to his religion he added fresh ice each time.

The weather could not have been better. Hot had become balmy with the setting of the sun. The air was still, but the movement of the ship generated a gentle breeze. And the combination of a clear sky and full moon gave them plenty of light. It helped that the iron beneath their feet was painted white.

When nothing but ouzo remained, Calix slid aside the brass clasps that held the antique humidor's lid in place. He lifted it and extracted three cigars, looking at Katya as he did so. "*Vamma Del Sol*, Greek sunshine. The best my country offers. Care to try?"

She politely held up a palm.

Achilles was not asked.

After re-latching the lid to keep the humidity inside, Calix slid open the left drawer and extracted two items. A cutter and a torch. He clipped both cigars, then handed one to Achilles. A minute later, both Coronas were burning bright.

"I'm going to do a bit of stargazing," Katya said, rising.

Achilles watched her walk as close to the corner edge as comfort would allow, maximizing her distance from the boys with their suicide toys; then she lay down on her back and laced her fingers to form a pillow.

"How many containers are on this ship?" Achilles asked.

Calix refilled their glasses. "This one's rated for five thousand TEU, twenty-foot equivalent units. So five thousand twenty-foot containers will fit. Of course, the vast majority are forty-footers. I'll leave the math to you."

"You grow up on ships?"

"Ships, boats and submarines."

"Do you think of yourself as a sailor, or a smuggler?"

Calix took a long puff, then studied the glowing tip with half a smile. "I don't have a business card, but if I did, it would say *Entrepreneur and Problem-Solver.*"

For a few minutes they silently studied the stars, which were bigger and brighter out on the sea where the celestial lights were the only ones around. Achilles enjoyed a long-forgotten connection to the universe and gained a fresh appreciation for the sailing life. Not that he could ever go that route. His spirit was too restless.

What a day! he reflected. He'd gone to bed in Kazakhstan, gone to work in India, crash-landed aboard a Russian plane in Turkey, and was now with a Greek atop a cargo ship at the eastern end of the Mediterranean Sea. All of it in the service of the president of the United States.

He'd earned a cigar.

They smoked in silence. Once his reward had burned down to the band, he rose and tossed it far off the back of the ship. He watched it disappear into the propeller wash, knowing it would degrade within a day. "I'm going to check on my wife."

Katya hadn't fallen asleep. She was staring up at the stars, wearing a big grin. As he drew near, she raised a hand. He took it and pulled her up into his arms.

"We did it," she said before giving him a kiss. "You need to brush your teeth."

"You need a shower, major."

"You think they'll let us take one together?"

"You think they could stop us?"

As the happy couple walked back toward the hatch, Katya added, "Seriously, thank you for bringing me."

"I'm glad I did."

"You really shouldn't have," Calix said, rising from his chair.

"Why not?" Katya asked in a mock defensive tone.

Calix raised a gun.

Chapter 27

The News

WILLIAM ZACHARIA ENJOYED COOKING. It relaxed him. He liked the predictability of it, the simplicity and the reward. *Do this, get that.*

With the ingredients arranged and apportioned in advance by his household staff, and by using equipment that was tried and true, WZ had only two variables to contend with: time and temperature. Get those right and everyone was happy. Add a bit of artistry, and people would take pictures.

If his business were as easily mastered, he wouldn't have a care in the world. Except money, of course. Chefs were compensated quite differently from CEOs. It was William Zacharia's ability to bring predictability to chaos that had made him a wealthy and powerful man.

That and an endless supply of grit.

Truth be told, he was weary of the constant crises, the incessant emergencies, and the ever-popular force majeure he faced as a chief executive. He was eager to move on to the next phase of his life. To reap the rewards he'd sown.

Come that day, he'd still split his time between his Dallas home and the Lonestar Lodge. He'd just reverse the schedule and only visit the city on weekends. Changing his active address came with another bonus: the company he kept.

William Zacharia was tired of wasting time on transactional relationships. He was sick of the corporate dance, of patting backs, puffing egos, and kissing ass. As far as peers went, Ben and Luci were fine, but WZ wanted to be warming croissants and cooking omelets for family.

What he craved, pursued and would soon achieve come hell or high water was the life of a living legend. He wanted to see his beloved fire pit surrounded by grateful and adoring relatives. The first of many generations who would proudly claim his name.

Now that the requisite multi-generational wealth was but weeks away, William Zacharia felt himself starting to salivate. Not unlike the guests who, at that very minute, were waiting for the product of his omelet pans.

He had three of them going, rather than the typical egg-station two. Three was manageable when you didn't have to prepare for the next people in line, and desirable when you wanted everyone synchronized.

"You never shared the genesis of your genius idea," WZ said, as he slid a mushroom, onion, tomato, egg-white omelet onto Luci's plate. "How did you concoct something so out-the-box as Operation 51?"

Luci enjoyed the first steamy bite before beginning to answer. "The political landscape has fundamentally changed over the past few years. The rise of social media and decline of peer-reviewed news has made it possible to sell just about any idea. When you can bypass experts, facts and logic cease to be the driving determinant of what's generally accepted as true. They get replaced by the emotions and impulses of the masses. Manipulating those is just a question of marketing."

"I'll buy that," Ben said. "But it's still a big leap from *we can sell any story* to *Operation 51*. As William Zacharia said, it's way outside the box."

Luci set down her fork and took a sip of coffee. "Actually, the two of you inspired me. As a new CEO, I wanted to do something big. Something transformational. Looking at it through pragmatic lenses, I saw the C3 as a powerful new tool. That got me thinking about growth in the defense and construction industries in addition to energy. I created a Venn diagram to show where the sectors overlap, then did a bit of brainstorming. Operation 51 wasn't that big a leap."

As Luci returned to her omelet, William Zacharia weighed her words. With hindsight, it was easy enough to make the connection. But that kind of foresight required a talent he simply didn't possess. The admission brought no shame. Luci was one in a billion.

The buzzing of his special phone interrupted WZ's self-reflection. He answered, listened, and smiled.

"What is it?" Ben asked.

William Zacharia raised his mimosa. "That was one of my agents, calling from a cargo ship. The prototype DelMos missile is now aboard, and the only people who can connect it to Rex have been buried at sea."

Chapter 28

The Conclusion

WHEN YOU CLIMB CLIFFS without ropes, you put your life on the line. One slip, one miss, one late reaction—you're dead. That's the bottom line. The calculation every free-solo climber has to accept and become comfortable with.

Assuming said climber is not insane (those don't last) or idiotic (those don't last either), reaching that comfort level requires three things: the right type of body, the right frame of mind, and practice.

When Achilles came to climbing, he was a recently retired Olympic athlete. A biathlete to be precise. A shooter and a skier. A person with great physical strength, cardiovascular conditioning, and neuromuscular control. It takes an extremely steady hand to shoot a bullseye when the clock is ticking and you've just been sprinting through the snow.

His retirement had not been voluntary. An injury had forced it upon him. He had earned bronze at an early age but was robbed of his planned attempt at gold. So he poured his frustration, surplus energy and athletic prowess into another great sport prevalent in his home state of Colorado: rock climbing.

When his courage, conditioning and mental control caught the eye of a CIA recruiter visiting the nearby Air Force Academy, the government opened the door.

Achilles leapt through. He welcomed the unexpected opportunity to exercise old muscles, develop new ones, and serve his country.

CIA operations differ from Olympic biathlons in that the foreign competition is shooting at you rather than with you. An important distinction, and one that forced Achilles to develop new skills. Olympic-level skills. Lifesaving skills. The ability to predict better, anticipate earlier, and react faster than the competition.

Before Calix's gun came into view, his body telegraphed intent. He sent signals that Achilles was trained to detect. Signals from his face, shoulders and feet. Even in the dark, even after the ouzo, Achilles remained wired like a cat.

Working in his favor during that split-second interval was the basic calculation: one on one. Working against him was the distance. The gun gave Calix the ability to project power further and faster. Achilles had to take the weapon out of play. He also had to take Katya off the board as a target.

Before Calix got the gun high enough to do damage, before he even understood that a race was on, Achilles executed his first two moves. With his right hand, he shoved Katya aside. Hard and fast. His palm to her shoulder. With his feet he charged forward, one step, two, then a kick. Not a football punt. More like a sprinter clearing a hurdle. His target was the humidor, his goal to distract Calix with a two-pronged attack. To buy himself the second of distraction required to close the remaining gap, to get one hand wrapped around the Greek assassin's throat while the other ripped away his gun.

Despite having instigated the attack, Calix reacted like a startled soldier to Achilles' lightning onslaught. He initiated a quick but clumsy mix of offensive and defensive moves. He simultaneously swatted the humidor away and pulled the trigger of his handgun, releasing one three-shot burst, then another and another. His weapon was a machine pistol. No wonder he'd been so confident. Achilles had been lucky to catch him holding it one handed. The repetitive recoil would ruin his accuracy.

But with that many bullets, bad accuracy was good enough.

As Achilles barreled into the assailant and bullets ricocheted off iron, Katya cried out and went down. Way down. Off the back of the ship and into the night.

The scene hit Achilles with the impact of a magnum round. Shock, anguish and disbelief struck him like a triple-tap to the gut. Then Calix's fists chimed in.

C C C

Calix cursed his earlier oversight even as he leveraged the good fortune that had killed one opponent and stunned the second. He whipped the machine pistol around, eager to finish the task. Job done. Problem solved. No one need ever know that he had almost blown it by being a second too slow to fire.

His arm responded with less speed than it should have. Fending off the flying humidor had temporarily dulled its nerves. Not a big deal under normal conditions, but a life-threatening disadvantage in circumstances like this. Before he recovered enough to take proper aim, the man he'd been paid to kill was at his throat.

Calix was no stranger to street fights. No weakling either. He'd grown up hauling fishing nets, huge blocks of ice, and catches that weighed hundreds of pounds. He'd come of age fighting on the slippery decks of fishing vessels and in the back alleys of port cities. He knew how to defeat larger men, those with more mass and a longer reach. He knew to take them to the ground.

As his Beretta 93R clattered to the deck, Calix also went down, pulling his soon-to-be-dead assailant with him. They barreled into one of the beach chairs, bending the aluminum frame and sending it skidding across the deck.

Predator and prey rolled across the deck as well, with fury and momentum propelling them ever closer to the edge.

Knowing that the victor was usually the most savage, Calix sought to keep them rolling like jungle cats until he could deliver the decisive strike. A crushing knee to the nuts. A blinding thumb in an eye. A pulping forehead butt to an unguarded nose. Or a windpipe-severing clench of his jaw.

But the American showed a similar grasp of the street fighter's craft. He gave no opening. Took no risk. In fact, he seemed intent on keeping them rolling as well. That made no sense—for a second or two.

As they crashed into the humidor hand-crafted by his great grandfather, sending it flying over the edge, Calix caught on.

His opponent wasn't trying to win.

He wanted them both to lose.

He wanted to go over the edge.

He wanted to die with his woman.

Emotions overwhelmed Calix a millisecond after that insight struck, because a second thought followed. A chilling conclusion he could not shake. *There was nothing he could do to stop it.*

THE MEDITERRANEAN SEA

Chapter 29

The Fall

THE RECORD FOR CLIFF DIVING, set at the Cascata del Salto waterfall in Switzerland, is 193 feet. If that doesn't sound high to you, try climbing out the window on the nineteenth floor of a building. Achilles knew the statistic because he'd planned to introduce Katya to cliff diving on their trip to Fiji.

Which meant she knew it, too.

Or at least the statistic lived in her brain. Her big brain.

Active recall was another matter. Instantaneous recall in the face of death another matter still.

But Achilles believed in his wife. At that point, he had no choice.

While seven stories and half-a-hull certainly felt high, it was only about half the record. In fact, the cargo ship's top deck was right around cliff-diving competition height.

They'd watched one of the Red Bull World Cliff Diving Championships on YouTube while discussing the trip. Achilles remembered selecting that particular competition because it had been won by a Russian. The show hadn't convinced Katya to give the sport a try, but it was impossible to forget.

Wearing nothing but bathing suits, men and women competed for points by throwing themselves off natural rock formations in scenic locations. Despite the impressive aerial acrobatics that followed, the commentators' talk was all about the entry because that's where the danger was. The divers hit the water at speeds of 55 to 60 mph, so form was what separated glorious victory from agonizing defeat. Life from death. And form was always the same. Chin tucked, toes down, body straight as a pencil.

He prayed she remembered that crucial conclusion in time.

Cliff divers aimed to slice through the water, knowing that it wasn't the fall that killed you, but rather the sudden stop. Organs splattered like tossed tomatoes when one didn't decelerate at a reasonable rate.

He prayed she remembered the announcer's poetic words.

And that she was conscious.

And that her bullet wound wasn't fatal.

In short, Achilles was praying for a miracle as he gripped Calix tight and rolled over the edge. But that prayer was only in the back of his mind. In the front, he was playing out the sequence he'd instinctively choreographed as Katya fell overboard.

By his calculations, that little bit of planning, that crucial ounce of preparation afforded him by forewarning, would decide the battle. It would allow him to live, whereas his opponent would almost certainly die.

If all went as Achilles planned.

And if the sailor wasn't familiar with cliff diving skills.

Achilles would know in less than three seconds. That was how long they had before impact. That was why foreknowledge was so crucial. The fall would be over before Calix could comprehend and react.

Achilles never stopped moving. Never stopped executing the preprogrammed sequence playing out in his head. The twist that sent them over the edge morphed into the thrust that propelled them apart. A two-palmed push where a pull had just been, straight into his assailant's chest.

Calix was unprepared to resist. Shock had zapped his brain. As they cleared the rim, his limbs flailed open and out in a reflexive attempt to find balance, freeing Achilles to continue his choreography.

The instant there was air between them, Achilles somersaulted into a rigid pencil position the way platform divers do. He cleared his mind of everything but form and reminded himself to resist the urge to inhale on impact.

The fall was over before it started. One second he was snapping into form, eyes clamped shut, the next he heard sea water rushing past his ears.

He had survived.

Or at least the fall hadn't killed him.

Had it been a cloudy night, he might have struggled to orient himself, to know which direction was up. But the moon was bright enough to give him the choice between pitch-dark and dim. The swim to the surface seemed to take forever, more because the salt water separated him from Katya than from the air he needed to breathe.

She was the oxygen he required.

The instant he broke through into the moonlight, Achilles began multitasking more intently than at any other time in his life. His ears went into overdrive, only to be frustrated by the sound of his own frantic breathing. He enlisted his biathlon skills to get that under control and listen for his wife. Fortunately there was little competing noise resembling a human voice.

His eyes began scanning. First for the ship and the line of its wake as a means of orientation. Then for objects poking above the surface. By his calculation, no more than thirty seconds had separated his fall from Katya's. Fifteen was probably more accurate. Maybe less. Mental time stretched during stress. Clock time didn't budge.

He'd lost his phone during the kerfuffle, but his watch was still strapped to his wrist. Achilles checked to see if it had survived the plunge, if Apple's marketing was more than hype. Finding the face still glowing, he initiated an open-water swim. It would track time and distance, providing invaluable input to his initial search and their ultimate salvation.

He began swimming away from the ship, back along its path, head above water, eyes scanning, mind working the math. Twenty-five knots worked out to just under half a mile a minute. That equated to an eighth of a mile every fifteen seconds. Call that six hundred fifty feet, or four laps in a competition pool.

The calculation hit hard.

There was no way he could cover that distance before she drowned.

Not if her lungs were already full of water.

He swam faster.

If she had been right there, even unconscious and broken, he could have saved her. He could have flipped her on her back, turned her head and compressed her chest. He could have administered mouth-to-mouth.

But she wasn't right there.

She couldn't be.

The ship had moved an eighth of a mile.

He swam faster.

Thank goodness the water was warm. For being stranded at sea, you couldn't beat the Mediterranean in late July. Most other seas, any other time, Achilles wouldn't have been able even to save himself. Not that far from shore. Hypothermia would have claimed him within hours if not minutes.

They were also blessed by calm seas and clear skies. He had visibility. He could swim without restraint and navigate. The direction of the current was an unsettling unknown, and it was an awfully big sea, but it could have been worse. Much worse. Unless she was already dead.

He swam faster.

He marked time by counting each right-left stroke cycle as a second. After the first minute, he stopped to call, look and listen. "Katya! Katya! Katya!"

Nothing.

After another minute, he tried again.

Nothing.

How long should he keep going? When should he start to circle back? Not yet. Not yet.

He saw her! No, he didn't. What was it? After swimming like a man possessed, which was exactly what he was, Achilles rescued the humidor. While disappointing, it was good news. A sign that he was on the right track. And it was the equivalent of a mile marker.

He checked his watch. He'd swum ninety yards in just under two minutes. Since the humidor had gone over midway between them, Katya should be roughly another ninety yards away.

As he plowed on over the gentle swells, following the wake of the ship, Achilles replayed the deck-top skirmish in his mind, paying attention to the clock. Trying to refine his estimate. Second one: the gun had come out and he had sprung. Second two: he had kicked the humidor and launched toward Calix. Second three: Calix had swatted the humidor and fired his gun. Second four: Achilles had struck Calix and a bullet had struck Katya. Second five: all three of them had gone down—Katya dropping much further. Second six: Achilles had begun maneuvering Calix toward the edge. From there, events began to blur along with the timeline.

In the front of his mind, Achilles had been defending against debilitating attacks, protecting his soft targets by blocking, tilting, scrunching and squeezing. And he'd been rehearsing his airborne moves. The separation, somersault, pencil and entry. In the back of his mind he'd been pursuing his objective of taking them over the edge. How long had all that taken? Less than fifteen seconds for sure, and more than five. But he couldn't get any more accurate than that. Still, knowing that Katya had hit the water no more than six hundred fifty feet before him was encouraging.

"Katya! … Katya! …"

"Achilles."

Chapter 30

The Find

KATYA DIDN'T KNOW if she was hallucinating, but she answered as if the cry were real. She said the word that would likely be the last to cross her lips. "Achilles."

She found that saying it did more than bring hope to what was otherwise a hopeless situation. It actually made her feel happy. Was she going mad? Slipping into insanity as the blood poured from her veins?

No, not insanity. Love. Pride. Hope. She was the wife of a wonderful man. A unique man. One in a million. A hero who would move the heavens and part the seas to find and rescue her.

Lying there on her back, a bullet hole in her calf, bleeding out into an endless sea, Katya knew without the slightest doubt that Achilles would hold her in his arms again. That gave her great comfort. She just hoped her body and soul would still be united when it happened.

"Katya! Katya, Katya, Katya!"

It wasn't a hallucination! Achilles really was near. Near enough to hold her when she passed. "Achilles! Achilles, I'm here." In her mind, she was shouting, but in her semiconscious state she couldn't be sure that her lips were actually moving.

Then he was there. His hands running over her cold skin. His voice calming her nerves. "Katya, I'm here. I've got you. You're going to make it. We're going to make it. I love you. I love you so."

"You got your wish," she said, her mind blissfully fading. "Cliff diving."

"You remembered. I prayed you would. I've got you now. You just relax. Save your energy. I'm taking you home."

Katya managed to say "my left calf" before the darkness overtook her.

C C C

Achilles found himself fighting back alternating waves of grief and relief as he felt for his wife's carotid pulse. Finding her alive had been one of the greatest joys of his life, but watching her slip into unconsciousness—there, alone on a dark sea—had nearly crushed him. Achilles knew he could not allow grief or rage or anguish or despair to lodge their cruel claws in his heart. In order to save Katya's life, he'd have to defend his own mind as much as her body.

His breath returned when he felt her heartbeat, weak but steady. She'd lost a lot of blood. She was losing it still. Stopping the flow was his most-urgent priority.

Rather than desperate hugs and frantic kisses, finding her wound had sucked up the first few seconds of their reunion—and the last before she closed her eyes. Given the limited light, the search had not been easy. He could smell the blood, but he couldn't see it. Her mumbled "my left calf" had done it.

Achilles marveled at his wife's quick wits and composure. Despite the extremely rapid devolution of events on the ship, the mere seconds she had to think between the gun coming out and her crashing into the water, Katya had recalled and reacted. He shuddered to think what would have happened had they not watched the cliff diving competition over homemade cioppino and a bottle of rosé. Then she had the presence of mind to float rather than swim, slowing her heartbeat, knowing he would come. And then when he did, to deliver the information he most needed to know.

One simply couldn't let a woman like that leave the earth.

The bullet had done more than graze her leg. It had penetrated through and through. But it had missed the bone. That slice of luck would spare her a mountain of pain and help to avoid both infection and shock. Assuming he could stop the bleeding. Not a trivial task when bobbing in the ocean.

Achilles was wearing neither belt nor socks, so he used tooth and claw to rip a two inch strip off the bottom of his t-shirt. He tied it around her calf as tight as he could, then positioned the knot over the exit wound. That would help, but it wouldn't suffice. Not with her first sip of water likely to be days ahead.

The problem was that blood doesn't coagulate in water. That was why suicide victims slit their wrists in the bathtub. You bled out.

Ideally, he would elevate Katya's wound. *Not much chance of that.* The nearest footstool was— Achilles cut himself off mid-thought. *The humidor!* And the antique wasn't just a makeshift buoy. It held a cutter and a torch.

All he had to do was find it.

For now at least.

In the back of his mind, Achilles knew that stopping the bleeding was but the foothill before the mountains to come.

Knowing that the smart move was to focus on taking one stroke at a time, he gently grabbed his unconscious wife and started swimming. Head up, eyes ever scanning the enormous dark rolling surface for the bobbing corner of a wooden box.

Despite the odds. Despite the demonic, titanic, infuriating injustice that put him and his beloved Katya in that precipitous position, Achilles was happy. His wife was in his arms—alive. And he could still fight.

Oh, could he fight.

Chapter 31

The Humidor

THE FIRST FLOATING OBJECT Achilles found wasn't the humidor. It was Calix. His white shirt reflected long flashes of moonlight as it rolled with the swell. Fortunately, the shirt's owner was face down. Achilles did not need another fight.

He wondered briefly whether the turncoat had died from the fall or had drowned. Achilles' money was on the fall. Most sailors are good swimmers. While they are also taught how to abandon ship, how to jump to inflate their clothes and land without breaking bones, that training presumes a planned evacuation. Calix had been given no time to prepare. No opportunity to shift gears. One second he was brawling, the next he was falling, by the third it was all over.

Katya, by contrast, was wary of falling from the very start given her proximity to the unfamiliar precipice. And she was primed by their Fiji prep. Mental jumpstarts like that made all the difference.

While mentally thanking the Almighty for giving them calm seas, Achilles removed Calix's shirt and pants—pocketing his wallet in the process. He tightly tied off the pant legs close to the bottom, grabbed the garment by the waist and swung it through the air until it ballooned. Then he crashed it to the water, trapping the air inside the legs. By cinching the waist shut, he created a U-shaped air pillow. The construction wasn't particularly robust, but slipping it around Katya's neck added a bit of buoyancy. He would be happy to have all the float he could get if the wind picked up or the weather turned.

Since the humidor had gone over the edge between Katya and Calix, Achilles knew he had swum too far. He doubled back and quickly spotted the polished wooden box in the moonlight.

Rather than immediately open it up, he first lifted the humidor out of the water to judge whether it had leaked. The big top compartment felt dry. That was no surprise. It was hermetically sealed to keep the cigars at a healthy humidity level. The drawers felt like they'd taken on water. One was empty. Presumably, it had held the Beretta 93R. The second contained a cigar cutter, torch, wet matches and soggy cedar sticks.

Happy with his treasure, Achilles went about lashing the antique beneath Katya's wounded calf. For rope, he used Calix's shirt. It wasn't ideal, but it got the job done. After satisfying himself that the binding was snug enough, he inspected the wound. Blood was still trickling.

He gave the torch a few violent shakes to dispel all clinging water, then tested the ignition. It failed once, twice, three times. He gave it another shake. On the fourth attempt it sparked to life.

Holding the cigar cutter's finger rings under water, he blasted the blade tips with the torch, then inserted one into the bleeding wound like a cautery tool.

The sizzle and smell tore at his heart like steel talons, but the heat did the trick. Fortunately, one application from each end sufficed.

With his wife no longer leaking blood, Achilles paused to look up at the moon while taking a deep breath. As crappy as their situation appeared, as unfair, unjust, and potentially inescapable their predicament, he knew he was blessed. He was alive and healthy. Katya was breathing and stable. The rest was just noise he needed to ignore. For now.

He had to disregard the pain and anguish and seething anger because a new race was on. This one against dehydration. He repacked the torch and cutter, oriented himself toward the north using both watch and stars, then started swimming.

In his mind, Achilles zoomed up over the water like an ascending drone. He rose ever higher until at last he could picture the topography like a fuzzy satellite shot. He recalled the Mediterranean Sea being about three times longer east–west than north–south, with the Strait of Gibraltar at the western pointy tip, the Suez Canal at the squashed southeastern end, and the Italian and Greek peninsulas dangling down in the middle.

Their ship had sailed from Mersin, Turkey, which was near the Mediterranean's northeast corner. It was heading for the Atlantic Ocean via the Strait of Gibraltar. They'd only just set sail, so Turkey was undoubtedly the closest country. Head north and he'd hit it.

But how far north? How far would he have to swim?

Cyprus, the big tadpole-shaped island whose tail pointed toward Mersin, was about fifty miles from the coast. If the cargo ship was sailing midway between the two land masses—a relatively safe assumption—that left Achilles looking at twenty-five miles in either direction, give or take. A maritime marathon.

If his geography was correct, and he swam straight, he could make it to shore in a day at just one mile per hour. That sounded easy enough for a man in his physical condition—if the sea remained calm and surface currents didn't fight him.

Achilles was confident that he could swim nonstop for a day. Doing so simply required forcing nerve impulses to fire— regardless of pain and fatigue. He knew the drill. In fact, he'd already put himself in robotic mode, separating his mind from his body and regarding his flesh as a third party.

Now he focused on increasing his speed. A ten percent boost would cut his swim time by two and a half hours. The obvious move was putting the hand holding Katya's hair into the propulsion business—without letting her go.

He just had to figure out how.

It didn't take long.

He cut strips from Calix's shirt and fashioned them into a tow rope which he looped under her arms and tethered to the back of his pants. He was concerned that the lack of a direct flesh-on-flesh connection to his wife would make him less sensitive to any change in her condition, but figured he'd be as primed to pick up those signs as any mother with her newborn baby.

That one move probably boosted his speed by fifty percent. Pleased with the progress—despite the lack of any discernable change in his position—he looked for other opportunities to move faster.

One was obvious. The humidor created significant drag. Achilles estimated that the big floating box was cutting his speed by one quarter. That was a lot. Perhaps a life or death amount. Katya's wound was probably stable, but he still hesitated to let the humidor go. It was both his Plan B and his insurance policy.

If a ship were to sail into view, either day or night, he could signal it with lit cigars. With smoke or flame. A weak signal to be sure, but much better than merely waving his arms. That knowledge fed his soul. It gave him hope. The warmth of a safety blanket.

But the humidor was a drag.

If the seas got rough or his tank ran dry, the humidor would serve as a life preserver. It might make the difference between staying afloat and slipping beneath the waves. Looking forward in time, he couldn't help but picture the climactic scene of the movie Titanic.

But the humidor was a drag.

Hours from now, when the knock of fatigue became a banging on the door, he could take a break. Enjoy a cigar. Put some stimulant in his blood. Soldiers had used that trick for centuries. Millennia.

But then and there the humidor was a drag.

An impediment to progress.

It would work against him for as long as conditions remained unchanged. Would they change? Achilles had to ask himself if he was feeling lucky.

He considered the circumstance that had put them in the water in the first place—then dismissed it. That wasn't luck. That was premeditated skullduggery. Pure treachery. Exactly who had ordered that betrayal remained to be determined, but luck had not played a role. The fact that both he and Katya had survived the fall, that involved luck. The fact that his wife's wound was manageable, that was luck. The facts that he found her, that the seas were calm, the moon was full and the stars were visible, those were luck.

He *was* feeling lucky.

He rechecked Katya's wound and found it stable.

His decision made, Achilles removed the drawers from the humidor. He pocketed the torch and cutter then punched out the bottom boards. He stacked the thin sheets of plywood like a sandwich and wedged them under Katya's shirt behind her back, creating a smooth plane with a bit of buoyancy.

Satisfied that he'd made his towing arrangement as aerodynamic as he could get it, Achilles turned back to the vast expanse of open water that separated him and his wife from the rest of their life, and let the humidor go.

Chapter 32

The Shape

ACHILLES WAS NO STRANGER to endurance exercise. Or danger. The trick to coping with both was to calmly abstract yourself from your situation. To detach your mind and make it a third-party observer. Oddly enough, that's exactly what your gray-matter was. The pain processed by the brain was experienced elsewhere, in a rumbling stomach or cramping calf. Ignoring those inputs amounted to disregarding a signal sent from a distance.

The easiest way to sever a mental connection was to focus on something else. Something cerebral and compelling. Of course, in times of danger, the mind tended to wander to all the things that could go wrong. To the sharks that might be circling. Fortunately, Achilles had mastered that mental switch-flipping skill during his Olympic-training years, and exercised it by climbing cliffs without a rope.

Normally, he would focus his thoughts on formulating plans and solving puzzles. He had plenty of those on his mind at the moment. But he decided to put them off until morning. The smart move was to rest his brain while the sky was dark and his muscles were fresh.

He let his mind wander into a meditative state, its fuzzy focus shifting slowly between his breath and the stars. Given the low light and the warmth of the undulating water, his relentless swim soon morphed into the rough equivalent of sleepwalking.

Achilles would snap out of it every fifteen minutes or so to check on Katya and stretch his limbs. But once he resumed, the monotony quickly sucked him back in.

And so it went, through the night until morning. When dawn's rosy fingers first tickled the eastern horizon, Achilles paused long enough to look around. To scan for ships and land. Nothing but waves caught his eye, not so much as a bird or plastic bottle.

The first stab of doubt struck his heart.

All his effort appeared to have yielded exactly nothing.

Not one whit of discernible progress.

He and his wife remained exactly where they'd been some eight hours earlier: stranded in the middle of an endless sea.

Achilles pushed doubt's knife aside and plowed on, stroke after endless stroke. When the sun came into view on the eastern horizon, he found himself craving coffee. The desire for eggs, bacon and French toast drowning in maple syrup soon followed. He pushed them back out and bolted the door, but knew his temples would soon start throbbing from caffeine withdrawal and dehydration. It would be the skull-splitting kind of headache that movement would exacerbate.

He would ignore it! He would plow through the pain as surely as he would the waves, which fortunately remained modest swells.

They'd been in the water for about ten hours. He'd been swimming north for nine. That should place them about eighteen miles from shore—if his net-speed calculation was correct. And his heading had been true. And his estimated starting position accurate. *Less than a day to go*, he told himself. *You can do anything for a day.*

After he reoriented and recalibrated, Achilles' trancelike state gave way to a contemplative one. Not about reaching land, but rather what he'd do once they did. Once they were rehydrated and Katya had received adequate medical care.

He made a mental spreadsheet. The first two rows, the only two that really mattered, both got checked. They were together, and they were alive. After that, things became considerably less grand. Basic survival and sustenance questions had no easy or obvious answers because the threat to their lives remained both omnipresent and unidentified.

Where should they go? Into hiding? Straight to the White House? Surely not home?

What should they do? Call the police? Collect intel? Report back to Rex?

Achilles quickly concluded that everything hinged on one key question. Until they answered it, they couldn't proceed with their lives. They couldn't even risk being identified. Not safely, at least. That question: Who had hired Calix?

Presumably, Achilles and Katya were serving President Preston Saxon. At the very minimum, they were working for Rex Rowe, White House Chief of Staff. But Rex wasn't directly managing the operation. There were at least two levels between him and them.

Directly below Rex was Aladdin. The procurement officer extraordinaire. Further down the chain of command were the hacker, aka The Invisible Man, Sergeant Belikov, and Calix. Whether the three were in direct contact with Aladdin or some reported to others, Achilles didn't know. In either case, there were plenty of points where a hostile force could have intercepted and subverted the wishes of the White House.

But was that likely? Was it more probable that the White House had been thwarted, or obeyed? Achilles had to go with the odds on that one, particularly since he didn't know either man personally. Nine times out of ten, chief executives and chiefs of staff were obeyed. Working conclusion: Rex Rowe had likely given Calix the kill command.

Likely, but not certainly.

To be verified.

Swimming on, stroke after endless stroke, Achilles shifted to a different angle of mental attack. He took aim directly at the principal question: Why?

The broad answer to why the unidentified commander wanted Katya and Achilles killed had to be one of two things, either eliminating witnesses to the original crime, or perpetrating a new one. Either the White House wanted to sever the only link between itself and the missile theft, or a knowledgeable third party was leveraging the White House operation to steal the cutting-edge armament.

Achilles found his head swimming along with his body. The list of powers that would want a prototype of the world's most advanced missile was long and nefarious. He could name a dozen within a thousand miles of his present position.

But for a theft to happen, the thief had to know the plan. The White House had gone to great lengths to minimize the number of people with that information. Still, Rex Rowe had outsourced procurement operations. He had created layers of cracks. Although The Invisible Man might well have been told nothing more than to serve Achilles, Aladdin had to know the big picture. And Sergeant Belikov knew several critical parts. As a participant, he had to know them. And he was a Russian mercenary. That made for more of a chasm than a crack.

Finding the uncertainty frustrating, Achilles paused to check on Katya and make her a protective mask. He wanted to shield her face from the rising sun. To do that, he used the cigar cutter and a remnant of Calix's shirt. He sized a piece of fabric to cover her face, then cut a hooded hole through which she could breathe.

Once satisfied that he could do no more to help his wife, Achilles tried to verify their northerly orientation with his watch, only to discover that it had died. Whether the water had killed it or the battery was just out of juice, he couldn't tell.

The loss of his compass and distance-tracking app was unfortunate, but far from his greatest concern. Orienting himself by the sun instead, he waited for a swell, then propelled himself vertically like a dolphin lifting a ball. At the apex of his ascent, Achilles thought he glimpsed a shadow on the horizon.

Hopeful but not convinced, he repeated the move. It was there! It was definitely there! A discernable shape. Land.

PART II

Chapter 33

C4

REX ROWE had expected a ranch-hand to run out, meet his flight, open his door and carry his bag. But nobody approached the Steel Shield helicopter as it touched down at Lonestar Lodge. The pilot kept his grip on the stick, and the man himself remained at the edge of the helipad. What kind of operation was the defense contractor running?

Rex shrugged off the slight. He should have known better than to transfer Beltway norms to the heart of Texas. Where he came from, the waiter boned your fish tableside. Down here, people took pride in baiting their own hooks.

Rex hopped out, pulled his bag from the stowage compartment, and rolled it toward the big man who was now extending his hand.

"Pardon the unusual reception," William Zacharia said as his helicopter departed. "I'd have mentioned it when I called, but as you know, the less said on the phone the better."

While Rex did indeed prize discretion, his host had taken brevity to a new level. Calling last night during Rex's drive home, the Titansized Texan had insisted that Rex cancel any Saturday plans and be ready for a 6:00 a.m. pickup.

Now Rex raised his eyebrows rather than voice the obvious question.

"A career working around intelligence operatives has made me a cautious man. I dismiss my domestic staff whenever the discussions will be sensitive. The last of the help left yesterday when the others arrived. It will just be the four of us this weekend."

"Well, you got lucky on the timing. With the president on vacation, everyone is taking the weekend off. I was looking forward to clearing my desk."

"Better to clear your mind. You can't beat this location for that."

Rex nodded politely while pausing to soak in his surroundings. He hadn't spent any time in rural Texas, and wanted a second to recalibrate before continuing toward the main building.

He'd done business in Dallas, Houston and Austin but hadn't ventured beyond the city limits on those visits. When boarding the Steel Shield helicopter, he'd expected it to fly him to a place resembling the set of a Clint Eastwood movie. Cactus, mesquite and red sand, all baking beneath a blazing sun on land flat as a flour tortilla. But the landscape below and around him was lush, with rolling hills and languid lakes.

The pilot had pointed out when they crossed the border onto William Zacharia's 64,000-acre property. Looking down, Rex had spotted no demarcation line. No road, river, fence or guardhouse. He'd seen no sign of civilization at all until the hunting lodge appeared atop a commanding hill like a modern castle.

"Ben and Luci are waiting," WZ prompted.

Rex had hopped into his sponsor's limo at 6:00 a.m., his plane at 6:30 and his helicopter three hours and a time zone later. He'd demonstrated a level of respect and obedience he normally reserved for POTUS alone. But Rex had not called off his Saturday night poker game. He was intent on making it. With that in mind, he decided it was time to show a bit of spine. To remind William Zacharia Bubb that the White House Chief of Staff was not his employee.

Standing his ground, Rex shielded his eyes from the rising sun and asked a casual question. A throwaway, but an ego stroker. An I'll-take-my-time-thank-you-very-much question. "How close is your nearest neighbor?"

The former Marine couldn't help but puff up. "Nearest property line is five miles from where we're standing. Nearest structure is a fire tower on unincorporated land. It's six miles out." He pointed northeast with his hefty hand. "Nearest house is seven." He threw a thumb southeast over his shoulder.

"Reminds me of Camp David," Rex said, simultaneously complimenting his host and referencing his own seat at the pinnacle of political power.

"I think you'll find my weekend hideaway considerably more comfortable than the Aspen Lodge. It wasn't built during the Depression with thin government dimes."

Rex appreciated his host's masterful comeback. It comforted him to see that the person who had commanded his appearance could wield more than a checkbook.

William Zacharia led him through soaring arched oak doors and an impressive atrium into the great room at the heart of his hideaway. With an open kitchen and dining area on one side and lounging configurations complete with a wet bar on the other, it featured an indoor fire pit as the central focal point.

Watching his entrance from two of the four leather lounge chairs situated around the dancing flames were the other members of the cabal that controlled him, Lucille Ferro and Benjamin Lial. Both held hefty coffee cups and wore concerned expressions. Neither rose as he approached.

Be that way, Rex thought.

He turned his attention to the odd indoor climate created by open flames battling with air conditioning. While it clearly wasted copious amounts of energy, the combination did kill the oppressive early August humidity and create an atmosphere that was at once stimulating and relaxing.

"For the last nine years, there have been three chairs around my fire," William Zacharia said, prompting the others to rise. "As of today, we have a fourth. Welcome to the C4."

"Thank you. It's an honor to be here," Rex said, already eyeing the door. Did they not realize he spent his days bouncing between the Oval Office and the White House Situation Room?

William Zacharia handed him a hot mug, and they all sat. Three sets of eyes instantly turned Rex's way. After a moment of awkward silence, WZ said, "We have a problem."

Chapter 34

Pedestrian Plans

LUCI SET DOWN HER MUG but kept her eyes on Rex. As much as she hated to hear that her grand plan might be suffering a serious setback, she was relieved to have the spotlight swing toward someone else.

She was also pleased to have the chief of staff aboard.

Although efficient, she found the C3's small size to be stifling. Expanding their membership brought a welcome bit of elbow room. And since C-4 was also the abbreviation of a popular explosive, it was doubly descriptive.

Rex helped himself to coffee and savored a long sip before catching the kickoff ball. "What's the problem, William Zacharia? And how can I help?"

His question sounded a tad taunting to Luci's ear. Or was that just wishful thinking?

"We may have a security leak, specifically with your recruit," William Zacharia said.

"Achilles?"

WZ nodded. "And Katya."

"I thought they'd be shark shit by now. Is that what you call fish feces, or is there a more appropriate term? I never had reason to think about it before," Rex said, looking around.

He wasn't going to make this easy for William Zacharia.

Luci was loving it.

"They may well be. Probably are, in fact. But we can't bet the barn on it."

"And why is that?"

"They're no longer aboard the cargo ship, but neither is our assassin."

"All three went overboard?"

"Apparently. Calix was last seen escorting them up top to do the deed. Gunfire was heard a few minutes later. But nobody came down. The ship was searched bow to stern. No blood, no bodies."

"And no other boats were nearby?"

"None. They checked the security camera feeds."

"But the missile is aboard? Safely hidden away in a container?"

"Yes. Mission accomplished."

Rex leaned back and laced his fingers behind his head. "You said gunfire was heard. How many shots were fired?"

"Probably the entire fifteen-round magazine from the assassin's machine pistol."

"And where, exactly, was the ship when your man was spraying lead?"

"Twenty miles from the Turkish coast. Thirty from Cyprus."

"And what time was this?

"The sun had just set."

Luci recalled the warning Rex had issued when proposing the former Olympian and CIA agent. "He's an ideal candidate and we have the perfect hook, but be careful. Once I wind him up, you'll have to manage him masterfully. Don't underestimate this guy." She wondered if Rex would remind them of his warning directly. Probably not. Fish feces gibe aside, he was too politically savvy for such a pedestrian remark.

Rex summarized the situation. "So shortly after the assassination attempt went bad enough that your man was firing in panic, he and his two intended victims all went overboard."

"Falling or jumping from a height of a hundred feet," WZ clarified.

"If they didn't climb down first. Remember who you're dealing with. In any case, you haven't heard from the assassin, correct?"

"Correct."

"He clearly didn't defect. We're the ones with the money. So he's definitely dead. He also clearly panicked before he died, given the way he unloaded his weapon. That means Achilles got wise to him. Therefore, the safe assumption is that our agent and his wife are alive and hell-bent on revenge."

"Safe, but not probable," WZ clarified.

Rex gave the CEO a withering look. "The man's an Olympic athlete. The Mediterranean is calm and warm this time of year. Don't get comfortable."

"If we were comfortable, then we wouldn't have asked you to join us."

"I can't intervene. The minute I do, I lose deniability. I can't ever mention Kyle Achilles' name, much less use my position to have him hunted."

"You don't need to use names," Luci said, having tired of watching WZ get walloped. "Give physical descriptions and reference *an American couple who went missing from a yacht*. Your law enforcement contact will assume they're influential donors and make it work."

Rex clapped his hands down and shifted forward in his seat. "You surprise me. I thought the three of you would know better, but you're making a typical civilian mistake."

"And what mistake is that?" Ben asked, speaking up for the first time.

"You assume *The Government* exists, and it's a machine. But it doesn't and it isn't."

"What in hell's blazes are you talking about?" William Zacharia asked.

"There's Interpol. And there's the Turkish Coast Guard. And the Cypriot Coast Guard. And there are an assortment of police departments along the coasts in question. And public hospitals, and private clinics. And dozens of other relevant organizations. All of them have their own systems and structures. All have outdated equipment and overworked employees. None of them report to the same person. Some of them have no links at all."

Luci felt foolish. She really had made an amateur mistake. Why were people so eager to embrace simplistic solutions? To ascribe inflated abilities to others? That didn't matter now. What mattered was getting back on track. "What would you recommend, Rex?"

"Old-fashioned footwork. Hire a bunch of private investigators and dangle big bonuses. Give them photos and fat expense accounts. Have them spread some money around while a hit team is standing by. You'll have your answer within seventy-two hours— and with any luck they'll be dead within seventy-three."

The three stared at him for a while before Ben said, "We could have done that without you."

"Exactly. You could have. Kindly recall that helicopter. It's poker night in Washington."

Chapter 35

Fighting the Tide

SWIMMING TOWARD SOMETHING you can see feels very different from swimming in search of rescue. The ocean is the same, the mechanics are the same, but the psychology is entirely different. Everything moves from the abstract to the concrete. The progress being made. The distance being covered. The time remaining.

It's like flying when your plane has a mechanical delay. When takeoff is uncertain, you're just praying it won't be canceled, that you will actually, eventually arrive. Once the flight's back on, however, it's all *how fast can I get there?*

Swimming for the shoreline he'd spotted, Achilles tried not to think about the distance he still had to cover and the myriad things that might yet go wrong. He tried returning to an automated trance, but his subconscious mind was too active. It nagged like a child who couldn't sleep in the backseat. It kept asking, "Are we there yet?"

On the upside, spotting land made it easy to dismiss his thirst and fatigue. With the solution in sight, they were but temporary annoyances, not life-threatening complications. And he was much closer to land than initially anticipated. Whether that was due to an advantageous starting position, faster swimming, or kind currents, he would never know. But he would be forever grateful.

The reason he couldn't calm his subconscious was Katya. Before sighting the shore, he'd been able to suppress his overwhelming anxiety. He'd smothered it with his gratitude for finding her alive and in relatively stable health. He'd told himself that with her circulatory and respiratory systems working, she'd be fine.

But that hadn't been entirely honest. The truth was, his wife had been unconscious for ten hours. That was a long time. In all likelihood, it was just her system coping with the low blood supply. But he couldn't be sure and that doubt was the devil's pitchfork.

He needed to get her hydrated.

Are we there yet?

Rather than swim against that unstoppable river of consciousness, Achilles diverted his flow of thought by mentally engaging Katya in conversation. He imagined working with her to solve the puzzle of the year. Namely, how did they end up there?

"Do you think Sergeant Belikov sold us out?" she asked.

"No. That just doesn't compute. He might have been in on it, but he wasn't behind it."

"Why do you say that?"

"He could have killed us on the plane and flown the missile wherever he wanted. No need to mess with involving a third party and the crew of a cargo ship."

"So the command to kill us came from above, either Aladdin or higher?"

"To be safe, we have to assume the White House ordered our execution."

"That's disheartening. It also complicates our next moves."

"Exponentially."

"Do you think killing us was Rex Rowe's plan all along?" the voice of Katya asked. "Or did something change that made it necessary, politically speaking?"

In his mind, Achilles shrugged, even as his real arms continued stroking. "I don't know, but one thing is certain. Politicians like Rex don't think twice about sacrificing others to save themselves—or their principal. To them, such moves are no more a transgression than when a lion eats a gazelle. It's just the natural order."

"But what does your gut say?"

"I'm not inclined toward the something-changed scenario."

"Why not?"

"Two reasons. One, the extraordinary secrecy surrounding my meeting with Rex. And two, the fact that Rex encouraged your participation. It's not normal to involve an operative's wife. Quite the contrary."

"I thought I was invited to enhance your cover?"

"Yeah, at the time that fit the picture, but now I suspect a different motivation."

"Namely?"

"Containment. If I had disappeared on a mission initiated by the White House, you would have investigated. Relentlessly. But with the two of us gone, any questions could have been swatted away with canned answers. We have no family, so nobody would care enough to press back, not against the United States government."

"I see your point. But if containment was such a big concern, why invite you to the Oval Office in the first place? Why didn't President Saxon just call and recruit you on the phone? That would be considerably simpler and less conspicuous."

As Achilles entered what truly looked like the last mile of the swim, he believed he had the answer to that crucial question. "Rex used the Oval Office as a proxy for the president."

"I don't follow."

"Holding a meeting in the Oval Office conveys presidential authority, but it doesn't actually involve the president. Not at midnight."

"Why is that important?"

"Suppose President Saxon actually knows nothing of our mission. Suppose Rex is running it—either for his own ends, or more likely at the behest of someone else."

"Why is someone else more likely?"

"Because the White House Chief of Staff has no use for a stolen missile, but he surely knows plenty of people who do."

"You're just speculating."

"Granted. But for safety's sake that's going to be my operating paradigm until data drives me elsewhere."

"It's going to severely hamper our ability to act."

"I know. It will make every move awkward, inconvenient and inefficient. But until we prove otherwise, staying safe means avoiding any activity that might make the White House aware that we're alive."

Katya fell into his groove at that point, in Achilles' mind anyway. "So we can't use our real names or any of our mission aliases. You can't use Calix's ID either. That leaves us with just the cash you took from his wallet."

"And the money we transferred from Rex Rowe's slush fund to a new offshore account."

"Right! That's close to a million dollars—if we can get to it. How familiar are you with the Turkish banking system?"

"Not very."

As the land began looming large, Achilles pondered the acrobatics it would take to turn them from near-penniless anonymous castaways back into potent international operatives. He also adjusted their trajectory to take them ashore on sandy ground rather than the marginally closer forested peninsula. His goal wasn't dry land, it was reaching civilization. More specifically, medical attention.

Unfortunately, the beach before them appeared to be deserted.

Chapter 36

Fire Escape

KATYA DREAMED OF RAIN. Not a downpour or a misting, but the occasional drip drop signaling that the heavens just might let loose. Ironically, that was good news. The only bright spot on her bleak horizon, in fact.

She was stuck in a bear trap. Her calf clamped by an iron jaw. And as if that weren't bad enough, she was slowly dying of thirst.

She stared at the bulging black clouds and prayed for them to rip. Wouldn't that be grand? The last time she'd tasted rain, she'd been six years old and running around the backyard of the dacha while her father yelled for her to come inside and her poodle leapt like a circus performer.

Katya tried pushing her tongue out, but it didn't want to go. It wouldn't respond.

Her father shouted again. "Katya. Katya, can you hear me? It's me. I'm right here."

"I know," she said. "Just let me catch the rain."

The drops came again, heavier this time, but she still couldn't move her tongue. Then something stroked her face and the clouds cleared. Disappointed, she opened her eyes.

It wasn't her father's face that greeted her. It was Achilles. His nose just inches from her own. "Hello, beautiful."

With those two words, reality shoved the dream aside as if it had never existed. "Hey. Why are you so sad?" Her throat felt painfully dry as she spoke.

His face contorted, then he kissed her forehead. "I'm not sad. I'm the happiest man alive."

His touch made her more aware of their surroundings, though most of it was still coming into focus. They were in a dim room, one lit only by the glow of tiny lights. "Where are we?"

"We're in a Turkish hospital." He paused there, as if waiting for her reaction.

One second his words made no sense, the next the context struck. The cargo ship. The stolen missile. Ten days to sail home. "Something happened on the ship?"

"You were shot in the leg and fell overboard. I followed you down and swam us to shore, then carried you to a road where a kindly passerby brought us here in the back of his pickup truck."

She bolted up in bed as the full force of consciousness came crashing down. Aside from a parched throat and a sore leg, she felt fine—if not a bit woozy. There was an IV in her left arm and a thick white bandage wrapping her left calf. She wore a hospital gown. "I don't remember. Who shot me? Are you okay?"

Achilles used a button to raise the back of her bed, then handed her a Styrofoam cup with a protruding straw. "I'm fine. Calix shot you."

She took a long, steady sip. Then a second. Her mind was racing in a dozen different directions. "How long was I out?"

"From the time you passed out in the water until you woke up in this bed, about thirty-two hours. It's 4:00 in the morning here in Turkey."

Katya wanted all the details, but instinct told her there was more pressing business to discuss. "Why did Calix shoot me?"

"He was hired to kill us. By whom, I'm not entirely sure. But whoever it was probably thinks we're dead, and we need to keep it that way. I told the hospital staff that we're Latvian. Your name is Anna Annina. I'm Anton. Got that?"

"Anna Annina. You're Anton. Were you worried I had brain damage?"

"I was keeping it simple. Not to match your mind, but because we have plenty of other issues to occupy our thoughts."

Katya drained the cup and then bought a few additional seconds of digestion by looking around the room. It was a basic private hospital suite. With no external cues coming through the curtain-covered window, they could have been in Mexico, Moscow or Memphis.

A pair of aluminum crutches propped up by the door caught her eye. "Can we leave?"

Achilles refilled her drinking cup from a pitcher on the bedside table. "We'll talk about that when you're feeling better."

"I've had thirty-two hours of rest and I've just been doused with a big bucket of ice-cold news. I'm ready for action."

"Let's test that theory, in case it's just the pain-killer talking," Achilles said, retrieving the crutches. As he lowered the side rail, he added, "Keep your left leg raised."

Katya slid to the edge of the bed while her husband managed the IV line, then she gingerly maneuvered herself onto the crutches. So far, so good. She ambled slowly across the room, turned and returned but didn't sit. "Satisfied?"

"You really feel fine?"

"I'm not ready for kickball, but I'm not going to pass out either."

"Good. I believe the staff has instructions to call the authorities when you wake up. I suspect the police will stop by first thing in the morning regardless. It would be nice to avoid that entanglement."

"Didn't the police question you already?"

"They did. I told them it was a spearfishing accident. We were scuba diving and I grabbed the gun the wrong way and the next thing I knew you had a spear through your leg."

"Did they buy it?"

"They seemed skeptical. I don't know what the doctor told them. Given all the time you spent in the water, he probably couldn't be definitive. In any case, they definitely want to talk to you."

"I'm glad they didn't wait around."

"They did at first, but another call came through. It's peak vacation season for locals in this part of the world, so they're probably understaffed."

"But we'd better not push our luck."

"My thoughts, exactly."

Achilles disconnected the IV, then produced two sets of green surgical scrubs and some matching rubber clogs. As they started changing, he said, "I got you moved to the end of the hall by asking for a quiet room. Since your condition doesn't require much monitoring, they were accommodating. There's a fire escape stairwell across the hall that the staff use for smoking breaks."

"What about the bill?"

"We'll have to settle that later. The soggy wad of euros I took off Calix won't cut it."

That minor issue brought the big one front and center. "What are we going to do once we get out of here?"

"Don't worry, I have a plan."

Chapter 37

Missing Memories

ACHILLES DIDN'T ACTUALLY HAVE much of a plan. Not for the short term. Not for the long term either. What he had was a basic set of objectives and tactics. Don't get caught. Do turn the tables. Use the big bank balance at their command to wage a clandestine operation the likes of which the world had never seen —not from a married couple who didn't own a castle at any rate.

He had not been this furious since an injury ended his Olympic dreams. He had burned off that all-consuming anger by climbing a Colorado cliff without a rope. No sport could help him this time, however. Back then, his frustration had been directed at fate, so it eventually diffused into the universe. This time, his rage took aim at a very real target. An as-yet-unidentified individual or group. An adversary that would soon become intimately familiar with the sharper side of suffering.

Achilles had fought powerful enemies on plenty of prior occasions, people who used underhanded tactics to obtain their evil ends. But never before had a war felt so personal. That was the big difference, he decided. In the past, the lines had been clearly drawn. Each party had fought for its side. This time it was different. This time, Achilles' own team had turned on him. This time, he had been betrayed.

Betrayal was an escalating force. A dirty, indecent, provocative action. It took the situation, and what he would do to correct it, to a whole new level.

On top of all that, they had shot Katya. His innocent partner, his wonderful wife, the love of his life. For that alone they would rue the day they'd first heard his name.

"You feeling okay?" Katya asked. "Am I hurting you?"

He was descending the third of three flights of stairs, with Katya draped over his shoulder in a modified fireman's carry. It was easier than attempting a quick getaway on crutches. "Not in the least."

"I thought I felt you tremble," she pressed.

Achilles chuckled at her misinterpretation as he pushed through the fire exit and out into the night. "Just a bit of emotional release. How about you? Are you okay?"

"I don't envy potato sacks, but I'm not complaining."

"Once there's a building between us and the hospital, I'll put you down and we'll give the crutches another try."

"Are you saying we don't have a car? We're making our escape on foot?"

"We have no ID. No credit cards we can use. I don't have a computer or phone with me and I wasn't about to leave you alone, so for the moment I'm afraid walking is our only option."

Katya paused a beat. "Where are we headed, on foot?"

"Away from the hospital. Beyond that, we'll be opportunistic. An all-night diner, a cheap hotel, or perhaps a taxi waiting outside a fancy hotel. Any of those would do."

"To what end?"

"As a stepping stone toward Antalya."

"Antalya. The popular beachfront resort city?"

"It's about a hundred fifty miles up the coast. There's probably a bus, or maybe we can negotiate a ride once it's light. In the meantime, we don't want to be wandering the streets." He tapped her thigh. "We don't want to be wandering at all."

The night sky was cloudless and the light breeze was balmy, at least seventy-five degrees. But the air right there stank from the cigarettes discarded in an ashcan.

Achilles headed toward the ocean, walking as quietly as he could. The clogs were comfortable enough, but loose shoes always made him feel uneasy. You couldn't effectively run, climb or fight in them. Still, he was happy his feet weren't bare.

"What time is it?"

"It's about 4:15. My watch died."

"The battery, or did it drown?"

"I'm not sure, I don't have a charger to check. I put it in waterproof mode after my initial plunge, but then swam for hours. Yours definitely didn't make it."

"I surmised as much. Does that mean you might have lost the recording you made at the White House?"

Achilles smiled with relief. His wife's mind was sharp as ever. "I'm not sure about that either. My phone is at the bottom of the ocean, so the sync is irrecoverable. I don't recall if that app backs up to the cloud."

Once they'd cleared the corner of a building, blocking their view of the hospital and vice versa, Achilles slowly set Katya onto her good leg.

After a few seconds of fidgeting, she tested the aluminum crutches. "This will work."

They put another block between them and the hospital and were working on a third when a light blinked to life a couple of blocks ahead. Red letters on a white oval read TOTAL. "There we go!" Achilles said.

"A gas station?"

"Exactly. What kind of driver is going to be filling his tank at this hour? I feel stupid for not having thought of it earlier, but I'm happy to settle for lucky."

"I'm not feeling very lucky," Katya said, looking down at her leg.

"Really? Because I feel like we won the lottery."

Katya stopped hopping and glanced his way. She asked a question with the tilt of her head, but she was obviously already working the problem internally. "My memory goes from being a hero enjoying a mission-accomplished celebration to waking up in a hospital bed with a gunshot wound and people wanting me dead. That seems like a pretty crappy shift of circumstance, but now I realize that's only because I didn't experience what we went through in-between."

Achilles felt himself tearing up. "Consider yourself lucky, and leave it at that. For now, anyway." He gestured toward the TOTAL station. "It's time for a bit of role play, and you've got the lead."

Chapter 38

Mistaken Identity

KATYA FELT FAINT as she stepped from the hot panel van onto the shady pavement. She'd been obliged to engage with the chatty driver for much of the four-hour ride up the Turkish coast, despite the hundred euros they'd chipped in for gas. Common courtesy.

Achilles' plan to find a car heading north and offer to split the gas had quickly yielded a catch. At that early hour, most drivers filling up had long hauls ahead, and Antalya was the nearest major city. Having a girl on crutches as bait probably didn't hurt. But that was where their good luck ended. The driver spoke both English and Russian, so Katya couldn't discreetly grill her husband on the details of what had happened and what he had planned. On top of that, the van's air conditioner was broken.

"Thank you so much, Arman. We really appreciate it," she said, over the rumbling of the old motor.

"I hope they take good care of you."

They were under the portico of the Medical Park Hospital in Antalya. She would not be registering when the van pulled away, but it had been a fitting destination to cite, and would be the perfect place for people dressed like them to catch a local taxi.

"I'm going to run in and grab some supplies from the pharmacy," Achilles said, motioning to a nearby bench. "Do you mind waiting?"

The shaded bench appeared positioned to offer a marina view and catch the sea breeze, plus she probably wouldn't have to make polite conversation. "Not one bit. Don't be surprised if I'm asleep when you get back."

"I won't be that long." He kissed her and headed inside.

"You weren't kidding about that nap," Achilles said, seconds later. Or so it seemed. Judging by the big bag in his hand, it had been considerably longer. When she didn't reply immediately, he added, "Are you feeling okay? We can have you checked out if you'd like."

"No. I'm just tired." Her leg was actually feeling more painful by the minute, but she figured that was just the painkillers wearing off.

He held her eye for a few heartbeats. "Okay. Here comes our cab. I had reception call it."

He helped her to her feet and into the backseat before addressing the yellow Toyota's driver. "We need an economy hotel that has a computer guests can use."

"This is Antalya, there are dozens. You want a pool? A view? A balcony?"

"Doesn't matter, so long as they take cash. Someplace close, preferably in town."

The driver let his eyes drift to Katya. "Okay, let me think."

Five minutes later, the taxi pulled to a stop before the Yazar Lara, a charming white and blue boutique hotel in a business district a few blocks from the waterfront. Ten minutes after that, they walked into a cheery room with a sea-view balcony. As the door closed behind them, Achilles swept her off the crutches and carried her to the bed.

"Are you thirsty?" he asked.

She'd drunk a liter of orange juice and two bottles of water in the van. "Actually, I'm ready for the bathroom."

"Of course." He scooped her back up and then left her to her business. "Holler when you're done."

Katya decided to test her leg rather than request a lift. Her calf was seriously sore but not blindingly painful. If she kept the muscle loose, it was easy enough to ignore. Alas, she soon discovered that there was no way to put pressure on her foot without involving her calf.

Achilles sprang to his feet when she opened the door, but she hopped through and over toward the bed. "I'm okay."

He'd been busy laying out his pharmacy purchases. There were about a dozen items designed to keep her leg happy. One box on the bedspread caught her eye. It didn't fit. A box of pills. Not pain killers. She pointed. "Am I reading that label correctly?"

Achilles didn't need to follow her finger. "Yes."

"Isn't Rohypnol the date-rape drug?"

"That's an off-label use," he said with a mischievous smile. "It's intended uses include insomnia and anxiety. It's legal here."

"I think I'll pass all the same."

"I didn't buy it for you. I saw an opportunity and seized it."

"I don't follow."

His smile faded. "We're in a covert war. Rohypnol is a covert weapon. It's colorless, odorless and tasteless."

"You bought a knock-out drug just in case?"

"I bought Ketamine too."

She'd initially ignored the small vial, assuming it was an injectable antibiotic. "The veterinary anesthetic? Why?"

He answered her question with one of his own. "Don't you cringe every time the victim in the movie fails to grab the gun off the floor? Or snag the axe or fire extinguisher from the wall?"

"Sure."

"I'm trying not to be that girl."

Katya couldn't help but smile at the comparison. "Nobody would ever mistake you for her."

"Thank you. I think. May I inspect your leg now?"

"Fine. What are you looking for?"

"Infection. The doctor got the wounds cleaned up, and the nurses treated it with ointments and injections. I just want to make sure it hasn't deteriorated since we left the hospital. Feel free to get comfy and close your eyes. If it looks good, I'm going out for intel and supplies."

"What if it looks bad?"

"Close your eyes, picture the Spanish fountain in our backyard, and ask me again in five minutes."

Katya closed her eyes, but quickly realized she wouldn't be able to distract herself with calming images. "What intel and supplies?"

"We need normal clothes and toiletries. Plus, if our money stretches, I need a business outfit."

"What for?" Normally, Katya would work it out herself, but she was groggy and preferred to keep her husband talking while he worked her wound.

"Initially, for a bank visit. Once I've identified a suitable establishment with a local office, I'll transfer the operating funds from Singapore. Then we'll really be in business."

"What business?"

"The rev—, the *justice* business." Achilles probed around the edges of her wound as he spoke. The pressure was painful, but far from excruciating. "Your wound looks great! Minimal swelling and inflammation."

Katya lifted her head and opened her eyes and saw that her husband was smiling. She flopped back down as he went to work with salves and fresh bandages. "What makes a bank suitable?"

"The bank we want will work with numbered accounts, so no identification is required. It will issue checks on the spot, put cash in our hands, and get us debit cards within a day or two."

"You think you'll find one fitting that bill here?"

"I'm pretty sure. This part of the world tends to be flexible when it comes to business arrangements."

Katya believed it. Banks made fat profits for doing little more than moving numbers around cyberspace. Since the banking transactions themselves were generic, the banks had to differentiate themselves on customer service. Under those circumstances, most institutions would go as far as the law would allow. Some further.

"Once we have the money, then what?"

"Then I buy us passports and charter a jet."

Chapter 39

Zeki

ACHILLES HAD PARACHUTED from a few jets. It was a very different experience from jumping out of a helicopter or propeller plane. Rather than falling, you felt like you were getting sucked up into a vacuum cleaner. Or swept up by a surprise tornado.

Achilles wasn't wearing a harness and he hadn't just jumped off a plane, but he felt that way now.

He had been cruising home, mission virtually accomplished, when *Wham! Bam!* he and his wife were dropped into an entirely new set of circumstances. Disastrous, disorienting, dangerous circumstances. Circumstances from which there was no clear, quick or easy escape.

Oddly enough, Achilles wasn't unhappy. Or at least that emotion wasn't registering. Not at the moment. Right then and there, with Katya healing and in good spirits by his side, a high-stakes challenge before them, and considerable financial resources at their command, he was content. Grateful even.

He'd heard that the three things you needed to be happy were *someone to love, something to do,* and *something to hope for.* At the moment, he could put big bold checkmarks next to all three boxes.

But the specifics of the last two would change.

They had to change.

Because his life was out of balance. Way out.

Restoring equilibrium would require an equal and opposite reaction. Violent, vicious and surprising moves matching the destabilizing ones. Achilles felt prepared to deliver those blows. He could sense the anger seething like lava beneath the surface of his skin. Red hot and raring to explode.

He would keep it tamped down—until an eruption was appropriate. Then he'd obliterate his opponents with the force and fury of Vesuvius.

Patience, Achilles. Patience.

Arriving at their hotel room from the store, he quietly cracked the door and slipped through, careful not to snag any of his shopping bags on the frame.

Katya wasn't on the bed.

He immediately gave the air a good sniff. No gunpowder or blood. No cigarette smoke or sweat.

He looked around. No signs of struggle, but no note either. She must have stepped out without thinking. He had been gone a long time. Surely, she wouldn't have gone far. She must have gotten hungry, or—

Achilles set down his bags and ran downstairs to the nook the hotel called a Business Center.

"I was starting to worry," Katya said as he appeared. "Nice suit. Did you stop to get it tailored?"

"It's off the rack. I have one for you too—up in the room. Sorry I took so long. I kept thinking of more things I needed to buy and do. I would have called but I hoped you'd be sleeping. How are you feeling?"

"Fine. I found our ship."

Achilles was stunned. "How's that possible?"

"I looked it up on marinetraffic.com. The website displays a map with live GPS tracking of all oceangoing vessels. It's amazing. They even have a phone app."

"How did you know what ship to track? They had the name covered with tarps hanging like laundry when we boarded. At the time, I assumed it was to keep nosey neighbors in the dark, but now we know better."

"I saw the ship's name on several documents while we were passing through the bridge. I'm sure you did, too. But even if I hadn't, it wouldn't have mattered. The website stores historic data."

Achilles had noted the name, but he was trained to do that type of thing. It was second nature. He had not discussed it with his wife. "You never cease to amaze me. Where is the *MS Sea Star*?"

"Middle of the Mediterranean latitudinally. Longitudinally, it's between Greece and Sicily."

"Halfway from Mersin to the Atlantic Ocean."

"Exactly."

"Great work! And just in time. Our plane to Istanbul is in four hours."

"Istanbul? Don't you mean Gibraltar?"

"We need passports. The supplier I know resides in Istanbul."

Katya crinkled her face. "By *supplier*, you mean…?"

"No worries. Zeki is a printer, not a mafioso. He looks like a stiff wind would blow him over, although he does talk like a bulldozer pushing rocks uphill. That always catches people by surprise. Anyway, he's already working on our passports, but I need to send photos. If you're done here, let's go up to the room. We'll take headshots with our new phones."

As they made their way upstairs, Katya asked, "How does Zeki create fake passports? Given all the imbedded security measures these days, I'm thinking we're way beyond acetone and razor blades."

Achilles was pleased to see his wife coping with her crutches and managing the pain. "There are three main methods the modern suppliers use. The best is creating a real fake. Like the passports Rex Rowe gave us. That's done by bribing someone either at the manufacturer or an office that can order them. Another method is building one from scratch, usually using supplies obtained out the back door of the original materials suppliers."

"That's possible?"

"Sure. If you think about it, making a passport is simply a sophisticated book-binding operation. And a high-volume one. Most countries crank out thousands every day. With that level of throughput, screwups at every stage of the manufacturing process are inevitable. Those mistakes create waste, which savvy employees quickly turn into gold.

"Zeki has spent decades cultivating his supply chain. Rumor has it that when he runs low on a specific item, a page type or security strip or whatnot, he simply orders it. His contact then arranges a mishap that generates the required product."

"What's the third forgery method?" Katya asked as they stepped back into their room.

Before answering, Achilles dug into the Apple Store bag and extracted a charger. He was anxious to learn whether his watch had survived. He plugged it in and placed his watch on the magnetic disk.

Nothing happened.

Disappointed, he answered Katya's question. "The third method is brokering an existing, legitimate passport. Suppliers pay desperate people to order real passports and turn them over. They'll have them alter their appearance for the photo in order to make it easy to approximate. Things like shaving their head or adding a beauty mark or wearing a wig and moustache that can be used by the passport purchaser. Visual distractions that the customs agent will naturally focus on."

"Clever."

"Very."

"I assume this means I'm going to get yet another name?"

"Already assigned. You're Katerina Kakos."

"Sounds Greek, not Turkish."

"That's intentional. Turks need a visa to visit the U.S. Greeks don't."

"I don't suppose you're Achilles Kakos?"

He chuckled, then embraced her. "I'm Kostas. We're Kostas and Katerina Kakos. Should be easy enough to remember."

Katya pointed over his shoulder. "It's charging."

Achilles turned to see green symbols illuminating his watch face. It had survived! "Excellent!"

"How long will we be in Istanbul?" Katya asked, bringing him back to the moment.

"Not more than half an hour I hope. Zeki is going to meet us at the private aviation terminal."

"Then what?"

"On to Gibraltar, as you predicted. We've got a ship to intercept."

Chapter 40

Human Nature

KATYA ACCEPTED her new Greek passport from the flight attendant and inspected it closely as their Falcon jet began taxiing toward takeoff at Istanbul Ataturk International airport. To her amateur eye, it looked perfect. She hoped the embedded electronics were similarly flawless.

She turned toward her husband, who was busy inspecting his own fresh document. "How did we manage to fly here without presenting identification?"

"We presented money instead," he said with a wink. "But seriously, that's all you need for a domestic charter flight. I told them we'd left our passports in Istanbul, and needed a quick stopover to get them before flying overseas. Zeki and the charter company took care of the rest."

In her mind, Katya replayed their brief interaction with the forger. "You were right about Zeki's voice. Kinda freaked me out."

"I know, right?"

"How much did the passports cost?"

"I paid fifty thousand for the pair."

"Wow!"

"Not our money. Our enemies' cash. And we've got hundreds of thousands more."

About three quarters of a million dollars by her count. "There's something poetic about that. It feels good."

"You deserve some feel-good."

"So things went smoothly at the bank?" They had so much to catch up on.

"Very smoothly. The branch manager at Yapi Kredi Bank was bending over backwards to please me. Got everything I wanted plus caviar canapés and a glass of champagne."

"Yapi Kredi?" Katya asked, just to taste the name.

"I know. Sounds silly to our ears, but this isn't a prestige play, and they're highly regarded by offshoring advisors."

"I'm not being snooty. In fact, I hope they have a Palo Alto branch. Silly makes me smile."

Achilles gestured toward her leg. "How's the healing coming?"

Katya had her ankles resting on the seat facing hers. While a bit awkward, the pose kept her wound elevated without compressing it. "As well as could be expected. It hurts, but it's not a searing pain. More the grin-and-bear-it kind."

"Prettiest grin I ever saw—on the toughest girl I ever met."

Katya couldn't fight back a smile, so she went with it. "The doctor did a good job. What were you doing while she was fixing me up? I saw you dialing a number after you excused yourself." Achilles had paid a concierge physician to visit their hotel room and tend to her leg.

"We're tight on time, so I found a virtual personal assistant service and gave them a call. They cater to the wealthy of Gibraltar. I asked for the best they had, and was skillfully assured that Maribelle would fit the bill."

"What did you ask Maribelle to do?"

"I gave her a shopping list, our travel plans and our new credit card number. I told her my schedule was tight and inflexible, my product requirements exact and non-substitutable, but there would be a two hundred percent tip for flawless execution. She perked up like a peacock on espresso and assured me that I would get it."

Katya was pleased to see her husband so visibly upbeat, and amused by his colorful imagery. "You're enjoying being rich, aren't you?"

He chuckled. "It sure makes life easier. And we were due a big helping of easier."

"I sense a 'but' coming."

"It's nothing."

"The plane's going to be doing all the work for the next few hours. We've got time to talk. Unload. Tell me what you're thinking."

Achilles reclined his chair a bit more. "*But* I'll be happy to blow through the whole cash windfall getting out of this mess. As sweet as having money to burn sounds, I cringe to think what we'd ultimately lose if we had no wants or needs. I don't think people are designed for that."

Katya's interest was piqued. "I agree with the sentiment, but I'm not sure I follow your last point. Isn't *the easy life* a near-universal goal?"

"It may be, but I contend that living things are designed to grow, not rest. I mean every living thing, from plants to insects to animals. Growth is what separates the living from the dead. We grow bigger physically. We grow bigger collectively—through reproduction. And in the case of homo sapiens and perhaps a few other species, we grow our cumulative knowledge base."

Katya saw that her husband was on a roll, so she urged him on with an attentive nod.

"We grew from stone caves and wooden clubs to freestanding huts and tilled fields. Then from huts to houses and from villages to cities. From horses to wagons to cars to trains to planes. Now we're transitioning to a world that's automated, digitized and computer controlled. It's what humans do. Our nature.

"Seems to me that if we're not growing, we're not in harmony with our programming. I figure it's hard to be happy when you're fighting your genetic identity."

Katya cocked her head and thought out loud. "You're saying that we wither when everything we desire gets delivered upon command."

"Exactly."

Katya spent a minute processing her husband's words. "I think I understand now, for the first time, what really propelled you into the Olympics."

He gave her a quizzical look. "It's the same impetus that earned you a PhD in mathematics."

She agreed that it probably was, and the thought made her happy. She was due a helping of happy. She decided to savor it, knowing what lay ahead.

Chapter 41

A Safe Assumption

AS THE JET CLIMBED to cruising altitude, Katya studied the lights below. So much rich history had played out on that landscape. Greece was to the northwest, Turkey to the southeast, and the North Aegean just ahead. This was the land of mythology, of Olympus and the Odyssey, Ithaca and the Iliad. It was the birthplace of Socrates, Pericles, Plato and Alexander.

The dark sea drew her eye. So much blackness. The largest ships were just pinpricks of light, like stars on an inky sky. The thought that she'd been bobbing in the middle of an even bigger sea just forty-eight hours earlier was difficult to wrap her head around. Achilles was right. They were incredibly lucky.

Especially her.

She'd gone into the Mediterranean with the one guy in ... a thousand? ... a million? who had the skills and stamina to save her. And now she was looking down on the waters that would have been her grave—not from heaven, but from the comfort of a private jet.

Katya glanced over at her husband. The marvelous man to whom she'd tethered her life. He was deep in thought.

Sensing her gaze, Achilles turned to meet her eye.

"You have it all figured out?" she asked.

"Nowhere close. But I have a plan to get there and I know our next moves."

"You ready to share?" When they weren't covertly running, he'd been frenetically prepping, so they had yet to discuss the evolving details of his plan.

He took a deep breath and slapped both palms down on the cream leather armrests as if punctuating the final sentence of his plan; then he launched into a pitch like a professor at a whiteboard. "We know that there's a stolen missile on a cargo ship. It doesn't have a warhead yet, but it's probably the most advanced delivery system in the world. Extremely fast and precise and probably destined to be delivered from an unexpected location. Bottom line, once the owner arms it, he'll have the ability to obliterate any city within hundreds of miles."

"In other words, some terrorist cell, radical government, or criminal organization just gained the ability to alter world history," Katya mumbled, as the stakes of their situation came crashing into focus.

"Yes, and not just because of the missile's tactical capabilities, but also because of its muddy provenance. Who gets blamed when a prototype weapon secretly stolen from a Russian-Indian joint venture is used?"

Katya felt a chill run down her spine. "I don't know."

"I'll tell you who. Blame will fall wherever the mastermind behind the theft wants it to fall. Where there's ambiguity, there's room for spin. And we're undoubtedly up against master politicians. Although we can't name our clever adversaries and we don't know their ultimate goal, I'd bet our house that we've been used to implement a very sophisticated plan."

Katya took a drink from the bottle of Evian in her armrest. "You say we aren't certain of the players, but also that we're up against master politicians. You're describing Rex Rowe."

"Among others, but he's the safe assumption."

Katya took another swallow. "What do you mean by safe?"

"Rex is an apex predator. If we prepare for him, we'll be ready for anyone."

"Isn't President Saxon the ranking predator?"

"Yes and no. The president technically has the power, but he's always in the spotlight. The White House Chief of Staff wields supreme executive authority from the shadows. That makes him more dangerous in clandestine affairs."

Katya saw her husband's point. She didn't like it. "Where does that leave us?"

Achilles took a sip from his own bottle. "The simple fact is this: We can't go home while Rex Rowe remains White House Chief of Staff."

The revelation hit Katya like a knee to the nose. How could they possibly dislodge such a powerful man? Can't go home! She took a deep breath and let it out slow. "What's our next tactical move?"

"I want to put a GPS device on the missile container, then give the tracking code to law enforcement."

"What agency can you alert, if our opponent is the White House Chief of Staff?"

"Some organization that's less political than Homeland Security. Maybe the Coast Guard—and a reporter or two for good measure."

Katya loved the idea of passing the military part of the operation off to law enforcement, although frankly she was a bit surprised that her husband would do so willingly. He wasn't one to relinquish control. Perhaps her presence was tipping the scale. Or maybe she was getting ahead of herself. "How, exactly, do you plan to put a GPS tracker on the container?"

"We know the *Sea Star* is going to be passing through the Strait of Gibraltar. And thanks to that website you found, we know exactly when it will be there. Just before dawn the day after tomorrow. We also know which container the missile is in—not by serial number unfortunately, but by location."

"I surmised that much," Katya said, feeling a bit breathless despite being seated. "What I want to know is how we're going to attach a GPS tracker to a container that's a hundred feet above the water on a fast-moving ship?"

Achilles smiled. "With a faster boat and some quick, clandestine climbing."

Chapter 42

Maribelle

ACHILLES BREATHED a sigh of relief when a town car pulled up to meet their jet as it parked at Gibraltar International Airport. The black Mercedes' presence indicated that Maribelle, the virtual personal assistant he'd engaged, was on the ball.

The famous rock loomed large as they descended the airstair. To Achilles, it looked like a lone giant canine tooth that had been decapitated with an enormous broadsword.

"No bags," Achilles told the attentive driver. "How far to the hotel?"

"Forty-five minutes."

"I thought Gibraltar was only a few square kilometers in size?"

"We can certainly find you a room in Gibraltar if you wish, Mr. Kakos. That is not a problem," the chauffeur replied in proper British English. "But I fear the quality will not excite you. Maribelle booked you at the Finca Cortesin, one of the finest hotels in all of Spain. I'm confident that you and your wife will be most comfortable there."

Achilles had never been one to outsource. He was an independent performer. An Olympic biathlete. A free-solo climber. He excelled because he paid attention to the details and took nothing for granted. Some might consider him a control freak, but one couldn't do what he did any other way—and expect to live.

The chauffeur continued, "I believe some items you requested are en route to the hotel via overnight delivery. We could pick them up and bring them to you here, of course. Whatever you wish?"

Achilles decided to roll with the recommendation. With Maribelle on the job, they had the time. And they could use a bit of pampering. Plus, a place like the one described could surely arrange for a doctor to inspect Katya's leg and change her bandages. He looked over at Katya who returned a nod and a smile. "The Finca sounds fantastic."

Fantastic it was.

Maribelle had booked them a pool suite, which, as advertised, had a private pool on a large terrace that looked out over the golf course toward the sea. Granted, neither of them was anxious for any more time in the water just yet, but the atmosphere was idyllic.

After the bellhop's quick tour, they returned to the bedroom, gave each other knowing nods and dove beneath the puffy white duvet. Both quickly surrendered to Somnus. It had been a long day, and a longer one would begin within hours.

Achilles awoke at first light and found Katya still sleeping soundly. He slipped on a hotel robe, brewed a black coffee and retreated to the terrace, hoping to get Maribelle on the phone.

It was just 7:30 a.m., but the personal assistant picked up on the second ring. "Mr. Kakos, how may I be of service?"

"Good morning, Maribelle. I wanted to check the status of my orders."

"As it happens, I was just preparing a text when you called. The rope, gloves, shoes and harness will be arriving at your resort by 10:00 a.m. The lifting magnets and GPS trackers are guaranteed by

11:00 a.m. Both are already listed as *out for delivery*. I've asked Francisco, the Finca's head concierge, to have them brought to your room the instant they arrive."

Achilles felt his shoulders relax, although he hadn't been aware that they were tense. "Outstanding. That's really good to hear. How about the Zodiac?"

"The MilPro FC 470 will be delivered to the Alcaidesa Marina and fully fueled by 3:00 this afternoon."

"And the captain for hire?"

"I found two naval special operations veterans, one a Brit, the other a Spaniard. The Brit will be in the lobby at 11:30. The Spaniard at 12:30. Given the time pressure, I thought lunch meetings might be efficient."

"You think of everything, Maribelle."

"That's my job, Mr. Kakos. And my pleasure to serve."

"What did you tell the two candidates?"

"As instructed, I conveyed that you had a twenty-four-hour Zodiac piloting job requiring grace under pressure and expert tactical skills. Dangerous but not illegal, and worth ten grand."

"Perfect."

"I will keep an eagle eye on your packages. Is there anything else I can help you with at the moment?"

"I'll be sure to let you know if there is. Thank you, Maribelle. You're a credit to your profession."

Achilles set down the phone and studied the distant sea as he sipped his coffee. It was the opposite end of the Mediterranean from where they'd boarded the *Sea Star*—back when their world wasn't inverted.

"What are you thinking?" Katya asked, catching him by surprise.

Achilles turned to see his wife standing in the doorway, looking lovely as a spring sunrise in her matching white robe. "I'm wondering if the world will be right-side-up again by this time tomorrow."

"You spoke to Maribelle?"

"Yes. She's done a splendid job in getting everything arranged. It's almost too perfect."

Katya hobbled closer, without the aid of crutches. Achilles sprang forward to help her but she held up a halting hand and asked, "Is it possible that they got to her?"

"To Maribelle? No. We wouldn't have woken up in our bed this morning if they had. We'd either have been hauled away in the night, or—"

"We wouldn't have woken up at all," Katya said with a stern nod.

Achilles didn't elaborate further.

Standing there staring at his beautiful wife, he wanted to promise that he would keep her safe, but he couldn't, and she knew it. He'd been by her side when Calix nearly killed her. The truth was tough to take, but they'd be fools to ignore it. Their lives were in serious danger.

Chapter 43

Defensive Measures

THE SPANISH SAILOR proved to be the more personable of the two candidates. He had a roguish charm that reminded Achilles of Han Solo. Working with him would likely be both memorable and a joy.

Achilles passed.

He went with the somber Brit instead.

This wasn't going to be a pleasure cruise. It was a stop-the-bomb, don't-get-your-wife-shot mission. Achilles wanted the guy with the most impressive combat CV driving the boat, and Jaxon had that by a mile.

Selecting him was an insurance policy. Better to have it and not need it than the other way around.

Their operation wasn't going to be an outright assault. They would be surreptitiously engaging the enemy. But if their incursion was discovered, it could get very ugly, very fast. Water cannons could come out. Bullets could start raining. Nets could be fired, slippery foam sprayed, or high-tech deterrents like lasers or acoustic cannons engaged. In short, avoiding disaster in a crisis would demand the kind of captain who could remain as calm, cool and collected under fire as Achilles did when free-solo climbing cliffs.

It didn't hurt that the Brit had a 9mm Browning Hi-Power he was willing to loan out.

Captain Jaxon had them spend the afternoon practicing with the Zodiac on the open water. He piloted the 15.5-foot assault craft all the way to Morocco and back, just to give them the feel of the entire playing field. The ride was far from a pleasure cruise. The rigid-hull-inflatable had more in common with a raft than a yacht. But it was very fast, exceptionally reliable, and invisible to the *Sea Star's* radar.

"The strait is basically a mighty river connecting the Atlantic Ocean with the Mediterranean Sea," Jaxon explained as they bounced from wave crest to wave crest. "Eight hundred thousand cubic meters of water pass through it each way every second, with the fresher, lighter ocean water flowing eastward above and the heavier, saltier Mediterranean water flowing westward below. Complicating things is a huge speed bump in the middle of the strait. It's an underwater mountain called the Camarinal Sill that makes the calm surface dangerously turgid underneath. We'll be wise to intercept the *Sea Star* well to its east."

Achilles nodded his agreement. "What about ferry traffic? Does it cease after dark?"

"No. There are half a dozen ports on both the European and African sides of the strait, creating quite the crisscrossed network of routes. Several run continuously around the clock, leaving every two or three hours, depending on the length of the route. But I know their preferred corridors, the ferries are big and the weather will be clear, so they'll be easy to avoid."

Once the introductory session was behind them, the three hit the marina café for a quick fish and chips dinner. Then Katya and Jaxon used marinetraffic.com to plan the exact intercept course while Achilles made his way to the dry dock to practice hiding GPS transponders on containers, and climbing steel hulls.

The lifting magnets that would give him grip looked like yellow metal bricks fitted with U-loop shackle-hooks on top and activation levers on one side. Each weighed seven pounds and would support 220 when properly affixed. Achilles roped both to a waist harness, then worked one with each hand. It was awkward at first, pressing the magnet against the hull while simultaneously engaging and disengaging the lever, all with a single hand. But once he got the technique down, a rhythm developed, and soon the repetitive nature made it faster than climbing irregular rock.

"Do you want to practice out on the water, against a less-hostile ship?" Captain Jaxon called out from below.

"Not worth the risk of getting spotted," Achilles replied.

"It's just that I've never seen anyone attempt what you're planning. I get the theory, but I can't help believing that the practice may prove to be an entirely different animal. It will be dark, wet and windy, and it's a long way up the side of a cargo ship."

"I've got the climbing covered."

"One little slip could plunge you into the path of the propeller. They're the height of a house on a ship like that, you know. Weigh about a hundred tons apiece. Spinning at 120 rpm, those blades will slice through you like a deli ham."

Achilles could have done without that image, but he appreciated Jaxon's motivation. The last thing you wanted in the midst of an operation was a what-have-I-gotten-myself-into revelation. "Really, climbing is my thing."

Jaxon raised both hands in surrender. Hopefully the one and only time Achilles would see the move. "If you say so."

Chapter 44

In the Spotlight

THEY SPOTTED THE *SEA STAR* at 4:14 a.m. It was a bit surreal, being out on the open water in the black of night, watching a ship they were tracking on a laptop slowly materialize on the real horizon.

The wind had risen since their earlier run, creating modest waves but killing sound. Overall, he couldn't complain.

As Jaxon set an intercept course, Achilles couldn't help but contemplate the increasingly large role that hunk of floating iron was playing in the story of his life. Unlike his first bike or car, however, the cargo ship would not star in a favorite chapter. Not yet anyway. With luck, it would become the place where he and Katya helped avert a nuclear disaster. For now, however, it was the setting where they had been completely betrayed and nearly killed.

The forty-foot shipping container holding the stolen missile was stacked in the forward bay, middle row, top tier. In other words, front and center. That made it easy for Achilles to find and access, but it also increased the odds that he would be spotted.

The *Sea Star's* cruising speed was twenty-five knots. The Zodiac pushed sixty. That combination meant the distance between them was shrinking at over eighty knots. An adrenaline rush to be sure.

Jaxon was handling their black inflatable like a pro. As soon as they passed over the *Sea Star's* bow wake, he throttled way back on the engine and made a smooth U-turn, putting them in the ship's shadow. While he closed in on the side of the starboard hull, Achilles gave his gear a final check.

By the time Achilles was poised to leap, the hull was looming over them like a moving mountain.

"Don't get dead," Jaxon shouted as the Zodiac kissed the painted metal. "You've got far too fine a woman to live for."

Achilles readied himself for the most critical moment of the mission, trying to time it right. If he got a good hold on the hull, one high enough to keep his legs out of the water, the ascent would be relatively simple. If he didn't, if he missed the mark or the magnets didn't grip, well, look out for that propeller.

As he prepared to synchronize his spring with the rhythm of the waves, a spotlight burst to life, illuminating the water just two meters ahead of their position. Achilles glanced up and saw that it originated on the main deck, amidships.

It homed in on the Zodiac.

"Zip around front to the other side," Achilles commanded into his throat microphone. "I'm going to try to board before they reorient."

Jaxon reacted without hesitation, rocketing the Zodiac to full speed and sending it screaming toward the bow.

Achilles shifted to the other side of the inflatable boat and prepared to jump with a magnet in each hand. Katya came up behind and helped brace him as they bounded over the wake and crossed mere meters before the prow.

"The port spotlight's not on yet," Jaxon shouted, stating the obvious but critical condition. "Hold on!" He whipped the boat around, putting it back on a parallel course while pulling closer.

Achilles didn't have the luxury of timing his leap. As soon as the two vessels touched, he went for it. He slammed the right magnet against the hull as the Zodiac was dipping. He flipped the lever, felt it slip, then grab, and shouted "Go!"

Chapter 45

Bad Position

WHILE THE ZODIAC PULLED AWAY beneath his feet, Achilles slammed the left magnet beside the right and flipped its lever. Then the boat was gone and the sea stepped in to rock his world. He was way too low. His legs were dragging in the water.

The saline assault was so ferocious that for a few seconds, Achilles found himself afraid to climb. Afraid that a single magnet might not hold against the tremendous force. He did his best barnacle impression as the waves pounded and the current sucked and the image of the big deli-slicer in back began looming large.

He'd leapt into an untenable position.

Thinking quickly, Achilles discarded the idea of climbing hand-over-hand and instead pulled himself up on the magnets like he was mounting parallel bars. This lifted his legs out of the current and immediately took the pressure off, but it left him in a position not suited for climbing. It locked his elbows and dumped all his weight into his shoulder joints. It also put his hands atop the magnet housings, rather than around their faces, making it awkward to operate the grip/release levers.

Nice, Achilles. Nice.

Fortunately, the news wasn't all bad. The rushed boarding procedure that put him in this pickle had also saved the mission. By the time the port spotlight sprang to life and started sweeping, the Zodiac was out of gunshot range. Achilles risked a glance over his shoulder and saw it rocketing away on a perpendicular course, giving the appearance of a spooked child.

A flashlight ignited on the Zodiac while he watched. Katya was trolling for the watchman's eye. "Smart move," he whispered, as the spotlight reacted.

Achilles turned his attention back to the hull. It was time for his next leap.

To free one hand, he had to go from hanging between two magnets to straddling one. From the parallel bars to the pommel horse. An easy move in a gym, less so when dangling between two nubs in an onslaught of the elements. He rehearsed the move a few times in his mind, then flexed his elbows and used his arms to spring to the preferred position.

He stuck the landing.

Propped up on a single stiff arm, Achilles released the unburdened magnet and repositioned it some five feet higher. Then he transferred his weight, released the lower grip, and put himself back in the climbing business.

Let's not do that again anytime soon.

From there on, the hours of repetitive shipyard practice paid off in the form of smooth moves. After a few more hand-over-hand repetitions, he turned to watch the action on the water. The spotlight was finally extinguished when the Zodiac neared the horizon.

Plunged into the relative dark with his team no longer in sight, Achilles suddenly felt all alone.

He and Katya had been uncharacteristically quiet in the hours leading up to the assault. Both intuitively understood that speaking what was on their minds would rile up emotions. Agitate nerves that were best left undisturbed before beginning dangerous missions. Besides, each already knew everything the other had to say. They were a team, a couple, a matched set. Interlocked and intertwined, now and forever.

Achilles strained his ears and detected no voices. Between the wind and the waves there was a lot of interference. That camouflaging effect would work both ways, but he stayed off the microphone just in case.

With the excitement of the botched leap behind him and his pulse now normal, Achilles decided that he probably didn't need to worry about the initial encounter. In busy waterways like this, smaller craft likely came close to cargo ships on a semi-regular basis. Security guards would regard them as houseflies. Annoying, but not a threat.

He continued the ascent, arm over arm, with rhythmic, repetitive motions. Release, reach, engage. Click, clunk, clack. Release, reach, engage. Click, clunk, clack. Soon he was hanging just below the main deck.

He positioned the lifting magnets where they'd be hard for a passer-by to spot but easy for him to find—hopefully less than five minutes from now.

Although he could not see his wife far away in the dark, Achilles was confident that she was watching. With the spotlight off, she was free to turn the binoculars in his direction without giving the game away. He waved for her benefit before slipping over the rail.

He landed on what was called a lashing bridge. One of the framed side-to-side passages that were walled fore and aft by tall stacks of containers. Jaxon had called them the honeycombs of the ship's worker bees.

Guards could be anywhere within them. Roaming, patrolling, playing cards or smoking dope. While theirs would be boring work, and therefore not attention-riveting, the men who did it night after night would be instinctively attuned to the natural rhythms of the ship. Discordant notes would register like faulty piano keys.

Knowing that he had to be careful, Achilles set out slowly, silently climbing the ladder to the next level. While not technically challenging, it was the equivalent of a room breach, since he couldn't see who might be inside.

It was clear.

But the danger would increase as he closed in on his prize. The next breach would put him in the long, tall, open ravine between the first and second container bays. That was where the smart watch would be posted—if the mastermind back in D.C. or Moscow, Baghdad, Beijing or Riyadh had ordered one.

While he didn't know who had or had not ordered a special guard, Achilles did know that cargo ships had only about twenty-five crew members. Jaxon had confirmed his research in that regard. Given that low total, they felt confident that there would be no more than half a dozen souls on active duty at this early hour. Six people to run the ship and cover its six exposed container decks, each one the size of three football fields. Achilles liked those odds—but he didn't think they applied.

Calix had been an add-on, and Achilles had to assume that when he disappeared, the mastermind had reacted by setting up a system that could keep a covert watch 24/7. Whether that system involved adding human eyeballs or electronic ones was an open question. Therefore Achilles had to outmaneuver both. He had to keep quiet and move quickly. Get in and out before anyone could react.

Fortunately, he wasn't trying to steal the missile. He didn't even need to open the container. All Achilles had to do was hide GPS transponders in a couple of the corner castings without anyone noticing. Like a magician performing sleight of hand.

Should be a piece of cake.

Chapter 46

Background Noise

KATYA BARELY BREATHED from the moment the spotlight hit the Zodiac until it was extinguished a few minutes later. Her diaphragm was just too tense to exhale.

The violent pounding of the raft against the wake didn't help.

Fortunately, she appeared to be the only one thus affected. Achilles and Jaxon had taken the surprise discovery in stride, like a hole in the sidewalk they could step around. Or rather sprint past. The speed and precision with which they reacted reminded her of firemen hearing an alarm.

Now that the Zodiac was in the dark, Captain Jaxon cut the motor and they picked up binoculars. "The watchman is still standing behind the spotlight, but he's not looking our way and he just lit a cigarette," Jaxon reported.

"Achilles is working his way aft, toward the gap between containers," Katya replied, much relieved. Her husband's initial grip on the hull of the ship had looked low and tenuous, but she hadn't been free to follow his progress for fear of guiding hostile eyes his way.

Now she watched with an odd combination of trepidation and pride as Achilles moved with the casual ease of a monkey in a tree. He quickly added altitude and disappeared over the rail before she'd fully caught her breath.

Suddenly she was blind again.

The three had agreed to maintain radio silence during the operation, unless there was crucial information to report. Achilles didn't want to risk being overheard either directly or through electronic intercept. Not on such a quick in-and-out mission.

Katya had agreed without reservation. She supported anything that decreased the risk to him. But sitting there in the dark on a small boat in a big sea while her husband vanished into enemy territory, the same terrain on which she'd been shot just a few days earlier, Katya wished she'd thought to have him wear a body camera.

Although Achilles had clad himself head-to-toe in black, he had not geared up like a soldier or SWAT team member. He had not donned body armor or a tactical vest full of kit. Just a miniature inflatable life vest. "Lean and light" was how he phrased it. Besides the climbing magnets, he carried only the GPS transponders and Jaxon's semiautomatic. Adding a camera would hardly have tipped the scale.

Jaxon keyed the motor, reversed course, and began closing back in on the *Sea Star*. But not very fast. In fact, quite slowly.

"Is there a problem with the engine?" Katya asked, as a dark splotch on the *r* of *Sea Star* momentarily drew her eye. It was just a blemish, not a climber.

"No problem. I'm trying to time it right. Your husband estimated a five-minute operation. Two minutes to ascend six levels. One to place the transponders. One to return to the main deck. One to descend the hull. Ideally, we'll pull alongside just as he's ready to jump."

"What do we do if they spot us first?"

"Depends on where we—" A distant crack! cut Jaxon off. A crack with a metallic ring. Katya heard it through her earpiece. A gunshot! Three more followed.

"Kostas is taking fire," Jaxon said.

It took Katya a second to register Achilles' cover name. "How do you know he's not the one shooting?"

"The earpiece report would be a lot louder. Those are handgun shots coming from more than a few feet away. Someone spotted him. Someone professional enough to aim each shot. But they're missing."

"How do you know?"

"You can hear the bullets hitting containers. He's fine. Don't distract him," Jaxon added. "Let him focus."

"How do you know he's fine?"

"He'd have yelped if he'd been hit. Speaking of which, there's no shouting in the background. That indicates there's just one guard engaged."

Katya could hear the rustling of rapid movement coming over Achilles' throat mic, then a short silence followed by a burst of noise she couldn't identify. Then nothing. Nothing at all.

Katya keyed her microphone. "Achilles! Achilles, say something!"

No reply.

She realized that she'd used the wrong name as she turned to gauge Jaxon's reaction. The captain's eyes were buried in his binoculars.

"What was that noise?" she asked.

"I'm not sure."

"What should we do?"

"What can we do? We can't board the ship. We can't stop the ship."

"Can we call the Coast Guard?"

"And tell them what?"

"A man was shot on the Sea Star."

"The Sea Star is transporting a billion dollars' worth of cargo through international waters. The Gibraltar Coast Guard isn't going to wade into that bureaucratic swamp on behalf of a foreigner committing a crime."

Katya felt gut-punched. Disoriented and breathless. How had she suddenly become so powerless? How had her husband failed to foresee this possibility? Once again her world was completely upside down.

She studied the side of the ship and the surrounding waters, hoping against hope that Achilles would appear.

He didn't.

They kept searching. Scanning the side of the ship. Sweeping the trailing water.

Achilles was nowhere to be seen.

What else could she do? She couldn't seek help from the authorities. She couldn't even let them know that her husband was alive.

Chapter 47

Shadow Ops

KATYA SUDDENLY became aware that Jaxon had cut the Zodiac's engine. Had it just happened? She'd been deep in thought, her processor churning at supersonic speed in search of a solution. A means of rescuing her husband. Of securing his freedom or at the very least providing him with medical attention.

The sudden change of atmosphere made her wonder if she'd missed the obvious. Was Jaxon in on it? Another Calix? Was he about to crack her skull and toss her to the sharks? "Why did you stop the motor?"

"To listen," Jaxon mumbled without turning.

Katya stopped herself from asking the obvious question. The act would forestall or perhaps even quash his quest—whatever it might be.

While the captain remained still and silent, Katya strained her ears.

"There! Did you hear it?"

Katya heard wind and waves and the light lapping of water. Nothing more. "Hear what?"

"More gunshots."

How could she have missed those? Was he listening to his earpiece, or the air?

Jaxon started the motor and immediately took the Zodiac up to full speed. Katya held on, keeping her jaw clenched to avoid biting her tongue as they bounced over the waves. Until she noticed something wrong. "Why did you change course? Why aren't we heading to intercept the ship?"

"You didn't figure it out?"

"Figure what out?"

"The acoustic clues."

Why was he toying with her? This was hardly the time for guessing games. Surely he knew that. Katya snagged on her own words. Surely he did know that, so why be obtuse? The answer was obvious. Or at least the sentiment. Either Jaxon didn't want to deliver bad news. Or he didn't want to give false hope. Or he wanted to keep her preoccupied while he verified his hypothesis.

She reflected on what he'd heard. Achilles had been close to the container when shots rang out. Four of them. Without warning or dialogue. Then she'd heard a burst of activity, her husband moving quickly, then a short silence before an odd burst of noise and the end of transmission. Some seconds later, Jaxon reported having heard gunshots. Meanwhile, they hadn't seen Achilles since he slipped between the cargo bays. And now Jaxon was steering the boat not to intercept the ship, not to pick up her husband as he made his escape, but on a shallower angle. Either to a place the ship had been, or to a unseen point on the Spanish shore.

Could Achilles be in the water? She'd been watching with unwavering attention and hadn't seen him. Surely Jaxon hadn't either, or he would have said something.

The answer struck like a two-by-four whacking her between the eyes. In a good way. She'd been too nervous to think clearly. "He jumped off the far side. The gunman spotted him in the water and kept shooting. Then he stopped." The final phrase caught in her throat like a barbed fishing lure as the second shoe dropped. The shooter stopped—and the ship kept going.

Katya turned to the cagey captain as her stomach shrunk to walnut size. Jaxon pointed in the direction they were headed.

Katya looked for a floating shadow, a black hump rising and falling with the waves, but she didn't see anything. It was still too dark. Clearly, the captain had trained his eyes to pick out anomalies on the familiar terrain, like a safari guide scanning the Serengeti.

A second later, everything changed. She caught sight of two circular objects moving through arcs. Moving! Her hopeful brain instantly identified the activity. Achilles waving his arms. His open palms. The only part of his body not covered or painted in black. "He looks all right!"

"Yes, he does."

"I'm okay," Achilles called as they closed in.

Katya practically lifted him out of the water herself. Then she squeezed him like a sponge that needed to be wrung dry.

"I missed you too," he said.

"What happened?"

"A guy was waiting for me. I should have been better prepared for that possibility. I should have aimed to identify and neutralize him, rather than relying on stealth and speed. In retrospect, what I did was easy to anticipate."

"No, it wasn't," Jaxon said. "Climbing the hull of a Panamax container ship moving at full speed is definitely outside the envelope."

Not if you know Achilles, Katya thought. But she and her husband both let it go. "Did you get the transponders in place?"

Achilles shook his head. "I was spotted when I was still a container away. The guy must have installed a motion detector, because I was silent as snowfall. I heard a device begin to beep above me and then a face peered over the rim of the missile container. A gun arm followed. The guard was probably camped out up there in a sleeping bag."

"At least you got away unscathed," Katya said.

"Why did you retreat to the opposite side?" Jaxon asked.

"It was darker, making me harder to spot. The moonlight was filtering through on the port side. As you recall, we initially approached from the starboard for that reason. We just switched to port when the boat was spotted."

"Of course," Jaxon said. "I should have anticipated your move."

"No harm done," Achilles said, removing the U-shaped auto-inflated life preserver from around his neck, and peeling off the ruined mic.

Speak for yourself, Katya thought. At least now she could better appreciate what her husband had gone through after she'd been shot.

Not wanting to dwell on unpleasant past experiences, Katya turned her focus to their future. Without a GPS tracker to identify the one correct container out of the thousands aboard, they couldn't involve the authorities. Not anonymously. The threat wouldn't be specific or credible enough to force the immense bureaucratic burden or justify the great financial expense of inspecting so many containers.

As she thought about it, Katya had no doubt that the *Sea Star* would use its cranes to reposition the incriminating container while crossing the Atlantic. A simple insurance policy, so to speak. The result would be the equivalent of shuffling a single joker within dozens of decks of cards.

And that wasn't the worst of it.

The bad guys, whoever they were, would surely hear of the black-clad intruder who climbed aboard in the middle of the night. It wouldn't take them two seconds to connect the dots. Therefore, they now knew that Achilles was alive.

Offensive measures would increase.

Defensive measures would increase.

The odds of beating them would plummet.

Speaking in Russian so Jaxon wouldn't understand, she asked her husband the pivotal question, "What now? How will we ever get our lives back?"

Chapter 48

Leapfrog

AFTER BLOWING THE MISSION, Achilles wanted to kick himself from Morocco to Gibraltar, but he didn't have that luxury. The clock was ticking and his wife needed him. Still, he simmered with that special sort of anger people reserve only for themselves.

Katya had broken cover by speaking Russian, but at that point it hardly mattered, and she was probably right to trade a bit of transparency for expediency at that particular moment. By being spotted, Achilles had already let the big cat out of the bag. The bad guys in D.C. or Moscow, Baghdad, Beijing or Riyadh would soon know he was alive.

As to her question about their next moves, Achilles saw only one workable option. Replying in Russian, he said, "We stick with the plan to alert the authorities, but shift the timing."

"I don't understand," she said.

"We follow the ship. We watch the unloading process. And when we see the missile container come off, then we tell the authorities exactly where it is."

Katya deflated before his eyes. It was like his words had ripped a hole in her hull and her soul was starting to sink. "Don't you think they'll shuffle the containers at sea, now that they know we're alive?"

"They probably will."

"So how will we be able to identify the missile container?"

"I got the registration number. The last three numbers and the check digit, anyway. 413 7. The others were in a shadow. And we know the container's color. That should be enough."

She brightened. "Yes, it should. Assuming they don't move the missile to a different container."

"I very much doubt they would. That would be tactically risky, given that they'd be doing it on the open water. And more importantly, it would reveal the cargo to the crew. At the moment, the most any of the sailors know is that there's a container onboard getting suspicious treatment. That's very different from knowing that they're clandestinely transporting a hypersonic cruise missile."

"But the missile is in a tube," Katya pressed.

"A very military-looking tube marked DelMos II, and displaying the Russian and Indian flags. With information containment as our enemies' chief concern right now, they're not going to risk letting anyone see inside that container."

"Won't they try to unload it early, now that they know we're in pursuit?"

"It's possible, and we'll have to be prepared to counter that tactic, but I doubt it. This is a very sophisticated operation. I'm sure it was months in the making. They'll resist deviating from the plan. They're also not going to want to get another ship and its crew involved."

"So how will they respond to what just happened?"

"They'll use the same strategy that brought them tonight's victory. They'll anticipate our likely moves and put countermeasures in place."

"I don't like the sound of that."

"Me either. But forewarned is forearmed."

Achilles glanced back at Jaxon, who was busy minding his own business, steering the Zodiac. He'd been a good find.

Katya followed her husband's gaze, then studied the waters ahead. In five minutes, they'd be back at the marina. "Where do we go when we get off the boat?"

"We go back to the hotel and have Maribelle charter us a jet while we clean up. Then we begin a game of leapfrog."

Katya took a second to process the leapfrog reference before confirming. "We keep one step ahead of the ship, depending on its heading, so we're sure to be present wherever it unloads."

"Exactly. We assume it's headed for the U.S., but we're not certain. And the U.S. is hardly a specific destination. Will it be Washington? Miami? Boston? New York? Or will they stage a shell game at some island along the way? Perhaps try to hide it on a small one?"

Katya raised her eyes in recall. "So first we fly to the Azores, then Bermuda?"

"You've been studying the map."

"Like a kid prepping for a geography exam. I want to win our life back."

Achilles wrapped both arms around his wife. "We will. I promise."

He meant it and she knew it. He also knew she'd help him do it. Alas, neither of them knew how they were going to identify, much less neutralize, the powerful people behind the proverbial curtain.

Chapter 49

Repositioning

REX THOUGHT he had successfully restructured the power dynamic last Saturday, when he'd shown himself to be the superior tactician. But a second summons had proved that to be wishful thinking.

He was still grumbling to himself as the helicopter touched down. Despite his silver tongue and sterling reputation, they had him. The simple, inescapable fact was that he owed his current plum position to the C3. They had placed him in the White House and they could pluck him out—shifting him from wunderkind to has-been at the speed of D.C. gossip.

But it wasn't pride or fear that had put him back on that helicopter. Ambition had. Specifically, the driving desire to have them do for him what they'd done for Preston Saxon, to make him president of the United States.

And then there was the money. The thirty million he'd be due when Operation 51 was done. His modest share of the loot. The fee he'd negotiated for serving as strategist, facilitator and watchdog.

A ranch hand was waiting by the helipad this time. The burly cowboy ran out, opened the door, and retrieved Rex's roller-bag in proper fashion. But after proffering the extended handle, he hopped into the seat Rex had just vacated.

A minute later, the big bird was back in the clouds and Rex was standing alone on the side of the helipad.

The White House Chief of Staff hadn't lied when he told WZ that he found the setting reminiscent of the president's official retreat. Both were leafy sanctums a half hour helicopter flight from home. The service at Camp David, however, was far superior. When one arrived at the president's place, he was met by a polished car and a deferential driver. Here, visitors walked.

Fortunately, the path to the lodge was lit, because beyond the low glow of those trail lights, the setting was midnight black.

Rex had studied the surrounding landscape while flying in, attempting to verify William Zacharia's no-neighbors claim. It held up. He had not seen a single photon for the last few minutes of flight. When the lodge did come into view, it stood out like a lighthouse.

Rex made his way up the path and through the big oak door. The three CEOs were seated around the fire when he walked into the room, as if they'd never left. Only their faces looked different. With nothing but the fire for illumination, they appeared older and more mortal.

This time, they stood as he approached. This time, they offered him a whisky tumbler.

"Thank you very much for coming," William Zacharia said, as Rex enjoyed his first sip. "I'll get right to it, knowing you don't have much time. Kyle and Katya Achilles are alive, and they're investigating."

Rex had expected as much, given the timing. Therefore he had thought things through. But before presenting his preliminary conclusions, he wanted to factor in everything they'd learned. "Tell me what you know and how you know it."

William Zacharia opened a laptop and paused with his finger poised to play a video he had queued up. "This is security camera footage from the *Sea Star* taken last night while it was passing through the Strait of Gibraltar. This container holds the missile." He pointed to the forty-footer in the middle of the row furthest from the bridge. "And that is our surviving operative camped out atop it."

"Why is the picture so grainy?" Rex asked.

"This is a digital zoom. The camera is on the bridge, some seven hundred feet back. Plus it's night so there's low light. Watch." He hit Play. A few seconds later a red light began flashing behind the sentinel. An alarm positioned at the container's aft end. He rose and readied his handgun, then inched toward the edge. A few seconds later, muzzle flashes erupted. Spaced and selective. Two directed portside into the rift between the rows followed by their man jumping back. Presumably after hearing return fire. Again he crept forward. Again he fired two shots, this time starboard as he tracked his target toward the edge. The entire encounter lasted only six or seven seconds.

None of the shots had hit their mark, Rex was sure. Not because of anything he'd seen, but because they'd summoned him. "What did your man report?"

"He said the intruder was incredibly fast. Under the conditions, it was like trying to shoot a black cat in a coal pit. A very quick cat."

WZ opened another video file. The still on this one appeared to have been taken from an aft camera. It showed the back of the ship and the churning wake that stretched out far behind. This time the Steel Shield CEO pointed to a dot in the water on the starboard side. "That's the man who triggered the alarm—alive and well."

He opened a third video. This one looked out over the whole ship from the bridge. "This is the camera that captured the shooting sequence. The footage is from a few minutes earlier."

As Rex watched, the water on the starboard side was illuminated by the beam of a powerful spotlight. The light homed in on a black raft racing across the water toward the ship's bow where it was soon hidden from sight. William Zacharia didn't stop the show, so Rex kept watching. About twenty seconds later the raft briefly reappeared on the port side as it sped off camera.

"That's when the intruder boarded," Rex said. "The timing and the angle don't match that of a straightforward escape."

"Yup."

"How did the intruder get aboard? Did an onboard accomplice lower a rope?"

In answer, WZ opened up two video stills, one of the raft in the starboard spotlight, the other when it was portside in the dark. Both showed a large figure at the tiller and a smaller one seated near the front. But only the illuminated photo included a third person, a large man clad in black.

Despite the fact that Rex could see only a black blob against a black background, he had no doubt. "It's Achilles."

William Zacharia nodded somberly as he closed the photos. "He climbed the hull, hand over hand, using magnets like suction cups. Your super spy is now working against us."

Chapter 50

Watch Out

BEN WAS USED TO STRESS and uncertainty in his business life. Construction contractors lived lives of feast or famine. Either they won the big job, or they didn't. Either he had too few workers, or too many. Either insufficient equipment, or a costly surplus.

Under normal circumstances, he used professional planners and sophisticated software to manage the business. Under extraordinary circumstances, he sent particularly pesky problems to their graves using much more primitive methods.

Unfortunately, regardless of his tactics, many forces remained beyond Ben's control. There were too many governments and agencies and special interests in the mix to make life fair or predictable.

All of that had taught Ben resilience. When he took a blow, he didn't waste time whining; he focused on his next punch. When Kyle Achilles moved from the asset to the liability column on Operation 51, Ben listened not with anger or frustration, but with an ear for opportunity.

"What do you think Achilles was trying to do?" Rex asked. "Why board the ship? Why approach the container?"

"To destroy it," William Zacharia replied. "He's furious at having been used, and by the assault on himself and his wife. So he wants to deprive us of our prize."

"I trust you drained their operating account?" Ben asked. It was a housekeeping question. The equivalent of *Did you turn out the lights and lock the door?* But William Zacharia reddened.

"They transferred the funds out of the account early on."

"How much?"

"The whole two million."

The room went still as a tree stump until Ben finally pressed forward. "How could you let that happen?"

"No way to stop it, really."

"You should have foreseen that possibility," Luci said, chiming in. "You financed our enemies. You put everything at risk."

William Zacharia bowed his head. "You're right. I should have. I could have doled out the money as they needed it. But at the time I was more concerned with making sure our agents didn't face financial constraints. It was no simple task, figuring out how to steal that missile. I didn't want to jeopardize the whole operation by forcing them to factor in money. Not a mere two million anyway."

"How much do they have left?" she pressed.

"We know they spent one million of the two we gave them on the Russian airplane and soldiers, because I set up that deal. I don't have insight into their other expenditures, but they probably have at least half a million left."

More than enough, Ben thought.

Rex changed the subject by pointing to the laptop. "Do you have a video of the missile being loaded into the container?"

"Yes, it's in here somewhere." WZ moved the cursor over an array of files before selecting one and hitting play. The video opened to show the missile being strapped into the container while Achilles and Katya watched. "Calix shot this on his cellphone."

The CEOs watched as their Greek operative approached and explained that the Americans would be riding to the port inside the container.

"Pause it," Rex commanded a couple of minutes later as Calix was preparing to close the container door.

WZ complied.

The frame captured the entire container opening, with the missile in the middle and Achilles and Katya seated on the right.

Achilles had a handgun in his lap and bolt cutters beneath his folding chair. Katya held two bottles of water.

"Look at the missile tube," Rex said. "The end cap is attached with eight baseball-sized bolts."

"What's your point?"

"It would take one monster of a wrench to expose the missile. Which he'd need to do if his goal was to destroy it. And Achilles wouldn't have been able to scamper like a cat if he was hauling twenty pounds of top-heavy steel. I take it he didn't leave any tools behind? Didn't drop anything to the deck as he fled?"

"No," WZ said.

"Why would the end cap have to come off?" Luci asked.

"So he could put the bomb inside the tube. If he put it outside, the explosion would likely just blow the top off the container. It's made of a much weaker material than the tube, and it's a less resilient shape. Explosive force escapes through the point of least resistance."

"In general, I agree," WZ said. "But a shaped charge could slice through the tube."

Ben raised a finger. "Yes, but shaped charges have to be directed."

WZ caught on immediately. "Creating the same problem as the wrench. Achilles would have been hobbled by a heavy and awkward load. A long section of angle iron."

"So what was Achilles attempting?" Luci asked.

Ben leaned forward to answer. "He's a man of action, right? The kind of guy who grabs the bull by the horns?"

"That's an understatement," Rex said.

"But he's also constrained by a lack of proof. If he told his story, it would be his word against yours. That's a nonstarter. You have far more credibility, and the ability to quash Achilles' story."

"Keep going," Rex encouraged.

"Achilles has to acquire and present proof in a way that won't allow you to intervene. That means swiftly, decisively and publicly. You follow?"

"Sure," William Zacharia said.

His tone expressed the apprehension Ben was also beginning to feel. "So Achilles climbs aboard the ship, intent on one: verifying the missile's presence, and then two: taking the bridge by force."

"To what end?" Luci asked.

"Summoning the Coast Guard. 'This is the *Sea Star* calling to report discovering a stolen missile in our cargo hold.' The Coast Guard can't ignore a call like that, and they won't need to run their reaction up the chain of command. They'll just converge on the ship and search the container. By the time they realize that the man who called is not the captain, they'll have the missile and it won't matter."

"Exactly," Rex concurred.

"But he didn't do either," William Zacharia said. "So we're safe, for now. Achilles has no proof. Plus now we know he's alive and attempting to expose us, so we can crank up both our offensive and defensive activities."

Ben found himself studying the projector screen while processing the implications. Staring the enemy in the face, so to speak. That was when he saw it, and his heart sank.

He rose and walked over to the screen, so he could study the image up close. So he could be sure. The others ignored him until he turned around and his expression caused concern.

"What is it, Ben?" Luci asked.

"We're wrong."

"About what?"

"About the whole scenario. He probably already has proof."

"What are you talking about?" William Zacharia asked.

In response, Ben raised his wrist and manipulated his watch. The tiny speaker wasn't powerful, but the sound quality was clear. *"What is it, Ben?" "We're wrong." "About what?" "About the whole scenario. He probably already has proof." "What are you talking about?"*

Everyone stared until WZ finally spoke. "You've been recording us?"

"I always record my meetings. It's a best practice. But that's not the point."

"What is your point?" The Texas drawl had developed an edge.

Ben held his arm up to the screen so his watch was beside Achilles'. "Note the matching logos. Achilles records his conversations too."

Nobody spoke for what felt like a full minute. Then, one by one, the other two followed Ben's lead and turned to look at Rex, who had closed his eyes to concentrate. The three remained silent while the White House Chief of Staff dredged his mind, traveling back to the beginning. When finally his head dropped, they felt slapped in the face. When he spoke, they felt kicked in the crotch. "Yes. Achilles was wearing his watch at our Oval Office meeting."

THE NORTH ATLANTIC

Chapter 51

Five-Star Frustration

KATYA WOULD NOT HAVE THOUGHT that island hopping on private planes could be anything but delightful. Not when the sun was shining and her husband was by her side. Not when she had her health and the best hotels were affordable. But she was finding that, no matter how spectacular the present might be, it simply wasn't enjoyable when the future was so uncertain. When everything she'd worked for and owned might disappear. Her home, her job, her name.

If they didn't somehow outwit and outmaneuver the unidentified masterminds, then they couldn't return to the United States. They couldn't reclaim their lives. Achilles couldn't climb and she couldn't teach—not professionally at least.

And that was just their personal loss.

If she and Achilles failed to prevent a conspiracy involving a cutting-edge cruise missile, millions might suffer or die. The weight on her shoulders was difficult to bear.

Even stretched out in a plush cabana at a five-star beachfront resort.

By leapfrogging the *Sea Star*, they were positioning themselves to be in place when and where the missile was finally unloaded. They did this by tracking the ship online and flying ahead to the next island in its path.

Turned out there were surprisingly few ports in the North Atlantic that could accommodate a vessel of the *Sea Star's* size. They'd flown from Gibraltar to the Azores, and then to Bermuda.

The *Sea Star* had not approached either island chain. In fact, the big cargo ship had sailed nowhere close to Bermuda.

Once it passed the Azores, Achilles and Katya selected the British island chain as a sensible intermediary stop, based on its proximity to the U.S. Eastern Seaboard. But given the *Sea Star's* northerly heading, a better pick would have been the large Canadian island of Newfoundland.

Katya glanced up from her laptop and spotted Achilles returning from a two-hour run. Windswept brow and sweaty skin aside, he looked fresher than when he'd left. "Good run?"

"Even better than The Dish."

Katya appreciated her husband's attempt to show the silver lining of their predicament, but she was too distracted to dwell on it at the moment. She pointed to her computer screen. "Looks like we should fly to Newfoundland."

"Agreed," Achilles said.

"What aren't you telling me?"

"While running, I was wondering if it would be wise to have The Invisible Man hack the shipping company and get us the *Sea Star's* itinerary."

Katya hadn't seen that suggestion coming. "The Invisible Man works for our enemies."

"I seriously doubt that he works for them directly. In fact, it's unlikely that they've met. Elite hackers who don't work for a government agency are almost always reclusive freelancers."

"Why is that?"

"Because those who aren't quickly end up behind bars."

"What makes you think he's not working for the government? The White House Chief of Staff pointed you to him. Through Aladdin."

"In addition to the obscene amount of money he's making, his email makes me think that. It's neither a .gov nor a throwaway. It's a professional calling card."

"@JackGriff.in," Katya recalled, accepting the argument. "But wouldn't he have instructions to keep Aladdin in the loop? By asking him, wouldn't we be telegraphing our intentions."

"That's a good point. You're likely right on both accounts. Do you recall the email address we were initially given?"

Katya would never forget. Not after the movie discussion it spawned. "vapor+blue_horseshoe@JackGriff.in."

"Right. With the blue_horseshoe being the project designator."

Katya caught on immediately. Subtraction operations were in her wheelhouse. "Which we could omit, thereby contacting him anonymously. Sounds worth a try."

"Especially since we wouldn't be giving anything away. The bad guys already assume we're tracking the ship. I'll buy a fresh burner with cash as soon as I've booked our flight to Newfoundland. But first I'm going to grab a shower."

As Achilles turned toward the hotel, Katya said, "I had another thought."

He reversed course and plopped down beside her on the shady lounger. "I'm all ears."

"Given all the complicating factors that have arisen since Gibraltar, shouldn't we take another look at using your Oval Office recording?"

Achilles answered without pause. "If I thought we could put it in the mail, so to speak, and then hide out on the beach until the authorities cleaned things up, I'd seriously consider it."

"Why only seriously consider?"

"It would be slow. You'd likely lose your job waiting for it to be safe to return home."

"Oddly enough, I hadn't thought about that," Katya said.

"And you don't need to. That tactic won't work."

"Why not?"

"In a word, timing. Anyone serious enough to do something with the recording will also be professional enough to demand verification. Technology has made voice recordings very easy to forge. Even video can be convincingly faked these days. There are ways to authenticate recordings, but they take time and resources. Who's going to invest those without evidence of a crime? Remember, Rex Rowe didn't do anything he could go to jail for in America. The crime our government cares about won't occur until he uses the missile. We assume."

Katya caught on. Better late than never. "The value of the recording is in convicting Rex afterwards. We can't use it to prevent a forthcoming catastrophe."

"Exactly."

"Which makes us a threat to some very powerful people," Katya mumbled, suddenly feeling a chill despite her tropical surroundings. "They need to eliminate us, and erase the recording."

Achilles nodded.

"What about taking the recording to former President Silver? He trusts you. He'll believe you. And he's still well connected."

"Well connected is not the same as being in power. Saxon has the power now."

"But Silver has a microphone."

"He's not going to pick it up without rock-solid proof. And when was the last time you saw a former president attack an incumbent? It doesn't happen. Even when they're in opposing parties, they're still members of a very elite brotherhood. It binds them like blood. And visiting Silver in Monterey is not an option anyway. He's in Japan for the week, vacationing with his former counterpart."

"How do you know that?"

"I considered the idea earlier. Did a bit of Googling and saw an announcement in *The Japan Times*."

"Can you call him?"

"I don't have his cell phone number, just his home."

Katya struggled not to sigh in frustration. "So what do we do now? We only have two avenues of action, right? Either we follow the missile, or we reach out to some authority and hope they act on what we tell them. That's a very finite set of variables. Easy to defend against when you have the U.S. government and unlimited financial resources at your disposal."

"Actually, the list of available options is even smaller than that while the ship's in international waters. We can't credibly make an anonymous tip with something so vague and no identifiable imminent threat. We'd have to go to the authorities in person. At which point two things will happen—if they take us seriously. They'll detain us, and they'll involve more people. Neither is acceptable. So, for now, our only available option is to follow the missile to wherever it's going, then alert the affected authorities once we know exactly where it is."

"The first time we tried that, you were almost killed. And that was before they knew you were alive. Now they know you're out there, and they know you're coming for them. I don't see how you make the math work."

"What's the alternative? A life in hiding?"

"If you get caught or I get shot, you're going to think a life in hiding looks pretty darn good."

He took her hands. "If this were just us, I'd probably agree with you. But some very bad and extremely powerful people have just stolen a cutting-edge cruise missile. If I can save ten thousand lives by jumping on a grenade…"

Katya felt hot tears roll down her cheeks.

Achilles pulled her closer and let her cry.

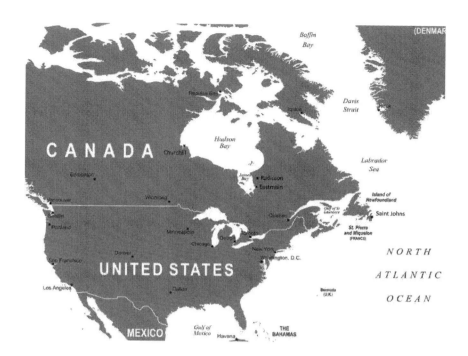

CANADIAN WATERWAYS

Chapter 52

Devious Detour

AFTER FLYING TWELVE HUNDRED MILES north from Bermuda to Newfoundland and reconnecting to Wi-Fi, Achilles was surprised to find that they were still south of the next land mass on the *Sea Star's* heading. Katya's expression told him that she was similarly stumped.

"I can't believe it's not going to the United States," she said, scooting closer.

Eager to get online immediately after their charter flight, they'd grabbed a table in the Maple Leaf Lounge at the St. John's airport.

"Or even Canada," he added, pointing to the map. "It's already sailed past the turnoff to the Gulf of Saint Lawrence."

"So what's left? Putting a missile at the North Pole? Would that be a big deal?"

"The North Pole is a point on the map, it's not a land mass. There's ice, but it moves. The Russians have had a research station there for nearly a hundred years, but it drifts with the ice and has to be rebuilt annually. Adding a missile would surely cause a stir, but I don't see any advantage to it. There's not a single valuable target within range." He winked at his wife. "Besides, the moon is where you'd put a missile if causing controversy was your goal."

"Getting there would be a bit of a stretch for a cargo ship."

"Same for the North Pole. You need a nuclear-powered ice breaker to reach it." As he spoke, Achilles found his words opening up new channels of thought. "The Northwest Passage is accessible this time of year, making northern Russia and Asia possible destinations."

Katya hopped aboard his thought train. "Would firing Russia's own missile at Moscow be the perfect crime?"

"Moscow is too far inland for the DelMos to reach. Saint Petersburg would be within range, but the Kremlin is surely prepared for that. They own the waters up there, militarily speaking. And cargo ships are the opposite of stealthy."

The couple sat in silence for a few seconds before Katya said, "Did you hear back from The Invisible Man?"

Achilles checked his new dedicated burner and found a text. "$5,000 job to be paid from a $100,000 retainer. Reply to vapor+fogbank@jackgriff.in."

Katya whistled. "He clearly doesn't want to mess around with anyone not in the big leagues."

"He's also defending against law enforcement sting operations. Only the big boss would be able to authorize an expenditure of that size, and people at that level tend to be politicians. Politicians use their discretionary budgets on visible projects with broad constituencies, so it would be very unlikely to get funded outside the Pentagon or Langley."

Achilles sent "Account?" to vapor+fogbank@jackgriff.in.

The account number arrived almost immediately. "He must have set up an autoreply."

"The man's a pro."

"Yeah. With that in mind, I'm going to set up a new account at a different bank and make the transfer from there. I don't want the world's best hacker knowing where the bulk of our money is."

"Good idea."

Achilles texted back, "On it," then pulled out his laptop and went to work.

"The *Sea Star* is definitely on course for the Labrador Sea," Katya said.

"Remind me of the geography," he asked as he went to work establishing a new Swiss bank account.

Katya waited for him to finish before answering. "It's north of Canada between Newfoundland and Greenland. Whereas the Gulf of Saint Lawrence is further south in Canada. It's between Nova Scotia and Newfoundland."

Once he had the account, he initiated the transfer. "Where does the Labrador Sea lead?"

Katya turned back to her computer. "Three places. Baffin Bay is to the north, Hudson Bay is to the south, and the Northwest Passages go through the islands in between."

Achilles pictured the globe. "I'm thinking we can rule out Baffin Bay. There's nothing up there, right?"

"Nuuk is there, the capital of Greenland."

"I'm sure Nuuk's a nice place, but from a global perspective, it's insignificant. So that leaves the northern Russia or Asia options, and Hudson Bay. What's on Hudson Bay?"

"Give me a few minutes and I'll let you know."

While Achilles waited, he received confirmation from Switzerland that his $100,000 transfer to fogbank was complete. He also got a surprising text.

"The Hudson is the second largest bay in the world," Katya continued. "It's nearly half a million square miles in area. Bigger than Texas and California combined. But it only has one port."

"The Port of Halifax?"

"No. The Port of Churchill. Halifax is in Nova Scotia. The *Sea Star* already passed it."

"I thought so, but The Invisible Man just texted 'Port of Halifax' as the *Sea Star's* destination."

"Sounds like we just wasted a hundred thousand dollars."

"Five thousand, and wait a second. There's a second text. 'Arriving August 16 from Mersin.'"

"August 16 is a week away."

Achilles voiced the obvious implication. "The ship is making a seven-day detour to drop off the missile."

"Apparently."

"That's an expensive delivery charge. I read that large cargo ships cost about ten thousand dollars a day just to operate. Plus the delay will take some explaining."

"Seventy thousand dollars is nothing to these guys. You just spent a hundred thousand of their money for a bit of information. And they can easily explain the delay by claiming that something required repair. Ships break down, same as trucks and planes."

Achilles saw her points. "So what's three and a half days from Halifax and on the *Sea Star's* current course?"

Katya turned back to her computer. "Well, Russia and Asia are definitely out. And there's very little civilization on Hudson Bay. It's too far north. Churchill has the only port that's big enough to accommodate the *Sea Star*. The only cargo port, period. But it has a population of 899. As in less than a thousand. You can't even get there by road. Only plane or train."

"Crap."

"What?"

Achilles shook his head. "Only accessible by plane or train. You know what that sounds like?"

"What?"

"A trap."

Chapter 53

Geographical Constraints

AS KATYA SET DOWN her burner phone, reservation in hand, words from the famous Eagles song *Hotel California* crossed her mind. "You can check out anytime you like, but you can never leave." Despite that eerie association, she found herself smiling. Her to-do list was complete. Her missions accomplished.

Hopefully, Achilles had been similarly successful.

After taking photos of her notes for backup, Katya returned to her laptop. She shifted screens and verified the *Sea Star's* position. It remained on course for Churchill.

Why Churchill? Why Canada for that matter? Their speculation yielded nothing compelling. The remote destination was one more mystery. Especially given that cruise missiles had ranges in the hundreds of miles, not thousands.

Her husband entered their hotel room a few minutes later while she was massaging her calf. He had a black backpack slung over one shoulder. He hadn't left with it, and yet it clearly wasn't new.

"I finally found us a plane!" she said, referencing her most important accomplishment.

Flying direct from St. John's, Newfoundland to Churchill, Manitoba took about five hours. The same trip would take the *Sea Star* more than three days. Assuming they'd correctly guessed where it was headed. Since they didn't want to fly to Churchill early, and they needed to be ready to react to course changes, they required pilots who were willing to stand by with the motor running, so to speak.

Achilles set down the backpack and kissed her cheek. "That's great. Where is it now?"

"An hour away, on Prince Edward Island. It's a Cessna Citation owned by a husband-and-wife pilot and copilot team. Cheryl and Robert. Guess what their company's called?" she asked, putting a playful lilt in her voice.

"No idea."

"Cher-Bert Charters. Can you guess what their logo is?"

Achilles smiled. "An ice-cream cone?"

"You got it. I also booked us and them hotel rooms in Churchill, just in case we're there overnight. I'd worried that rooms would be scarce in a town of that size, but they aren't. Turns out Churchill draws about ten thousand ecotourists a year."

"Ecotourists?"

"People seeking polar bears and northern lights. Count your blessings that it's August. We might see the comfortable side of sixty degrees. In January, the mean temperature is twenty-six below zero. Anyway, for accommodation I got to choose among the Iceberg Inn, the Polar Inn, the Aurora Inn, and the Polar Bear BnB."

"A regular Disney World."

"On ice."

Achilles laughed. "Given all that ecotourism, I trust you had no trouble renting us an SUV?"

"Got us a Ford Explorer."

"What about a helicopter?"

Not knowing whether the opposition planned to move the missile onward from Churchill by train, plane or helicopter, Katya and Achilles had to be prepared for all three options. If a train, they'd stow aboard, tag the container with a GPS beacon as originally planned, and call the Canadian authorities. If a plane or helicopter, they'd follow in one of their own and call the Canadian authorities. It seemed a solid plan suitable for all foreseeable alternatives, but it required having both a plane and a helicopter on standby in Churchill.

"Did that, too. I have a Sikorsky flying up from Winnipeg."

"From Winnipeg. What's its range?"

"Eight hundred miles. It's a search and rescue model."

"Sounds perfect! You've been busy."

"Phone calls are easy. Easier than obtaining illegal handguns, I'm sure. Judging by the backpack, I take it you were successful?"

"Got two Beretta Picos. They're .38 caliber and hold six rounds but are just five inches long and three quarters of an inch wide. Easy to hide in the small of your back with the right holster. I got those, too."

"Nice job. I don't suppose we can practice?"

"Not on a range. But we'll take them into the woods. I got two hundred rounds of ammo and a bag of red apples."

Katya was not into guns or knives any more than cars or can openers. They were tools she used as required—with proficiency but without passion for make or model. She reserved her zeal for people. Protecting herself, her husband, and the children she hoped to have.

Achilles glanced toward her computer. "How far is the *Sea Star* from the mouth of Hudson Bay?"

"About a day and a half. It's in the Labrador Sea nearing the Hudson Strait."

Once the ship turned into the Hudson Bay—if it turned into the Hudson Bay—the trajectory would telegraph its destination. Churchill was in the southwestern corner, about 550 miles from where the *Sea Star* would enter.

Katya and Achilles wouldn't fly to Churchill until they had that confirmation. Not given the knowledge that the tiny town likely held a trap.

Achilles moved to where he could see her screen, then traced the distance between St. John's and the *Sea Star*. "I'm not comfortable being so far from the ship. Even with the plane standing by, we're hours away if something should happen."

"What else can we do? Civilization doesn't extend up there."

"Nothing smart. Everything I can think of would raise our profile and thus aid our enemies."

"So what now?"

Achilles picked up his backpack. "We take our mind off it with a long hike. First up to the tower on Signal Hill where we'll catch the best view around, then into the woods to make applesauce."

Chapter 54

Swaps and Surrogates

USING THE WEB BROWSER on his phone, Achilles kept an eye on the *Sea Star's* progress for the remainder of their time in St. John's. He theorized that the filed schedule might be a ruse to lure them to the end of the earth. That the *Sea Star* might suddenly turn back toward the Gulf of Saint Lawrence, which had plenty of ports and was packed with shipping traffic. But the cargo ship remained on course as it left Newfoundland in its wake.

Given that reassurance, Achilles emailed vapor+fogbank @JackGriff.in with another assignment. He asked the hacker to access the *Sea Star's* inventory management system and get him the position and full serial number of every container whose last three serial numbers and check digit were 413 7.

The Invisible Man replied within the hour. Two containers matched. One at Bay 12, Row 07, Tier 05, and one in Bay 01, Row 00, Tier 62. Their complete serial numbers were provided. Ten thousand dollars was debited from the retainer.

Achilles recognized the serial number of the second container when he saw it, as well as its location. "They didn't move it," he said as Katya emerged from the shower. "The missile is still front and center on the top tier. At least in the ship's computer."

"Huh. Could they have done an unrecorded swap?"

That was Achilles' first thought as well. "I seriously doubt the ship's software would allow it. A container mix-up would be a big deal. Those are exactly what cargo management systems are designed to avoid. Consider the logistics of rapidly loading and unloading thousands of containers—and the potential costs of getting them confused.

"I grabbed the wrong bag at the airport once and didn't notice my mistake until I went to unpack the following morning. It was a time sink for me and a major inconvenience for the poor soul I screwed. I gotta think cargo companies install bulletproof systems to prevent human error."

"And tampering," Katya added. "Don't forget theft."

"Right."

"But if they didn't move the missile to a new container, or the container to a new location, then the missile is right where it's always been. That doesn't feel right."

"It doesn't—until you think about what happens next. Remember, Halifax is the ship's destination. Churchill is just a diversion, and it's a tiny town. I doubt the ship will unload more than a dozen containers. Probably just two or three."

Katya started nodding. She got it. "No point in shuffling a container around to hide it when they're going to produce it anyway."

"Exactly."

"Which means they have some other method of making it disappear."

Or us, Achilles thought. "It does. That's my chief concern at the moment. They know something critical that we don't."

Katya became contemplative.

Achilles waited.

When she refocused, he knew she'd latched onto something. "Isn't that the very nature of warfare? Both sides structure systems and activities around plans and anticipated actions, never knowing exactly what their opponent is up to until a battle sorts things out."

"I suppose you're right, professor."

Katya didn't react to his quip. She was on a roll. "You and I will personally be at the battle of Churchill, adapting to the situation on the ground minute by minute. Our enemies, by contrast, will remain in Washington or wherever. They'll be sending surrogates."

Achilles had sensed the point she was driving toward, but hadn't consciously articulated it. "Giving us a tactical advantage. Have you ever considered becoming a motivational speaker?"

"I'll be very happy if I can just continue teaching math."

"Well then, we'll be sure to wrap this up before September."

Chapter 55

Surreal Experiences

KATYA FOUND the early morning charter to Churchill surprisingly scenic. She glanced out the Cessna's window during takeoff to enjoy the sunrise and ended up spending most of the five-hour flight studying the landscape below. It boasted myriad lakes and endless miles of coastline, all accented by trees whose leaves were at peak green, making for a relaxing distraction.

Achilles, meanwhile, stayed focused on the inside of his eyelids.

She was contemplating the unpredictable nature of life when a container ship came into view. A majestic vessel plowing through the dark blue waters of Hudson Bay, leaving a lighter trail behind. It had to be the *Sea Star*. The only other big boats marinetraffic.com showed on the bay were oil tankers.

She found it a surreal experience, seeing the setting of so much stress reduced to the size of a postage stamp. It reminded her that most problems were relative—and only as big as you make them.

The town of Churchill came into view minutes later. As they descended and details of the waterfront community became discernible, Katya thought it looked like an outpost at the end of the earth. A small airport to the east, a small seaport to the west, and a tiny town without much meat sandwiched in between. While it presented in vibrant shades of green and blue beneath the August sun, it was easy to picture the scene as it persisted for most of the year: a flat white landscape where polar bears roamed.

The change of engine tone that signaled descent brought Achilles around. He looked over at her and smiled with sleepy eyes before closing them again.

She turned back to the window. The airport had one long runway and a shorter perpendicular one, with a small tower by the corner. The adjacent terminal building was a big blue box that could have been mistaken for a Walmart if there had been more parking and different signage. The only other object that caught her eye was the large Sikorsky helicopter off to one side. She'd been advised that it had arrived last night, but seeing it was a comfort nonetheless.

Katya unlocked her phone and saw that it had a signal. She opened the marine traffic app and checked on their favorite cargo ship. "Achilles, the *Sea Star* is pointed straight at Churchill. It's about two hours and fifteen minutes out. I actually saw it from the sky."

"Well, hallelujah! That's one thing that has gone as predicted."

They'd planned their arrival to allow sufficient time to canvass the tiny town, but not so much as to become conspicuous. Two hours was perfect, they'd figured. Add forty-five minutes to unload the missile and they should be in a happy place just three short hours from now.

Katya couldn't wait. To be done with this. To return to her life. To reclaim her real name and her real job.

The plane taxied into the only open service hangar. After shutting down the engines, Cher emerged from the cockpit to open the door and lower the airstair.

"I'll call you as soon as I have an ETD," Achilles said. "Could be as soon as three hours from now, but four to six is much more likely."

"We booked you a room at the Polar Bear BnB," Katya added. "In case we have to stay the night."

Cher gave a quick glance toward the desolate landscape. "We'll refuel and resupply so we're ready when you are."

Katya and Achilles walked over to the waiting Sikorsky and gave the crew the same speech about takeoff timing and the reserved room.

Katya found the entire situation surreal. They had two private aircraft on standby. A jet and a helicopter. Had she married a billionaire or movie star, that might seem normal. But as life constantly reminded her, there were no norms when one's spouse was a spy. Some days you chartered jets, others you abandoned ships. Sometimes you dressed up and sipped champagne at diplomatic balls, other times you strapped illegal weapons to the small of your back and smuggled yourself across international borders. Oddly enough, she found herself evolving to the point where she wouldn't want it any other way.

Despite the inherent ups and downs, Katya realized that she was blessed. After a few years by Achilles' side, she doubted that a predictable life with ordinary problems would seem fulfilling. Not at their age anyway. Then again, it did greatly decrease their odds of learning what it was like to grow old. Or even see the next sunrise.

Chapter 56

Orderly Orthodontia

THEY DROVE their rental SUV straight to the center of town and parked in front of a coffee shop. The Last Drop was one of those cozy establishments with mismatched wooden chairs and used paperbacks on homemade shelves.

The bald, bespectacled barista smiled as they approached the counter. "Welcome to Churchill, and The Last Drop."

"Thank you. Charming place you have," Achilles said. "We'll take a large black coffee and chamomile tea."

"Coming right up."

"Is it always this busy?" Katya asked.

"I tend to do all right. Ship days are better than most. The excitement brings people out." He leaned closer. "Doesn't take much, to be honest."

"What's coming in?" she asked.

"We don't know. It's not our usual monthly shipment. People are excited to see."

"What do you mean?" Katya asked, keeping her question vague so he would reveal whatever was top of mind.

The barista removed his glasses and cleaned them with a plaid handkerchief, buying a few seconds to think. "It's kinda like seeing a big box under the Christmas tree with no tag."

Katya was pretty sure nobody was dreaming of a missile for Christmas, but kept that to herself. "Nice analogy."

"Not mine, but I like it too. Overheard it earlier this morning." He smiled and went to work preparing their drinks. Two minutes later, she and Achilles were back in the rental car.

Their main objective was finding the best position for watching the *Sea Star* unload. A location where they'd have a clear binocular-assisted view but wouldn't be noticed. A setting conducive to rapid reaction, by car, train, helicopter or airplane—depending on what they saw. A place from which they could easily escape, if required.

The seaport was situated just two miles from the airport on a peninsula serviced by a single road. Achilles had called it "a bottleneck leading to a dead end." Looking at it live while driving around, Katya thought it was worse than that.

A century ago, when the prospects for Churchill had been much grander, the government had constructed the port on an enormous pier that ran parallel to the shoreline. It was a concrete behemoth connected to the mainland only via a dogleg at its eastern end. Tactically speaking, that made it a maze on a dead end accessed by a bottleneck.

Given its dilapidated state, the pier obviously saw precious little business in the modern age. They'd spotted a couple of guys in orange hardhats and vests placing safety cones and referring to clipboards while going in and out of a makeshift office, but saw no other signs of life. No semi-trailers with open beds waiting for loads. No train carefully backing in along the tracks. No ancient forklifts emerging from the ramshackle garages.

But there was still time.

"This isn't going to work," Achilles announced, his eyes glued to their 20×80 binoculars.

They were parked on the side of the road running parallel to the port, the closest land-based vantage point of several they'd tested.

"We're just too far from the action side of the pier," he continued. "The rangefinder clocks it at nearly five hundred yards, so objects look like they're seventy feet away even at maximum magnification. If the angle's not just right, we won't be able to see serial numbers. And we can forget about scanning facial expressions."

The instant they had put the Ford in Park, Katya had worried that the distance was too great. Unfortunately, the landscape offered precious little wiggle room. The intervening area was filled with railroad tracks and a marina. "We can't edge closer without either standing out or boxing ourselves in."

"I know. We'll have to take our chances on the pier."

"Maybe that's why our enemies weren't worried that we could follow the container. They knew we'd be vulnerable when we got here."

Achilles said nothing.

Katya motioned toward the trunk. "What about the telescope? You get sixty-four power magnification with that, right?"

"Yeah, but it's not good for tracking moving objects, like people or containers suspended from gantry cranes. We need to move close enough to get by with the binoculars. Or better yet, our bare eyes."

As Katya considered the prospect of moving to the port proper, insight struck, assuaging some of her fear. "There's nothing going on here, right? School's out, it's not the tourist season, and with just nine hundred residents, the entertainment infrastructure must be extremely limited."

"Right…"

"Combine that with the barista mentioning that people are excited about the unexpected cargo ship. It's kind of a big event for them. Having looked around, I'm thinking it might be the highlight of the week. Maybe the month."

"Like the Wells Fargo wagon pulling into an old western town," Achilles said, catching on.

"Nice day like this, I bet the locals will walk over to the port to watch."

"And we can attempt to blend in with the crowd."

Achilles turned the binoculars toward town and did a bit of back and forth. "The edge of town is about a thousand yards away. The center about a mile. Easy to walk. I bet you're right. In fact, it looks like a small group is already on the move."

As he spoke, Katya's eyes were drawn to the horizon over his shoulder. "There's the ship!"

Achilles turned and raised the binoculars. After studying the scene for a second, he handed her the Nikons and grabbed the telescope from the trunk.

Katya turned to watch the curious, oncoming crowd as her husband set up the tripod and brought the *Sea Star* into focus.

"No! No, no, no!"

"What is it?" She asked, releasing the binoculars and turning toward him.

Achilles slowly backed away from the tripod so as not to jiggle the instrument. "Have a look."

Katya put her eye to the lens and read the bow. *Sea Star*. The port side *r* had the blemish she'd observed in Gibraltar. They hadn't pulled a switcheroo. Her eyes went high to the top tier of containers. It was orderly as an orthodontist's smile—except that it was missing a tooth. Her heart sank. "The missile's not there."

Chapter 57

Mental Math

ACHILLES PONDERED THEIR PREDICAMENT as Katya consulted the marine traffic app on her phone. Where was the missile? Was it still on the ship? Had it simply been hidden? Was the whole Churchill trip a diversion? A way of throwing off pursuit when it was headed for Halifax all along?

"Achilles, look at this." Katya's tone snapped him out of his circular speculation.

He whirled around. "What is it?"

"It shows the *Sea Star's* position seven hours ago."

"Shortly after we took off from St. John's?"

"Exactly. Now watch as I play it forward." She began clicking the mouse. "It stops in the middle of the Hudson Bay and a much smaller cargo ship, the *Sakami*, pulls up alongside."

Staring at the screen, Achilles felt the cold finger of inferiority poke him in the eye. "They unloaded our container when they guessed we wouldn't have Wi-Fi. Where is that sneaky little ship now?"

Katya changed tabs. "It's passing Flaherty Island. Looks like it's headed for James Bay." She used the mouse to circle a large appendage on the southeastern end of the Hudson Bay.

"What's there?"

Katya Googled. "A few Inuit communities. Some hydroelectric development and a bit of fur trapping."

While a remote hydroelectric plant was mildly interesting, it didn't grab Achilles' attention. "Does the Canadian highway system connect to James Bay anywhere? Or is it as isolated as Churchill?"

Katya clicked away on the keyboard. "Nope, it's cut off. Wait. There is a James Bay Road, but it doesn't actually connect with the bay. Nowhere close. It ends at a town called Radisson … which has a big hydroelectric plant … and connects to the James Bay via the La Grande river."

"Is the La Grande big?" Achilles asked, realizing the stupidity of his question as the words rolled off his tongue.

Katya hit the hyperlink without calling him out. "It's the second largest in Quebec. Six hundred miles long."

"How far inland is Radisson?"

"Looks to be about fifty miles from James Bay."

"Does it have an airport?"

Another click. "The La Grande Rivière Airport is twenty miles southwest. Wikipedia says it's used primarily by Hydro-Québec employees. There's nothing else around."

"Pan out on the map so we can see both Churchill and Radisson."

Katya complied.

Achilles consulted the scale in the bottom right corner. "It's about seven-hundred miles. That's a two-hour flight. And the *Sakami* is what, about five hours from Radisson?"

"Round about."

He continued calculating out loud. "We'll need about two hours to watch the *Sea Star* unload and get to the plane, plus two to fly. Throw in the drive from the airport to the river port once we get to Radisson and we'll be cutting it really close. If we wait to watch the *Sea Star* unload and things don't go perfectly, then there's a good chance we'll miss the *Sakami* unloading."

"We could split up." Katya kept her voice steady as she spoke, but Achilles saw her lower lip tremble.

So did his heart. "No. Not this time. Not while we're being hunted on hostile turf. We need to watch each other's backs."

Katya's phone began to vibrate as they met each other's eyes. She diverted her gaze to the screen, which displayed Cher-Bert Charters. "Hello."

"Hi. It's Cher. I'm afraid we have a problem. The airport's fuel pump isn't functioning. The fuel line appears to be blocked. We've been working at it with a local mechanic without success. Looks like we may have to make alternative arrangements. Things are still developing, but I wanted to let you know."

Achilles leaned into the phone. "There's no backup system? No spare parts?"

"No. It's a very limited facility, as you might imagine. It's just a self-serve pump with a very long hose. That's the norm at small airports."

Achilles supposed that self-service made sense, given the low traffic volume, although in the back of his mind he'd assumed that airports would have technicians running the fuel pumps. Probably because most of his experience was with large commercial facilities. "Is there a workaround you can think of?"

"Nothing that wouldn't violate safety regulations and void our insurance policy. If we can't render a mechanical fix with our limited resources, we'll have to have fuel brought in."

"Please keep us posted."

Katya hung up and turned to him. "Sabotage?"

"Almost certainly."

"I'll see if the Sikorsky got fueled before the pump was sabotaged."

"Great idea."

Katya called and was soon smiling. "So it's fully fueled. Great, thank you."

"Score one for the good guys," Achilles said.

His good mood lasted about two seconds. "Call them back."

"Why? What?"

"Helicopters are much slower than airplanes. Find out how long it will take to fly to Radisson, Quebec."

Katya made the call, got the answer, and asked the pilot to hold. "Five hours."

"Of course," Achilles mumbled.

"We have to choose," Katya said, also deflated.

Achilles thought out loud. "Is the *Sakami* the diversion? Or Churchill? Which is the false trail? I can't believe our future hinges on a coin toss." He paced a bit then said, "Call up the big map again."

Katya did.

Achilles traced it with his finger. "Radisson is about seven-hundred miles southeast of us. The James Bay Road runs four-hundred miles south from there to Matagami. It's the only road. They have to take it. So if we flew direct to Matagami from here, literally cutting the corner, we'd easily beat them to Matagami and could then fly north to intercept the truck as it's bringing the missile south."

"Matagami is too far. It's out of range even for our rescue helicopter. We could probably make Eastmain Airport, though." Katya pointed to a dot midway between Radisson and Matagami.

"How big is it?" Achilles asked, encouraged by the name.

"It's a tiny Cree community. Even smaller than Churchill."

"Great. And it's only half as far south as Matagami, so we'd lose that buffer. Plus it's not on the James Bay Road. It's a hundred miles west along a smaller road, which adds risk."

"Do the math," Katya suggested.

"Although helicopters fly at less than half the speed of planes, they move at more than twice the speed of trucks. And the truck carrying the missile from the boat toward Matagami will be on the road for about one hundred and fifty miles before it passes the off-road to Eastmain." He did some mental math. "That should work —if everything goes right."

"When do we need to leave? What should I tell the pilots?"

"Sixty minutes is all we can afford. Tell them to pick us up at the seaport in exactly one hour. That will allow us to watch the containers unload if the *Sea Star* doesn't delay."

Chapter 58

Slow Pace

TO HELP BLEND IN with the Churchill locals, Achilles and Katya grabbed baseball caps, then mingled with a group walking to the seaport for the show. To further enhance their cover, they split up, each walking and talking with a different clique.

For the entire walk, Achilles ensured that Katya was never more than three steps away. Although she was exceptionally perceptive and quick to react, and she too had a Beretta strapped to the small of her back, it was crunch time. Peak danger. This would be the turning point—for better or worse.

While superficially engaged with a trio of high-school teachers, Achilles scanned near and far for signs of danger, particularly snipers. Nothing pinged his radar. By the time they completed the slow quarter-mile stroll from the edge of town to the seaport, the crowd had doubled in size, but no one who joined struck Achilles as suspicious.

Normally, unaffiliated pedestrians were prevented from entering ports, but if Churchill had ever used gate guards, they were long gone. There wasn't so much as a chain running across the entry road.

The pier looked as long as a runway and many times as wide, but was in a sad state of disrepair, with rusted braces, crumbling concrete and thriving weeds. The three-story operations building that anchored it all had clearly been closed for years. Its condition explained the temporary office. Achilles suspected that the historic building would have been covered with graffiti if not for the fact that spray paint could be easily traced in such a small, remote town.

Overshadowing the water's edge was the massive conveyer system once used to move containers between trains and cargo ships. Although one walking companion bragged that it was "a marvel of modern engineering in its day," the monstrosity struck Achilles as a rusting eyesore.

While he found the setting depressing, the people brightened his mood. They seemed to have remained pleasant and stalwart despite the stark economic situation and harsh climate. At least the locals who walked out to meet the ship.

Four mismatched container trucks rumbled past shortly after the walkers stepped onto the pier, sending a wave of excitement through the crowd. The trucks made U-turns down near the new office and parked in a line about twenty feet from the water's edge.

Something about the sight bothered Achilles, but he couldn't put his finger on it. He considered walking up to the first driver and asking what they were expecting and where they were taking it, but figured the odds were very long that he'd be told anything truthful or useful. It was far more likely that he would be dangerously misled than helpfully directed. He might have asked anyway, just to get more mental ammunition, but he didn't want to draw attention.

The crowd continued along to a spot some fifty feet back from the trucks behind a string of orange cones. Apparently, that was the extent of the safety system and the locals all knew the drill.

The drivers remained in the trucks while two men in orange hardhats and vests walked back and forth between the cabs and the refrigerated container serving as their office.

Achilles confirmed that it was the same two guys he and Katya had seen earlier while watching from the side of the road, then casually made his way to stand by his wife. He kept his gaze on the bay when he got there, both for camouflage and because he'd noted a disturbing development. He raised the binoculars to block the view of his mouth and spoke softly. "The *Sea Star* seems to have slowed. We might run out of time."

"At least we learned that four containers are coming off, and they're going onto trucks," Katya replied. "Could there be more missiles? Or a launch platform?"

"That's a scary thought, and a good question," Achilles said, scanning the pier. "Nobody I talked to knows what's in them."

"I got the same story. The mystery has everyone excited. Are you seeing any sign of the opposition?"

"I see nothing but a sleepy town enjoying a bit of action. And when a landscape is this bleak, there just aren't many places to hide. I'm becoming concerned that the helicopter will arrive before the containers are unloaded, forestalling any illicit activity and putting us in the spotlight."

Katya edged closer. "Do you want me to push back the pickup?"

"No. We can't be late for the Radisson intercept."

"So you're okay with leaving before we see if the missile and three associated containers come off the *Sea Star*?"

"No. That would be foolish."

Katya cocked her head at the apparent contradiction, but quickly did the math. "You want to split up?"

Achilles turned to his wife and took both her hands. "No. I'm not letting you out of sight until this is over. Come with me. I want to see if we can speed things up."

Chapter 59

Fruitful Frustration

KATYA COULDN'T FATHOM how her husband could possibly speed up the *Sea Star's* unloading. Not when it hadn't even docked. It wasn't until he intercepted one of the hard-hatted men to ask a question that she caught her false assumption.

Raising a finger and flashing a smile, Achilles said, "Excuse me. Is there any way for you to check if a particular container is aboard that ship?"

The dockworker stopped and gave them an appraising glance, but didn't immediately reply.

Achilles had obviously anticipated the burly man's thought process, as he subtly flashed two hundred-dollar bills while adding, "We'd be most grateful."

The man ran his tongue across the inside of his lip. "You have the ID number?"

"We do."

He did the tongue thing again then turned toward his 'office.' "Follow me."

The refrigerated container was positioned parallel to the pier, with the doors facing the far end, which maximized privacy and minimized noise. Despite the fact that her life had revolved around shipping containers for what felt like an eternity now, Katya had never really contemplated them. She knew they were eight feet wide and eight-and-a-half feet tall, but it wasn't until she saw the homemade desk (plywood straddling two dented filing cabinets) and twin visitors' stools that she realized it was roomier than her also-windowless office at Stanford. Even with two ugly oil drums in the corner by the door and large racks of old binders along one wall.

"Have a seat," the man said while skillfully making the proffered bills vanish. He dropped into the rolling chair behind the desk and grabbed the mouse of an old desktop computer. He clicked it a few times then asked, "What's the container ID?"

Speaking from the edge of his stool like an eager pupil, Achilles recited the full sequence he'd learned from The Invisible Man.

The dockworker typed, then frowned. "Say that again."

Achilles repeated the seven digits.

Katya had also memorized the identification number. She confirmed that he had it right.

"Gimme a minute." The man rose and walked around the desk.

As he passed their chairs en route to the door, Achilles sprang up and clocked him hard in the side of the head. Fist to temple, out of the blue, like a line drive catching a distracted infielder. The sequence was so fast and fluid that Katya would have missed it if she'd sneezed.

The dock worker wobbled once and dropped to the cold steel floor. *Crack! Thump.* No cry of protest. No scream of pain. His nervous system had crashed before it became aware of the threat.

Staring down at the limp lump of flesh, Katya couldn't tell if the man was stunned or dead. For the moment, it didn't matter. She jumped up and looked around, suppressing both question and scream as she sought the signal that had launched her husband's fist. The trigger. The red-flag warning.

Nothing caught her eye.

Achilles grabbed the fallen man's right wrist, then began to frisk him while providing Katya with an explanation. "Process of elimination. And his accent. He's from New York. No way a New Yorker his age is living here. He had to have just flown—."

"Freeze! On your knees or I shoot your wife!" A voice boomed from the doorway. "Three ... two ... one—"

Achilles crouched and raised his hands.

Katya turned to see the second dock worker standing in the doorway. He had forearms the size of footballs and held his handgun rock steady. The muzzle was pointed at her heart. "You too, lady."

She dropped to her knees.

Popeye kept his weapon on her and his eyes on Achilles. To his credit, he had accurately identified both the greatest threat and the best means of neutralizing it. "Is he dead?"

"He just stopped breathing," Achilles replied. "He needs CPR."

"Lace your fingers behind your head. Do it now. Do it slowly."

"Seriously, your partner is dying."

"Lace your fingers behind your head. Do it now. Do it slowly."

Achilles complied.

"Good boy. Now, for your second gold star, I want you to plant your face on the floor without moving your arms or legs. You can do that as fast as you like. But if you do anything else, your lady gets a bullet in her beautiful chest."

Achilles slowly lowered himself to the ground.

"Very good. Now, remove your watch and let it drop to the floor."

The request puzzled Katya for a second, but she caught on as Achilles carefully complied. They were after the Oval Office recording. But how could they possibly know about it?

While that mystery would take time to solve, she now knew why the first man hadn't shot them the instant they entered the container. He had orders to neutralize the recording. To learn what Achilles had done with it, and to delete all copies, no doubt. Unfortunately, that didn't lead to a particularly healthy prognosis for their condition. Once everything was understood and erased, Popeye could pull the trigger, lock the doors, and effortlessly send their corpses to China. Or the bottom of Hudson Bay.

With Achilles face down on the ground, the assailant inched closer. "Lock your fingers and look away. You twitch, I shoot, she dies."

Again Achilles complied.

Slowly and smoothly, without averting his eyes or his aim, the man extracted the Beretta from beneath Achilles' sweatshirt. He pocketed it, then plucked the watch from the floor and backed off. Once he was three paces away, he strapped it to his own wrist. "What's the passcode?"

"Seventy-four, oh-eight," Achilles lied.

It wasn't just the lie that caught Katya's attention, it was the format. Two double-digits rather than four individual ones. That was the phrasing they used in their numerical scrabble game.

She began working the numbers.

Although there were ten digits on telephone keypads, only 2 through 9 had letters assigned, with A, B and C placed under the number 2, D, E and F placed under the number 3, and so on. Most numbers had three letters assigned, but 7 and 9 had four. This was done to spread the load on a percentage-used basis, going by the frequency with which letters appeared in English words.

The letter E topped the list, appearing in a whopping 12.7% of words. The next most common wasn't a vowel, but rather the most popular consonant. T appeared in 9.4% of words. A, O and I followed with 8.2%, 7.5% and 7.0% respectively.

When you combined the percentage scores of letters assigned to each keypad number, 3 was of course the winner as it contained E, along with D and F. 3 appeared in 19% of coded words. The loser was 9, with a total of under 5% for the combination of W, X, Y and Z.

Achilles had used neither a 3 nor a 9, but he had used a 0. While not assigned a letter on the keypad, in their game they used 0 for O, leaving 6 for just M and N. So the third of the four letters was an O. The first was a 7, meaning almost certainly an R or an S, as P and Q were low-use. The second was likely either H or I, as G was only a third as likely to appear in any given word. And the concluding 8 was almost certainly a T, as V was rare and U didn't end words. So seventy-four, oh-eight was R or S plus H or I then OT. RIOT or—

"Wrong code. Don't mess with me!"

"It's seventy-four, oh-eight," Achilles replied, his voice calm and cool. "You must have typed it wrong with those big fat fingers of yours."

As Popeye reentered the four-digit code, as he focused on getting it perfect, Katya SHOT him, center mass.

Chapter 60

Coming Up Short

ACHILLES WAS ON HIS FEET before the second body smacked the floor. He immediately snatched the fallen gun and bolted toward the doors. As much as he wanted to embrace his wife, to comfort her after her heroic but traumatic move, he wouldn't make the same mistake twice. Although virtually certain that the entire hit-squad was dead, the prudent move was to check.

Nobody was outside the container.

Nobody was approaching.

All four drivers were still seated in their trucks, looking bored. Apparently, the container had sufficiently suppressed the sound of the single gunshot.

With that knowledge, he ran back to his wife. He wrapped both arms around her and pulled her close.

"I'm all right," Katya said, her voice steady.

Achilles didn't let up. He didn't back off.

"It may hit me later," she added. "Post-traumatic stress or guilt for taking another life. But for now, there's simply no room in my mind for complications like that."

"You're sure?"

Katya gently pulled back. "I'm certain we don't have our lives back. I can't return to Stanford. We can't go home. You can't competitively climb. And the key to recouping everything may well be just a few feet from this bloody container. So let's stick with the plan."

Achilles wanted to tell his wife what a remarkable woman she was and how much he loved her, but he didn't want to stir any more emotion, so he said, "Well all right then, let's go get our lives back."

"What do I do with this?" Katya asked, holding up the Beretta Pico. "Should I get rid of it?"

"Just the opposite. I want you to hold it in your jacket pocket until we're on the helicopter." She was wearing an oversized windbreaker to help hide her pancake holster. "At this point, convenience takes priority over concealment. If you're okay with that?"

She nodded.

Achilles reclaimed his watch and repositioned his own handgun before they stepped out into fresher air and better scenery. He was about to close the container door behind them, sealing their problem inside, but stopped himself as he considered their next move. "Give me a sec."

He went back in and took the hardhat and orange vest from the first phony dock worker. The one who had died from a single blow to the head. Probably rapid onset cerebral edema or a subdural hematoma. Probably the result of aggravating an existing condition. Definitely not something Achilles would lose any sleep over.

He didn't know whether they'd brought the makeshift office with them, or it had already been on the pier, but if it was the former, then it might be a long time before their bodies were discovered. That was his hope anyway. His life could do without additional complications at the moment.

As Achilles headed back toward the door dressed as a dock worker, the two drums in the corner caught his eye. The lids were in place, but not sealed. He peeked inside the nearest one and saw the future. The path not taken. The one his enemies had planned. Each barrel held nothing but a bag of lye.

You needed water to turn lye into a flesh-dissolving agent, but there was no cooler or plumbing at hand. As he contemplated this whole new meaning for the phrase "bottom of the barrel," Achilles remembered a lesson he'd learned from a colleague working mob crimes: urine worked almost as well.

He wouldn't mention his find to Katya.

He could have done without that image himself—although on the bright side it favored his preferred answer to the question of the makeshift office's origin.

"The *Sea Star* has docked," Katya said as he latched the door.

That was good news, and it made sense. "I bet the captain was asked to hold back in an attempt to smoke us out. Once we approached the first guy, the second one gave the ship the go ahead. Probably asked the captain to hurry in order to provide a distraction. Bet that's why he was delayed."

"You're giving 'them' a lot of credit."

"I haven't been giving them enough," Achilles said with a shake of his head. "They just outwitted me on the battlefield. They put their men in place early and hid them in plain sight. A big dockyard setting like this, you expect to see guys working. Lots of guys. Had there been twenty, I'd have looked for the imposters among them, the hidden agents. But since there were only two..." He shrugged.

"Do you think they killed the real workers, or there weren't any to begin with?"

"I don't know. And at this point, I'm not about to inquire."

"I hear you there," Katya said, gesturing skyward. "Here comes the first container. It's not ours."

The missile container was dull green in color. The one being lowered onto the lead truck was a faded burgundy, and fortunately the labeled end was pointed their way. Achilles raised his camera to photograph the serial number, thinking he might have The Invisible Man look into it later.

He stopped short.

He looked down at the lead truck. Then at the three behind it. "I've been an idiot, and my stupidity almost cost us our lives."

"What?"

"The missile is definitely not going to be among the four containers coming off."

"How can you be so sure?" Katya asked.

"Look at the trailers on those trucks. They're twenty-footers."

Chapter 61

Eastmain

KATYA HEARD THE HELICOPTER before she saw it approaching from the east. A mighty and majestic beast that seemed oversized for the tiny town, much like the pier on which they stood.

Achilles took her hand. "Come with me. We've nothing to lose at this point."

He led her to the closest truck, the last one in the line.

The driver rolled down his window as they drew near and raised two squirrelly eyebrows. "He'p ya?"

"Morning. What you picking up today?"

"Sugar."

"The sweet stuff?"

"Twenty tons worth."

"Huh. Where's it going?"

"City Hall."

Achilles hadn't seen that coming. "What does City Hall need with twenty tons of sugar? I mean, how much coffee can the mayor drink? The man can't be that busy."

Squirrelly-eyebrows chuckled. "You're funny. This here's food aid. We got rice, flour, potatoes and sugar." The trucker pointed to the three other rigs and then to himself as he spoke.

"Who sent it?"

"Gov'ment. I s'ppose."

"HHS?"

"What?"

"Health and Human Services?" Achilles clarified.

The trucker referenced the clipboard on the seat beside him. "Farmers United."

Katya caught the address. 1400 Independence Avenue, Washington, D.C.

"Thank you very much," Achilles said.

"Well, all right then. You have yourself a great day."

Achilles turned toward the helicopter, which was landing further down the pier, well clear of the crowd.

"Do you want to double-check with another truck, just to be sure?" Katya asked.

"No need. I already got the message."

"Message? What message?"

"Farmers United. F. U."

Katya had missed that subtlety. "What about 1400 Independence Avenue?"

"Address like that, situation like this, it has to be some huge federal agency. Health and Human Services, or Agriculture, I'd guess."

They ran toward the helicopter, which was waiting with rotors turning.

"It was a smart move. A good cover operation," Achilles said, speaking as much to himself as to her. "Delivering food aid to a remote, hard-hit town. Nobody questions someone going out of their way to do a good deed. Looks good on the books, and probably made the crew proud. Might even make the trip tax deductible."

Katya replied, "F. U. indeed."

The helicopter was by far the largest Katya had ever been in, although that wasn't saying much. It reminded her of a big pickup truck in that it was clearly a workhorse vehicle with the equivalent of an extended passenger cab. Although instead of protruding fenders covering a second set of tires, it had gas tanks sticking out like little wings.

It wasn't more luxurious than your average pickup either. The seats folded down from the walls, so they could be folded up to make room for cargo, and there were no nonessential niceties. But she wasn't complaining. She was thrilled to have found a helicopter capable of making the long, remote trip.

The big bird lifted off as soon as they were aboard, and the pilot addressed them shortly thereafter, speaking through wired headsets they'd found on their chairs. "Good evening and welcome aboard. This is Grant, your pilot. Beside me is Yvan, your copilot. We've got about twelve hundred kilometers to cover. Will take us about five hours and put us at Eastmain Airport by 6:30 pm."

"How long will refueling take?"

"We're going to burn through almost the whole tank getting there and this bird drinks three-thousand pounds of fuel, which is about four hundred fifty gallons. The refueling operation will take about fifteen minutes, wheels down to wheels up—assuming there's not a line."

Grant had a sense of humor. Achilles liked that. "When does the sun set in Eastmain?"

"Just a minute… 8:45."

That was good news. Their best guess was that the truck hauling the missile would pass the turnoff to Eastmain at 8:00, plus or minus an hour. That meant they were in good shape whether it was early or late.

Since the Sikorsky was a search-and-rescue helicopter, they could even search after dark. They could identify trucks from high above the road then swoop down and shine the spotlight on the container ID and the truck license plate.

Katya prayed it wouldn't come to that.

Much better to make the identification without alerting the truck driver. Then the Royal Canadian Mounted Police could catch them by surprise—while she and Achilles watched the show from far above. Like from the sky box at a sporting event—without the hot dogs and beer.

As she reveled in that scene, Katya realized she'd forgotten to release their airplane. Not that Cheryl and Robert could have left if she had. Not without fuel.

She checked her phone, hoping to see signal bars. The helicopter was flying well below ten thousand feet. Closer to one thousand, probably. But the top of the screen was blank. No cell towers, she was sure.

Given that virtually the entire flight path lay over Hudson Bay, they would likely be cut off for the next five hours. Hopefully the mechanics would fix the Churchill fuel pump just as the helicopter reached the Eastmain cell tower, and Cher-Bert would be on their way without Katya having added to their delay.

She looked over at Achilles and saw that his eyes were closed. Probably a smart move. *Sleep while you can* was the soldiers' motto, and they were both clearly combatants now.

She closed her eyes, determined not to think about the man whose life she'd ended—or any family he might have left behind. Fortunately, his death had been instantaneous. She must have hit his heart or spine because he'd just dropped. No screaming, no flailing, no staggering about. No nightmare to run on a repeat loop in her mind. It was like she'd flipped a switch rather than pulled a trigger.

Better his switch than her husband's, or her own.

With that thought front of mind, Katya focused on her breath. In and out. In and out. The next thing she knew, the pilot was announcing their landing. She cracked her eyes and glanced over at Achilles. He appeared wide awake.

"You slept like a log," he said.

"I guess I did."

"That's a good sign."

"Yes, I suppose it is."

"Your yoga instructor would be proud."

Given the big picture, Katya wasn't convinced of that, but she let it slide.

A small twin-engine Beechcraft was taking off as they approached. Perhaps the pilot hadn't been joking about waiting in line for fuel.

The Sikorsky touched down in a clearing cut from evergreens. Eastmain Airport was nothing more than a long grassy strip with a fuel pump and tiny building. It reminded her of a highway rest area, without the highway. Just a small connecting gravel road.

"You might want to take advantage of the facilities," Grant suggested, as he and Yvan disembarked.

She followed Achilles out the door.

The airport facility was tiny but clean, and only had cold water. Nonetheless it felt good on her face. She managed to smile at herself in the mirror, partly in acknowledgment of the bizarre circumstances that had brought her to this remote dot on the map, partly from relief at still being alive, and partly from pride. Not everyone could or would do what she and her husband had done.

Achilles was waiting when she emerged and linked her arm for the stroll back to the helicopter. As they drew near, she detected the sound of frustration. Katya didn't speak French, but could recognize cursing.

"What is it?" Achilles asked the pilots.

Grant turned with a frown on his face. "The fuel pump isn't working."

Chapter 62

Contingencies

WILLIAM ZACHARIA looked down at his hand as he reached for the bottle of his favorite whisky. It was trembling. That had never happened before. Not while walking onto the field to quarterback the Cotton Bowl in front of 73,000 screaming fans. Not after barely escaping the Beirut barracks bombing that killed 220 fellow Marines. Not during any of the half-dozen times he'd testified before congressional committees out for his blood.

So why now?

Was it age? They say the human body's warranty runs out at forty, so he was nearly twenty years into the red.

Was it the booze? His consumption had increased considerably since the start of Luci's grand plan.

Or was his subconscious picking up on something his conscious mind had yet to realize? That was the possibility that scared him.

Whatever the reason, he couldn't let the others observe his infirmity. He excused himself. "Ben, would you mind doing the pouring? Nature's calling."

WZ spent a minute staring at the mirror, psyching himself up before flushing. "You went on to win the Cotton Bowl. You survived Beirut and earned a Silver Star. You kept your head cool and your spine straight before scores of scornful congressmen. You can crush this, too. You *will* crush this. You and your three friends."

Were they his friends? Were Ben, Luci and Rex friends? Or just members of his new team? Was there a meaningful difference? Was the C4 different from the Longhorns or the Marines? All were elite groups. Their battles were of a very different type, but the other members were fighting on his side, by his side. And they would share his fate. Some might say that made them more than friends.

Holding onto that thought, William Zacharia raised a steady hand in the mirror and nodded to himself. Problem solved.

He returned to the fire pit, skipped the small talk and ignored the waiting whisky. Without further delay, he began the meeting by popping open a can of contention. "Kyle and Katya Achilles appear to have escaped our trap in Churchill. I'm not one hundred percent certain, but the assassination team I sent is missing in action. Incommunicado. Given our experience in Turkey, the safe assumptions are that Achilles outsmarted them, and that he and his wife remain at large and in possession of the incriminating Oval Office recording."

WZ paused there. Having spat their problem out onto the table, he indulged in a healthy swallow while waiting for the well deserved backlash. The caustic reminder that he had made the same mistake a second time.

Rex was the first to break the silence, but he did so with a question. "When will you have confirmation?"

WZ leaned forward. "My investigator will arrive in Churchill this afternoon."

"Your investigator?" Ben blurted. "One man? Shouldn't you be sending in an entire assault squad? Seal Team Six? Shouldn't they already be on the ground? If the targets survived, they'll be stranded, right?"

William Zacharia realized that he was subconsciously shielding himself with his glass. He set it down, calmly. "One woman, actually. And she's taking the train. The same train the troublesome couple will almost certainly board to escape Churchill if they're still breathing. It only runs twice a week."

Ben appeared anything but mollified. "What will she do if she spots them? She can't very well shoot them, either on the platform or aboard the train, because she can't escape. Heck, the three of them might be the only passengers aboard. Hard to hide in a crowd of one. They'd catch her red-handed, meaning they'd catch us red-handed."

William Zacharia maintained a calm tone. "First of all, like all the contractors, she has no idea who hired her. Secondly, you needn't worry about anyone being caught red-handed. When the train was in Winnipeg, she installed explosives beneath the passenger compartments. If she sees them board, she'll detonate when the train's a couple of hundred miles into the journey. If they don't board, she'll remove the ordnance when it's back in Winnipeg."

"Is there a chance they got out?" Ben pressed.

"I hesitate to rule anything out. Time and again the couple have proven to be highly resilient and resourceful. But with no connecting roads and their airplane disabled, it's hard to see how."

"They could charter another plane."

WZ shook his head. "Only if they find one that has some fuel left over from a previous flight. To account for that contingency, my saboteur is taking out all the airport fuel pumps between Churchill and the tiny town seven hundred miles southeast where the missile will actually be unloaded. So they'll just get stranded again in the middle of nowhere. Bottom line, they absolutely, positively will lose track of the missile."

Luci clunked her glass like a gavel. "I'm absolutely, positively sensing a bit of hesitation in your voice."

Embarrassed at being caught and called out, William Zacharia couldn't help but bow his head for a momentary reprieve. "In their first report from Churchill, the assassination team I sent mentioned that a Sikorsky search-and-rescue helicopter arrived shortly after they did. It came from Winnipeg with only the crew aboard, so I dismissed it."

"But?"

"But then I put myself in Achilles' shoes and something occurred to me. He doesn't know what we have planned for the missile. He'd want to be ready for any situation."

"Which might include having a helicopter on standby," Luci said.

"And?" Ben asked, impatiently prompting him on.

"I called the Churchill airport and talked to the facilities manager. The Sikorsky took off around the time the *Sea Star* departed. He didn't see if anyone boarded, but it headed southeast. My fuel-pump saboteur is watching for it just in case." William Zacharia felt a phone begin to vibrate as he spoke. It was a dedicated burner, so he had no need to check the screen as he pulled it from his pocket. "Speak of the devil and he doth appear. My saboteur is calling."

Chapter 63

Zayn

PILOT ZAYN BARBARY had been harboring hope that his latest gig might turn into something bigger. It was more of a feeling actually, an instinct. One born from sensing the sweet combination of deep pockets and growing anxiety. So when he quite literally spotted an opportunity, he was primed to take it.

Probably.

Instinct was also telling him it might cost him what was left of his soul.

Staring at the satellite phone on the empty passenger seat of his Beechcraft Baron, Zayn took a moment to reflect. He had been on a downward spiral for years. Since December 20, 2006 to be precise. That was the day his side business with Afghanistan's cash crop had gotten him kicked out of the Royal Canadian Air Force and into a three-year stint at "Club Ed."

After prison, when no commercial airline would hire him, Zayn had begun scraping a living by doing odd piloting jobs. They would have paid his modest bills if he owned a plane, but as it was, the aircraft rental fees took most of the haul—on above-board work. The hunting trips and ecotourism gigs.

Smuggling jobs put steak on the table, but there weren't nearly enough of those.

Then the other night, while he was finishing up his second can of Labatt's, a knock on his Thunder Bay apartment door left Zayn looking at an unexpected package. At first, he was sure the delivery was a mistake. The box contained twelve cans of quick-set insulating foam spray that he definitely hadn't ordered—and a satellite phone. While he was contemplating what a pawn shop would pay for the phone, it began ringing.

"Hello."

"'Zayn Barbary?"

"Yes."

"I have a job for you. It requires flying about two thousand miles tomorrow. It pays twenty dollars per mile." The man spoke with a Texas accent.

"Do I know you?" Zayn asked, at once skeptical of and excited by the math. Texas was full of oil, right?

"No, you don't know me, but I know about you. I know that if you're not looking at an open can of Labatt's, you wish you were. I know that you're a good pilot who's had a rough ride. I know you're willing to do what it takes to earn extra money, so I'm asking you how forty thousand dollars sounds?"

"It sounds pretty darn good. So does the flying part. What's the cargo?"

"You're looking at it."

Were they smuggling narcotics in foam spray cans now? "I only see twelve cans."

"That's right. You're going to leave one at each of twelve airports around Hudson Bay. And you're going to be flying with your transponders turned off."

Hudson Bay? The airports up there were lifelines to communities that would otherwise be cut off. "You're going to pay me forty thousand dollars to deliver a can of foam spray to each of twelve airports tomorrow? I don't believe it."

"Are you interested?"

"Sure I'm interested."

"Can you do it?"

"Hell, yes. Which airports?"

"There's a printed list wedged between the cans. You're to visit them in the order listed, making the deliveries as close as possible to the times noted."

Zayn found the sheet. It included the flight distances as well as the airports, most of which were little more than grass landing strips servicing isolated native settlements. He'd be flying virtually nonstop, with little time on the ground. "Am I being met? Or is there a drop box for the, uh, cargo?"

"Neither. You're going to be emptying the can into the fuel pump at each airport. Use a cork to keep the foam from regurgitating before it dries, so your handiwork won't be easily detected."

"I'm fresh out of corks."

"No, you're not. Take another look at your welcome mat. You'll find a box containing corks, rags, solvent, a can of white spray chalk you can use to temporarily conceal your tail number, a debit card you can use for anonymous refueling before you disable the pumps, and a ten thousand-dollar prepayment for your services."

Whoever the caller was, he seemed to have thought of everything. That was a good sign. A very good sign. "When do I get the remaining thirty thousand?"

"You're to call me as you complete each job, leaving a message if I don't answer. If you finish all twelve by this time tomorrow, you'll find the rest of your payment waiting when you get home."

Zayn had hit Churchill Airport on time. Then Shamattawa, Fort Severn, Attawapiskat, Kashechewan and Fort Albany. All without problem. Then a lingering Cessna Skyhawk at Moosonee set him back two hours, and the untimely arrival of a pump truck at Kuujjuarapik delayed him further still.

Midway through, his employer had begun answering the calls. He wanted to know if Zayn had seen a Sikorsky search-and-rescue helicopter in Churchill. When Zayn reported that it had been there when he arrived and left, his employer got aggravated. Had he seen it since? No, he had not.

That was true as of their last call five minutes earlier, but Zayn had spotted a Sikorsky flying into Eastmain as he was flying out. He grabbed the satellite phone and hit *Redial*.

"That was fast," his employer said.

"I'm not in Waskaganish yet. I'm calling from the air to let you know that I spotted the Sikorsky flying into Eastmain as I was flying out."

"Just now?"

"Just now."

Silence followed. Long and awkward, like teenagers on the doorstep at the end of a first date.

Zayn closed his eyes and asked the big question. "Do you want me to offer them a ride—then take care of your problem?"

"Can you?"

"I can."

"How?"

"When flying into remote areas like this, I've learned to come prepared for bears."

Another delay, then, "I see. Have you ever shot a *bear* before?"

"I've practiced enough to know that I can pull the trigger if given sufficient reason."

"What would you consider a sufficient reason in this case?"

"How many bears are we talking about?"

"One male, one female."

"Are these bears members of an Italian family, or anything like that?"

"No. They're loners. But clever."

"I can be clever, too. Where are they going?"

"I'm not sure. Probably the U.S. What are you thinking?"

"I could land at Waskaganish and wipe the spray chalk off my tail number. Then I could spray over my plane's pin strips so it won't look like the Beechcraft they just saw. Then I'd fly back to Eastmain."

"Sounds smart. What will you do with the meat?"

"I'll leave it for the wolves in the woods around Nemiscau. Of course, the plane will get messy, and it's a rental. I'd probably have to buy it."

"I see. What would a fair fee be under those circumstances?"

"Hard to say, so why don't we keep it simple? Call it an even million?"

"I appreciate simple. Send me a clear picture of both bears and your money will be waiting when you get home."

"I'm afraid that since this is our first hunt together, prepayment will be required."

"Prepayment takes time."

"They're not going anywhere in the next few hours, right? That's the whole point of my job, right? I'm sure you can find a bank somewhere in the world that's open. It just so happens that I have an offshore account." His old Cayman account had a ten-dollar balance, but this guy wouldn't know that. Zayn dictated the number, then said, "Send me the details when it's done."

Chapter 64

Legal Limitations

ACHILLES HAD BLUNDERED twice in one day. He couldn't remember the last time he'd been so mad at himself. First, he'd failed to anticipate that every dock worker might be an enemy agent; then he'd fallen for the same crippling strike twice.

Sabotaging rural airport fuel pumps was a cinch to pull off, he realized in retrospect. Nobody was around. A single person could visit every airport in the region and put its pump out of commission in seconds, stranding any aircraft that followed.

But Achilles wouldn't waste time on self-flagellation now.

He wasn't beaten yet.

If he could get to the James Bay Road in the next ninety minutes, the odds were fifty-fifty that he'd be there before the truck drove past. They'd already beaten much worse odds on this mission. "Can you drop us at the James Bay Road? It's only a hundred kilometer drive, so probably eighty as the crow flies."

The pilot's expression popped Achilles' balloon before he spoke. "I'm afraid we don't have the fuel. You asked for maximum speed so I took us to the edge of the fuel reserve requirements."

"We're really in a bind here. Can't you push it a bit more? I can't go into details, but this is a *really big deal.*"

"I'd love to help you," Grant said. "Truly I would. But if I take off now, with the fuel tank where it is, I'll lose my job and probably my license. I'd be putting our lives and this five million-dollar aircraft at risk."

Katya interrupted. "There's no cell phone coverage."

"Better and better," Achilles mumbled before beginning to think out loud. "I have an hour and a half to get myself a hundred kilometers east along a very remote road. Running is out. Hitchhiking would require a miracle. How far is town?"

"About two kilometers," Grant said.

"You keep working the pump. See if you can get it going. If you can, great. Take my wife to the intersection, then fly back along the road. If you see a car racing east, you'll know I got a ride. If not, wait for me back here."

"Roger that."

Achilles turned to Katya. "Stay at the intersection and video every truck rolling past. Be sure to capture the license plates. If you see ours, find a phone and call the Royal Canadian Mounted Police. Then make your way to a hotel in Matagami. I'll find you there. On the other hand, if I get to the road before you, I'll film until I see our truck, then alert the RCMP, then make my way back here. That work for everyone?"

They nodded.

He began running.

There was only one road, so getting lost wasn't an issue. And the terrain was relatively flat coniferous forestland, so it wasn't problematic. In fact, the run would have been delightful under different circumstances.

Achilles reached the branching gravel road connecting Eastmain to the James Bay Road in about eight minutes, by which point the town was already in sight. There were precious few lights visible, but among them was the Eneyaauhkaat Lodge. *Say that three times fast.*

He found nobody at reception, but a sign on the counter directed him to one of the rooms. He knocked on that door, perhaps a bit too aggressively.

The peephole darkened a minute later and an elderly male voice called, "Oui?"

Achilles knew a bit of French, but not enough to convey his complicated situation at the speed required. "Speak English?"

"Une minute."

"Yes?" This time the voice was younger and female.

"I'm in a bind and need a ride to the James Bay Road right away. I'll pay a thousand dollars for your trouble, but I need to leave right now."

The woman translated his words into French for the man. There was a bit of back and forth before she asked. "Where on the James Bay Road do you need to go?"

"Just drop me at the intersection. I have to be there one hour from now."

The woman answered directly. "It takes three hours to get to the James Bay Road."

"Three hours is no good. Does someone in the village have a faster car?"

"The car is not the problem. The road is the problem."

Again, Achilles felt the urge to kick himself. Again, he had no time. "What about a motorcycle, or an airplane?"

"No airplane. Chogan has a motorcycle, but the tire is flat. Ripped."

Achilles knew a dead end when he saw one. He couldn't believe it. It was hard to fathom that after chasing the missile from Turkey to Gibraltar to the Azores to Bermuda to St. John's, Newfoundland to Churchill, Manitoba, they were going to lose it because of a fuel pump problem in Eastmain, Quebec.

And yet he could believe it.

He could believe it because the opposition had outsmarted and outmaneuvered him every step of the way. Never before had he been so consistently frustrated by a single adversary.

He thanked the woman and slipped a twenty-dollar bill under her door. Then he turned and began the run back to the airport.

His only hope was that the clever rescue-helicopter pilots had cleared the fuel line.

He didn't get far.

Not even to the road. Achilles was just a few steps down the driveway when he spotted two small silos nearer to the center of town. One gray, one white. He ran close enough to read the lettering and inspect the setup. One tank was labeled Petrol, the other Kérosène. One was for powering vehicles, the other for stovetops and space heaters. A big enough supply to last a long winter.

But it wasn't winter.

The roads were open.

They could get more.

And kerosene had another name: jet fuel.

Achilles ran back to the airport even faster than he'd come. Time was terribly tight. When he arrived, nothing appeared to have changed. Katya and the pilots were all still huddled around the pump.

"They have kerosene. A big tank full. Probably fifty thousand liters. The hose isn't nearly as long as this one, but I think we can push the helicopter close enough."

"Can't do it," Grant said.

"Then we'll find a hose. Hell, we can cut this one off and use it as a bridge. It's ruined anyway."

"It's not the hose that's the problem, although that is as well. I can't risk a very expensive helicopter and four lives on a questionable liquid. Who knows what's really in that tank and how pure it is? I can probably get approval if the kerosene checks out, but that's not going to happen in the timeframe you require. You'd need to track down whoever's responsible for the tank, and you can't do that until morning."

The pilot was right. The helicopter wasn't a private vehicle, and Achilles didn't have the resources to buy it.

He just wasn't one to surrender.

Katya put her hand on his shoulder. "We'll figure something out. Some other angle. Some alternative approach. We won't let them win."

Achilles put his hand atop his wife's. Despite this blow, and all the others they'd suffered over the past eight days, he felt blessed. He turned back to pilot Grant. "What's the plan?"

"We've radioed Winnipeg. They're looking into getting us fuel."

"What about tonight?" Katya asked.

"We sleep in the Sikorsky. There's plenty of room and we've got the essentials—this being a rescue helicopter."

Achilles liked the pilot's attitude. "I'm guessing you guys are vets?"

"RCAF. You?"

"I spent five years working for the federal government."

"Enough said," Grant replied, catching on. "Only thing I need to know is where we'll be going next?"

Achilles glanced at Katya. "I don't know yet. But we'll figure it out before the fuel gets here."

Chapter 65

In The Stars

ACHILLES DID NOT LIKE the idea of spending the night in the helicopter. It was an obvious move when stranded at a predictable place in the middle of nowhere. It turned him and Katya into sitting ducks. So he gave the pilots a story about wanting to sleep beneath the stars on a fine August night, and took a stack of blankets to the best observation post he could find—the flat roof of the hut that housed the fuel pump.

From that elevated position, he would be able to hear anyone approaching in the night. At the moment, the only noteworthy noise was the world's number-one least favorite sound: mosquito buzz. He'd have to be creative when arranging the blankets—and would probably have to sacrifice his nose.

Insects aside, the air was delightfully invigorating. Crisp, fresh and heavy with a pine scent that reminded him of childhood summers at the family cabin. His innocent days—forever gone, but not forgotten.

As he made his makeshift mattress on the bunker-like concrete canopy, it occurred to Achilles that under the circumstances, a missile strike wasn't completely out of the question. While this was Canada, not Kandahar, he couldn't help but picture a black-and-white satellite shot of the airport with crosshairs highlighting the helicopter. Without warning, it disappears in a huge cloud of smoke. Then the camera pulls back, exposing nothing but forest and the village for miles around. Take out the Cree settlement too and explosions would be like the falling trees that nobody hears.

That image was still in his mind a minute later when Katya emerged from the helicopter carrying more blankets under her arms and something in her hand.

"Up here," Achilles called. *Your brilliant husband is preparing to sleep atop a thousand pounds of liquid explosive—just to be safe.*

He climbed down as she walked over.

"Brought you a can of bug spray, and some company."

"You're a good wife, Katya Achilles," he said with a playful kiss.

They applied the repellant with enthusiasm, then climbed up and settled in.

"This could almost be Fiji," Katya said as they took in the stars. "We've just got the breeze swishing the trees rather than the sound of crashing waves."

"That's exactly what I was thinking before you appeared," Achilles lied.

"We could move there, if this doesn't work out."

"It will work out."

"I know it will, but a girl can dream. Have you decided where we should go tomorrow, assuming the helicopter gets fueled?"

"I'm thinking Niagara Falls. It's a good-sized touristy town right on the border. Tons of back and forth traffic over multiple bridges to America. There's probably no easier place for an innocent-looking couple to slip through."

"Like hiding a grain of sand on the beach," Katya said.

"Exactly."

"But they'll still check our passports, right?"

"Sure. Since our documents are Greek, we'll get more scrutiny than people with North American passports. But given our appearances, it should still be cursory."

"So long as the agent doesn't speak Greek."

"A chance we'll have to take."

"Then what?" Katya asked, shifting onto her side. "What's the big plan?"

Achilles rolled to face her. "We have a couple of crappy leads, and one solid one. On the crappy side, there's the captain of the *Sea Star*, and the owner of the estate where the ship docked in Turkey. If we're lucky, one of them will provide a name that leads to another name that may get us somewhere. Far from ideal.

"The only solid lead, as you know, is Rex."

Katya nodded. "Do you still believe President Saxon was not involved?"

"I do, but I'm not certain. Call it seventy-thirty. There really was no need to use the Oval Office if the president was actually involved. Not given the additional logistical hassle."

"But Rex would anticipate your reverse logic, right? He's the brilliant manipulation specialist."

"He is, but he also spends all day, every day, dealing with people desperate for a piece of the president. Rex is bound to be a bit blind in that area."

Katya kept playing devil's advocate. "I'll concede that, but remember, this is an off-the-books assignment. Can't Saxon's absence be construed as self-protection? As giving him credible deniability?"

"If that was Rex's goal, he definitely wouldn't have kicked things off with an Oval Office meeting. And if the convenience of the White House was important to Rex, meeting in his West Wing office was hardly something I could snub my nose at. But politics isn't my thing, and maybe Saxon had planned to be there but was called away, so seventy-thirty."

"Okay, let's assume Saxon's not involved and Rex is our lead. How do we turn that conclusion into an action plan for getting our life back? How do we, in hiding and on the run, gain access to the right hand of the most powerful and well-protected man on the planet? And what do we do once we're in a room with him?"

Achilles kissed his wife. "Two excellent questions. I'm going to meditate on them tonight and hope to have answers in the morning."

"Something tells me you will." She kissed him back. "Good night."

As Katya closed her eyes, Achilles turned back toward the stars. He focused on the supergiants forming Orion's Belt and thought of his inevitable, pivotal and final clash with Rex Rowe. He didn't know where it would be, or when, but the chief of staff had definitely messed with the wrong man.

Chapter 66

Yin and Yang

ZAYN AWOKE to a ringing phone. He'd been fitfully attempting to sleep in the plane at the clearing in the woods referred to as Waskaganish Airport, which was about a hundred kilometers south of the clearing in the woods known as Eastmain Airport. The fitful part was not due to the cramped accommodations or cool northern weather, but rather the winds of change.

In a few hours, his life was going to pivot and launch on a new trajectory. With a single act, he'd achieve his long-held ambition of owning his own airplane and living without debt. Alas, that same act would also make him a murderer. Why was there a give attached to every take? A yin for every yang? Who made that rule?

With those philosophical questions still spinning around his sleepy mind, Zayn answered the phone. "Yes."

"Check your bank account. You now have a seven-figure balance."

Zayn couldn't check. There wasn't a Wi-Fi hotspot within 500 kilometers of Eastmain, and his satellite phone didn't have data. But the rich man with the Texas accent likely didn't know that. Northern Canada was much more desolate than most people realized. "I'll do that. Assuming I'm happy with what I see, I'll wrap things up within the next couple of hours."

"Good. Call me back the moment you do."

While trying to fall asleep, Zayn had pictured the scenes to come. He'd devised his story and imagined his moves. How he'd silently slip his Smith & Wesson from his aviation bag. How he'd position and hold it so his victims couldn't see. The man wouldn't even hear the bang if Zayn's aim was true. The woman would suffer a second or two of extreme shock, a rousing jolt of electrifying fear, but it would quickly pass.

Zayn would wait for the right time to do the deed. He'd hold off until both had settled back and closed their eyes. Two quick trigger pulls would end their lives in their sleep, and begin his dream.

Well, after a bit of cleanup.

That shouldn't be too bad.

He'd drop the bodies into a dense section of woods that hadn't felt human feet for a hundred years. There were plenty of places like that up here. Millions of acres in fact. As for the blood...

He wasn't going to fool himself about the blood. It might take a while to wash away.

It was 4:00 a.m. as Zayn caught sight of Eastmain's runway edge lights and began his last landing as an aircraft renter. By 4:04 he was cutting the engine, parked alongside the fuel pump.

Two men in flight suits emerged from the Sikorsky and began walking his way.

"Morning. Sorry to have woken you. I didn't expect anyone to be here."

"Not your fault. We didn't expect to be here. We're stranded. The pump is out," the closest pilot said, nodding to the instrument now in Zayn's hand.

"Bone dry?"

"Broken. How are you on fuel?"

Zayn replaced the nozzle on the pump. "I've got half a tank. I was planning to top off before flying to Windsor. I'd offer to help you out, but I don't think I can spare enough to get you very far," he said with a gesture toward their big bird.

"That's all right. We've got fuel coming. But if you have room for our passengers, I think they'd be mighty grateful."

"I've got room. Would be my pleasure."

"That's kind of you," a voice said behind Zayn's shoulder.

He whirled to see a large man standing before a beautiful woman. They appeared to be late-twenties or early thirties and were definitely officer material, as his Air Force peers used to say. Bright-eyed and athletic, with friendly smiles. Zayn had been expecting drug mules, or maybe mafia enforcers. Puffy faces, dead eyes and frowns.

The man cupped his hands around his eyes and peered into the back of the Baron.

"You have a lot of luggage?" Zayn asked.

"There's just two seats," the man replied.

"I take the back two out to save weight when I don't need them. You'll appreciate the extra leg room."

"We've got fuel on the way. No need to put you out," the man said.

Zayn hadn't expected pushback. They were supposed to be desperate for a ride. He needed time to think, but didn't have it. "You wouldn't be putting me out. I'd appreciate the company. Where are you headed?"

"Churchill."

Churchill was 700 miles northwest. He'd told them he was going to Windsor, which was a thousand miles to the south. Hadn't they just come from Churchill? Zayn felt his new life slipping away. "It will be a lot easier to get a ride to Churchill from Windsor than anywhere around here."

"You're probably right. Thank you. We'll grab our stuff."

As they walked toward the helicopter, Zayn opened the Beechcraft's passenger door. He stood there staring at the two seats that would soon be covered in blood. Once the couple buckled in, they'd be fish in a barrel. Except they weren't fish. They were human beings, with bright eyes and smiling faces.

He'd met plenty of people the world would be better off without. Thieves who would break a car window to grab a quarter from the ashtray. Drug dealers who would hook teenage kids on heroin. Thugs who would shatter kneecaps for fifty bucks. But the couple now walking his way with two small roller bags bore no resemblance to the lowlifes who'd crossed his path. They were nothing like the trash he'd expected to take out today.

Zayn climbed in and locked the door behind him. He hopped into the pilot's seat, checked to ensure that the man and woman were clear of the propeller blades, and started the engine.

The couple stood quietly. Not waving, not shouting.

He gave the Beechcraft gas, turned it onto the runway and began accelerating toward a new life. He had Tex's million bucks. He'd toss the satellite phone out the window in a few minutes. Later today he'd return the clean plane, transfer his dirty cash, and buy a one-way ticket to Bermuda.

Chapter 67

In Your Face

KATYA WATCHED the twin-engine airplane disappear into the pre-dawn sky—without them aboard. "What just happened?"

"I'm not sure," Achilles replied.

"Why did you let him get away?" she asked.

A few seconds earlier, while they were grabbing their suitcases, Achilles had warned her that this was a trap. He told her to play along until he turned the tables. He said he wanted to interrogate their would-be assassin.

"I decided he didn't know anything."

"How on earth did you decide that?"

"I got the impression that we weren't what he was expecting. And I figured that if he didn't know about us, then it was very unlikely that he would know anything useful to us."

"Whoa, slow down. How did you determine that he was sent to kill us in the first place, much less what he was expecting?"

"Look at where we are," Achilles said, gesturing around. "Trees outnumber people a thousand to one, and it takes three hours to drive to the nearest paved road. What are the odds of an airplane landing on this airstrip at 4:00 a.m.?"

Katya attempted the math. She couldn't help herself. The tiny settlement probably got one or two supply deliveries a month. Throw in a visitor and you got one plane every ten days or so. But how many of those would be in the middle of the night? One in ten at best. One in a hundred was more likely. So the odds were less than one in one hundred. Less than one percent. "Very low, but not low enough to convict a man without a trial, so to speak."

"Agreed. But besides the math, the man said and did things to give the gig away."

"I agree that he seemed a bit uneasy, but who isn't a bit uneasy picking up a hitch hiker?"

"I'm not talking about his body language. It's what he said and did."

Katya didn't recall him saying or doing all that much. Nothing had raised her antennae in any case. "Specifically?"

"Look at our helicopter. What strikes you about it?"

Katya glanced over at the Sikorsky. It was a magnificent piece of machinery, in the engineering sense. A very capable beast. She thought she knew where Achilles was going. "It's big."

"Yes, it is. You could fit twenty people in there. Yet when our pilots asked if he could give their passengers a ride, how did he respond?"

Katya thought back. "He said something like, 'it would be my pleasure.'"

"That's right. He didn't ask how many passengers, despite having removed half of his airplane's passenger seats."

"Nice insight."

Achilles shrugged. "I spent yesterday feeling guilty about using the Sikorsky for just the two of us. You look at that huge bird and you intuitively expect four passengers, minimum. But he didn't ask."

"Because he knew there were just two. Specifically us, no doubt."

Achilles didn't comment.

Katya cocked her head. "You also said he *did* something that gave the gig away?"

"Yeah. When the pilot told him the fuel pump was broken, he put it back without giving it so much as a bang or poke. He didn't even look at it. What guy does that?"

It was a rhetorical question, but Katya answered anyway. "The guy who broke it in the first place."

"Exactly."

"What do you think his orders were?"

Achilles raised his right hand in a gun gesture. "We'd have been helpless as caged kittens."

Katya pitied the fool who mistook her husband for anything less than a tiger under any circumstance, but she accepted the argument. "So why did he run away? Did he find you intimidating, despite the caged-kitten scenario?"

Achilles surprised her with his answer. "I honestly think it was your face that made him think twice."

While Katya was contemplating that twist, the pilots reemerged from the Sikorsky. "What just happened?" Grant asked.

"He's going to Windsor, but we need to get to Niagara Falls," Achilles said.

Grant gave Yvan a quick glance, but didn't comment on the decision. "Well, you're in luck because the fuel truck is scheduled to arrive at 7:00 a.m. We can have you in Niagara Falls by noon."

Chapter 68

Surprising Expression

WILLIAM ZACHARIA had an uneasy feeling in his stomach as he reconvened the C4 meeting. The discomfort had begun when he woke without having heard from Zayn. He'd gone through the hassle of making an after-hours transfer in order to ensure that his volunteer assassin could catch the couple before they slipped yet another noose. And he'd asked to be informed the minute the deed was done. Enough time had since passed that some deed was sure to have been done, but the silence left him fearful that it wasn't the one he wanted.

He tried calling Zayn, but got no answer. He checked the GPS coordinates of the satellite phone he'd provided the pilot and got a surprise—one he pondered over hot coffee and cold cereal.

He was only halfway through his breakfast when Rex walked into the kitchen and got straight to business. "Did we get them?"

"Good morning. How'd you sleep?"

"Just fine. Are we happy?" Rex pressed.

William Zacharia held up a hand. "Let's wait on Luci and Ben before diving into business."

"We're here," Luci said, walking in beside Ben.

Seeing the two of them together first thing in the morning gave WZ pause. Was it a coincidence, or something more? Their bland expressions favored the coincidence option.

"Coffee is ready, and I've set out yogurt, fruit and cereal. Help yourselves and join me at the table."

They did, and all eyes were soon on him again.

"The situation in Northern Canada does not appear to have gone as planned. My saboteur didn't call to inform me that the deed was done. And now his satellite phone is sitting stationary in the woods about fifty miles south of Eastmain Airport."

"You think they caught on to him, and the ensuing fight crashed the plane?" Ben asked.

"That's a reasonable conclusion and one I'd like to believe is true, but given our experience with Kyle and Katya—"

"It's probably wishful thinking," Ben said, completing the thought.

"Better to assume they escaped yet again and be pleasantly surprised than the other way around," William Zacharia said.

Rex was next to chime in. "If the plane crashed, wouldn't the phone have been destroyed—along with Achilles' watch and the incriminating recording?"

Luci shook her head. "The fuel doesn't always ignite when planes crash, and even when it does, objects can be thrown or blown clear."

In a rare sign of humility, Rex dropped his gaze. "I wish I'd never found President Silver's letter. We'd already be in the clear if I hadn't gotten Kyle Achilles involved."

Again, Luci shook her head. "That assumes we'd have found a way to steal the missile. As you'll recall, our brainstorming exercise got us exactly nowhere. We needed Achilles." She turned back to their host. "You've had some time to think this through, William Zacharia. Tell me, what does this unfortunate situation do to our plan?"

"It puts pressure on our timeline. It will be very awkward if the recording receives media attention before Operation 51 begins. On the other hand, if it comes out after, it will be but one drop in a flood of conspiracy buzz. My conclusion is that all will be fine if we launch before the recording goes public.

"Fortunately, Achilles doesn't know that. At the risk of underestimating him for a fourth time, I'm going to say there's no way he could guess our plan. But he is likely to equate a missing missile to a ticking bomb and feel compelled to move quickly. Bottom line: we have to act faster than Achilles."

"How fast is that?" Luci asked.

She was the gating factor, and everybody knew it. They needed the nuclear warhead to give Operation 51 the required bang. William Zacharia didn't go there. Despite the urgency, he sensed that the smart move was to be gracious, to give his colleague a break. "As you know, I've had my hacker monitoring multiple agency databases. If Achilles or his wife makes a travel reservation, scans a passport, gets a speeding ticket or uses a credit card, I'll be notified within minutes.

"Achilles undoubtedly assumes that's the case, so he's operating off the grid. In other words, he and Katya are handicapped—and in all likelihood, stuck in Canada.

"On top of that, I'll be crippling them further. Later this morning, I'll ask the chief of the Dallas police, a fine Texan who's sat around my fire many a time over the years, to put out an APB for Kyle and Katya Achilles. Soon, any interaction with any law enforcement officer in North America will get the couple arrested."

"What will you tell the chief to justify the APB?" Ben asked, his voice still elevated by frustration.

"I'll indicate that I have an embarrassing situation in which some top secret information is missing. He's a friend, and of course he knows that as a defense contractor, I'm steeped in confidential national security stuff, so he won't press. Fortunately, you don't need an arrest warrant or even a good reason to issue an APB. The chief once issued one for an escaped cougar."

That brought a chuckle, but the levity didn't last.

"An APB is a predictable move, so it's not likely to catch our antagonists. But it will slow them down. Hopefully, enough for us to finish."

"So it remains a race," Ben said.

"Overlaid with a battle of wits," Rex added.

Seizing that remark as a good transition point, William Zacharia grabbed a magnum bottle of champagne from the refrigerator. While the others looked on with curiosity in their eyes, he said, "Let's take this discussion over to the fire."

Once the cork was popped and the champagne poured, he raised his flute in a toast. "Regarding the race, some very good news did just come in. The missile is finally free and clear and under our control on North American soil."

As congratulatory words erupted all around, William Zacharia felt the champagne begin to work on the knot in his stomach. On the most important issue, he had delivered! The trek had been steeper and more serpentine than anticipated, and he'd tripped a time or two, but like a good Marine, he had completed his mission, and he had done so on time.

Ben was the next to speak, and he added fuel to the festive atmosphere. "I also received good news overnight. The stage is set! Construction is now complete—at both sites."

The C4 were on a roll.

Once again four flutes were raised and sweet words were said. After the excitement faded for the second time, all eyes naturally turned to Luci, the chief executive responsible for the third and final physical component of their plan.

She sat stoically for a few short seconds, absorbing energy, betraying nothing. Then, to William Zacharia's delight and surprise, she smiled.

Chapter 69

Sparking Ideas

LUCI HAD BUILT HER LIFE around the pursuit of grand, strategic plans. Stepping stones to ever-higher plateaus of power, wealth and accomplishment. From high school valedictorian and junior national tennis champion to the Air Force Academy. From the armed services to the aircraft industry. Up the corporate ranks to the executive suite. Then over to the mother lode: energy.

Sure, she'd sabotaged rising rivals and paid to keep a few failures quiet along the way, but for the most part, it was Luci's grand plans that had propelled her ahead.

Each leap followed the same pattern. She'd set an ambitious goal, then devise an audacious plan. A maneuver that crushed her competition because they never saw it coming. In the midst of every campaign, her mood would fluctuate up and down as obstacles arose and fell. She got stressed and occasionally depressed, but she never let herself start doubting or stop thinking. Inevitably, she landed intact and on target. Every time.

Operation 51 would be her last leap. The one that would take her to the ultimate plateau. A position defined by legacy, wealth and a prominent place in history. Once they launched the public phase, she'd be as good as there. Sure, there were thousands of variables and millions of players, but people were so predictable and the strategy was so solid that there could only be one outcome. Modern history made victory a lock.

All they had to do was launch.

As far as she could see, only a single obstacle remained—now that her part of the plan was set to deliver.

"The warhead is on the way. It left the Russian port of Naryan-Mar two days ago on a nuclear submarine and will reach Hudson Bay in three days." She turned to William Zacharia. "From there, I trust you can arrange transport along the same corridor the missile used?"

"Yes, that's easy enough to orchestrate. There's no serious border control up north. Everything's on the honor system. How is the transport being masked from the Russian Navy?"

"With an inside man, of course. A close friend of General Gromov's. The warhead was loaded alongside other nonessential spare parts in a crate labeled Anchor Chain."

"That's not suspicious?" Ben asked.

"Not in the least—when you consider the beast. Modern nuclear submarines are longer than football fields. There's tons to maintain. Forty-eight thousand tons to be precise. And submariners pay much closer attention to the critical components and food coming aboard than redundant, routine hardware, as you might imagine."

"How will it be unloaded?" Ben pressed.

"It will go off as trash."

"Outstanding," William Zacharia said. "That's the last piece. We have the missile, the warhead and the military installations. If assembly goes as expected, we can launch next weekend." He looked a bit awestruck.

Luci was feeling that way herself.

Ben didn't appear quite so jubilant and was quick to voice his concern. "A week is plenty of time for our former agents to interfere—if they're alive and on the move."

Rex turned to their host and asked, "How do you suggest we stop them?"

Luci found it odd that the politician was asking William Zacharia, since he had already botched the job twice. But at the same time she was curious to hear his answer.

"The fact that they followed the missile despite the danger tells me they don't feel they can go directly to law enforcement. Maybe they don't have the recording. Maybe it's incomplete. More likely, they've correctly deduced that they'll be totally outmatched within the legal system—and lethally exposed by the attempt. Do you follow?"

Luci nodded along with the rest. What he said made sense.

"With that in mind, I speculated regarding their next step. I asked myself: *Without the missile to chase, what's left?*" William Zacharia waited while everyone reached the same conclusion.

Luci and the others all turned to Rex.

"I am," the chief of staff said.

"Exactly. They'll be coming at you like a heatseeking missile. All we need to do is keep you out of reach for a week."

Could it really be that simple? Luci wondered.

"Can you get out of Washington?" Ben asked.

Rex shook his head. "Not for more than a weekend. My duties keep me tethered to the West Wing."

"Leaving town wouldn't help anyway," Luci said.

All eyes turned to her. "If Rex is clearly out of reach, Kyle and Katya will quickly move on to Plan B."

"What's plan B?" Ben asked.

"We don't know, and that's a problem. Therefore, Rex has to remain in Washington—and vigilant." Luci turned to address Rex directly. "Stick to the White House while awake and don't sleep anywhere besides your home."

"No problem," Rex replied. "More days than not, that's my regular routine anyway. But I want to do more than hide and wait. Why don't we set a trap?"

Luci stood and grabbed the cool end of a burning log. She raised it high, then dropped it into the flames, showering sparks. "Funny you should mention that. If they're alive, I know how we can catch them."

Chapter 70

Two Steps Back

WITH THE ARRIVAL of the fuel truck, Katya felt their situation morph from one form of nervous tension to another. From the stress of being stranded to the strain of entering back into the battle for the rest of their lives. She and Achilles were once again flying toward an unknown future in search of justice.

He slept for most of the flight to Niagara Falls, Ontario. She spent much of it in contemplation. Achilles had said he thought it was her face that changed their would-be assassin's mind, meaning that she appeared innocent. That killing her would cross a line.

But she had killed a man just hours earlier.

As Katya contemplated the incredible new entries being written in the book of her life, her mind kept going back to the genesis of this dark chapter—in the Oval Office. The idea that a politician had *used* her, had *changed* her, had *made her a less-sensitive person* left Katya feeling angrier by the minute. She vowed to reclaim a heightened sense of humanity when this was all over. To make her current mindset a temporary accommodation to an atrocious situation. Meanwhile, she would use her anger—for good.

Exactly how, she wasn't sure. The five-hour flight wasn't long enough to figure that out.

The Niagara Falls Heliport was a busy one with all the sightseeing tours taking place. She and Achilles both profusely thanked the pilots for their service and flexibility before melting into the crowd that was staring down at the whirlpool. Within seconds of leaving the helipad, they became just another couple vying for the best place to take selfies before one of the Seven Natural Wonders of the World.

For security reasons and with a lack of internet connection, they hadn't attempted to reserve a room in advance, so they walked along Niagara Parkway in the direction of the Horseshoe Falls looking for something inviting. As they neared the Rainbow Bridge, which connects Canada with the United States, Achilles gestured to a large, historic-looking limestone building up the hill to their right. The Crowne Plaza. Apparently, he was in the mood for a bit of balancing luxury. She didn't mind.

The lobby had the kind of grand sweeping staircases that beg to be photographed, along with crystal chandeliers and a ceiling painted to resemble the sky. It also offered free Wi-Fi.

Katya read about the hotel on the login screen while they waited in line for a room. Marilyn Monroe had stayed there while filming *Niagara*, and every table in the restaurant boasted a falls view.

"We're looking for a room for the night," she told the receptionist.

"For how many people?"

"Just me and my husband."

"With falls view, or city view?"

"Falls would be nice." Why not? Rex was paying.

"King or suite?"

"Suite would be nice. I read that there's one where the whirlpool tub has a view?"

"Suite 707. It's taken. But a cancellation has left another suite available on the seventh floor. You can see the falls from the spa by looking in the mirror."

"We'll take it," Katya said, handing over their Greek passports and matching credit card.

The receptionist worked quickly. As she was handing Katya the room key, Achilles interrupted. "I'm sorry. We're not going to be able to stay."

The receptionist looked at Katya.

Katya didn't miss a beat. "Can you cancel that? I'm sorry. My husband's father has been very ill."

"Of course. I'll reverse the transaction."

Katya reclaimed their documents and Achilles immediately led her out a side door and around a corner onto a busy pedestrian back street lined with museums and gift shops. After a good minute of brisk walking, he said, "I got an email from Zeki. There's an APB out for Kostas and Katerina Kakos."

"No! How could they have learned our false identities?"

"I was just thinking about that. Man, they're clever. They pulled on the one loose thread I forgot to tuck away."

"What thread?"

"The plane that was stranded in Churchill. We chartered it using our new identities."

Achilles was obviously mad at himself.

Katya changed the subject. "How did Zeki learn about the APB?"

"He monitors the identities he creates. It's in his interest to keep anyone he supplies from getting caught, since law enforcement would inevitably ask where the forged documents came from."

"Lucky for us."

"Yeah. We'd have been sitting ducks."

Katya pictured them naked in the hot tub, soaking in the romantic atmosphere as the door burst open and the room filled with Mounties. That was a scene she could definitely do without. And, she realized with no small amount of distress, it would remain a likely scenario until they concluded this thing. Unfortunately, a favorable conclusion had just become even more difficult to achieve.

She looked around the busy sidewalk, wondering how many cameras were capturing their every move. "Are we safe now?"

"Depends on whether the hotel reservation was voided before our names hit the system. In any case, we're stranded outside the U.S. without passports. Again."

Chapter 71

Game Changer

ACHILLES OPENED the door for Katya, then followed her into the independent taxi. They had to get off the streets and away from the Crowne Plaza in case the hotel booking had triggered an immediate response. "St. Catharines, please."

"Anyplace in particular?" the driver asked.

"Do you know the city well?"

"Born and raised."

"We're looking for a quiet BnB. Someplace privately owned. More grandma than government if you know what I mean?"

"I know exactly what you mean. And I know the perfect place. Have you there in about fifteen minutes."

The driver began fidgeting with his phone as they fought the traffic surrounding the falls, making Achilles wary. At the next light, while Achilles had one hand on the door handle and another holding Katya's, the driver made a call. "Lily, it's Norman Jensen. How are you? Wonderful. I have a lovely couple in my cab that are looking for a place like yours. Do you have room? Excellent. I'll have them there in a tick."

Achilles relaxed both hands and gave a grateful nod as he met Norman's eye in the mirror. Then he went to work typing an email on his phone while Katya watched. After hitting SEND, he turned to his wife and said, "I hope Zeki was anticipating our request. I'm worried about the timeline, now that the package has been delivered."

Katya kept it simple. A taxi wasn't the place to vent or discuss operations strategy. "Me too."

They cut clear across the city on Queen Elizabeth Way and then a mile into the country before Norman pulled onto the gravel drive of a large old farmhouse. The hand-painted sign posted by the turnoff was both playful and descriptive. Katya read it aloud. "Inn the Pines."

"You'll like it here," Norman said. "Quiet, personable, and the food doesn't get any fresher."

Achilles paid twice the meter and thanked Norman for his kindness.

Lily met them at the door and invited them into a parlor with lace curtains and antique furnishings. Once she quoted the rate and options, he pulled out enough cash to pay for a full week's room and board, but kept their passports in his pocket. Best to predispose her to be flexible, he figured. Harder to be a stickler for the rules of registration when a fat stack of cash was dangling within reach.

Five minutes later, having finished the tour and learned the rules, 'the Joneses from Virginia' closed the door on a delightful room with a fireplace and hardwood floors. Achilles immediately emailed Zeki their assumed name and the inn's address.

"Will the rollercoaster ever end?" Katya asked with a relieved shake of her head.

Despite the question's casual construction, it was a serious one. Geography aside, they were no closer to regaining their lives than they'd been when he'd carried her unconscious body ashore in Turkey. In fact, it could be argued that they'd lost ground, having burned through their best lead and alerted their opponents to their status and intent. Achilles equated the last two weeks of their lives to running hard on a treadmill set a little too fast. "Let's talk about it in the shower."

"Excellent idea."

They soaped up and scrubbed off the sweat of two frustrating days, blowing through all three tiny bottles. It wasn't until they were waiting for the hair conditioner to work that Achilles confessed, "I haven't figured out how we get to Rex."

"Does he get Secret Service protection?"

"Not under normal circumstances. But he spends about eighteen hours a day in one of the most secure buildings on the planet. And I'm sure he has a panic button. Plus people are contacting him all the time. He'd be missed almost immediately if he disappeared during the week."

Katya stepped under the spray and rinsed her hair while processing the news that her husband had failed to formulate a plan. After wrapping one of Lily's fluffy white towels around her head and drying herself with another, she had her next question ready. "What would you ask Rex if he were here now, in this room?"

Achilles didn't need to think about his answer, but he did anyway out of respect for his wife's deliberative process. "I'd ask Rex, *Who are you working with?* and *What's your plan for the missile?*"

Katya gave him a satisfied smile. "So you only need the answers to two questions?"

"Basically, yeah. Although the more I think about it, the more I become convinced that going after Rex is a fool's errand. Messing with the White House Chief of Staff is just too risky. The odds of getting caught are very high, and the consequences…"

"Would be severe," Katya said, completing his thought. "I agree. On the other hand, I think your approach is flawed."

"How's that?"

"I think you should ask yourself a different core question."

"And what question is that?"

"How else can you get the answers you need?"

Achilles liked the idea. To help himself think, he repeated the questions he most wanted answered. "Who is Rex working with? What's their plan for the missile?"

"Break the problem down. Take the questions one at a time," Katya suggested.

"Who is Rex working with?" Achilles said, continuing to think out loud. "The White House visitor logs aren't available through a Freedom of Information Act disclosure. That's been widely reported. And FOIA requests take too long in any case."

"Could The Invisible Man get them?"

"Now there's a great idea. Let's find out." Achilles shot off an email.

The Invisible man had always been quick to respond. This time his reply was so rapid that it made Achilles wonder if the hacker was actually a teenage girl. He read it aloud. "Can't do it."

Katya grew a contemplative look. "Inconvenient though that might be, in my heart, I'm glad to know that there are limits on his power."

"I hear you there."

"Keep brainstorming. How else can you discover who Rex associates with?"

"Direct observation isn't practical. I'd likely be spotted before I figured it out."

Achilles thought back to the night he'd visited the White House. Was there a way he could sneak into Rex's office and rifle through his records? Perhaps detach from a tour? Would Rex even keep those records in his West Wing office?

"That's it!"

"What?" Katya asked.

"You're a genius!"

"What?" she repeated with a smile.

"Rex keeps a personal phone in his car. One he doesn't take into the White House so that it isn't subject to recordkeeping protocols and he doesn't violate the statute against conducting private business in federal offices. I saw it after the meeting when he dropped me at the Hay Adams."

"That sounds promising."

Achilles felt his skin start to tingle. "It's a game changer. It means we don't actually have to get to Rex. Just to his car. That's an entirely different proposition. A much less risky one."

Katya inclined her head. "I like the sound of that, but we still have to cross the border without being detected, make our way to Washington, and figure out how to access the White House Chief of Staff's car—before he executes his secret plan."

Achilles retrieved his phone, checked the email and got another hit of good news. "Zeki will have our new documents on a direct flight from Istanbul tomorrow. It arrives in Toronto at 6:45 p.m. We're to meet his daughter at international arrivals."

"His daughter? Wow. What did you do to earn that kind of service?"

"I'll never tell."

Katya elbowed him. "Do you know her?"

"Never laid eyes on her."

"Then how will we recognize her?"

"She has our pictures. They're in the passports."

Katya reddened, then elbowed him again.

As she withdrew her arm, an idea struck Achilles.

"What is it?" she asked, apparently sensing his shift in mood. "Did I hurt you?"

Achilles began nodding to himself, temporarily adding to the confusion that he then wiped away with a grin. "With a little luck and a bit of bold, I think we can turn this latest twist against Rex and his friends."

Chapter 72

Hotel Hopping

KATYA THOUGHT the University of Toronto resembled Stanford in that it looked like an elite university in an urban setting. Tree-lined pedestrian pathways, well-maintained classical buildings, and a vibrant atmosphere packed with purpose and painted with optimism.

The fraternity houses were similarly reminiscent on that midsummer Sunday evening, with some students pretending to be reading on outdoor furniture while other, more honest if less earnest brothers played games in the front yards.

When she was athletically dressed, Katya was occasionally mistaken for a sorority girl during the twilight hours. But there wasn't much chance of that today, and no need really. Fraternity boys weren't that discriminating with their attention.

Katya spotted a brother with the right look chatting in the yard of the third house she passed. She sauntered up the front walk, then cut across the trampled grass toward the Ping-Pong table. Once seven sets of eyes were looking her way, she raised a stack of hundred-dollar bills and said, "I've got seven thousand dollars for your boldest, most adventurous brother."

The reaction was delayed.

The offer was so unexpected that it took a moment to process. Seven *thousand* dollars? *From* her?

Then the books and paddles were cast aside and two seconds later all seven students were lined up and clamoring for her attention.

Katya made a show of appraising each, head to toe, although in truth, only one was a suitable candidate. Maybe a second, she decided with a closer look. She and Achilles had agreed that this competitive approach was far more likely to succeed. Make the chosen one feel more fortunate than suspicious, and throw in peer pressure to boot.

"You," she said, stopping before the biggest of the bunch. "What's your name?"

"David. David Kennedy. No relation," he said through a suppressed grin.

"Do you have a car, David?"

Her question garnered a chorus of approving *Ooohs* from the others.

"I do," David said, losing the battle with his smile.

"And how flexible is your schedule, this coming week?"

That really got the brothers looking wide-eyed at each other. *A whole week!*

"My evenings are free," he said.

"Excellent. Would you mind stepping to the curb so we can talk in private?"

The others didn't follow, but their attention didn't wander either.

"Here's the deal," she said, producing Kostas Kakos's passport once they were suitably isolated. "My friend Kostas needs to appear to be living in hotels this week, while he's otherwise occupied. I need you to check into those hotels, pretending to be him. Here's a map of their locations, with the date you need to be at each. This seven hundred dollars will cover the cost of the rooms." She waved the money.

David was blinking rapidly, as if his eyes were activity lights on a computer processor, but he didn't speak.

"As soon as you check in, you're to mess up the bed and bathroom so they appear to have been used by two people, then leave. Do that immediately, then take off. No more than five minutes from check-in to take-off. Got that?"

"You said something about seven thousand dollars?"

"I did. Take a selfie in front of each hotel, then a picture of the messed-up room with the receipt on the bed and text both photos to me. I'll Venmo you a thousand dollars each time. Got that?"

He blinked a few more times. "I think so."

"Can you do that, David? Look at the map?" The cheap hotels were all within a hundred miles of Toronto. All near border-crossing points.

"What's this about?"

"I told you. My friend Kostas needs to appear to be living in hotels this week. There's nothing illegal here. There's no law against checking into a hotel room under a fake name. Do you want the job, or shall I ask one of your brothers?"

"I want the job. May I see the passport?"

Katya knew what was coming. "There are plenty of other candidates around campus. And the clerks at cheap hotels never look closely, not when people are paying cash."

"How do I know this passport isn't stolen?"

Smart question, but then he was a university student. Katya turned and raised her hand.

Achilles emerged from behind a tree across the street and walked over to join them. "No worries, I promise," he said, holding out his hand. "Do we have a deal?"

Chapter 73

RollJam

THEY DECIDED to drive to D.C. Driving was lower-profile than flying, and Washington was only about five hundred miles from Toronto. Plus both she and Achilles were over their monthly limit of airplane and helicopter miles.

When neither of them was sleeping, they brainstormed on the best way to discover where Rex Rowe garaged his car, and how to get their hands on his cell phone once they did. The former was the tougher nut to crack.

They considered using a drone to follow him home from the White House, presumably late at night. They considered having Katya approach his car at a red light along that route, so she could slap on a tracker while propositioning him. They considered hitting a bar popular with journalists and working the crowd. That last line of thought led to the final and, in retrospect, obvious solution: asking The Invisible Man.

By the time they—Mr. and Mrs. Matthias, according to the fresh Greek passports delivered by Zeki's attractive daughter—checked into a Washington hotel, they had Rex's address. The Invisible Man also provided the phone number for a local hardware hacker, which Achilles immediately dialed.

"Speak."

"I need a phone cloning device and two RollJams, one for a garage, one for a car," Achilles said. "Today."

"Where are you?"

"D.C."

"Can you be on the southbound platform of Farragut North in an hour, wearing a baseball cap backwards, and holding a manila envelope?"

Achilles set the sixty-minute timer on his watch and replied using the same abbreviated style. "What should I put in the envelope?"

"Two thousand dollars."

"I'll be there."

"What's a RollJam?" Katya asked as Achilles pocketed his phone.

"It's a device that opens garage doors and car doors that are locked using rolling-code remotes."

Katya was familiar with the modern technology, it being mathematical. With older technology, burglars could record the signal coming from a remote, then replay it to open a door. Rolling-code systems defeated that tactic. They were programmed to transmit and accept thousands of complex codes, but only once each. They required an unused code every time, so recorded ones were useless. Katya couldn't immediately figure out how to defeat that setup. "Interesting. How does it work?"

"RollJams block and capture the transmitted OPEN signal, emphasis on the block. With the signal blocked, the receiver doesn't mark it as used and of course the door doesn't open. The inevitable result is that the user presses the OPEN button a second time. The RollJam blocks that too, but it also releases the first code, opening the door. In that way it captures the fresh second code for future use."

"In a continuous jam-and-release cycle. A roll-jam. Clever," Katya said, speaking slowly as she pictured the process. "Meanwhile, the user suspects nothing. He assumes the first push didn't transmit."

"Exactly."

Katya admired the innovative thinking. It reminded her of a mathematical proof in its elegance. "It's at once a simple and sophisticated idea."

Achilles smiled. "You can actually grab instructions off the internet that show how to build one from readily available components, but we don't have the time or tools to mess with that."

"How do you know this stuff?"

"Samy Kamkar presented RollJam at the DefCon conference in Las Vegas a few years back. He's a famous hacker."

"Hackers have conferences?"

"Sure. They're important to the industry. They stimulate innovation. Inventing this stuff isn't illegal—although using it can be. Which is why guys like the one I'm meeting keep a very low profile."

"You think that hacker technology can defeat Rex's security system?"

"His car's an older model, and his house was built in 2003. I think we're safe."

On that note, Achilles left for Farragut North and Katya hit the mall. She needed to buy black clothes. Something perfect for the modern burglar. It took a bit longer than she'd anticipated, so Achilles beat her back to their room.

"That's a lot of clothes," he said as she walked in holding two big bags.

"I want to go with you."

Achilles crinkled his brow. "It's a one-person job. Plus the only leverage we'll have if I'm caught is that you'll be on the loose. Free to hire a lawyer, talk to the press, or otherwise fight back."

"I can help you avoid arrest without risking getting caught myself by serving as a lookout. I'll hide somewhere across the street and alert you if a car is approaching or a light goes on."

"My cover is a jogger," he said, looking at her leg.

"So I'll be a walker," she shot back.

Achilles didn't look convinced, so Katya pressed on. "Walk me through your plan."

"You know the plan."

"Humor me."

Achilles shifted modes, as she knew he would. "Burglar alarms tend to focus on the house. not the garage. So—"

"Even when it's attached?" Katya interjected. Rex had a 4,500-square-foot Italianate home with an attached two-car garage, fifteen minutes northwest of the White House near Georgetown University and the Potomac River.

"Yes. Typically, systems are configured to alarm the door between the garage and the house, not the side door into the garage. Point being that I should be able to enter the garage without tripping an alarm."

"Won't Rex hear the garage opening?"

"I'm hoping to enter through the side door, not the roller door. I'll only use the roller door if I can't pick my way in through the side. Likewise, I'm hoping to find Rex's car unlocked."

"So what are the RollJams for?"

"If the car is locked, and/or I can't get in the side door, then I'll plant the RollJam devices. Unfortunately, we may lose a day if that happens because the RollJam won't capture the car-unlocking code until Rex uses his remote in the morning."

Katya took a second to process that logic before asking, "How long will you need, once you're inside?"

"Probably just a few minutes. Rex keeps his personal phone on a magnetic base attached to the center console. I know he plugs it in with a wire, because it comes to life when he starts the ignition, but I didn't see where the wire goes. It was far from my focus at the time. It probably either wires into an outlet in the glove box or on the center console. All I need to do is insert this device,"—he held up a flash-drive sized object—"between the charging cable and the power source, and it will copy everything on Rex's phone within a few minutes of him plugging it in, enabling us to clone it."

"So you install the device tonight, he plugs in the phone tomorrow, then you retrieve the device tomorrow night and Rex never knows."

"Exactly."

"Sounds like a great plan. If you're quiet, the only thing you need to worry about is a silent alarm. Which I can shield you against by standing watch. When do we go?"

Achilles smiled in defeat. "We leave at 1:00 am."

Chapter 74

Plan C

ACHILLES FELT LIKE SWEARING, but chuckled instead as he drove past Rex's street.

"What is it? You missed the turn."

"They say the first casualty of any battle is the plan of attack, and ours just died. Rex posted guards at both ends of his block."

"How do you know? We're not even there yet."

"I saw an SUV parked exactly where I'd put one. I'm going to drive around and go past the other end of the street to confirm."

"Can't you just drive past his house without slowing down?"

"I could, but if they're top notch, they'll video every passerby and compare what they see to our mug shots."

"Mug shots?"

"Figure of speech. Whatever photo Rex supplied."

"So what's Plan B?"

"Please pull up the satellite shot of Rex's house."

"Give me a sec."

Before Katya had the picture, Achilles confirmed his theory. "There's the second SUV." He continued a few more blocks, then pulled to the side of the road behind another parked car so they'd blend in.

Katya handed him her phone. "Here's the satellite picture."

Achilles had studied the neighborhood already. "The lots are large and wooded, which works in our favor. Plenty of places to hide, and sounds won't echo. The fences are more for basic privacy and decoration than security. I'm going to approach the back of Rex's house from the neighboring block." He drew a path with his finger. "You're going to approach the house directly across the street from Rex's, also from behind." He pointed out another path, then two side-yards. "You'll stand watch from either there or there, in the shadows between houses. You'll be looking for lights or excitement in the SUVs."

"What if there's a dog?"

"Good point. That's a big variable. Rex is a bachelor who works all the time, so it's fairly safe to assume that he doesn't have a furry friend. His neighbors are less predictable, but given the sleep deprivation that accompanies the workaholic D.C. atmosphere, I doubt anyone would tolerate a neighbor's barking dog. But you never know. We'll just have to play that by ear. Assume there are dogs around and move accordingly. Slow and silent. That will help with the other big variables too: motion-detecting lights and hidden guards."

"Okay. Will we be able to talk?"

"Another good point. We need to keep conversation to a minimum. Use single words when possible. People question their hearing when sounds don't repeat."

"Got it."

He put his arm around her shoulder. "You sure you're up for this? Normally I'd use tonight for recon and go in tomorrow night, but I hate to lose another day."

"Another?"

"We have to come back tomorrow to retrieve the cloning device."

"Right. Yes, I'm up for it."

Achilles met her eyes and saw that she was. No surprise. Not from his Katya. "Okay. We'll walk together to your insertion point, then I'll continue on alone unless I hear a dog, in which case I'll circle back."

"Thanks." Katya kissed him and they got out of the car.

"I'm leaving the key on the front tire." They'd rented a black BMW with D.C. plates. A ubiquitous vehicle that would evoke more deference than suspicion from the typical patrol cop.

Aside from their phones, which were connected in a call, Achilles had a slim black fanny pack containing the tools and equipment he'd need. Both of them had day-and-night vision monoculars. To casual observers, the couple would easily pass as fitness fanatics, despite the solid black wardrobes being a tad suspicious. D.C. schedules were crazy, and late-night joggers were far more common than burglars in these affluent neighborhoods.

Katya broke off into the shadows as they passed the pre-identified house and Achilles carried on, converting to a jog. He had to add a block to avoid the parked SUV, but still reached his objective in under ten minutes.

Before ducking into the shadows, he said, "I'm about to leave the sidewalk."

Katya did not reply.

He hadn't heard a dog bark or a trashcan topple or the muttered expletive of someone blindly stumbling into thorns. But he knew Katya was there from the occasional rustle.

The house backing up to Rex's was a large white colonial surrounded by big leafy trees. It had a redwood fence with an unlocked gate and a deep backyard with a rectangular swimming pool. Aside from the lack of any sign of children—a basketball hoop, a jungle gym, a stray ball or forgotten bat—it was the kind of house that epitomized the American dream. Hopefully the residents would never know that their neighbor had masterminded a nightmare—because it wouldn't happen.

Achilles paused at the rear fence to study Rex's backyard with the monocular. He did not expect to see security, but avoiding the unexpected was the only way to survive the spy game.

Aside from the SUVs watching both ends of the street, Achilles figured Rex would have a bodyguard or two inside. That was the key, the advantage he was counting on. Bodyguards, not security. They were there to protect their charge from a specific individual assailant, namely him. They were not there to prevent theft. Or the opposite thereof, which was Achilles' intent.

After confirming that the backyard was clear of bodyguards and the windows were not concealing watchers, Achilles looked for electronic security devices. He spotted a motion activated light beside the back door, and cameras beneath the eaves on both corners.

Once satisfied that he had thoroughly assessed the threat, Achilles rolled over the fence and landed behind a bush. To avoid attracting electronic or human attention, he moved slowly and silently along the perimeter, staying behind the ornamental trees and bushes where possible. The larger vegetation gave way to flowers for the final thirty feet before the garage side-door, so Achilles slipped to the ground and low-crawled.

Once he reached the door, a bit dirty and scratched, he risked a whispered question. "All clear?"

Katya immediately whispered "Yes."

Achilles knew how to pick locks, but he was far from a pro. He would practice on occasion while chilling before the television, but not religiously.

The garage lock was a Baldwin, a good brand, but it looked older. Not the new Prestige 380 which typically took minutes rather than seconds to defeat. Achilles grabbed a pick and tension wrench, then silently went to work. A shadow in the night, quiet as a mouse.

He'd been asked more than once in casual conversation why people didn't put sophisticated locks on their mansions. The answer was obvious if you thought about it. *Would you rather have a thief pick your lock, or break your glass?* Rex had a very nice house, but it wasn't in the bulletproof-glass category, so the hardware matched.

Achilles ignored everything but the feeling in his fingers, including the time. He had Katya to keep watch and she was silent.

The cylinder finally turned after about five minutes of failed attempts. It was a sweet feeling.

He cracked the door but didn't open it. He just gave it enough push to let the latch release into the air. Only when no audible alarm followed did he risk slipping inside.

Rex had a typical suburban two-car garage with cabinets along two walls and tools tacked up on the third. All the essentials for maintaining a house and yard. The only thing missing was his car.

Chapter 75

Roses and Thorns

KATYA WAS WORKING a thorn from her thumb when Achilles' voice broke the silence. "No car." She was still processing his message when two vehicles turned onto Rex's road, clarifying everything. A silver Cadillac with just the driver inside followed by a black SUV with at least two occupants. She said, "Cars coming now. Looks like Rex and guards."

Achilles didn't reply.

Moments later, both garage doors began to rise and light flooded out from the growing gap. Katya used her monocular to scan for feet, but saw no movement before the cars pulled in.

It was nearly 2:00 a.m. Rex was working killer hours. As was his security detail.

The pale yellow house with white accents had a simple but elegant design that struck Katya as classically European. A solid rectangular facade with five large, evenly spaced windows on the second floor, and four parallel windows below separated by an arched main entrance in the middle. The single-story garage, bumped off to the right, had two rolling doors that were arched in the same pleasing style. The roofs were topped with steeply sloped tiles that resembled slate but were probably gray concrete shingle. The summation was regal without being ostentatious. The perfect choice for a successful politician.

Katya listened intently for any sound of discord. A raised voice, a slammed door, gunfire. She heard nothing before the garage doors began to close.

Interior lights started coming to life, first two ground-floor windows, then one on the second. She couldn't tell if the garage light had gone out, because it had no windows facing the street and the roller doors were solid. She couldn't see into the house either since the blinds were drawn. "Lights indicate Rex upstairs, guards downstairs."

Achilles didn't reply.

Katya watched and waited.

Five minutes later she reported, "Upstairs light off."

"Downstairs lights off," she added shortly thereafter.

Achilles still said nothing.

It was just after 3:00 a.m. when her earpiece finally came to life. "Meet me at the car."

Katya slowly extricated herself from the copse of shrubs that had hidden her for the past hour and a half and backed up to the fence that separated her from the house's side yard. As good as it felt to move, she wasn't looking forward to the retreat.

When coming in, Katya had climbed three fences and crept slowly along two fence lines in order to avoid triggering the motion sensor-activated floodlights. All in the dark on unfamiliar terrain. The first house had been relatively painless, but the owners of the second had a passion for roses. For tomorrow's repeat performance, she'd wear jeans and gloves.

On the upside, neither house had a dog.

Once she made it out of the second yard, complete with a fresh collection of thorn pricks, she said, "I'm on the sidewalk."

"Me too. Talk in the car."

Achilles was waiting when she got there. Apparently he'd been enthusiastic when it came to using jogging as a cover. She, meanwhile, was hesitant to put any unnecessary strain on her recently healed wound, despite the fact that her calf felt fine.

She slid into the passenger seat and he hit the gas. After they were free and clear on Foxhall Road, Achilles held up the cloning device he was supposed to have planted.

Her heart sank. They'd failed. Yet again, fate had raised her hopes only to dash them. "What happened? Was it too risky? Did the RollJam malfunction?"

He turned and smiled. Before he said a word, she knew he'd been toying with her. "Rex left his phone in the car. I don't know if it's because he got home so late or it's just his usual practice to deal with private business during the commute, but it really doesn't matter. I got it. I copied everything."

"We don't have to go back?"

"No, we're done."

Katya let out a long, slow breath. "What's on it?"

"I don't know. Maybe nothing. Hopefully everything. Shall we brew some coffee and find out?"

"Achilles!"

He jumped in his seat. "What?"

"You know I drink tea."

Chapter 76

Emergency Procedures

ACHILLES PLUGGED the cloning device into a waiting smart phone, while Katya used the in-room Keurig to brew coffee and tea.

The data transfer was very fast. Too fast, it seemed. Did Rex delete his phone records daily? Was he that disciplined? That was a best practice, but few abided by it. Especially those with multiple balls in the air. People whose memories needed electronic assistance. Still, the transfer hadn't taken very long.

Achilles paused with his finger hovering over the duplicate phone's RECENT CALLS button. This was a momentous event. A pivot point that might set the future course of their lives. Katya should bear witness.

"What's on it?" she asked.

"Come join me and we'll see."

Katya didn't wait for her tea to finish brewing. She grabbed his coffee off the credenza and joined him on the couch.

Achilles opened the call log.

"It only goes back a couple of weeks and there's only one number listed," Katya said, sounding as disappointed as he felt. "All the entries are from this month."

"Rex's phone was a generic no-name. Undoubtedly a burner. I bet he changes it out the first of every month."

"All the calls are incoming. Not a single outgoing. Where's area code 972?"

"It's a newer exchange. Dallas, I think."

Katya grabbed her laptop to check.

Achilles opened TEXTS and things got a bit more interesting. The number that made the calls was listed there, designated WZ, as were two others with 972 area codes, one labeled Luci, the other Ben.

The discussion gave Achilles an idea. He navigated to the settings. "This phone has a 972 number as well."

"You're right about it being Dallas. Do you think that's where the phone company is, or where the callers reside?"

"The callers, I'd guess. They may not be in Dallas, but I bet they're in Texas. People tend to want to be associated with either their own ZIP code or the one they aspire to, so that's what providers sell."

"I doubt Rex's colleagues have to do much aspiring."

"I hear you there. Listen to this." Katya read the first text aloud. "August 1 from WZ to Rex: 'Cancel any weekend plans and be ready for a 6:00 a.m. pickup.'"

Achilles recognized the date. "That was just after Calix disappeared. We were in the Mediterranean Sea when that text went through. August first was a day I'll never forget—and one you'll never remember."

"There's another emergency meeting with a 6:00 a.m. pickup just three days later," Katya said, continuing to read. "That was right after the unfortunate events in Gibraltar. Why aren't they worried about leaving a text trail?"

Achilles knew that answer. "No need to be, they're burner phones. The messages don't use full names. They don't say anything meaningful, not in a legal sense anyway. And phone companies don't store text messages for more than a few days or months, if at all." He was throwing out fingers as he spoke, counting the reasons. One, two, three. "The text messages essentially only exist on the phones, which I'm sure these guys destroy monthly when they swap them out."

"Really? I thought texts were permanent, like internet posts?"

"Nope. You're safe if you physically destroy your phone without having backed it up to a computer or the cloud."

"I'll keep that in mind," Katya said with a wink.

The third and final text was the most interesting. It was sent August 6, to multiple recipients, a Luci and a Ben as well as Rex. Achilles read it aloud. "Confirming no meeting tonight. Meet 13-15 as usual. Help gone by 19:00."

"The fourteenth and fifteenth were a Saturday and Sunday. These guys meet for the weekend starting Friday nights," Katya said.

"I like the 'help gone' part. That implies they meet alone," Achilles said, thinking ahead. "Which makes sense. You don't want witnesses when you're plotting to start a war."

"Not when the witnesses are earning servant wages," Katya agreed. "But what about security?"

"I'll need to know more about who they are and where they meet before hazarding a guess. 'Help gone' indicates a residence rather than an office. In any case, odds are they meet where the leader is comfortable. Someplace private. A location where the exclusivity lends security. How much personal protection they employ will depend on how threatened they feel in general. If they're drug kingpins or major celebrities or billionaires afraid of being kidnapped, they probably keep guards around all the time. If not, they probably do without. Guards are a burden. A hassle. And ironically, a potential threat. People don't hire them without good reason—unless they're exceedingly paranoid or vain."

"What about Rex?"

"There's no way he'd allow a Secret Service agent to witness his treason."

"No, of course not," Katya agreed.

Achilles pictured the scene. Four titans plotting the future of a nation from their makeshift Mount Olympus. Lots of ridiculously expensive liquor and plenty of backslapping. Probably a humidor full of fancy cigars. Maybe they were on a yacht or in a penthouse or at a country retreat. In his experience, the behavior of the rich and powerful tended to fit the stereotypes.

Katya interrupted his reverie with an excited question. "With Rex's phone cloned, we'll get notified of any additions or changes, right?"

"We'll receive his messages, and see whatever he sends." Achilles was excited about that as well. The phone in his hand wasn't quite the equivalent of an Enigma machine, but it might win them the war nonetheless.

If they could act quickly enough.

The weekend was just three days away.

He opened the CONTACTS tab. It listed the numbers for WZ, Luci and Ben, but no last names and no other contacts. The other tabs were all blank.

They stared at the screen in silence for a while. Achilles felt his mental processor spinning in place. Despite the sugar rush from the sweet news, and regardless of the caffeine boost, he was fatigued.

Katya yawned. "That's good intel, but I'm not drawing any grand conclusions. Are you?"

"Conclusions, yes. At least three. But no grand solutions."

"What are your conclusions?"

It was Achilles' turn to yawn. "First, we know they meet to discuss business face to face and probably only face to face. That's smart when you're doing something as ambitious, sophisticated and illegal as they undoubtedly are. Second, we know when they get together: weekends and emergencies. Third, we know their only emergencies this month coincided with our escapes from the ship."

"But not our escape in Churchill," Katya interjected.

"Which confirms the second point. They had no need to text or call an emergency meeting for our Churchill escape because it happened on the weekend when they were already together. As usual."

"Of course," Katya said with a shake of her head. "Sorry, my brain's running on empty. What's the value of that insight?"

"It indicates that the requests we sent The Invisible Man didn't get back to them."

"You're right! That is good to know." Katya was clearly excited, but losing her fight with the sandman. She looked like he felt when it was very late at night and he was glued to a good book.

"So what do we do now?" she asked. "It's Wednesday morning and we need to be in place and ready to execute Friday night. If we're not, we probably have to wait a week, and this is likely to be over by then."

"I know. Right now, I'm going to ask The Invisible Man to get the history of all four phones' physical movements. Then we're going to get some sleep. When we wake up, we should have everything we need to figure out who and where they are."

Chapter 77

Cui bono?

KATYA HIT THE PILLOW pondering her husband's last pronouncement. "When we wake up, we should have everything we need to figure out who and where they are." By identifying and hacking the cell phone carrier, The Invisible Man could give them a history of which cell towers the four phones had connected through and when, creating a time-map of movements. That would be helpful, but it wouldn't tell them who owned the phones or precisely where they'd been. The phones were burners. Anonymous. They didn't have the apps that fed the phone company GPS coordinates. Katya figured she must have missed something, but she wasn't about to wake Achilles up to ask what it was.

Sleep came fast and deep.

It took her a moment to orient herself when she opened her eyes. The bed was strange and Achilles wasn't by her side. She spotted him a few feet away, seated before his laptop at a hotel-room desk. The kind with a lamp and phone and a services directory pushed off to the side. The room itself was artificially dark due to heavy blinds. They were in D.C. It was all coming back. Boy, she'd really been out.

"What time is it?"

Achilles turned and smiled. "Just past noon. You slept about seven hours."

"And you?"

"About six and a half." He motioned to his laptop. "The Invisible Man came through."

"For the low, low price of?"

"Twenty thousand dollars. Five per phone."

"Was it worth it?"

Achilles walked around the bed and slid between the sheets beside her as Katya propped herself up against the cushioned headboard. "The four phones are all from the same batch of burners, which means they were bought at the same time. No surprise there. We'd inferred as much from Rex's limited usage history."

"Go on."

"Three of the owners spend their weeks in Texas. One in Dallas, one in Fort Worth, and one in Houston. The fourth resides here in D.C."

Katya knew where this was going. "But on the weekends?"

"They come together on unincorporated land roughly midway between the Dallas–Fort Worth area and Houston."

"What's there?"

"I can't be completely certain due to the cell tower placement, but given the way the three travel there, I'm pretty sure they're on a ranch that's about ten miles square."

"A cattle ranch?"

"No livestock as far as I can tell. Maybe a hunting ranch. In any case, there's just one complex on the property. A large house located on a hilltop near dead-center, with a few surrounding support structures."

"The ultra-rich version of the middle-class cabin-in-the-woods."

"That's my best guess, going from the activity we've seen and Google's satellite shots."

Time for the big question, Katya thought. "So who are they?"

Achilles closed the laptop. "The cellphones provided nine pieces of information in addition to what we already knew about Rex and our other clue. Namely, three partial names, three rough business locations, and three rough home locations."

Katya recalled the data she'd seen a minute earlier. "WZ in Dallas. Ben in Fort Worth. And Luci in Houston."

"Exactly."

"Those are major cities and relatively common names. Ben and Luci anyway. WZ has potential, I suppose, if Z is the first initial of a last name. But I bet there are still at least a hundred candidates."

"Z is for Zacharia, a middle name."

Katya was shocked. "How did you figure that out so fast? You only got up half an hour before I did."

Achilles raised his eyebrows.

Katya didn't need long to catch on. "You mentioned a clue we already had. What is it?"

"People in Rex Rowe's league."

"Of course," Katya said, nodding to herself. "But what did you use as a search parameter? Rich? Famous? Powerful? Politician? Donor?"

"None of the above," he said with a smile.

"I don't follow."

"Google does that for you. A name and location was enough. The phone owners weren't on page one of the search results, but all three showed up within the first four."

"So who are they?"

"William Zacharia Bubb is the founding CEO of Steel Shield, a defense contractor. Benjamin Lial is the CEO of construction contractor Grausam Favlos. And Lucille Ferro is the CEO of KAKO Energy. All three companies are industry leaders."

"Huh. Leading defense, construction and energy sector CEOs collaborating with the White House Chief of Staff at an isolated hunting lodge. That sounds like a Breaking News headline," Katya said, as much to herself as to Achilles.

Her stomach grumbled while she began digesting the news. "Can we continue this conversation over brunch? I'm starving."

Achilles smiled. "Room service or restaurant?"

"Let's find a place where we can sit outside. I feel the need for sunshine and fresh air."

"Okay. But we need to be quick. Our flight to Dallas is in three hours and I'd love to hit the National Mall on the way to the airport."

"Fine with me, but why?"

"The memorials are a good reminder of what we're fighting for, and that despite appearances we're not alone."

Katya was touched by his sentimentality. Her husband was so tough that sometimes she forgot he was really a softy. "I'd like that."

Given the size of their expense account, Achilles phoned the Hay Adams *just in case* while she dressed, but the rooftop restaurant had a two-hour wait. However, he was able to snag an outdoor table at Farmers Fishers Bakers, which was just a short walk away.

Achilles went with the house special fish and chips, patronizing both the farmers and fishers. By her logic, Katya figured she was duty bound to support the bakers, so she ordered a chocolate croissant to accompany her Country Medley salad. Fair was fair.

Just knowing that a bit of sinful food was on the way gave Katya the energy to tackle the key question. "So what would three big-league CEOs and the White House Chief of Staff want with a cutting-edge Russian/Indian missile?"

"If we'd gotten in at the Hay Adams, we probably could have just stood up and asked the restaurant. I'm sure it's packed with lobbyists, plus a few politicians and reporters. But since we're here with the tourists, we'll have to see what we can work out on our own.

"WZ, William Zacharia Bubb, might be a good place to start. He placed the incoming calls and owns the property where they meet, which indicates that he's their leader. And he's a defense contractor."

Katya didn't need a chocolate assist to predict where her husband was going. "So WZ gets the missile, and Ben gets something construction related and Luci gets something energy-related? All using Rex's connections, in exchange for their support."

"Arrangements like that aren't unusual," Achilles said, but he didn't look or sound convinced.

"Does Steel Shield make missiles or missile-defense systems?"

"No, they're in the soldier-for-hire business."

Katya asked a question she'd long wondered about. "Why does the United States need soldiers-for-hire. Don't we have a huge army?"

"We do. The second largest after China. But we use a ton of mercenaries nonetheless. There are two reasons for that. The first is that they put a lot of money in play, both for the company that supplies them and for the politicians who rely on defense-contractor contributions to fund their election campaigns. Contract soldiers often bill out at ten times what their enlisted counterparts earn, so there's plenty of pork for sharing. The second reason is that using soldiers-for-hire allows the Pentagon and White House to truthfully understate the number of troops deployed and killed."

"Isn't that trick transparent? And doesn't the cost make the graft obvious?"

"The CEOs and politicians word the contracts in ways that provide cover, but the real reason is that nobody sees the costs broken out. Military budgets are huge and far from transparent. For national security reasons, of course."

"Of course." Katya wished she hadn't asked. Politics always left her feeling dirty on the inside. Discussing it breathed smog into her soul. "So stealing the missile wasn't just a technology grab?"

"Definitely not. Remember, that's what Rex told me it was, so he wouldn't need to kill us to cover that up."

"Right. So why does Steel Shield want the DelMos II?"

"I haven't figured that out yet."

"Suppose that's the wrong question. Suppose it's not WZ and Steel Shield who want it, but the four of them as a group. What would defense, energy and construction CEOs and the White House *all* want with a stolen missile?"

Achilles smiled, big and broad. Then he stood and kissed her across the table. "When you put it that way, it's obvious."

"How so?"

"*Cui bono?*"

"*Who benefits?* From a stolen missile?"

Achilles shook his head. "Not a stolen missile. A launched missile."

"Launched where?"

"I'm not sure it matters."

Katya caught on after a second of thought. "War. Launching a missile could start a war."

"And who benefits from wars?"

Chapter 78

Where You Go

ACHILLES WAS NOT CONVINCED of his own conclusion. Launching a single missile to create a conflict didn't seem a grand enough outcome to justify the effort. These were very serious people, rich and powerful, and they'd gone to great lengths to acquire something very specific. Sure, the DelMos II was said to be cutting edge. But that just meant a bit faster or a bit further, right? Could it really do something no other missile could do?

Without a warhead?

And if a warhead was also on the way, what else was coming? Was the missile but one item in ten they were assembling? One in a hundred?

Katya peered at him with that crinkled-nose look she employed when trying to penetrate his mind. They were standing before the Three Soldiers statue on the National Mall, reflecting on what it was they were fighting for.

How had a country so grand—the land of Lincoln, Jefferson and Washington—fallen under the thumb of people so unscrupulous?

The power that We The People give the president was staggering, when you stopped to think about it. When you pondered the endless sacrifice and suffering required to embed and maintain the principles represented by the monuments surrounding them, when you considered the tremendous effort it took to create and nourish this democracy, this unparalleled union of ingenuity, opportunity and justice—then realized that it was all subject to something as fragile as a single human ego … Well, the thought was enough to freeze and shatter his heart.

Rex Rowe wasn't president. But he occupied a neighboring office. Close enough that it might make no difference, depending on the brains and backbone of the main man. Or the cunning of the confidant doing the manipulating.

Achilles did not have the measure of President Preston Saxon. Nor did he know for certain what Rex Rowe and his cabal were plotting for this country. But he did know that he would stop them —or go down trying. Some things were worth fighting and dying for, and the future of the home of the brave and land of the free was absolutely among them.

But so was the woman by his side.

Would it be right to involve her in what was to come? To have her participate in the bloody, brutal, mind-bending spectacle that had become no less certain than tomorrow's rising sun? Did he have the right to stop her?

"What on earth are you thinking about?" Katya asked.

Achilles shook his head as if trying to clear it. "I don't think I'm right regarding the missile launch. But I also don't think it matters. The actions I intend to take are going to be the same regardless. For the first phase anyway. They deceived me. They used us. They tried to kill us. For that, they're going to pay in a big way."

He gestured toward the statue and the black granite wall of the Vietnam Veterans Memorial beyond. "Whatever they're doing, it likely involves sending more boys like these to their graves. I can't sit back and allow that to happen. So they're going to tell me what they've put in motion. That, you can take to the bank. It's one hundred percent guaranteed."

"But?" Katya prompted.

He took her hands. "You shouldn't be present for the interrogation. It's not just that it's going to be very unpleasant. It's that I'll likely have to take actions no wife should ever have to see her husband perform."

"You may recall that in Churchill I did something no husband should ever see his wife do."

Achilles felt his cheeks flush. "I do recall. Believe me, I do. But this will be different. Less sudden. More intimate. There's a reason soldiers *go off* to war."

Katya didn't immediately reply. She just kept eyeballing him with that crinkled-nose stare of hers. Before she spoke, Achilles knew she'd set her conclusion in concrete. It was evident in her eyes. "To quote a wise woman from long ago, 'Where you go I will go.'"

"Katya, it's—"

She brandished a finger that cut him off like a knife. "You better get creative, Kyle Achilles, because I'm seeing this through by your side."

PART III

Chapter 79

Creating Waves

REX WAS MORE THAN READY to launch Operation 51. He was sick of the pregame tension, happy to have the Texas trips behind him, and eager to engage on his home turf. While the others would watch the action unfold from their armchairs like the spectators at a ballgame, he would be running the show from Washington. Steering ideas, setting talking points, pitching rebuttals, and, of course, appearing on talk shows. He'd do the entire circuit. ABC, NBC, CBS, PBS, CNN and Fox.

So would the Secretaries of Defense and Homeland Security, once he'd prepped them.

That wouldn't take long.

Rex had an advantage over every other talking head and policy wonk. Over every other strategist, lobbyist and tactician. He knew what was coming.

Sunday morning would bring something so unexpected and out of the blue that nobody else would be mentally prepared. None would have their positions or arguments formulated. None would have the relevant facts or precedents at hand. Certainly not NATO, the United Nations or the WTO.

That void would leave attitudes ripe for sculpting. With their well-reasoned arguments and, more importantly, their orchestrated onslaught of emotional manipulation, Rex and his surrogates would turn public opinion into an unstoppable tide long before cooler minds could construct appealing alternatives.

Luci really was a genius.

But her plan was not infallible, and the C4's position was not impregnable. Those adjectives would only apply after launch. Until then, they had one seemingly irrepressible vulnerability. Ironically but hopefully not fatefully, it was named Achilles.

Despite all their successful prep and posturing, Rex couldn't dismiss the threat that Kyle Achilles posed. Even forewarned and with bodyguards in position, Rex remained uneasy.

He had been optimistic when Luci made the observation that the new identities Achilles and his wife were using could be backtracked through their charter airplane reservation. Unfortunately, once again, acting on that insight had proved problematic. William Zacharia's agents had suffered one near-miss after another. First in Niagara Falls, then Toronto, Kingston, and Sarnia. Clearly, the fugitives were attempting to slip across the border. Just as obviously, they were getting tipped off in time.

Rex found the rollercoaster ride of now-we-have-them, now-we-don't to be both distracting and disheartening. For him, it was personal.

There was no White House record of Achilles' midnight visit to the Oval Office, and Rex had arranged an alibi complete with surveillance footage and witnesses. If Achilles tried to publicly introduce his recording through any official channel, Rex would get word in time to quash it. He was nothing if not well-connected. But as a politician with higher aspirations, knowing that it existed made him nervous. One drop of poison could turn an otherwise perfect politician toxic.

After the second near-miss, William Zacharia had theorized that the hotel check-ins were red herrings, that Achilles was paying someone to use the fake identities. But he went on to wangle a copy of the security camera footage from the Crowne Plaza in Niagara

Falls. It left no doubt. Their faces were clear, their emotions unmistakable. Kyle and Katya Achilles had begun registering with Greek passports when a cell phone message made them bolt.

After that near miss, their clever adversaries started using increasingly seedy hotels and paying cash in hopes of avoiding detection. But it wasn't working, and so far neither were their attempted border-crossings. Each subsequent check-in attested to that.

Rex speculated that the blips would soon disappear from the C4's radar screen, either when the couple gave up on hotels and began sleeping in tents, or when they successfully slipped across the border. Two very different scenarios. Not knowing which it was would be maddening.

Fortunately, it was almost too late to matter. In a few days, nothing Kyle or Katya could do would make any difference.

Sunday could not come fast enough!

Although Rex was counting on his co-conspirators' successors to make his presidential dream come true, he would likely never see WZ or Ben or Luci again. Certainly not before the dust settled some months or years from now. By then, the three former CEOs would all be living large in retirement. Perhaps William Zacharia would once again gather them around his fire so they could bask in their mutual genius. Revel in the glorious secrets that elsewhere might be suspected but could never be revealed.

But Rex doubted it.

They were neither family nor the sentimental type. They were the kind of people who waged war and moved on. It was safer that way. When you created waves, it was better for both body and soul to never look back at your wake.

Chapter 80

Bend and Break

KATYA KNEW SHE WAS ADDING RISK to an already perilous situation. By restricting her husband's interrogation options, she was handicapping him at a very dangerous time. They were up against a group of exceptionally intelligent and well-funded chief executives. Professional strategists who had outwitted and outplayed them in Turkey, Gibraltar and Canada. By baseball rules, they'd already be out.

But she knew hers was the wise move.

She knew that because she knew they would eventually get through these dark days. And with that knowledge, that certainty that comes from an unwavering faith, she felt it was her obligation as the nurturing member of the pair to get them to the other side free and clear of the corrosive darkness. She refused to drag it with them, to arrive in the light only to live in the shadow of what they'd done. To suffer from haunting images and blackened souls for the remainder of their lives. To be forever changed.

She would not let Rex Rowe or William Zacharia Bubb or Benjamin Lial or Lucille Ferro live inside her head. Once they were stopped and justice was served, she wanted to forget them forever.

"I keep thinking about Guantanamo Bay," Achilles said, pacing before the floor-to-ceiling window of their downtown Dallas hotel room. "Professional interrogators got nowhere with most of the Al-Quaeda terrorists for months. I'll have two days, max. And the CEOs will know that. Rex and the others will be well aware that come Monday morning, very serious, very competent search and rescue operations will kick into gear. That will give them hope the terrorists never had."

Katya looked up from her laptop. She'd been studying the geography surrounding William Zacharia's lodge. "The terrorists believed in what they were doing. They thought Allah was on their side. This group isn't driven by piety. They're almost certainly driven by greed. Greed for money or power or both. Figure out how to use that against them."

Achilles kept pacing. "I'll be asking them to confess to something atrocious. Probably somewhere between murder and genocide. Probably treason as well. Almost certainly enough to get them life behind bars, if not the needle. And disgrace. Disgrace is the big problem. The huge hurdle. You can bet that these guys are driven by ego. Once you've got a nine-figure bank account balance, if you're still in the rat race, you're working for pride."

"Are you sure they're wealthy? Maybe they have gambling debts or lost their fortunes in a divorce?"

"I asked The Invisible Man to investigate their holdings. He's pulling together detailed asset reports for us, but the quick and dirty calculation is that Luci has a high eight-figure net worth and the other two are well into nine."

"You're talking about them like a group, but really they're individuals. You don't need to break all four. Just one."

"I thought you weren't going to let me do any breaking," Achilles said with a wink.

They both laughed.

It wasn't funny, and neither was truly amused, but the pressure was bubbling over—and they loved each other.

"No breaking, no burning, no sanding, no slicing," she said. "Nothing that would make Torquemada proud."

Achilles clenched his fists in frustration. "We don't have time to break them down with sleep deprivation, and I don't have chemical interrogation agents—or training in their application."

"You have those pills you got in Turkey."

"The Rohypnol?"

"Yeah. That makes people more prone to suggestion right? That's why it's used in rape? Victims go along in the fog."

Achilles thought for a second before replying. "I'm not sure. Central nervous system depressants are tricky. If we had a week, I might be able to get the dosing right for interrogation. But with just two days, we can't count on simultaneously inducing both a loose tongue and a lucid mind."

Katya saw the logic in that, but refused to be deterred. She thought back over their conversation, looking for assumptions she could nullify or factors she could reverse. The key to solving complex equations often involved simplification and reorganization. Moving things around. "What if you changed the rules?"

"I don't follow."

"I'm thinking out loud. Right now, hope is working against us. Given the timeline and their status, they have a legitimate expectation of rescue. Suppose we took that away?"

"How?"

"I don't know. Get creative. When is hope all but lost?"

Achilles threw his arms up, but then his expression changed to the ponderous one she was looking for. Words soon followed. "Hope is lost when the hangman's rope goes around your neck. When your head goes on the guillotine block. When the straps cinch you to the electric chair. When the firing squad aims."

"Well, there you have it," Katya said.

"Have what?"

"The winning methodology."

"What do you mean?"

Katya was enjoying the thrill of solving a complex puzzle. "None of the things you mentioned actually do harm."

"Yeah, but you have to be ready to swing the axe," Achilles said, mimicking the act. "I could put the four in a circle, stand in the middle with a big blade held high and start asking questions. That tactic would pretty much guarantee three cooperative hostages— but first one head would have to roll."

"All right!"

"All right, what?" Achilles asked, clearly confused.

"You have your tactic. Now you just have to refine it."

The dark cloud cleared seconds later and his smile grew like a sunrise. "You're right! We can outsmart them. We can use psychological warfare to bend and then break the bastards."

Chapter 81

Battle Plans

ACHILLES SAT BOLT UPRIGHT in the middle of the night with an image stuck in his mind. A horrific scene. A nightmare to be sure. But not his own. While he floated down the river of sleep, a tactic that would crush his enemies had drifted before his eyes.

With that one picture now consciously burning bright, Achilles knew how to dangle hope and despair. How to create urgency and win enthusiastic cooperation with a purely psychological ploy.

He went to work drafting plans using a pencil and a pad of hotel paper. First a crude design, for brainstorming purposes, then the more detailed version required to create a shopping list. After cutting and grouping, stacking and binding, he calculated that the supplies would take up an area roughly six feet by two feet by one foot, and weigh about three hundred pounds.

A manageable load.

Ideally, he'd strap it to the roof of an electric utility terrain vehicle and drive it onto the remote Texas ranch from some side road or bordering property. That would be quick and quiet—but it wasn't really an option. Not given the security measures that he had to assume were in place.

Fortunately, those measures didn't appear to be extraordinary. Satellite photos showed William Zacharia's weekend retreat to be more house than castle. The hilltop location was clearly selected to maximize comfort and view rather than defend against marauding hordes. The design boasted walls of picture windows and scads of cushioned deck chairs, not watchtowers and battlements.

While Achilles had no doubt that there were electronic security measures in place, he figured they would be limited. Animals had to be accommodated. Big ones. At a ranch like that in a place like Texas, hunting would be a key attraction. Deer and antelope for sure. Probably feral pigs and bighorn sheep, too. Metallic vehicles like a UTV, however, might well trigger sensors. Clipping a fence to let a vehicle pass almost certainly would.

The smart move in a situation like theirs, when the stakes were sky-high and do-overs didn't exist, was to haul in his load like a mule. He could bind it like a wagon and rig it with lightweight wheels. Probably from high-end mountain bikes. As long as the terrain wasn't too steep, he'd be all right. And, come to think of it, he could pack an electric winch in case he got himself into a bind. Or a gulley. Or was just plain worn out.

Achilles completed his calculations before the sun rose. The battle plan was remarkably simple for something so sophisticated. The best ones usually were. He ordered them room service, then hit the shower.

Katya was up when he emerged, and breakfast arrived shortly thereafter. By the time he'd reached the bottom of his oatmeal bowl and Katya had finished her fruit, they were in agreement. "You're really okay with this? It's not the Spanish Inquisition, but it definitely is Edgar Allen Poe."

"I think it's perfect."

"So we'll be good?"

"Before, during and after," Katya confirmed.

Achilles didn't doubt his wife's sincerity, but he wanted to be sure she went into this with eyes wide open. "I once sat next to a guy on an airplane whose job was arranging social events for billionaires. Weddings and cocktail parties. Society stuff on a level we'll never know. We got to talking when they brought our meals. I couldn't give two hoots about the gossipy stuff, but there was one question I was eager to ask."

"What was that?"

"Are billionaires happy?"

"What did he say?"

"Without hesitation, he shook his head and said, 'No, they're not happy people.'"

"Why are you bringing this up now?"

"I just wanted to make the point that people don't always fit our expectations. Just as having money doesn't make billionaires happy, doing evil doesn't make criminals monsters. It's likely we'll find them quite sympathetic in person."

"And you think sympathy will weaken my resolve to carry through with the plan?"

"That would be natural. Do you still want to participate?"

"Absolutely."

"Good. Because we've got to roll. I need to hit a hardware store, an electronics store, a hunting store, a grocery store and a bicycle shop on our way south."

Chapter 82

Eye in the Sky

ACHILLES PULLED the big black rental SUV off the side of the road and parked in a dip behind a thicket of mesquite. They were five miles from William Zacharia's lodge, with nothing in between but rolling hills. At least according to Google Maps.

They'd picked this particular entry point for their approach because the terrain appeared relatively flat in satellite shots and it didn't force them to cross a river.

"If you'll get busy with the drone while it's still light, I'll scout on foot," Achilles said.

Katya hefted the lunchbox-sized DJI Spark bag. "You got it."

There was no fence visible from where they had parked, but Achilles figured one had to exist. Perhaps set back from the road as an aesthetic accommodation. He trekked a good quarter-mile without spotting anything manmade before turning and jogging back.

"How's it looking?" he called to Katya.

"We'd be okay going in here, but it looks better about a quarter mile up the road. What did you find?"

"Nothing. No fencing. No electronic equipment."

"I didn't see anything from the sky either. Kinda makes sense. What's the point if you're not keeping livestock in?"

"Keeping hunters and hikers and mischievous trespassers out."

"I suppose," Katya said. "But to enclose a place this size we're talking forty miles of fencing. Weigh the cost of installing and maintaining that over the inconvenience of maybe having someone wander past your house once a year. Bear in mind, he's five miles in. Most of it uphill."

Achilles thought about it. "You're right. It wouldn't be truly defensive in any case. Fences are easily climbed. A serious barrier would be ridiculously expensive. I've been picturing this property as an evil enemy's fortress, whereas it's really just a rich guy's weekend house. Let's move the car to the spot you found and get to it."

They re-parked a quarter mile down the road in a similarly concealed position, and Achilles went to work assembling his cart. The foundation-like frame consisted of six sheets of $\frac{3}{8}$-inch plywood, cut by helpful Home Depot employees to specified sizes, then drilled by Achilles in the parking lot. To the bottom board he added axles by mounting metal rods a foot from either end. He slid washers onto the axles and attached four mountain-bike wheels before piling on the rest of the wood. With that solidly arranged and strapped in place, he topped it off with a large, folded beige canvas tarp, then added heaps of hardware: traditional and battery-powered tools, dozens of spare batteries, and twenty feet of $1\frac{1}{2}$-inch PVC pipe. Much of it he stuffed into matching canvas bags. All of it he strapped down with black bungee cords. The resulting construction seemed solid. Whether it would prove robust enough to cover five miles of forested terrain remained to be seen.

They donned backpacks that held additional electronic equipment and camping supplies, then headed straight for the house on the hill. Well, as straight as the terrain would allow.

Achilles found irony in the fact that he was literally hauling a large load uphill. The physical challenge was an accurate metaphorical summary of the last three weeks of his life.

He hoped this would be the final climb. The campaign that yielded victory. He needed it to be.

He and Katya had remained competitive in their battle against the conniving corporate titans due largely to the big bank account at their disposal. But those funds were now running low. If they failed yet again, if Texas yielded no more success than Gibraltar and Canada, then they'd have little chance of ever winning.

Bottom line, this was their last, best opportunity to reap justice and reclaim their lives. He had to make it work.

Katya sent the drone up again as the sun sank. She took it high enough to catch sight of the house without risking detection. The main building was mostly dark, but one of the smaller surrounding structures was well lit. "The servants' quarters," Achilles said. "Take it a bit closer."

Katya complied and they soon got their first live shots of the campus. It consisted of a midsized barn, a good-sized shed, a separate garage, a swimming pool, a bocce ball court, archery and skeet ranges, and a helipad, in addition to the residential facilities. All were linked with flagstone paths and landscaped to the nines.

"How greedy do you have to be to want more than that?" Katya asked. "Seriously. It's a retirement dream if the traditional Texan lifestyle is your thing, which it obviously is for William Zacharia."

"I'm not sure," Achilles said, "but if all goes as planned, you'll have the chance to ask him."

Chapter 83

First Arrival

KATYA WAS SOAKED with sweat when the lodge finally came into view. Her husband appeared to be drowning. While planning the trek in their Dallas hotel room, with northern Canada's cool weather still fresh on their minds, they'd neglected to factor in heat and humidity. Central Texas was sweltering in August.

She and Achilles had paused every quarter mile or so during the gradual uphill climb to scan their surroundings with their monoculars and listen with a parabolic microphone. They'd spotted white-tailed deer, pronghorn antelope, raccoons, armadillos and an opossum, but no dogs, cows or people. Now they were just a hundred yards out and the lodge was discernible through the trees.

Achilles parked the cart and shucked his backpack. "Let's circle the house. Find the best place to set up."

"Suits me," Katya said, putting her own bag down. "But I thought we'd already decided to operate where the barn blocks the view from the house to the woods?"

"That's probably the best place, but we should check before we dig in. And since sound is no less of a concern than sight, we'll want to factor in the wind. Plus we want to be shielded from view as helicopters come and go from the helipad."

They each drained a water bottle before heading out, unencumbered but for their handguns, monoculars, and the parabolic microphone.

On foot they confirmed what the satellite shot and drone had shown. The tree line was trimmed back a good fifty yards from any structure, accommodating the landscaping plan and facilitating the lodge's 360-degree command of the scenery. They kept well within the trees to avoid being observed.

While walking the circuit, they found three paths leading from the facilities into the woods. Unfortunately, the one originating at the barn went right past the place that would otherwise have been a prime spot.

"Should we risk it?" Katya asked. "What are the odds the CEOs will be riding horses?"

"I don't know their routine, but the ranch hands will likely exercise the animals before leaving for the weekend. We shouldn't risk it."

"So where do we set up then?"

"The horse trail branches east, so let's go downhill to the west about fifty yards."

"That won't put us too far from the house?"

"I've got my makeshift cart, so distance isn't as critical as it would have been otherwise."

"It's your back. Lead on."

He did. They found a natural clearing surrounded by tall trees whose leafy branches provided significant overhang. They couldn't glimpse any part of the barn from there, but that limitation worked both ways. "This will do. Let's grab our stuff and——."

The thwap-thwap-thwap of an approaching helicopter interrupted him. Katya followed her husband beneath the shelter of a big tree to listen. The rotors grew in volume, then changed in pitch. "Let's go see who's arriving."

"Or departing," Katya added.

The helipad was east of the house, about ninety degrees around the circle from their current northerly position. They ran toward it, confident that the engine noise would cover the sound of their approach.

By the time they reached a spot that yielded a partial view of the helipad, the big mechanical bird was already on the ground. Its rear doors were open and large men were stepping out into the twilight. The one on the pilot's side was obviously a bodyguard. Big, beefy, body-armored and armed. The sight of him stepping out of that glossy black helicopter would have made a fine advertisement for Mercenaries Incorporated.

The man who emerged on the passenger side looked like the kind of backslapping, bravado-wielding CEO who had learned his management style quarterbacking football forty years back. Or maybe Katya was just projecting what she'd read on Wikipedia. In any case, he was easily identifiable as the owner, William Zacharia Bubb.

A couple of ranch hands met the bird. One grabbed the bags from inside, while the other removed boxes from the cargo hold. WZ's bodyguard simply looked on.

The helicopter departed once all four men were clear.

"Do you think it's going for more guests?" Katya asked.

"Probably. But if the schedule holds, it won't return until tomorrow night."

"I'm surprised there was only one bodyguard," Katya said. "Don't they usually work in pairs? When's he going to sleep?"

"They do, and I'm sure it's not a budgetary issue, so that probably indicates that William Zacharia feels safe here."

"Is that a good thing, or bad?"

Achilles waggled his hand. "If it's a result of the remote location, it's good. If it's because there's a hidden moat filled with flesh-eating bacteria, it's bad."

Chapter 84

The Other Kind

THE LODGE LOOKED to be about ten thousand square feet in size. Achilles had not seen the blueprint, and the real estate websites were no help since it had never been sold, but Google's satellite had supplied a helpful aerial view. In it, the front door appeared to lead into the rear of what was likely a great room, one that showcased a two-story semicircular southern vista. Wings off to both sides gave William Zacharia's hideaway a footprint that vaguely resembled the White House, although that was the extent of the similarity.

Other than the adjacent helipad.

Once the four men from the helicopter had walked up the path out of sight, Achilles said, "Follow me. I want to see where they go. Which rooms illuminate."

"Are you hoping to identify the rooms where they'll be sleeping?" Katya asked.

"Exactly. There are probably bedrooms in both wings, and that's a lot of territory."

"Are you planning to avoid the bedrooms, or target them?"

Achilles smiled at the question. "Avoid. Initially at least. My goal tonight is to figure out where they're going to meet, and how to get there tomorrow without being detected."

"You're picturing a study resembling an old gentleman's club, aren't you? Someplace with dark paneling and burgundy furniture? Perhaps a bar at one end and a fireplace at the other?"

"Where they can burn their notes before leaving," Achilles added with a wink. "Yeah, I suppose subconsciously I am. I don't know these people, and I've never hung out with their kind, but I suspect they're big on tradition."

"I agree. Leave the reconnaissance to me. You've got other work to do."

Achilles hadn't seen that offer coming. "Seriously?"

"Of course. We're a team, we divide the labor when we can—and I definitely prefer this division."

He leaned in and kissed her. "You think you'll be able to find our campsite?"

"I'll call you if I can't. Or if anything else comes up."

"You're the best. Take pictures of the lit rooms."

"Yes, dear."

Achilles hoofed it back to where they'd left their supplies. As he grabbed the looped strap he used to haul the cart, his body let him know it had not forgotten the hours of abuse he'd subjected it to earlier. He chuckled rather than wincing, knowing that by morning an entirely different set of muscles would also be complaining.

A phone buzzed in his pocket as he ran. A single vibration. A text, not a call. And not his primary phone. The Rex Rowe clone. Achilles checked the screen. The text was from William Zacharia's number. It read, "Good luck this weekend! We'll be here if you need us."

Achilles stared at the screen for a while, ensuring that he'd read the words correctly while analyzing each one. There was no ambiguity. He only had to prepare for three interrogations. He placed the phone back in his pocket and ran on.

Once he reached the campsite, Achilles immediately went to work prepping the ground by clearing debris. As he kicked an old log out of the way, a violent rattle sent lightning along his spine and something banged the sole of his boot. The impact wasn't overwhelming, but between it and the frightful shock he fell backwards onto the ground.

The rattle intensified as the snake studied him with bobbing head from a coiled position.

Achilles slowly slid his feet back from the frightened animal, keeping his boot soles up like shields. Once he'd retracted them as far as they'd go, he converted into crab position without letting his eyes leave the rattler. "I know you're scared, little fellow. Believe me, I am too. I'm just going to back away now, nice and slow."

Slow was difficult when your heart was racing at a million miles a minute. So was speaking calmly. Achilles had no idea whether the snake would find his voice soothing. Most of the reptiles he'd battled were the two-legged kind, and this fellow didn't even have ears. But he figured instinct was all about reading signs and he desperately wanted to transmit the friendly kind.

The rattling intensified again as Achilles lifted his rear off the ground, but he kept moving, slowly, oh so slowly, pushing backwards inch by inch.

A bite would end the mission there and then. Due to the potential lethality of snake bites, he'd have to go to a hospital immediately. Ironically, they'd need to call an ambulance to William Zacharia's house.

Achilles cursed himself for not being more careful. For neglecting to take something so critical into account. For being so focused on two-legged snakes that he'd forgotten to consider the slithering kind.

The stakes were too high to allow amateur errors. Tonight's attack was their best and probably last shot at stopping whatever tragedy was about to happen.

While Achilles' world teetered in the balance, the rattler slithered off. It just turned and vanished into the dark like the whole thing had been no big deal.

As Achilles exhaled in relief, he was surprised to find himself feeling like an assault victim. Oddly enough, that was a new emotion. He'd been attacked dozens of times in the line of duty, and outnumbered for plenty of them. Thinking about it, he realized that his unease didn't derive from the odds. It arose from the inverted hierarchy. This was the first time in his life he felt like prey.

He'd come back to that analysis and emotion at another time. It was worth exploring. For now, he had predatory work to do, and a lot of it.

Chapter 85

Boring

ACHILLES CAREFULLY FINISHED clearing ground around his worksite—with the aid of the shovel. Once satisfied, he pulled the electric auger from atop the cart and went straight to work. The manufacturer claimed, and the reviews confirmed, that the battery-powered device would dig a six-inch wide, thirty-six-inch deep hole in about thirty seconds, even in tough, dry soil. Achilles was very relieved to find that the assertion was accurate, given the quantity of holes he had to dig.

By the time Katya returned, Achilles was finishing up his twenty-fourth dig. He was a sixth of the way done. A few large roots had slowed him, but a Sawzall with a big blade advertised as The Ax had made short work of them. It was grueling labor, but he hadn't minded it a bit. Quite the opposite. Building battle sites on hostile land was cathartic. Seeing his enemy in the flesh for the first time since the treachery began also had a stimulating effect. He felt like a shark that smelled blood in the water.

"Wow! You've accomplished a lot," Katya said.

Achilles had decided not to mention the rattlesnake. "You didn't hear me working?"

"I could hear that without this," she said, pointing first to the reciprocating saw and then to the parabolic mic. But only when the wind died and because I was listening for it. I couldn't hear the big drill-thingy even with the listening device."

"Good. I'm afraid we got some bad news. A text from our host." Achilles gestured toward the lodge. "Rex isn't coming this weekend."

Katya frowned. "Does that change things?"

"We still proceed. We still interrogate. But with one of the four absent, the result won't be as clean or complete."

"Maybe we can use his absence to our advantage," she suggested.

That was a good idea. Achilles would process the tactical and strategic implications later. Meanwhile, he had more urgent business. "Did you identify the rooms they're using?"

"I believe so." Katya pulled out her phone and popped open her photos. "William Zacharia's room is in the southeast corner. His bodyguard is also in the east wing, but in a middle room on the north side."

Achilles memorized the lighting patterns. "And the help?"

"In the servants' quarters, here and here," she said, pointing to windows in the smaller house.

"Great. That leaves me free to explore the entire west wing without worry."

"I thought you'd be pleased."

He glanced back at the ground behind him. "Do you think you'll be able to sleep if I keep working?"

Katya set her tools down. "You'll wake me before you head out, so I can stand watch?"

"I will."

She glanced skeptically at the campsite. "Then I'll be more than happy to give it a try."

"You'll need to sleep high above the ground." He spoke a bit too aggressively as he remembered the rattler. Berating himself, he continued in a calmer voice. "Let's lay your camping mattresses out atop the plywood."

"Okay."

"Actually, you can use both mattresses. They're kinda thin."

"Why, what a gentleman you are, Kyle Achilles."

He mock-bowed to hide his relief. "I apologize in advance for the noise."

Once he had his wife situated as comfortably as conditions would allow, Achilles went back to work. He drilled the remaining 120 holes before removing his gloves for a break. The entire task required only three of the six batteries he'd brought. The electric auger was nothing short of amazing.

He hoped never to touch one again.

With the dirty work done for now, he stripped down and took a sponge bath from a water bottle. Given the humidity, Achilles knew he wouldn't stay fresh for long but it still felt great to wash the grime away. Once refreshed, he donned the black outfit Katya had bought him in D.C.

He packed his backpack, then shook his wife's shoulder. "I'm heading out."

"I'll take two eggs, over easy. Whole wheat toast, no butter. Some blueberries and a big pot of tea."

"You got it. Give me about forty-eight hours."

She smiled and sat up to kiss him.

He kissed her back, grabbed a set of tools that thankfully had nothing to do with digging, and headed up the hill.

Chapter 86

Irregular Features

BEFORE SNEAKING into the lodge, Achilles decided to inspect the grounds methodically, building by building, like a SWAT team clearing a crime scene. Fortunately, the moon was full and the sky was clear, so he had no trouble navigating without artificial aids.

A mistake many people make when walking around at night is turning on a flashlight. That practice reduces your view to the illuminated cone, and prevents your eyes from adjusting to the dark. Achilles would not have used artificial light in any case, but he was relieved that his night-vision device would not be required. Given the danger, he wanted his peripheral vision in play.

Achilles hit the shed, garage and barn in quick order. All were peaceful. He found nothing of interest—but was amused by the hundred-year upgrade in recreational transportation. While the barn had obviously housed horses in the not-too-distant past, it now contained nothing but electric vehicles. UTVs for work and ATVs for play. The owner had kept his sanctuary free from noisy engines.

Achilles found servants' quarters to be similarly unconcerning. The only sign of life coming from them was snoring.

Satisfied that the day's earlier activities had not triggered any alarms, and that there were no active threats he needed to neutralize, he sent Katya a text. "All quiet. Go back to sleep."

She immediately replied with a hug emoji.

He pocketed his phone and turned toward the danger zone. It was time to reconnoiter the lodge. His first order of business was dealing with the security alarm. From a pure roll-the-dice perspective, it represented the riskiest move in this stage of the operation.

For decades, home security systems had been hard-wired. But like most electronic apparatuses, they had swiftly migrated to more-convenient, less-costly wireless versions once that capability emerged.

Wireless security systems consist of three categories of components: wireless routers, wireless controllers, and sensors. The sensors tend to come in two types. Contact sensors are attached on either side of door and window openings. Motion detectors are strategically positioned in corners to survey rooms but not windows. When a contact sensor breaks or motion is detected, a signal is sent to the controller, activating the programmed sequence using the router if the system is active, or merely recording the activity if the system is passive.

There is a relatively easy way to defeat these systems. You just have to jam the signals from the sensors so they can't reach the controller. Service providers are well aware of this weakness and are working to counteract it, but they are constrained by battery-saving requirements among other factors.

Achilles' understanding was that you could still defeat even the most advanced wireless systems by transmitting that jamming signal next to a window for the short duration required to open and close it. He was about to test that understanding.

If William Zacharia was using a wireless system.

Or Achilles couldn't confirm otherwise.

His first move was to try to get a glimpse of the control panel. These are almost always near the door and sometimes placed where they can be seen from the outside. Given the number of picture windows in William Zacharia's weekend house, Achilles was hopeful.

He worked his way around the first floor, cautiously peering through the bottom corners of windows, searching for both people and a glowing panel. His phone vibrated about a minute into his search. Another text had arrived.

Shielding his phone so no light would escape, he checked the screen. "Can't sleep. Can I listen in?"

Achilles looked around, casting a net with his ears and catching nothing but the night. For the moment, there were walls and distance between him and every living thing.

He popped in a single earbud and speed-dialed Katya's number.

"Hey," she whispered.

"No horses here. Just ATVs," he whispered back.

She didn't laugh at his lame joke. She didn't reply at all. She knew this was no time for conversation.

Achilles continued his survey and struck pay dirt when peering through the next-to-last window in the circular array surrounding the enormous living room. It afforded him a direct if distant view of the alarm's digital panel, which displayed a green shield. "The alarm is armed, but wireless."

"Good luck."

With the security setup confirmed, he turned his attention to the floorplan. The great room housed the kitchen at the back, a bar at one side, and various view-oriented dining and lounging configurations scattered here and there. But the focal point was a fire pit in the middle. Not a fireplace. The feature wasn't surrounded by glass. An actual indoor fire pit.

Achilles turned his gaze toward the domed ceiling high above. With the aid of night-vision, he saw the large ventilation fan that made the feature possible. As his eyes moved down to the four leather armchairs that surrounded the careful arrangement of logs below, he envisioned the scene that was absolutely, positively certain to come.

Just as quickly, he concocted a plan.

Chapter 87

Risk and Reward

KATYA WAS STILL DIGESTING her husband's whispered "All done" when he walked into their camp and stopped to stand before her in the moonlight. He was wearing a contemplative expression she knew well. She stood and took his hands. "What happened? How can you be finished?"

"New information came to light, shifting the balance of risk and reward."

"What does that mean?"

"You know how the lodge is built around that large array of semicircular windows?"

"The panoramic view. Sure, what of it?"

"Right in the middle of that room, WZ has a fire pit. I'm talking hickory logs on an open hearth. Half the ceiling above is an evacuation vent, which makes it possible. Anyway, situated around it are four leather armchairs."

"Okay?"

"You get one look at it, and you just know that's where they have their meetings. You can practically see them sitting there, sipping single-malt whisky or aged French wine, and plotting their evil money-making schemes with imperious pronouncements and smug smiles."

"Okay, I'm with you. How does that help?"

"Now that I know where they're going to be, now that I can picture the scene, there's much less need to learn the lay of the land. If it were just a sixty-year-old CEO in there snoring away, I'd have risked it, but with a professional bodyguard, I went with discretion."

"So you didn't break in?"

"I found an unlocked bathroom window on the second floor of the west wing that I'll use when the time comes, but no, I didn't enter."

Katya leaned in and hugged him hard. "What are you going to do if the help doesn't leave, or they don't meet around the fire, given that you won't be familiar with the floorplan?"

Achilles checked his watch, confirming that it was early Friday morning. "Then instead of attacking this evening, I'll attack tomorrow morning, having done the reconnaissance tonight. We'll only lose about twelve hours."

"What if those are the crucial hours? What if tonight is launch night? Or early Saturday morning?"

"That is a risk. My gut tells me that whatever they're doing, they'll want to do it on a weekday, when patterns are more predictable, newsrooms are in full operation, and Congress is in session. But I could be wrong. Could well be the opposite. Perhaps they want buildings to be empty, skeleton crews on the news, and no one minding the government store."

"You're talking in circles."

Achilles took a step back and studied her face. "I know. You are, too. I thought my discretion would thrill you."

Katya felt her face flushing. "On the one hand, it does. On the other, I'd hate to feel that my presence is jeopardizing the mission by dulling your edge. Tell me, what's driving your instincts regarding the timing?"

"Good question. I'm stuck on the idea that one missile isn't big enough to make the kind of impact a high-powered crew like them would demand. They need an amplifier."

"Like a big crowd and a lot of coverage?"

"Exactly."

"There's not some major sporting event this weekend? Or political gathering?"

"Nope."

Katya looked up at the stars to think. Despite the local lack of light pollution they were nowhere near as bright as the Canadian version. Probably the humidity. In any case, they provided no answers. "So what now?"

"I'm going to get the noisiest work out of the way while everyone's still asleep."

"The power tool part?"

"Yup."

"How can I help?"

His expression turned sheepish. "Two things leap to mind. Which you choose depends on how physical you want to get. How *dirty*."

His emphasis on the last word sent her eyes to the shovel. "The drill-thing only got you so far," she said softly.

"The auger got us eighty percent of the way there. I'm thrilled that I thought of it. But the remaining twenty percent will still be draining."

Katya bent down and picked up the shovel. "I've got no problem getting dirty. In fact I welcome the opportunity to work out some frustration."

"You say that now. Come the morning, you may wish you'd gone with yoga."

Katya gave the worksite a studious appraisal. There was a lot of dirt left to move. She looked down at her slim arms and dainty hands, then over at Achilles. He wasn't an ape, but he was Tarzan. "What's the other task that leapt to mind?"

"I think we should develop a script."

"As in a detailed playbook for tomorrow night?"

"Exactly. Psychological warfare is no different from the conventional kind in that it pays to prepare multiple moves ahead. I have an outline, but you could take it to the next level." Achilles began nodding as he spoke. "In fact, given that the stages of psychological attacks are more predictable, you can plan each step with precision. Really refine my tactics to maximize pressure and tension. Pick the perfect words. Plot the optimal sequence. Flesh out the if-this-then-that strategies. All keeping in mind what we've learned about each individual."

Katya didn't need long to decide. She passed her husband the shovel and said, "Yeah, I'm going to go with option two."

Chapter 88

Two Fingers

BEN HAD ENJOYED his visits to Lonestar Lodge. Helicoptering to a luxury hideaway in order to mold geopolitics alongside his fellow elites was an ego rush on par with Aspen and Davos. But with all the recent visits, the shine had dulled. As the skids touched down, Ben realized that he would not cry if he never saw William Zacharia's helipad again.

Fortunately, he'd never have to.

This was it!

Game day had arrived.

With the work behind them and the ball passed to Washington, he expected to enjoy the weekend tremendously. Sitting around William Zacharia's fire would be like watching the Super Bowl from the owner's box. Or the World Series from the dugout. Or a championship boxing match from ringside seats.

They'd timed the launch of Operation 51 to hit the news early Sunday morning. After the papers were printed, but well before the Sunday morning political shows.

Rex would be their quarterback, their pitcher, their heavyweight. He'd get Saxon's Cabinet quickly aligned and oriented—thanks to the coordinated assistance and forceful support of three key Cabinet secretaries. Then they'd be off to the races.

Nobody met Ben's helicopter. The hired help must have taken an earlier flight. It was mandatory that they all be gone before the meeting began. With so much at stake, the C4 couldn't risk letting anyone overhear an incriminating word or spot a damning text.

Ben rolled his bag up the walk and into the flickering firelit lodge with the comfort and familiarity of a man arriving at his own second home. Oddly, William Zacharia and Luci weren't in their usual chairs. He was in her chair and she was in Rex's. Both were sitting with their backs to the door. "Good evening," he announced, feeling chipper.

As the words left his lips, a hand grasped his trailing wrist from behind. It forced Ben to release his bag and double over. Once his nose was near his knees and his shoulder about to dislocate, he felt a flurry of activity and heard an ominous ziiiiip. Then his left wrist was manhandled up beside his right and a second ziiiiip followed.

He'd been trussed like a pig! Or more accurately, plasticuffed.

He, Benjamin Lial, CEO of Grausam Favlos and soon-to-be billionaire, was suddenly someone's prisoner.

"Go join your friends," a familiar voice said. Then Kyle Achilles propelled him toward the fire pit.

"How did you—"

"Shut up!" Achilles barked. "You speak one more word before I ask you to and you'll be eating your teeth."

Ben didn't doubt the Olympian's sincerity. Or his ability. Achilles looked even more impressive in person than he did in photographs. Somehow larger and less civilized.

Ben quickly dropped into one of the remaining chairs. It was not comfortable, sitting with his hands cuffed behind his back. As he attempted to adjust, he saw that it was going to get worse. WZ and Luci wore ankle cuffs as well.

Thirty seconds later, so did he.

The fire was blazing much brighter than usual, casting off more light and heat. Someone had piled on the logs.

Achilles dropped into the fourth chair, William Zacharia's chair, but said nothing. He just stared them down, one by one. His gaze carried a grim message, like the crosshairs on a sniper scope. The silence continued for what felt like the longest wait of Ben's life. He couldn't verify how long it actually was, but it felt like fifteen minutes of holding his breath.

At long last, Achilles rose and walked to the whisky cart. He opened a fresh bottle of Blue Label Ghost and poured four glasses. Just two fingers, rather than William Zacharia's usual three, Ben noted, as though that mattered in the slightest.

Achilles set a glass on the table beside each chair. "Shall we drink?"

Ben remained stuck on Achilles' earlier phrase, the one that ended with anyone talking losing his teeth. Apparently the others were stuck there too as they silently nodded.

All eyes went to him and Ben quickly concurred.

Achilles produced a set of pruning shears from the cargo pocket of his black pants and went to work replacing the plasticuffs behind their backs with ones in front. While hardly cause for celebration, it was a serious improvement. And boy did that whisky look good.

Once he'd reapplied the cuffs on all three of his prisoners, Achilles dropped back into his seat and picked up his glass. "To a new partnership."

Partnership? What the hell was he talking about? Did Achilles expect to join them? Did he know what they were up to? He'd uncovered their secret meeting place, he had to know part of the story. But how much? And how?

Only three other people knew the C4's plan, and two of them were tied up beside him. Rex was the only insider not in the room. He was also the only member Achilles had previously met. His only known link to them.

Impossible though the possibility seemed, given Rex's protected position as White House Chief of Staff, Achilles must have captured him. Interrogated him. Pried the plan and the players' names from his flesh.

Ben dared not linger on the images his imagination conjured while picturing that scene, especially given the impressive physique and stern expression on the athlete now holding him captive.

Was Rex already dead? Their plan kaput? Achilles' mention of a partnership indicated otherwise.

Was this a shakedown? Did he want a billion dollars? That sounded like an attractive option to Ben at the moment.

William Zacharia was the first to react to the proposed toast. Ben guessed it was the proffered whisky that motivated him. Like preemptive liquid courage. He raised his glass in a two-handed grip and repeated, "To a new partnership."

When Achilles didn't leap to his feet and punch WZ in the mouth, Ben and Luci joined in.

Achilles took a sip and set his tumbler down.

Ben did likewise.

William Zacharia knocked the whole glass back.

Luci then did something unexpected. She extended her glass toward WZ. It was an awkward move, given that her hands and feet were cuffed, but she pulled it off with relative grace.

The big Texan eyed it hungrily, and when Achilles didn't protest, he accepted it with a grateful nod and a less-graceful grab. Once he had it in hand, he looked back at Achilles, a question in his eyes.

Achilles nodded.

William Zacharia restrained himself to a sip this time, and Ben decided he had the right idea. He took a second sip and carefully replaced the tumbler on the end table.

Achilles did nothing. Said nothing. He just sat there as if angrily waiting for a bus.

Ben looked at the others. They appeared equally baffled. Apparently there hadn't been much discussion before he arrived.

So what was Achilles after? Had he come to negotiate? Was he loosening them up with liquor, like this was just another business meeting? Let it be so!

Ben began fantasizing. If only they could steal a few seconds to talk among themselves. A minute to synchronize and strategize. Plan an attack, mental or physical. He understood why Achilles was keeping them from talking, but he didn't get why they were just sitting around. Was he waiting for the police to arrive? That could take some time, especially if it was federal forces.

Ben took another sip of his whisky. Then a third. And a fourth. The tension was getting to him. He held the liquor in his lap.

What was he missing? What had William Zacharia said before he arrived? Or Luci for that matter? Had Ben walked in at halftime? During the third quarter? For that matter, when did this party get started? Had Achilles waited for the help to leave, or were they hogtied in the servants' quarters? He had too many unanswered questions to formulate a plan.

Ben finished off his whisky.

William Zacharia also caught sight of the bottom of his glass. Luci's glass, actually.

Achilles continued to slowly savor his own drink while saying nothing. The whisky was unbelievably smooth. Ghostlike, as the name suggested.

Why wasn't Achilles talking? Buttering them up while the whisky worked its magic?

The answers to Ben's questions came all at once, wrapped in a single package and delivered with divine clarity. Achilles wasn't there to negotiate. He wasn't there to interrogate or arrest either. He was toying with them, like a cat with captured mice. He had come for revenge.

Chapter 89

In the Bag

LUCI KNEW what Achilles was doing. He was using silence as a weapon. He was waiting for them to independently arrive at the only logical conclusion: He had captured Rex and forced him to talk.

Obviously, Rex had not told Achilles everything. If he had, Achilles wouldn't be loosening their lips with liquor. What weak fools her colleagues were for imbibing at a time like this. They needed to be sharper now than at any other point in their lives. But she knew better than to say anything—to them or Achilles. Not just for fear of needing serious dental work but for strategic reasons. Best to retain every possible advantage—given what was undoubtedly coming.

She did not know the specifics of what awaited them when the whisky was gone, but she was certain it would not be pleasant. While she worked at keeping speculation from hijacking her mind, William Zacharia passed out in his chair. Luci bolted upright as his tumbler toppled to the floor. Had he passed out, or died? She studied his slumped figure and noted with relief that he was breathing.

Surprisingly, Ben did not look alarmed. In fact, he was also sleepy-eyed. He looked like a student trying to stay awake for a Latin lecture.

Achilles ignored the broken glass and the yawning guest. He got up. He went to the bar and grabbed her a fresh glass. While she watched, he poured two fingers of whisky and then, without sleight of hand or sign of shame, he added two small white tablets.

Luci immediately understood. For the first round, he probably had pulverized pills already waiting in the bottom of three tumblers. What surprised her were his words when he handed her the glass. "I'd strongly suggest you drink this one. I promise it won't shorten your life."

"What's in it?"

"Rohypnol."

Luci used the calming trick of exhaling a long slow breath before answering. "Why would I voluntarily drink a date rape drug?"

He answered her with the reasoned calm of a seasoned weatherman. "Best to sleep through what's to come. Save yourself an unpleasant memory."

Achilles didn't pull her head back by the hair and try to pour the liquid down her throat. He simply placed the glass in her hands.

She stared into the caramel-colored liquid. What a conundrum. She wasn't the first to face a fateful choice. But which one was it? Was she Alice in the rabbit hole? Neo in The Matrix? Or Francis Gary Powers behind enemy lines?

Not Alice, she decided. There was no way drinking the potion would enrich her life. Neo's red-pill, blue-pill choice was more like it. Two bad options in a brand-new reality. Unfortunately, that framework gave her no guidance. The U-2 pilot's situation was probably the best proxy. Powers had passed on the suicide pill, and although the subsequent ride in Soviet captivity had been rough, it had proved to be the smart choice in the end.

She poured out the whisky. Just twisted her wrists and let it splash onto the hardwood floor.

"Good thing your partner didn't see that," Achilles said, nodding toward William Zacharia. "I googled it. Blue Label Ghost costs $350 a bottle."

He grabbed another pair of plastic handcuffs from behind the bar and doubled up the bonds on her wrists. He ran the second pair through the belt loops above her hips, effectively securing her hands in the fig leaf position.

She did not consider it an encouraging sign.

"Can you believe they sell these on Amazon for a buck apiece?" he said, raising one of the thick black nylon straps.

Luci didn't reply, but knew she wouldn't be able to stomach the sight of zip-ties for the rest of her life.

Achilles began pulling knives from a countertop butcher's block and testing their edges with the pad of his thumb. After setting the first five aside, he settled on the smallest one, a paring knife.

Luci began regretting her decision to dump the whisky.

Blade in hand, Achilles walked to the nearest couch and selected a dark brown decorative pillow. Luci had seen criminals and spies use pillows as suppressors in the movies. While Achilles had a gun, he'd just picked up a knife.

He held her eye for a second before plunging the blade into the pillow at the seam. Once he'd sliced open two thirds of one side, he flicked the knife toward the ground, embedding it in the hardwood like an arrow. Then he pulled out the pillow stuffing, tossing it left and right while walking her way. Before she knew it, the makeshift bag was snugged over her head.

The fire-lit scene had been eerie enough, but the mood was infinitely worse when all she could see was an occasional flicker that leaked up from the bottom of the bag.

As her blood pressure spiked and she began to get dizzy, fear crashed down on Luci like a falling piano. Until that moment, the cozy setting and familiar company had kept her demons in check. Now she was isolated. Relegated to the dark, with her wrists and ankles tied.

WZ and Ben were effectively out of the picture.

Rex was probably dead.

Her only companion was a man they'd attempted to kill on several occasions.

Luci forced her thoughts to the military training she'd received long ago. As a pilot, she'd gone through both the U.S. Air Force's Survival, Evasion, Resistance and Escape (SERE) school and the shorter Evasion and Conduct After Capture (ECAC) course. Most of those lessons were now a blur, but one takeaway leapt out. The power of mental discipline. The importance of focusing on factors she could control. On opportunities for escape. On the health she still enjoyed. On a positive vision of her future.

Unfortunately, that motivational train quickly crashed into a crippling roadblock. The framework for those courses was Patriotic Duty. In those scenarios, she had been an Air Force officer defending her country against foreign fighters. On this occasion, the opposite was true. She was the hostile agent and her captor the patriot fighting for the USA.

Obvious though that was, the revelation shocked her. It was undeniably true. She wouldn't admit it in a press conference or a court of law, but she wasn't so far gone that she couldn't be honest with herself. At least not then and there, when critical decisions had to be made—with a bag over her head.

How had the reversal happened? Where had she gone wrong? All she'd ever done was battle her way to the top—using the same tricks as everyone else. Morally, she was no different from her peers. She'd succeeded where they'd failed; not due to different tools, but because she'd used them better.

The answer to her esoteric question was obvious. She'd strayed the same way they had. One small step at a time.

Listen to yourself! her inner voice screamed. *You sound weak and pathetic. Pull yourself together and find a way out of this mess. Save the philosophy for a sunny day.*

Luci snapped back to the moment with the realization that she'd heard nothing for a while. Was Achilles still in the room? Was the paring knife still stuck in the floor just a few yards away? Could she use it to escape? "Achilles?"

No answer.

She didn't ask a second time. Instead, she slid off her chair and rolled toward the abandoned blade.

Chapter 90

Taking out the Trash

LUCI COULD NOT FIND THE KNIFE. She rolled this way and that until she became totally disoriented. At some point she realized that she could shake the bag from her head, and chided herself for not thinking to do so immediately.

It took some wild head wagging, but she got it off—and found Achilles sitting right there. He was watching her with an amused smile on his face. In one hand, he held the paring knife. In another, a thick roll of gray duct tape.

Ben and William Zacharia were gone.

Achilles ripped off a foot-long strip and stuck it over her mouth. Once her lips were sealed, he placed the pillowcase back over her head, grabbed her by the collar and began dragging her across the floor.

She couldn't begin to fight. Not blindfolded and gagged with her wrists and ankles bound. Luci had never felt nearly so helpless in her life. Or degraded. She'd been reduced to cargo. A load to be hauled.

Probably to her death.

They went out the door and into the humid night. As her butt bumped over the doorsill, she caught the call of crickets and felt a light breeze. The degrading drag continued for a few more seconds and a half-dozen bumps, after which Achilles abruptly released her collar. While this made it easier to breathe, the reprieve was tauntingly brief. Before she could reorient, he hoisted her into the air and dropped her down between two soft but lumpy objects.

Ben and William Zacharia. Two pairs of feet in her face.

Luci's mind filled with images of mass graves. Corpses pushed by bulldozers. She tried to scream but the gag kept her quiet.

Soon they were moving. Rolling. She hadn't heard an ignition but now she caught the quiet, familiar hum of an electric engine. They were on the back of one of William Zacharia's glorified golf carts. A Utility Terrain Vehicle.

The cart bumped along for what was probably a few minutes but possibly not even one. Time distorted when your head was in a bag —and soon might be separated from your neck. The ride was smooth at first but became much rougher as they entered the forest, causing her unconscious co-conspirators to kick her face.

Scenes from mobster movies were the next to invade her mind. Walks into the woods or the Nevada desert. The condemned with a gun to his or her back. Did Achilles have the weapon William Zacharia's Greek assassin had planned to use? Had he kept it for them? Would he make her dig her own grave? Would he give her the chance to talk? To make this right? If he did, what could she tell him?

Suddenly, Luci knew what she needed to do. She needed to delay. She needed to slow Achilles down by a day and a half. From Friday night to Sunday morning. If she could do that, then the deed would be done. Revenge aside, there'd be nothing for him to gain.

Perhaps then bargaining could begin.

She could negotiate.

Achilles might even like her grand plan. It was quintessentially American. The concept had broad support. The Founding Fathers had been behind the idea, and everyone enthusiastically singing *America the Beautiful* gave it tacit support.

No, she decided. That approach was too risky. To recruit him, she'd have to reveal her plan. Regardless of its merits, Achilles wouldn't be favorably inclined to join them.

A scary thought struck, as if she needed another. She was assuming that he didn't know everything. What if he already did? What if this was just a twisted form of torture?

She swatted the thought aside. She couldn't think that way. She had to stay positive. To focus on escape.

Could she escape? Motivated as she was, Luci could run like the wind— if she could somehow sever her bonds. It was far more likely, however, that she'd have the opportunity to *talk* her way out of this. If she could spin a scenario that slowed things down, drag things out until Sunday morning, then Achilles might cut and run.

She really needed to know what Rex had revealed. Could she coax that information out of her captor before he did whatever it was he had planned? She would certainly try.

The UTV stopped, redirecting her focus from inside to out.

She felt Achilles step from the vehicle. Then another person. He wasn't alone! Someone lighter was with him. Katya maybe? That was a good sign, right? The presence of any allied woman, his wife no less, would surely make Achilles softer than he'd be alone.

Luci could feel the couple hovering over her. As her senses struggled to learn more, the bag was tugged from her head and she found herself staring up at a moonlit canopy of leaves. Not surprisingly, she was in the woods.

The scents of nature assaulted her now that the filtering bag was gone. Dead wood, fallen leaves and sunbaked earth. The crickets and frogs resumed their cheery symphony, oblivious to her mood.

Luci felt happy memories attempting to flood back, but all were stopped at the door. This was not a camping trip.

Achilles reached out, grabbed the duct tape, and peeled it off her lips like a big Band-Aid. As it uprooted all the attached hair, she couldn't help but wince.

Before Luci found the wherewithal to begin her pitch, Achilles produced the paring knife. Its silvery blade caught the moonlight, making it look larger than before. Regardless of the size, it was certainly sharp enough to slit her throat. Was that the plan? Was she to be slaughtered on a mossy granite rock or decaying tree stump? A sacrifice to the god of justice?

Achilles cut one plasticuff from her wrist. The one that ran through the belt loops of her jeans. Rather than move on to the second bond or down to the one at her ankles, he plucked her from the cart with the ease of a mother lifting a child.

He threw her over his shoulder and carried her across uneven ground, giving Luci an upside-down look at their environment. They were well into the woods, but it wasn't the surrounding shrubs and trees that caught her attention. No, her eyes locked on the ground. Specifically, on three fresh holes the size of graves.

Chapter 91

A Change of Perspective

WILLIAM ZACHARIA woke up slowly at first, then all at once. His return to consciousness began with that delightfully sweet feeling of being sucked into a bed, and ended with the mental equivalent of an ice water bath. He jolted up, but didn't get anywhere. Couldn't get anywhere. He was confined from every direction. His hands were bound. His feet were bound. His shoulders were pressed from both sides.

As his body slammed against the confining pine walls, the events of the evening came crashing back into his mind. His bodyguard and the last of the domestic help had left for the weekend an hour before Luci was set to arrive, giving him time to relax and prepare. He'd hit the treadmill and turned on the news. It had been an awesome feeling, watching television knowing that soon the only thing on any channel would be talk of his creation. That was power, and he had it. The power to change the world.

A quick shower, some fresh clothes, and he was off to start the fire. He liked it to be mature when the guests arrived, with hot coals, glowing logs and flickering light. The sweet scent of hickory in the air. Half the trick of charismatic leadership was learning how to put on a show.

He got the blaze roaring and turned around to find himself staring at the wrong end of a Glock 19. WZ had never been a big fan of the classic weapon's boxy look. He preferred something more stylish, a Springfield or Walther or his personal date-night favorite, a Whitney Wolverine.

The man holding the Glock was also the last person on the planet he wanted to see. Alive, anyway.

"On the floor, William Zacharia."

Achilles' words sounded so cold that WZ expected to see frost forming on his nose. He knelt down, then dropped.

Achilles bound his wrists behind his back, then moved on to his ankles. "Where are your guns?"

"There's a safe in the barn."

"No, your inside stash. One near the fire pit, I'm sure. Another in the kitchen, no doubt. Talk to me now or I'll hold you over the flames until you do."

WZ held no misconceptions about the irate Olympian's willingness to carry through with his threat. "They're hidden. I'll direct you. Take a seat in the chair facing the front door."

Achilles did.

"Use your middle finger to press into the end of the right armrest. There's a button beneath the leather and batting."

Achilles did as instructed. A side panel swung open revealing a Sig Sauer. He pocketed it. "Very nice. What about the kitchen."

"It's Velcroed under the cabinet with the crystal tumblers."

Achilles didn't move. "Where else?"

"That's it. One room, two guns, both strategically placed."

"You swear on your life?"

"I do," William Zacharia said without hesitation.

Achilles raised the Glock and aimed it center mass. Then he walked to the next armchair over and felt for the hidden button. A second Sig popped into view. He pocketed it, then repeated the move two more times while WZ attempted to melt into the floor.

Once all four Sigs were secured in his cargo pockets and the hidey-holes closed, Achilles crossed to the kitchen. He removed a fifth Sig from the place WZ had told him it would be, then a sixth from beneath a cabinet on a perpendicular wall.

"Do you know what you've done?" Achilles asked.

WZ needed more context. He'd done many things that Achilles might find concerning.

"You've proven that swearing on your life means nothing to you. That information is going to come in handy during the hours ahead."

Before WZ could chew through that tough wad of mental taffy, Achilles sliced through the plasticuffs on his wrists with a paring knife. He then flipped WZ's arms up so his hands were over his head and re-cuffed them. As the echo of the last ziiiiip died, they heard a helicopter.

Luci was landing.

"Who's that?" Achilles asked.

Was there any leverage in lying? William Zacharia wondered. Did Achilles know about Luci and Ben? Probably. Hard to see how he'd have arrived at this place at this time without also learning about their involvement. "Luci."

"When does Ben arrive?"

So he did know. "About an hour from now."

"What about Rex?"

Was that a trick question? Or the first sign of ignorance? Surely it was Rex who'd pointed Achilles to this meeting. There was no one else who could have. But if so, Achilles would know that Rex wasn't coming. "I don't know. He may not be coming."

Achilles moved closer and switched his aim from WZ's heart to his face. "Yes, you do."

"He's definitely not coming."

"Bet your life?"

WZ closed his eyes. "Yes."

Achilles backed up a step. "Wriggle your way up onto the chair that positions your back toward the door."

Once William Zacharia complied, Achilles slapped a long strip of duct tape across his mouth. "It's for your own protection. You're obviously too reckless for your own good. And too dishonest to be useful. Good thing I won't need you once I have Luci."

While WZ digested that fateful nugget, Achilles moved to an alcove that would allow to him watch Luci's approach, then catch her from behind as she came through the door.

He caught her.

And then he captured Ben.

Once they were all around the fire, Achilles ripped off the gags and poured the whisky. Bound wrists and ankles aside, it resembled a regular meeting of the C4—with Achilles substituted for Rex.

The next thing William Zacharia knew, he was waking up in a buried box. A pitch-black box. A can't-see-the-finger-that's-about-to-poke-your-eye dark box. And a small box.

He couldn't relax his shoulders or extend his legs. It was probably about six feet long and two feet wide. There was a bit of room for vertical movement and therefore the circulation of air, thank goodness, but not much. Call it two feet as well.

It smelled like fresh plywood and dirt, with touches of sap, mold and sweat thrown in. The air wasn't exactly fresh, but it wasn't completely stale either. The box had some ventilation.

As panic closed in like a vise tightening around his heart, William Zacharia tried pressing outward, upward and sideward. He gave it everything he had with his arms and his legs. The walls flexed more than the steel side of a battle tank, but not much.

He felt around the coffin's lid for the source of the air and found holes in the two corners he could touch. Each could accommodate two fingers. He longed to look through one to learn how deep he was, or to see anything at all, but he couldn't wriggle his eye close enough to the corner. No doubt that was by design.

He got his lips as close to a hole as he could, and began shouting. "Help! Help me! Help me, please!" Then he listened. For a reply. For vibrations. For anything louder than the beating of his own heart.

He heard nothing.

Could it be that he was already dead? Was this Hell? Purgatory? He doubted the devil could devise anything worse.

Suddenly, he felt cold. Bone cold. Cold to his core.

He started shaking.

Soon he, William Zacharia Bubb, was trembling like a private before his first firefight. He couldn't stop. The tears started flowing and he found himself sobbing. All the while, Achilles' last words played on a loop in his head. "I won't need you, once I have Luci."

Achilles was right. And because of that, WZ knew, sure as the sun would rise, that he would die cold, alone and cowardly in that box.

Chapter 92

Mental Health

ACHILLES ATTEMPTED to keep an eye on his wife during the evening's more dramatic moments, looking for signs of stress. He didn't pick up on any. In fact, she seemed every bit as psychologically balanced as he felt.

Katya watched the early scenes through the slats of the pantry door, ever ready to step in and save the day, gun blazing. But no one caught him by surprise and nothing went awry before the boys passed out and he blindfolded Luci, so Katya remained hidden. Like one of WZ's secret weapons.

Achilles' concern for his wife's mental health spiked during the burial phase. When the female conspirator opted to remain conscious, Achilles worried Katya might lose it. But again, she remained professionally placid.

Luci, by sharp contrast, completely lost control. When she caught sight of the open graves, she began screaming like a woman possessed and flailing like a fish out of water.

Achilles reacted by dropping her in the closest hole. It was only three feet deep, but he released her from waist-level, so she fell nearly seven. The impact was enough to wind her, which gave him time to toss on the lid and hop atop it.

Never in his life had he heard wailing of the sort that came while he was screwing down that plywood lid. You'd have thought he was skinning her alive. Luci's shrieking subsided after the last of the sixteen screws went in, but it resumed with even greater intensity once the first shovel of dirt hit the lid.

Ironically, those screams were a sound that Achilles would likely carry with him to his grave—hopefully many years hence. That didn't bother him, he decided while reflecting back on his night in the Mediterranean. Luci had earned the experience, and she'd been warned.

Achilles had drilled one air hole in each corner of every lid, allowing for the cross-flow of air between pipes that were just thirteen inches long. On account of them, the CEO's screams were audible even after he'd piled on and packed down a foot of dirt. But it was an oddly warped and muffled sound, one much too faint for her co-conspirators to hear.

Before entering the next phase of their long night, Achilles paused to actively take Katya's measure, lest his passive meter was misreading. An event that had been known to happen. "How are you feeling, Sweetie?"

She stopped rearranging the electronic equipment laid out before them and turned his way. "Relieved."

That sounded good. She looked good. "No internal conflicts you want to unload?"

"You know I want children, right? I mean someday, not immediately?"

Achilles hadn't expected anything close to that response. Maybe both their meters were off. More likely, he was just half-a-step too slow. "I know. I do, too."

"These people almost robbed us of that experience. And the world of our offspring. They made multiple attempts. So believe me when I tell you I have no problem with doing whatever we have to do to prevent them of robbing hundreds, thousands, maybe millions of people of their dreams—so long as it's creative."

Creative was a euphemism. One that he and his wife would likely forever associate with this night. "Well all right then. Who do you want to start with?"

"I think we should save Luci for last. She knows where they're buried and how they got there, so she may take longer to break. And I like the idea of letting William Zacharia sweat, since he's both the ringleader and likely the tougher of the two men."

"Okay, Ben it is."

Achilles plucked the high-end baby monitor labeled Ben off the UTV dashboard. He turned it on in Talk mode but said nothing. Instead they listened.

They had tested the systems earlier and found the microphones to be sensitive and the sound quality excellent. Just what you wanted with a baby monitor. Granted, their field test had been done without the dirt on the lids, but given the advertised thousand-foot range, Achilles figured that wouldn't matter. They were only about fifty feet away. Far enough that WZ and Luci couldn't possibly overhear the discussion with Ben.

He heard nothing coming from the monitor. No moans. No heavy breathing. Certainly not the anguished cries that had erupted when Ben awoke to the sound of dirt raining down on his coffin. But that had been two hours earlier. He and Katya had napped since then, and maybe somehow Ben had drifted off too. It was the middle of the night. Their biological clocks were at an ebb.

Achilles met Katya's eye and she gave a go-ahead nod. He began the interrogation with a question. "Bet you never once imagined you'd die buried alive in Mexico?"

"Hello! What? Mexico? Achilles, is that you?"

Apparently, Ben had not yet lost his marbles.

Achilles hadn't expected to find raving lunatics. His prisoners were highly accomplished CEOs. People of achievement. Fighters with brilliant minds, resilient spirits and stoic self-control. Still, the experience had to be soul crushing.

He'd spent about a minute in each buried box while they tested the sound systems. All three times, Achilles felt his stress hormones get an iron grip on his heart and begin to squeeze.

Was it possible Ben was made of tougher stuff than he? Had Achilles made a mistake by not beginning the interrogations as soon as his captives awoke? Police detectives tend to let suspects stew in a cell before questioning. Giving them an hour or so alone allows their depressing new reality to sink in and start fermenting. But perhaps in this case the reprieve had generated the opposite effect, allowing the CEOs to frame their circumstance as a hardship to be endured, like a ransom kidnapping or a prison sentence? The presence of air holes did clearly telegraph the intent to let them live.

Katya leaned in to whisper in his ear, "Don't second-guess yourself."

"Can you hear me?" Ben asked, his voice remarkably calm. "Where's the speaker?"

Achilles had attached the devices to the lids down by their shins, where they'd be away from hands, knees, and feet. He didn't want anyone inadvertently disabling their communication system by floundering around. He'd also covered the LEDs so they emitted no light.

But he wasn't going to tell Ben any of that. Best to keep him in the dark, literally and figuratively.

Achilles repeated his opening question. "Did you ever imagine you'd die buried in a box in Mexico?"

"No."

"Do you know who buried you in a box in Mexico?"

"You did, Achilles."

"After you tried to kill me and my wife, multiple times. You gave it your best shot when you were at the peak of your power, and yet there you are and here I am."

Experienced executive that he was, it didn't take Ben long to switch gears and start negotiating. "I can make you rich. Not just you, but your children and your children's children. I'm talking generational wealth."

"I'm already unbelievably rich," Achilles said, looking at his wife. "Stop stalling. The battery on the baby monitor won't last forever."

There was a long pause before Ben replied. When he came back on, his voice was notably strained. The battery revelation had clearly rattled him. No surprise there. Everyone had seen a flashlight die—but few had been the bulb. "What do you want?"

"I want you to tell me a story that's so delightfully packed with truthful detail that I'll be grateful enough to let you be the one who lives."

Chapter 93

In the Dark

BEN FOUND HIMSELF employing every trick in the book just to remain sane. He was buried alive! That had to be the greatest psychological pressure tactic ever invented. It piled on so many heavy rocks. Fear of the dark. Fear of suffocation. Claustrophobia. Arachnophobia. Loneliness. Hopelessness. Thirst and hunger. On top of which he'd already soiled his pants on both sides, leaving him suffering from foul stenches and pesky itches.

As if that weren't enough, he found himself further depressed by the thought that his bones would turn to dust in Mexico. Anonymous and undignified. He'd gone from the top of the social ladder to its bottom rung in the time it took to drink a single glass of whisky.

As he lay there absorbing the cruel blows, Ben knew he should be strategizing. Figuring out how to outwit and manipulate the man on the other side of the speaker. It was three-dimensional chess to be sure, because he also had to take Luci and William Zacharia into account. The three had to synchronize their stories.

There was no chance of that happening. Ben wasn't calm enough to competently attempt anything cerebral. And at the moment any coordination would require telepathy through a few meters of Mexican soil.

Would the others be any more composed than he was?

William Zacharia might. He was a former combat Marine, and in general one tough son of a bitch. Luci—who the hell knew? She was extraordinary on so many levels, and had probably gone through interrogation training as an Air Force pilot.

Ben found his conclusion as depressing as it was inescapable. He was the weak link.

Never in his life had he been the poor performer. Was he going to ruin that record now? Would the punctuation mark that ended his story be a question mark? Or an exclamation point?

What were his choices?

It took everything he had just to speak in a casual voice. He didn't have the wherewithal to convincingly lie his way through hours of interrogation. Not in his current condition. Not when his words could be so easily corroborated or disproved. So what was left?

Ben chewed through the skin of his lower lip before ultimately deciding that he had just two choices. He could stay silent, or he could tell the truth. Would Achilles let him out if he told the truth? Probably not. If Achilles was a cold-blooded killer, he would probably murder him whichever route Ben took. If Achilles wasn't, he'd probably let Ben out either way.

His captor had hinted at which it was. He had said, "Tell me a story that's so delightfully packed with truthful detail that I'll be grateful enough to let you be the one who lives."

"Let you be *the one*," Ben repeated to himself. Was that a bluff? Was this a competition? Were his odds of survival only one in three? Did he have any leverage? Achilles had rejected money outright.

The way Ben figured it, that left his options numbering exactly one. He gave it voice. "Get me out of here, and I'll tell you everything you want to know."

Achilles didn't reply.

The silence was maddening.

He waited.

Achilles still didn't reply.

Demons crept into the void. Taunting him. Teasing him. Dangling him before eternal darkness. Sucking his breath.

Scratching his flesh. Making him want to pound his way out of that damn coffin with his forehead.

As he inched toward madness, Ben detected movement. First vibration, then something rustling over his right shoulder. He heard it. He felt it. A shifting. Were they digging him out? Had someone else come to his rescue?

Ben waited for the sound to repeat.

It didn't.

"Help! Help! Help me! Help me, please!"

No reply. No repeat.

He continued waiting. Hearing nothing. Feeling nothing. But something had changed. What was it? There was a stronger earthy smell in the air, and the atmosphere itself seemed more stale.

An idea struck him like a punch in the nose. A terrible, horrible idea.

He strained to reach over his right shoulder. It wasn't easy, given his bonds and the structural constraints, but he managed.

The first thing he found was cool earth on his shoulder. Tiny clumps, like a fresh ant hill. The second thing was a fresh hole in the lid. Not truly fresh, just changed. As his fingers confirmed the find, his world seemed to shrink like a crumpled candy wrapper. Achilles had pulled out one of his air pipes.

Chapter 94

O Canada

KATYA WAS STILL PROCESSING Ben's surprising resilience when Achilles returned from removing one of his air pipes. As he slid into the driver's seat of their 'outdoor office,' she said, "I don't know how he kept his cool. If I woke up buried alive, I'd be hysterical."

"No, you wouldn't have been," Achilles said. "I've seen you in action. Your default setting is analytical. That's where you go when pressured. Ben's no different. While that's disappointing, I don't find it the least bit surprising, given his record."

"Should we be listening to him now?" Katya asked. They were keeping the coffin monitors turned off when not in use to help them save battery and avoid surprises.

"No. In situations like this, resolve is like porcelain, once it cracks there's no going back. Things aren't improving down there. So we're not going to miss out on a limited-time opportunity. Let him stew in silence."

Katya suspected that Achilles had actually turned off the speaker so she wouldn't be subjected to the buried man's sobs and pleas, but she let it go.

"Shall we move on to William Zacharia?" Achilles asked.

"I've changed my mind regarding sequence. I want to move on to Luci—and I want to interrogate her myself."

"Okay." Achilles handed her the Luci monitor without comment.

Katya felt the need to explain, if only to clarify things in her own mind. "I want to take a different approach with Luci. She's a blank slate, in that we haven't asked her any questions yet. She has no idea what we already know, and what we don't. What the others have confessed. She's been down there for hours, assuming the worst and lamenting her mistakes. I think I can use that situation to finesse the plan out of her."

"I think that's a great idea," Achilles said.

Katya set the monitor to *Talk*, then took a deep breath and traveled back to the scene of Luci's last human interaction. She would never forget the frantic screams that had filled the air as Achilles screwed down the lid on the female CEO's coffin. You'd have thought he'd dumped ravenous rats inside.

"Luci, it's Katya. The woman who risked her life to complete your mission. The woman you tried to murder."

Even though the words came without warning after hours of silence, Luci immediately replied. Her voice was strained and suffused with sorrow. "Katya, it wasn't me. Yes, I was part of the group but I wasn't—"

"You're going to die for your sins," Katya interjected. "But before you go. Before you waste away in an unmarked grave that may never be found, I want you to ask yourself a question—for your soul's sake. I want you to ask yourself if all the killing and conniving were worth the reward? If all the money and power you amassed during your career gave you comfort and peace? Do you think they made you happier than a typical schoolteacher?"

Katya was about to turn off the monitor, to let the earworm crawl for an hour or two, when Luci's rapid reply stopped her short. "It wasn't worth it. I wasn't happy. I was proud, and I was comfortable, but no, I suspect that I wasn't any more happy than a typical schoolteacher."

Katya looked at Achilles, who displayed a surprised smile and flashed a thumbs up. "Would you do things differently, if you could wind back the clock?"

This time Luci took longer to answer. Katya saw that as a good sign. It meant she was thinking rather than pandering or placating. "If I wound back the clock, I wouldn't know what I know now, but I'd still have the ambitious personality that's driven my life. So no, I probably wouldn't do things differently. Not without a … a … an event like this. An external shock to cause me to question both my values and my core identity. Not in our image-driven society. Not when the choice most companies give you is *climb* or *be the rung*. I'm too inherently competitive."

Katya again met her husband's eye. His face reflected the same emotions she felt. Surprise tinged with equal measures of hope and cynicism.

He prompted her onward with a nod.

She turned back to the mic. "What would you give to get a second chance?"

"Anything. Everything. I want to become a better person than I am today."

"Are you sure?"

"Let me ask you something, Katya. Do you believe that anyone has ever reflected on their life more intently than I have in this cold, dark pauper's coffin?"

Luci made a solid point. Katya decided to test it. "Tell me about the plan—from your perspective. Help me understand why you felt the need for such extreme action."

Luci didn't hesitate or push back. She dove right in, but chose a surprising pool. "Do you have any idea what it's like to run a company with hundreds of billions of dollars in annual revenue?"

"No, I have no idea."

"Of course you don't. Few do. But you do know what the CEO's job is, right? Pushing all the obfuscating, supplicating, feel-good, PR crap aside, it's really just one thing: to grow the share price. How do you grow a company of KAKO's size?"

"With something big," Katya said.

"Big would be nice. It's got to be gigantic. Few companies ever reach revenues of even one billion dollars, but I have to add twenty billion just to grow ten percent. If I do that, they pay me a fortune. If I fail, they fire me. That's the life of elite CEOs like William Zacharia, Ben and me."

"Thank you for the big picture," Katya said, her tone sympathetic. "That helps me understand. Now make it personal. Start at the beginning. Tell me the story in your words, from your perspective."

When Luci replied, her voice sounded a bit less stressed. "It began with a brilliant plan. One so big and bold that we'd never need to create another. One that would enable us to retire in wealth and glory."

Katya wanted to say, "Congratulations, you're retired," but she bit her lip and asked an open-ended question instead. "Give me your reasoning. Help me understand."

Again, Luci dove in an unexpected direction. "A few years back, your motherland annexed Crimea. This gave Russia a critically important warm-water port, and it slowed Ukraine's slide toward the West. Two huge wins for Putin. Do you know why the world let him get away with it?"

"The world didn't. There are sanctions," Katya said.

Luci chuffed. "Russia still occupies Crimea, right? That doesn't look like it's changing, does it? Putin got away with it. And the reason he got away with it was that Russia had enough of an excuse —given Crimea's history and ethnic demographics—that no other country was willing to go to war over it. Countries think three times before tangling with a military powerhouse."

Katya had no idea where this was going, but she was definitely intrigued. Luci was the last person on the planet who'd be interested in wasting time. "Go on."

"Big picture, all we're doing is replicating the Russia/Crimea situation in North America. Just bigger and better."

"Not really," Katya said.

"Yes, really. To see how it would work, all you have to do is ask yourself one question."

"I'm listening."

"What would happen if news broke showing that Canada was secretly constructing military facilities capable of obliterating many of America's major cities in minutes? Nuclear missile facilities which, due to range limitations, could only be used to attack the United States."

Katya's dropping jaw almost kept her from answering. "You tell me."

"Okay, I will. In the age of social media, public reaction would depend almost entirely on how the U.S. government decided to spin it."

"And you have the policy makers and spin machines under complete control," Katya said, as if nodding along with the logic.

"Putting them in our pocket was step one."

"So how do they spin it? What's the end result of your campaign?"

"Americans become irrepressibly outraged and understandably frightened. It's 9/11 all over again—even without the actual carnage—because tens of millions will learn that they were within missile range. That they were targeted and could have been killed at any time with no warning. Furthermore, Canada's betrayal will catch the American population completely by surprise, making voters viscerally angry."

"Keep going," Katya prompted, as fascinated as she'd ever been by anything in her life, but trying to sound bored.

"So the U.S. government acts swiftly to eliminate any possibility of a Canadian attack. The United States annexes Canada. This doubles America's land mass, thereby creating trillions of dollars of business for well-positioned U.S. companies in the defense, construction and energy industries."

"Specifically yours, Ben's, and William Zacharia's."

"As I said, it's a brilliant plan."

Chapter 95

Killer Deception

ACHILLES' HEAD WAS SPINNING like a roulette wheel at a cocaine convention. Luci's logic was sound, but the plot she'd exposed was so far beyond the envelope containing conventional thinking that he was struggling to find footing.

He looked over at his wife.

"I'll be right back," Katya said to Luci.

Once she muted the microphone, Achilles said, "I'm having difficulty processing Operation 51. Oddly enough, my first thought was that if Canada were to merge with the U.S. it would add ten states, not one. A state for each province."

"Operation 60 doesn't have the same ring to it," Katya said, her tone indicating that her thoughts were elsewhere.

"No, I suppose it doesn't."

Achilles studied his wife's expression. "You don't look nearly as surprised as I feel."

Katya sighed. "It's WMD and the Gulf War all over again. They're using a fabricated threat to justify a lucrative military action. Operation 51 is just a bit more ambitious."

"Just a bit," Achilles repeated with a roll of his eyes. "I'm at once skeptical that they could pull it off, and yet have no doubt that they're about to. I bet they gamed it out from dozens of angles and planned accordingly, planting plenty of false evidence while eliminating all real leads. I can't wait to hear the details. I already have a dozen questions and will probably have a hundred more before dawn, but the two most urgent ones are *When is this scheduled to happen?* and *What can we do to stop it?*"

Like him, Katya was clearly still chewing and swallowing. Luci's big revelation was a lot to digest. "You're right about our priorities, and I have no doubt about the public reaction. Outrage trumps reason when the rabble rousers control the microphone. But I'm not entirely convinced that Luci could achieve her predicted outcome. Surely Canada would fight annexation?"

Achilles did not share that particular skepticism. "They'll fight diplomatically, but they can't battle us in the conventional sense. The U.S. has the greatest military in the world, with Russia and China a distant second and third. Canada is something like twentieth. And it's an easy mark. More than half of the Canadian population lives on the relative sliver of land that's sandwiched between Michigan and Maine. Almost everyone else in Canada resides within one hundred miles of our border."

"So a few stragglers in the sticks aside, you believe they'd be swallowed in hours? That they'd have absolutely no chance?"

"I seriously doubt they'd even fight. The average Canadian would be both aghast at what their government was doing and loath to take up arms against their American cousins. Sure, some would call for a fight to the death to defend Canadian sovereignty, but the vast majority would vote to become part of the U.S. over the alternative. It's not like we'd be significantly changing their way of life. Certainly nowhere near as radically or traumatically as a war."

"You think it's that simple?"

"No, it would be a very bitter pill. And I'm certain that it would be both contentious and complicated. But the bottom line is that the Canadians would have no real choice."

Katya pressed on. "You're forgetting to factor in pride."

"Pride might cause the Canadians to fight *if* the U.S. just randomly decided to annex them. Heck, if there were no justification, other countries *might* even come to their defense. But by installing offensive nuclear missiles that are directed at the United States, Canada would have given the U.S. all the justification it needed."

Katya shook her head. "The missile or missiles might be there, but Canada didn't install them." The injustice of it all clearly had her rattled.

"The Canadian government will passionately deny any knowledge, of course. But given the photographic evidence, nothing they say or do will convince the scared and outraged American population that it wasn't them. Not when Canada can't credibly blame someone else."

Achilles continued thinking out loud. "The only question is whether Canada can convince another country to put their army in the path of American battle tanks—and keep the troops there long enough for the truth to emerge. Given the lack of foreign military reaction when Russia annexed Crimea, there's little chance of that happening. I doubt there would even be sanctions. Nobody wants to upset the sole superpower. Luci is right, their plan is brilliant."

Katya didn't look convinced, and she said as much. "I don't know."

Achilles understood. The idea of annexing Canada was so bold and original that it was hard to picture it being possible, even when the logic was all laid out in plain sight. But to Luci's point, bold and original was the business model these days. Just ask Uber's CEO. Or Airbnb's.

No doubt his wife also wanted to believe that justice would prevail. "Suppose sentiment sways toward believing that the Canadian government knew nothing about it. In that case, instead of being criminal, they're just grossly incompetent. All Luci's spin machine has to do is point out that gross incompetence can't be tolerated—not when it comes to protecting the American people."

Katya's expression changed as Achilles completed the big picture with that last puzzle piece. She slowly voiced the obvious conclusion. "So the result is the same no matter what Canada does. Our government still has to annex it in order to ensure America's safety. You're right."

She turned to face him. "We have to stop them. Immediately. I bet Rex isn't here because he's in Washington, preparing to steer the spin machine."

As Achilles nodded along, Katya flipped the monitor back into talk mode.

Chapter 96

Bad Conclusion

LUCI WAS ENDURING the most demanding and momentous day of her life. That was saying a lot for a woman with her record, but the competition wasn't even close. For the first time ever, she was questioning her own sanity.

She was in the midst of an event more traumatic than most could imagine. One that she probably wouldn't survive.

If she did live to see the outside of her coffin, the reprieve wouldn't be long, given that she'd committed crimes meriting capital punishment. And yet somehow, at that very moment, buried alive in a crate from which she couldn't possibly escape, Luci felt calm.

Had she snapped?

Was she so emotionally exhausted that she had nothing left?

Was she subconsciously relieved that her colleagues had spilled the beans?

Or was the catharsis of coming clean so powerful that it put her at ease?

Whatever the reason, she prayed the feeling would last. By all rights, she should have been furious, despondent or depressed. She'd come within hours of completing one of the greatest coups in business history, only to have victory yanked away—along with the spoils.

Canada was the world's fourth-largest producer of both oil and natural gas. After the annexation put its reserves in play, KAKO Energy—with its White House connections—would have locked in contracts worth hundreds of billions.

Speaking of lost spoils and unexpected emotions, she wondered if Ben and William Zacharia were also experiencing a calming catharsis. They too had lost big-time. WZ hadn't shared his calculations, but Canada was twenty times the size of Iraq and its location far more important to U.S. national security, so Steel Shield would surely have scored a staggering sum. As for Ben's windfall, the opportunities for construction contracts on a territory of that size and import were virtually limitless. The presence of a Russian missile would prove that the border was unacceptably porous. And it was a very long border.

A burst of background noise coming from the speaker attached to her coffin's lid interrupted her speculative self-reflection. Katya was back.

"Luci, what's the strategy behind the timing of the launch?"

"It allows for an emergency cabinet meeting to start and finish, and for talking points to be adopted before the morning talk shows begin."

"The Sunday morning politics shows?"

"Right."

"Who is going to be doing the spinning?"

The question jolted Luci like a log laid across the railroad track of her mind. In fact, it completely derailed both her presiding train of thought and her calm disposition. It was a request for fundamental information, rather than background perspective. And Katya wasn't just asking for an innocuous detail. She wanted Luci to name names. "Rex didn't tell you?"

Katya hesitated in her reply. When she did speak next, her tone was more telling than her words. "No, he didn't."

A shiver ran down Luci's spine. "What, exactly, did Rex tell you?"

"Not enough."

"And the others?"

"Not enough."

Luci knew evasive answers when she heard them. Katya's were telling. Concerning. They made Luci question her core assumption. Her critical assumption. Was she mistaken in believing that the others had already revealed the master plan—under duress or otherwise. No! That wasn't possible. At the very least, Rex must have cracked! There was no other way Achilles and Katya could have discovered the time and place of the C4 meeting.

Was there?

"How did you find us?"

Katya didn't answer.

"How did you connect the three of us to Rex? How did you learn about the C4 meeting?"

Again, silence.

Luci replayed their earlier discussion in her mind. Had she offered up any meaningful new information? Katya had asked her about her career and why she'd felt compelled to implement the plan. Luci had talked about her motivation and regrets. She'd highlighted the big picture, the grand design, corporate pressures and geopolitics. Stuff that would help them understand the *why* rather than the *what*. Information they needed to stand in her shoes before passing judgment.

Now that she thought about it, Luci realized that she had disclosed more. But was anything she said a revelation? New-to-them information?

Luci repeated her questions. "How did you connect us to Rex? How did you learn about the C4 meeting?"

She got no reply.

Katya had left her alone. Alone to face the truth. Rex had not spilled the beans on Operation 51. He had not cracked. He had not been captured and outwitted.

She had.

Luci had believed that her situation could not possibly get worse.

It had.

She was still alone in a pitch-black casket, but now she was buried beneath a shroud of failure and smothered by the shame of being beaten at her own game.

Chapter 97

Burden of Pride

ACHILLES TURNED to his wife as she switched off Luci's monitor for the second time. "That was great while it lasted."

"Yeah. I blew it when I asked who was going to be doing the spinning. I should have asked her to game out the spin campaign for me. The details would have slipped out as they did with the other stuff."

"Don't beat yourself up. You were remarkable, and we got enough."

Katya kept venting. "She clearly assumed that we had interrogated Rex, despite his status and security."

Achilles understood why. "She couldn't conceive of any other explanation. I'm not surprised. We did a lot of brainstorming before I remembered Rex's car phone and figured out how to clone it." He raised a finger as an idea struck. "Something else just occurred to me. Do you remember where she started her story?"

"Remind me."

"She began by explaining why the CEOs did what they did. At the time, I thought she was trying to paint herself as a victim of circumstance, but now I think it's because she assumed that we were blaming her for being the mastermind. She was looking for understanding. For sympathy and ultimately leniency."

"Why would we blame her? William Zacharia is the apparent leader."

"Because it's true, and she assumed Rex told us so."

"You think the scheme to annex Canada was her brainchild?"

"I do now. If you think back, when Luci disclosed the details, she did so with pride."

Katya thought about it. "Huh. I hadn't noticed, but now that you point it out, you're right. She did. So when I shattered her contextual framework by asking her one of the first questions we would have asked Rex, I not only pulled the rug out from under her reality, I dealt a severe blow to her already damaged psyche. I exposed her as the weakest link. The first conspirator to be duped. The traitor to the group. And intellectually inferior."

"That's my thinking. But psychology, particularly the female kind, is far from my area of expertise."

"You do all right," Katya said. "But tell me this. Do you think she was playing us? I note that the plan she outlined doesn't involve mass murder. There is no missile launch. There's just the threat. It's more Bay of Pigs than 9/11."

"It is, which lessens the crime and therefore sounds suspicious. But despite that red flag, I don't think she's lying. If her story is not entirely true, it has to be close. The plan she outlined is too tight and original to have been concocted minutes ago under duress."

Katya didn't immediately respond.

Achilles could see that she had picked up the ball and was intent on taking it further downfield. He sat silently and let her run with it.

"She referenced constructing secret military facilities capable of obliterating America's major cities in minutes. But we only stole one missile, and that was a prototype. DelMos hasn't even made enough missiles to hit all the big cities within hypersonic cruise missile range of southeast Canada: Boston, New York, Philadelphia, Washington, and Chicago. Have they?"

"I don't think so."

"Not to mention the big cities that would be out of range. Los Angeles, San Francisco, Houston, and Dallas for starters. But if you're using less sophisticated missiles, why bother adding a single cutting-edge one, at great cost and risk of exposure, especially when you're not actually going to launch it?"

"Those are great questions," Achilles agreed. "Rather than waste time speculating, I think we should interrogate William Zacharia."

Chapter 98

Detailed Disclosure

THE VOICE blasted William Zacharia back to consciousness from a trancelike mix of mental exhaustion and irrepressible fear. After hours of silently staring into the dark face of death, those words were the spoken highlight of his life. Sweeter than, "I do." More enticing than, "I will." More rewarding than, "It's you." Even though they were voiced by his enemy, rather than his wife, lover, or boss. Even though the speaker would be taking rather than giving. Because they were a sign of life.

"William Zacharia Bubb, are you ready to repent?"

His reply was immediate, sincere and enthusiastic. "Yes."

"Truly repent?"

"Yes. God, yes."

"Good. Answer all my questions truthfully, and you'll live to see daylight. But give me one misleading answer, try one deceptive trick, and—"

Achilles didn't finish the sentence. He didn't say anything. William Zacharia was left hanging there staring into the abyss. He couldn't help but ask, "And what?"

"I'll pull the pipes that deliver your air, then rake the ground. Even with dogs they won't find your body. Not that the Mexicans will be looking."

The Mexicans? Had they driven him across the border? Of course they had. Geographically, it wasn't far, but tactically it was a world away. The border separated them from his family, his lawyers, and his posse. Not that those would matter to a man who had no air. "I'll cooperate."

"We'll know if you lie. We already have the answers to half the questions. And hesitation will be equated with deception."

Power plays were familiar territory to William Zacharia. His terrain, so to speak. His only concern was getting out of that grave. Whatever that took. Locked up underground, he was helpless. Up top, he had the best lawyers in the world. And an army of mercenaries. "I understand."

"Okay. Here goes. What do you call your plan?"

"Operation 51."

"When does it launch?"

"Early Sunday morning."

"Why early Sunday morning?"

"So we're ready for the talk shows."

"Who will be spinning Operation 51 on the Sunday morning talk shows?"

"Rowe, Walker, Andrews and maybe McPherson."

"Use their titles, please."

So they were recording this. Smart move. Wouldn't matter. His lawyers would get it tossed. "White House Chief of Staff Rex Rowe. Secretary of Homeland Security Arlen Walker. Secretary of Defense Curtis Andrews. And Energy Secretary Meredith McPherson."

"What about President Saxon?"

"He's friendly, but he's not in on it."

"Have the three cabinet secretaries all been in on Operation 51 from the beginning?"

WZ hated this. Betraying his teammates was the last thing a Marine would choose to do. But they literally had him boxed in, so he couldn't even hesitate, much less negotiate. "Just Rex."

"What's your group's relationship with the others? The Cabinet secretaries?"

"They're friendly to us. To industry."

"But they're not in on the plan?"

"No."

"But you can count on them?"

"Yes."

"Did your group put them in place?"

"Yes."

"Did your group put President Saxon in place?"

"Yes."

"How?"

"The usual manipulations. Copious cash and good old-fashioned blackmail."

"But Saxon knows nothing of Operation 51?"

"No."

"If you're holding out on me hoping for a pardon, it won't work. We will put assurances in place."

"I'm sure you will. Saxon owed us for getting him elected. He paid that debt by letting us select Rex and the other three."

"So you're co-conspirators, but not colleagues?"

"That's the nature of modern presidential politics."

"What mechanism will you use to expose Canada's devious plan?"

"We're going to use the dark web to deliver a recorded, anonymous tip simultaneously to the FBI suboffice in Toronto and a variety of locations in Washington, including the Hoover Building and the White House. Plus, of course, *The New York Times*, *The Washington Post*, and other major news organizations."

"What will the tipster tell them?"

"He'll provide the exact geographic coordinates of the two secret missile installations Canada has constructed, complete with photographs."

"Whose land are they on?"

"The Canadian government's."

"How have you kept them hidden?"

"They're small needles in a huge haystack."

"Explain."

William Zacharia remembered an early C3 discussion on that very topic. "Did you know that there's a history of Mexican gangs planting fields of cannabis crops in U.S. national parks?"

"I've heard the news stories."

"Reports are they kept some fields secret for decades—and it's still going on. While that's hard to believe, take one look at a map and you'll be convinced. The parks are huge and the rangers are few. Well, Canada's population density is just one tenth that of the United States, and our launch sites are a hundred times smaller than those marijuana fields. Small needles, huge haystack."

"What will the FBI agents find when they arrive at the coordinates you supply?"

"New federal signs on old barbwire fences warning against trespassing. New buildings that appear to be old barns, housing missile launch facilities."

"How sophisticated are we talking?"

"Not very. Missiles of that category are typically launched from mobile platforms. Ships, submarines, aircraft and land-based vehicles. There's a steel launch structure and a control panel. The magic is all in the missile itself and the communications system, which is separate."

"How many missiles do you have?"

"One."

"How many nuclear warheads do you have?"

"One."

"How can you obliterate most major American cities with one missile?"

"We can't."

"So what's the plan?"

"Operation 51 doesn't require actual missile launches to work. It doesn't even require the ability to launch multiple missiles. To work, it only requires evidence of clear intent and credible potential."

"Explain."

"Canada is going to be caught in the act of preparing. There's no need to wait for their preparations to be complete. That's not just infinitely easier to orchestrate, it feeds the narrative Americans will want to believe. That their agencies are on the ball. Catching threats early."

"How does a single nuclear missile give you a strong enough story?"

"Easy. You make one missile look like it's the first of many to come by installing a bunch of other launch pads. Bear in mind, it's a fearsome weapon. Better than anything else out there. The DelMos II has a range of six hundred miles and a speed of six thousand miles an hour."

"Six hundred miles leaves a lot of the U.S. out of range."

"Six hundred miles gets us Boston, New York, Washington, Philadelphia, Detroit and Chicago from our base in Ontario. And Seattle and Portland from our base in British Columbia. But remember, without all the missiles present, there will be speculation as to which additional missiles are planned. San Francisco, Sacramento, Los Angeles, Denver, Phoenix, and Las Vegas come into play if you switch to a slower missile with a twelve-hundred-mile range. Speculation will be rampant, I assure you. Imaginations will run wild."

"What are you going to say is Canada's motive for doing this?"

"We're not. No motive is needed if you think about it. The threat is clear. The deception is clear. Canada is going to deny it, not explain it."

"How do we stop it?"

William Zacharia knew where this was going. He'd known it within minutes of waking up. What he hadn't known was whether he'd be the one to do it, or he'd be left there to die alone in the dark. Never again to see sunlight or hear another human voice. "I can stop it with a phone call."

"To Rex?"

"To Rex."

"What would you tell him?"

"I'd tell him we need to postpone for a week."

"And he'd listen?"

"Rex doesn't care. Not really. Sure, he gets a big bonus, but he's really in this because he wants to keep his job—and he wants us to do for him what we did for Saxon."

"He wants to be president?"

"Is there a politician or power broker in Washington who doesn't?"

"What will you tell him if he asks why?"

"I'll tell him it's complicated, and there's no time to get into it now but I'll call him back."

"Won't he be suspicious?"

"Of course, he will. But he won't go ahead on his own."

"Are you ready to make the call?"

"I've been ready for hours."

"I'm dialing."

William Zacharia could hear the phone ringing. He could see the pendulum of his life slowing to a stop and preparing to change direction. But that didn't happen. Rex did not pick up.

Chapter 99

Phoning It In

ACHILLES FELT like he'd arrived at the airplane gate seconds after they'd shut the door. The plane was still there, but he couldn't reach it, and in minutes it would be gone.

He wished his real situation were as trivial as that nightmare. Failing to connect William Zacharia with Rex would be far more consequential than missing a plane. If the email went out, it would open Pandora's Box. Closing it would not be an option.

Once the world saw pictures proving Canada's treachery, the pitchforks would come out. The media blitz and public frenzy that followed would blow up into an unstoppable torrent that would not end until Canada was no longer independent.

Achilles was brainstorming plans for breaking down the metaphorical airport door when William Zacharia chimed in. "I know his home number. It's a perk of being a big time donor."

"What is it?" Achilles asked, his heart still racing.

"I don't have it memorized. It's on my cell phone."

William Zacharia walked him through unlocking the confiscated phone and finding the contact. A second later, Rex's home phone was ringing.

"Hello?"

"Rex, do you recognize my voice?"

"Yes."

"Good. I tried your other number, but you didn't answer."

"I don't keep the *secure* phone on me," he said, discreetly highlighting the perilous nature of their current call. "What's so urgent?"

William Zacharia knew to play along. "That project we've been working on. Something has come up making it very important that we delay for one week."

"I see. Nothing big, I hope?"

"Just a timing issue."

"Does this have anything to do with our former colleague and his wife?"

"No. There's an issue up north."

"And we definitely have to delay? I'm concerned about that former colleague causing trouble."

"Me too. But we have no choice. Stay vigilant."

"Keep me informed." Rex hung up.

Achilles felt simultaneously euphoric and stunned. Like he'd won Olympic gold in absentia. He and Katya had just averted a major geopolitical realignment. They had literally saved Canada. The ultimate outcome was so disproportionate to the immediate input that it left him reeling.

But of course, their quest had only climaxed with a call. One relayed from a coffin through a baby monitor to a burner phone, then on to the residence of the White House Chief of Staff. Before that call came the transcontinental race. One fraught with uncertainty and danger. One forcing them to break laws and make controversial choices. One compelling them to outwit and outmaneuver some of the smartest and most resourceful people on the planet.

Suddenly the magnitude of what they'd done and how they'd done it came crashing down. The danger, the exhaustion, the sweat and sacrifice.

And they hadn't actually won yet.

They'd just earned a reprieve.

Making the peace permanent was the next step. That, and serving justice.

But first, Achilles had to hug his wife. He wrapped his arms around Katya and she around him and they cried. There in a UTV beneath a canopy of Texas trees in the middle of the night, with crickets and frogs bearing witness, but no humans walking the earth for miles around.

Achilles slowly released his love and turned back to the monitor. "Well done, William Zacharia."

"Shall we break out the champagne? After all this talking, I'm a tad thirsty." The defense contractor's voice was hoarse, as if trying to control his speech while talking through tears.

Achilles could easily imagine, if not sympathize. He too had woken up locked in a dark box once, depressed and completely disoriented. His makeshift coffin had been a bit bigger than the one WZ now occupied, but it was also underground. At the time, he hadn't been tormented by interrogators. His torture had been not knowing whether Katya was dead or alive.

He switched off the monitor and again embraced his wife.

"We did it!" Katya said, finally free to speak. "Unbelievable. I'm still in awe over the audacity and ingenuity of their plan."

"That was Luci's initial point, right? She called it the thing that most people can't comprehend, referring to the scale and stakes of hundred-billion-dollar businesses. The complexity of the schemes required to move the needle, and the extent to which chief executives will go to earn their nine-figure payouts."

"I remember."

"People subconsciously assume that those payouts are made because the CEOs' skills are so good, but at times it's because their souls are so bad. Some will do things others wouldn't ever consider."

Katya shook her head at the wonder of it all. "Ever since Luci's opening remarks, I've been pondering the forces and factors that come into play when the numbers are that big. It would take me a thousand years of teaching to earn a single CEO bonus. If I try to mentally compress a thousand years of teaching stress down to a single semester, I begin to get a feel for their shoes.

"I'm still a long way from forgiving them, but I'm closer to understanding them."

Achilles stroked his wife's wet cheek. Forgiving them? Katya was cut from different cloth than he if she could even consider it. Better cloth, he supposed. "What's your read? Should we close things out with William Zacharia now, or wrap it up with the others first?"

"You heard his voice. He's not exactly sounding authoritative at the moment."

"I suspect he'll snap back once we offer credible hope."

"You don't think the initial ask will kill him? Literally cause his heart to stop? Be the last straw?"

"He's tough. And frankly, either way I'm ready to find out."

"Your call," Katya said.

Achilles turned the monitor back on. "William Zacharia?"

"Yes."

"You've earned the right to buy your freedom."

Chapter 100

The Accounting

BEN WAS STILL BREATHING OXYGEN. After losing one of his air tubes, he had waited with unparalleled dread for a sign of suffocation beyond the anxiety he already felt. Giddiness, nausea or mental confusion. Rapid breathing or a tightness in his chest. Instead, he felt a touch of breeze near his feet. Probably thanks to a gust of wind. To his great relief, he realized that there were air holes in every corner of the coffin, not just the ones by his head.

He would not suffocate. Or at least, he had two more strikes before he'd be out. So life continued, such as it was. Trapped in absolute darkness with nothing but guilt, fear and dread to keep him company.

Achilles had put him in an impossible position. Literally and figuratively. Although the construction projects were bulletproof from the Canadian end, and all the launch site paperwork looped back to the Canadian government, and the facilities were hidden away on government land, there was a loose end. By tugging on him, Achilles could unravel the whole perfect plot.

The other C4 executives were also loose threads, of course. Had they talked? Or had they come to the same conclusion? Ben found the complete absence of information almost too much to bear.

"Ben?"

"Yes!" He shouted the reply as shock, hope and relief surged through his veins. He hadn't known whether he'd ever have human contact again.

"Your colleagues enlightened us regarding Operation 51 and your plan to rake in billions in government contracts from Canada's annexation."

Ben was so shocked by the sudden onslaught of confidential information that he didn't know what to say, so he said nothing as the implications overwhelmed his mind like marauders on a medieval castle.

"We're ready to take you up on your offer," Achilles added after a long and lonely pause.

Ben felt a rush of relief so strong he thought he might faint. He had been kicking himself ever since the last words he spoke had crossed his lips. *"Get me out of here, and I'll tell you everything you want to know."* Yet that bold gambit had somehow worked! Although given that the others had clearly caved, he didn't understand why.

He took a deep breath to calm his system down before replying. "I'm glad to hear it."

"We are going to reverse the timing, however. And alter the terms a bit. You'll get out after you tell us everything we want to know, and we come to an agreement."

Ben's heart sank.

Plummeted was more accurate.

He felt like Achilles had ripped the beating organ from his chest and tossed it off the Golden Gate Bridge toward the cold waters of the Pacific.

As silence followed and his heart sank beneath the surface, Ben couldn't refrain from venting the fear that filled his mind. "Why would you let me out after I tell you everything you want to know?"

"You'll understand that once you learn what we're asking."

The unexpected words halted his heart's chilling descent, and flashed a glimpse of the light far above. They dangled the hope that he might reach the surface before drowning. In a second, that hope would either be strengthened or dashed.

He began to tremble.

"What are you asking for?"

Achilles didn't hesitate with his comeback. "I'm asking you to repent. To shed your evil ways and become a new man. An honest man. A meek and modest man. That probably sounds like a line, but I'm sincere."

At the moment, Ben would have been excited to become anything but a man buried alive. "I'm listening."

"You're going to anonymously donate a hundred sixty-eight million dollars to charity. You get to choose which one, but it has to be a real, A-rated charity, not a lobbying organization. The Red Cross, Wounded Warriors, the Cancer Research Institute, for example."

A hundred sixty-eight million dollars! That was roughly his entire net worth. He didn't know the exact figure on his big balance sheet as his wealth was spread across various investment vehicles whose values fluctuated, but a hundred sixty-eight million was in the ballpark if all his stock options were taken into account. It was also a relatively precise figure. Not a hundred sixty million. Not a hundred seventy. A hundred sixty-eight indicated direct knowledge.

It also explained the true meaning of Achilles' meek-and-modest-man demand.

Once again, Ben cut to the crux. "What are you leaving me with?"

"You get to keep your primary residence and one million dollars' worth of liquid assets. The amount a well-educated, frugal and hardworking American of your intellect might have honestly accumulated by your age if he'd been fortunate."

From extraordinary to ordinary in the span of twenty-four hours. Not an attractive proposal, but one that beat the pants off his current predicament. Or cancer. "It's all a matter of perspective, isn't it?"

"Everyone eventually ends up in the box, Ben."

That they do. Oddly enough, the concept calmed him. "How is this going to work?"

"An accountant is going to show up at your door. You're going to enthusiastically cooperate with him or her to reassign your stock options and liquidate all assets other than your home. All but a million dollars goes to charity."

Ben hated to ask, but he had to. "Then what?"

"Then, so long as you stay on the straight and narrow, we don't have to give the FBI the recording."

"What recording?"

"The one you're going to make a few minutes from now, after you call Grausam Favlos to resign. In it, you will give a detailed timeline of Operation 51, with emphasis on the roles you, Luci and William Zacharia played in the plan to steal and smuggle nuclear weapons, with special emphasis on the repeated attempts to murder me and my wife."

The lump constricting Ben's throat turned his next words into a whisper. "What about Rex? He's wealthy, but not rich."

Achilles didn't reply immediately. When he finally did, his voice was practically a growl. "Forget about Rex. He made this personal. He betrayed me, my wife and the president—in unforgivable ways."

Chapter 101

Transformation

NOT SINCE LISTENING to her grandma read Grimm's Fairy Tales at bedtime had Katya been as fascinated by stories as she was when listening to those told by Benjamin Lial, William Zacharia Bubb, and Lucille Ferro. Every element was fascinating. Rex Rowe's discovery of the secret second page of Silver's letter to Saxon. Achilles' midnight recruitment in the Oval Office. The provision of their two-million-dollar operating fund and a genie-like "procurement officer." The purchase of a shelved nuclear warhead from a bent Russian general. The plot to kill them coming out of Churchill by blowing up a train. The stories went on and on in gripping and gruesome detail.

The taped confessions also yielded satisfying answers to all of Katya's nagging questions. *Yes*, William Zacharia was Aladdin. *No*, The Invisible Man was not a double agent. *Yes*, Sergeant Belikov and Calix were. *Yes*, Calix had an accomplice on the *Sea Star*, a Greek who went by Whistler, but *No*, the captain was not in on it. He was simply following orders from headquarters. Orders filtered down from parent company KAKO Energy, the office of the CEO, no less.

The same Steel Shield database of rough men ready to do dirty work for big bucks that had yielded the Russians and sailors had also identified the Churchill assassins and the pilot who first sabotaged the fuel pumps, then offered to kill them for a million bucks. William Zacharia assumed all three were dead. Achilles didn't correct him.

The secret launch facilities had been constructed in the middle of nowhere by Grausam Favlos affiliates. They worked like self-contained military units. All employees knew that their work was top secret, but none knew the genuine reason. Only the men who had placed the signs and misdirected the local law enforcement officers had known that their work was illegitimate. That display of ignorance stunned Katya, but Achilles assured her that big, bold moves typically sailed over the deception-detecting instincts of most people. The spy in him thought it was brilliant.

Katya found herself enthralled by these unscripted glimpses behind the curtains of power. The way the CEOs had changed the course of history by blackmailing the presidential primary frontrunner into endorsing her rival. The way they'd gained operational control over both the White House and three federal departments through that ballsy presidential quid-pro-quo.

Then there had been the less dramatic but more useful revelation of how they'd gotten the Chief of the Dallas Police Department to issue an APB for the arrest of Kyle and Katya Achilles. A situation which her husband immediately had William Zacharia rectify over the phone.

In the end, the political manipulations didn't shock her that much. She'd grown up in Russia, after all. What chilled her most was the disclosure regarding the nuclear warhead. The thought that a person could purchase a weapon with that destructive power was truly disturbing. Luci had assured them that it took more than an eight-figure bank balance. Close connections at the highest levels had also been required. That additional detail did not completely calm Katya's nerves, but since she was powerless to change it, she moved on.

She and Achilles made the three now ex-CEOs go through their stories three times on tape from the dark confines of their would-be caskets. The first to think it through. The second to flesh it out by adding in elements brought to light by the others. The third to deliver the complete story with polish.

Katya stopped the recorder as Luci finished her final retelling. She had proved the most unpredictable of the three. Her mind had worked differently from the others. Perhaps it was because she'd been conscious for the burial procedure. Perhaps it was because she'd been forced to fight harder than the men to get ahead. Maybe it was just her personality. Whatever the reason, she'd ultimately acquiesced. She'd done what it took to survive.

Katya closed by saying, "It may not feel like it now, but we're giving you a great gift. Something you've never had before."

"What's that?" a skeptical voice had asked.

"Permission to be ordinary."

Luci's final reply surprised Katya. "It's better than I deserve."

Achilles switched off the baby monitor.

"Do you think she means it?" Katya asked.

"I think spending hours staring into the black abyss of death is enough to change anyone, radically and forever. Most memories fade, but I doubt today's ever will. The process forced her to admit to herself what she'd done and who she'd become. How far she'd strayed from her own ideals.

"I can't say for sure, but I think we've given her angels the power to suppress her demons."

"Let's hope."

"I may do more than hope, if she strays," Achilles muttered.

They looked down at the dirt.

Katya reflected on how close she and her husband had come to being the ones in the boxes. She considered how easy it would be to pull the pipes, rake the leaves and walk away without leaving a trace. Physically, at least.

She didn't dwell on that idea. "How are we going to let them go?"

"Let's get everything loaded onto the UTV. The tools, the tarp, the wheels I used for the cart, and the bag with their laptops and cell phones. Everything but the cordless screwdriver and a shovel."

The packing and strapping didn't take long. While they worked, Achilles explained the rest of his plan. When they were finished, he turned on all three baby monitors. "This is the moment you've been waiting for. Your return to the land of the living. Your rebirth. We're going to dig Luci out, then leave it to her to free Ben and William Zacharia.

"Within the next few days, you'll be getting a visit from the accountant assigned to your case. Make sure you're home. He or she will remain with you until all your assets have been liquidated and duly donated. During that process, I will be getting regular updates. If I'm not satisfied, I will send your taped confessions to the media, and the FBI. If just one of you cheats, you all go down. Needless to say, the same sequence will occur if Katya and I come into any harm.

"Lest you fool yourselves into believing the wishful thinking that lawyers can get you out of this by claiming fruit of the forbidden tree or attempting other tricks—a pursuit I'm sure many law firms would be happy to attempt for a thousand dollars per billable hour —I want to point out that much of what you said can be independently corroborated. Witnesses will step forward. Records will surface. Not that it matters. The rule book won't apply. You committed treason. You conspired to acquire and import a nuclear weapon. Renege on our deal and you'll be locked in a maximum-security facility within minutes, back in a box, never to emerge again."

Chapter 102

Too Far

THEY DIDN'T ACTUALLY LIFT the lid off Luci. They just shoveled away the topsoil, then removed the sixteen screws and left. Achilles figured it was best to give her a clean rebirth. Alone in the woods with her maker. There was nothing to be gained by complicating that powerful moment with concern over appearances or awkward silences or penetrating glances. No sense in forcing her to stifle her sobbing cries or joyful tears. As far as Achilles was concerned, she was a new woman and Ben and William Zacharia were new men.

Walking away from the battleground in the dawn's early light, Achilles felt good about their act of magnanimity. For that reason, he was glad that Rex had not come.

Achilles didn't think he had it in him to forgive the chief of staff. Rex had directly and intimately betrayed him, and two presidents. He had stolen a sacred letter and perverted it for personal gain.

Whereas the three CEOs had ordered atrocities the way military generals do—anonymously and from afar—Rex had recruited Achilles face to face. He'd looked him in the eye and told the vilest of lies. Nonetheless, if that had been it, Achilles might have been able to get past the betrayal—if Rex had been close to the end of his career like the others. If his wealth and pride could be as easily and permanently stripped. But Rex wasn't and it didn't matter, because the chief of staff had also committed an unforgivable offense. He'd gone too far, and he'd made it personal when he involved Achilles' wife.

Achilles let Katya do the driving so he could send two texts and make two calls. Both texts were to The Invisible Man. With the first, Achilles requested the names of three specialized accountants. The kind The Invisible Man had used to track down and value the three CEOs' assets. People who could emerge from the ether to oversee the liquidation and transfer of those assets.

His second text was to request that The Invisible Man establish an impenetrable place in the cloud that would dispatch recorded copies of the CEOs' confessions if Achilles didn't log in to reset the timer once a month.

Both texts were met with affirmative replies. The second added that his retainer was drained. Any further requests would require another hundred-thousand-dollar deposit.

Achilles' first call was to Monterey, California. His second was to the Dallas Executive Airport to book a late afternoon flight—to Monterey, California. Both calls were also successful.

"That pretty much polishes off our operational budget," he said, hanging up on the charter service.

"We blew through the whole two million?"

"There's still enough to finance a first-class trip to Fiji."

"I should hope so," Katya said with a laugh.

They were both a bit giddy. The last twenty-four hours had been incredibly intense, and they knew they faced some tense times ahead. That was why he'd chartered the flight for the afternoon rather than the morning.

"Let's find a motel. The kind that takes cash. We'll grab a shower and a nap before heading to the mall and then the airport."

"The mall?"

"We need to upgrade our outfits."

Katya looked down at her filthy black sweats. "Good point. Why a hotel that takes cash? You're not completely confident that the APB has been canceled, are you?"

"I'm confident that it's canceled. I heard the Police Chief confirm it. But I'm not certain everyone got the word. Getting arrested before Monterey would at best be extremely awkward."

Half an hour later, they paid cash and were not arrested.

They took long showers and longer naps.

They hit the mall, shopped and changed.

Then they flew private from Dallas to Monterey. They slept for most of the three and a half hours, landed just before eight o'clock, and stepped directly into a waiting rental car.

Achilles called ahead when they were a quarter mile from the guard house. "We're turning onto your road now in a silver Audi A4."

"Give me two minutes."

They waited by the side of the winding, tree-lined coastal road for exactly that long.

The heavy iron gate opened as if triggered by their headlights, causing floodlights to come on. The illumination revealed a tall, lean man with aquiline features and a thick head of hair that matched his name. He was standing behind an ornamental barricade off to one side. He wore jeans and a sport jacket over a white polo shirt. The Secret Service agent to his right wore a dark suit, ear phone and sidearm.

President Silver said something to his bodyguard. Whatever it was, the agent didn't visibly react.

"Best to keep your hands in plain sight," Achilles told his wife, putting the car in Park and killing the ignition. The agents would move the Audi wherever they wanted it. He'd leave the key inside.

"Pleasure to see you, Kyle. Thank you for bringing your beautiful wife. Good to see you, too, Katya," Silver said, kissing her cheek after shaking Achilles' hand. "Are you hungry? I don't usually eat so late, but the Japan trip has my stomach off schedule."

"Very kind of you," Achilles said. "Our schedules have been a bit hectic of late as well."

Achilles hadn't known what kind of a reception to expect. Silver had so many acquaintances, literally thousands of people with whom he'd intersected over the years. Most had either donated to his campaigns or, like Achilles, had otherwise aided his administrations. Despite the magnitude of Achilles' contribution, it was hard to know what status that genuinely left him with in the former president's mind. What Silver really thought of him. He was a professional politician after all, and men of his stature surely weighed contributions on a gargantuan scale.

According to the preliminary evidence, Achilles' decided that his status was pretty good.

They sat in a dining nook rather than the kitchen or the formal dining room. Achilles was certain that it afforded a breathtaking view of the Pacific Ocean during the day, but the way Silver had the landscaping backlit also made it beautiful at night.

Three plates were waiting beneath silver domes. Evidence of domestic help trained to be invisible as elves. Silver set his lid aside revealing a steak salad. Achilles and Katya did the same.

The president filled crystal glasses with Napa Cabernet, raised his own and said, "Here's to the United States of America."

They touched glasses.

"That's why you risked coming to see me, I believe," Silver added after a swallow. "Despite the APB and Secret Service warning?"

"Yes, Mr. President. May we tell you a story?"

Forty-Eight Hours Later
Camp David

Chapter 103
The Judge

STANDING BEFORE A BIG WINDOW in a back room of the Aspen Lodge, Achilles watched with fascination as Marine One approached over the woods from Washington. A growing green object cutting across a backdrop of thunderous gray clouds.

He and Katya had seen the helicopter numerous times on TV. Most people had. But watching it live was a very different experience. Knowing the power of the machine and the men inside, Achilles felt the trepidation of a knight catching sight of a fire-breathing dragon.

An epic battle was coming. After weeks of skirmishes, the big clash was but minutes away.

President Silver turned from the window, not toward the door, but in Achilles' direction. "One last question before this begins. One I've been puzzling over."

"Please."

"You and I go way back. We've seen things. Done things. And we're both retired from government service now. We can be honest."

"Yes, Mr. President."

"Why are the three CEOs still breathing?"

Achilles relaxed as he mused at Silver's ironic choice of words. He had not shared the details of what happened at Lonestar Lodge.

Just the outcome. He didn't want that story circulating, for many reasons. For them, for him, for the country. Achilles also didn't care to share anything too intimate at that moment. Not while he was mentally armored up for battle. "In a nutshell, we decided that the world would be better served by half a billion dollars in charity donations than by one couple's revenge."

Silver raised an eyebrow. "You let them buy their freedom?"

"Practicality over pride. Besides, they've changed."

"Really?" Silver sounded skeptical.

"Trust me, they're not the same people they were a few days ago. And I assure you, one way or another, they never will be again."

Silver let that message percolate and its implications resonate before responding. "How did you do it? How did you get three of the toughest, smartest, richest people on the planet to confess to treasonous conspiracies and capital crimes on tape? There are some dedicated patriots over in Langley and down in Guantanamo Bay who would love to know."

"With all due respect, I believe it's best if they don't. Best if you don't know either, Mr. President."

Silver nodded slowly.

"Good luck, sir."

President Preston Saxon had agreed to his predecessor's request for an urgent but unspecified meeting at the official presidential retreat. A one-on-one meeting. Camp David was just a thirty-minute helicopter flight from the White House, but a five-hour jet ride from Monterey. The optics were right. The ego was right. The curiosity irresistible.

"How long do you think this will take?" Katya asked, once the door closed behind Silver. The waiting was going to be tough.

"I don't know and I hesitate to speculate. Could be minutes, could be hours. It's like a court deliberation with a jury of one."

"I think they call that a bench trial. Those use a judge, not a jury," Katya's tone implied an attempt to lighten the mood. She added, "Is a short meeting better for us, or a long one?"

"Hard to say. But if we catch sight of an approaching Marine fire team, that's almost certainly not a good sign."

Katya began browsing a coffee table book. "Did you know this place used to be called Shangri-La?"

Achilles did not. "I thought Shangri-La was a fictional location. Someplace in the Himalayas?"

"It is. The name comes from the first mass-market paperback book, the 1933 novel *Lost Horizon,* by British author James Hilton. President Roosevelt changed the retreat's name from Hi-Catoctin to Shangri-La after reading it. Eisenhower then renamed it Camp David in honor of his father and grandson."

Achilles grew a wry smile. "The use and abuse of presidential power has grown quite a bit since Ike's days."

They lapsed into contemplative silence, with Katya continuing to flip pages and Achilles practicing memory tricks with a deck of cards. It was an hour to the minute after Silver left when a lone Marine knocked on their door. He told them it would likely be an hour more.

The same Marine returned sixty minutes later, but this time he was accompanied by a steward toting a large tray of fruit, cheese and crackers. Plus fresh pots of coffee and chamomile tea. "It will likely be another hour."

The third hour came and went without sight of the Marine. He knocked for the final time midway through the fourth hour, then invited them to the big room before vanishing into the woodwork.

Country-style armchairs and couches surrounded a large square coffee table in the middle of the living room. The scene, like the rest of the lodge, reminded Achilles of rental-property photos he'd seen on Airbnb. Not the five-star celebrity retreats that went for four or five figures a night. The three-star listings you could snag in the off-season for a hundred bucks. It appeared so ordinary relative to the business that took place there, that it brought to Achilles' mind a phrase from the Gettysburg Address: "… *government of the people, by the people, for the people* …"

President Saxon was sitting in one of the armchairs.

President Silver was nowhere to be seen.

Chapter 104

The Marines

PRESIDENT SAXON LOOKED in their direction as Achilles and Katya drew near, but his mind's eye clearly remained elsewhere. "Please, sit down."

Saxon added nothing once they took seats on the edge of the couch. As Achilles attempted to divine the proper protocol for such a situation, a distant toilet flush cleared things up.

President Silver joined them some seconds later, reclaiming the armchair he'd obviously vacated after sending the Marine to fetch them.

Silver's return also brought Saxon back to the moment. The current president shifted in his seat so that he could face Achilles directly. "The missile you acquired is about to be airlifted to a Naval base in Rochester, New York. From there, it will disappear.

"Later today, two detachments from the Army Corps of Engineers will break off from their training exercises and begin dismantling the launch pads. They will leave nothing but the concrete floors and wooden shells behind. It is my sincere hope that the Canadian government will never know what was there."

Achilles sat silently, trying to maintain a neutral facial expression. He was certain that Katya was doing the same.

"Also later today, I'll be having a discussion with the Director of the CIA. I'm going to have him find a way to anonymously alert President Putin about the role a certain Army general and Navy captain played in making one of his nuclear warheads disappear."

Achilles was certain that the interrogation General Gromov and his friend faced would not be "creative." The Kremlin played by old-school rules using old-school tools. He had no problem with that, and saw by his wife's expression that she didn't either. They gave Saxon approving nods.

So far, it had all been good news, very good news, but the big news was yet to come.

In a sign that the main course was about to be served, Saxon glanced at his knees before looking back up. "Before the end of the year, Homeland Security Secretary Arlen Walker, Defense Secretary Curtis Andrews, and Energy Secretary Meredith McPherson will all resign. President Silver and I considered dismissing them later today, but that would put the investigative journalists into high gear.

"I will not be resigning. But I will not be seeking reelection either. I'll be throwing my full support behind Vice President Joy Hughes."

Achilles said nothing.

Katya said nothing.

He was pleased, and knew Katya would be too, but it wasn't really their place to comment.

Saxon continued after a slight pause. "I trust we can all agree that the country would best be served if the press did not get wind of Operation 51?"

That was the billion-dollar question, wasn't it? Achilles had his own opinion and he was certain that Katya had hers, but neither of them were experts in running a country.

One of Achilles' pet peeves was the way so many people trusted their gut judgment over the opinions of experts when it came to political affairs. They deferred to lawyers for legal issues and consulted doctors for health concerns. They called plumbers to unclog toilets and electricians to change fuses. But for some reason every Tom, Dick and Harry believed in his own ability to fix the infinitely more nuanced and complicated affairs of state.

Fortunately, Achilles had one of the world's leading experts on government sitting to his right. A venerated professional who had the added advantage of not belonging to President Saxon's political party. Achilles turned to Silver.

Silver simply nodded.

"We are in agreement, Mr. President," Achilles said to Saxon.

"Thank you, Mr. Achilles. Mrs. Achilles. I'm very glad to hear it."

With the big issue done and dusted, President Saxon picked up the phone on the end table to his right and said, "We're ready."

Seconds later, they heard a procession of cars come to a stop before the front door, then lots of doors opening and closing. Achilles looked at Katya and Silver. The former President seemed unperturbed. Katya displayed a touch of the anxiety Achilles felt.

Marines began trooping in through the front door. First two, then four. While they split to form a human corridor, Katya put her hand on Achilles' knee. As she did so, Rex Rowe walked into the room. He was followed by four more Marines.

Rex walked over to stand at the open side of the coffee table.

He was clearly attempting to look relaxed, but finding it difficult to ignore the two fire teams of Marines or the other three unexpected people in the room. "You sent for me, Mr. President."

Saxon didn't bother with introductions or a greeting. He got straight to business. "President Silver has just described to me in detail some treasonous recordings that have come into his possession. Four of them, to be precise. You star in one. William Zacharia Bubb, Benjamin Lial and Lucille Farro narrate the others. Shall we listen to them all together, or would you prefer to resign right now and save yourself the embarrassment?"

Dallas, Texas

Chapter 105

Invisible

CECILIA VON SPEE jumped in her seat as a grenade bounced off her desk and smacked against one of the framed movie posters on her office wall, cracking the glass over Gordon Gekko's face before thunking onto the thin gray carpet.

Marcus Devereaux followed his toy through her door. "Oh, jeez, Cece, I'm sorry. I got excited. Wasn't thinking. I'll have it replaced."

She shifted her gaze from the damaged *Wall Street* poster to the practice grenade on her floor, then back up to her visitor. Only at a defense contractor could you get away with a stunt like that. "Don't worry about it. What's got you excited?"

Her fellow digital spy stepped toward the cracked glass for a closer look. "At least it wasn't your favorite."

"It's all right. Time to rotate in a new poster anyway. Did you want something? I'm busy."

Marcus grew a grin. "Did you hear the news?"

Cece took a calming breath and closed her laptop lid. "What news?"

"They named Ellis CEO."

Steel Shield had been operating without a chief executive since William Zacharia's sudden resignation. His unexpected move had caught the board flat footed and left every employee nervous from the knowledge that whoever replaced the founder was sure to shake things up.

"It's a dream come true," Marcus continued. "With one of us in the big chair, Cybersecurity will finally get its due."

"You're probably right," Cece said flatly.

Marcus retrieved his toy and began tossing it hand to hand while studying her face. "You don't seem surprised."

She shrugged. "It was predictable. Our division may be relatively small, but it's both the fastest growing and the most profitable."

"I didn't see it coming," Marcus said.

He stopped fidgeting as an idea struck. "Hey, you'll probably get Ellis's job. You've always been his favorite."

Cece shook her head. "I don't want it."

"Yeah, right. VP's gotta pay close to half a mil, including stock options. Don't tell me you wouldn't take it. Greed is good, right?" he added, quoting Gordon Gekko.

Cece appreciated the *Wall Street* reference, but a different Gekko line was on her mind. *The most valuable commodity I know of is information.* "It's a work-life balance thing."

"Cece, you're single and you already work around the clock."

"By choice, on both accounts. Speaking of work, I need to get back to it." She tapped her laptop. "I have a very demanding client."

"Seems you always do," Marcus said, rising. "Plan on drinks at Midnight Rambler after work. I'm sure the team will be going out to celebrate." He stopped in the doorway. "Really sorry I ruined your *Wall Street* poster. At least it wasn't *The Invisible Man*."

One Month Later

San Francisco Bay Area

Epilogue

KYLE ACHILLES SLID the Fiji guide onto the *visited* side of their travel bookshelf. He loved seeing that section grow. Every inch of occupied space represented a victory in the great war. A win against the unconquerable foe called time.

"You were right about the sharks," Katya said. "I never would have thought that diving thirty meters beneath the waves to swim with carnivorous monsters could be a blast, but I was mesmerized. I'll never forget it."

"Glad you enjoyed it," he said, stepping in for a hug.

"Just promise me we won't swim near the carnivorous monsters circling the White House anytime soon."

"Only if you promise me to wear your bathing suit around the house. I can't get that little red one out of my mind."

Katya pushed him away, but he could see that she was pleased.

"Not all the time. Just when the sun is shining," he added.

"We live in California, Achilles. It's always sunny."

A loud knock on the front door turned both their heads. Achilles stepped around his suitcase and glanced through the peephole.

"Who is it?" Katya asked.

"Two men in dark suits."

"Mormons?" she asked with a hopeful lilt.

"They're wearing earpieces and coordinated lapel pins. Secret Service." He opened the door.

"Welcome home, Mr. Achilles. Mrs. Achilles. Please come with us."

"Now?" Katya asked. "Sorry. Stupid question."

The black SUV with tinted windows took Middlefield Road to the Oregon Expressway, then turned south on the 101. Fifteen minutes after the knock, they exited the freeway into Moffett Field, home of the historic landmark Hangar One. Normally, Achilles would have found his eyes riveted to the colossal Depression-era dirigible hangar, which had a footprint the size of six football fields and was tall enough to form its own atmosphere, but today his eyes went straight to an adjacent airplane.

While technically a Boeing VC-25, structurally the aircraft looked like a typical 747. The famous light-blue nose and stripe were what made it distinctive, while the round door seal and long bold fuselage inscription left no doubt: UNITED STATES OF AMERICA.

The driver parked before the red carpet at the foot of the airstair. The other agent opened the passenger door and let them out. As Achilles and Katya ascended, an attractive flight steward stepped into view—backed by two additional Secret Service agents. She addressed them with a smile as they stepped inside. "Welcome aboard Air Force One. President Saxon will see you in his office." She motioned to the interior stairway leading up from the middle of the room.

Achilles was not a fan of politics or politicians in general, and the revelations he'd heard in Texas regarding how Preston Saxon had become his party's nominee and who had financed his campaign, did not make Achilles particularly fond of this one. Achilles had been blunt about that with former President Silver during their flights to and from Camp David.

Silver had gone on to surprise him, twice. First by getting Saxon to agree not to seek a second term. Then, in a somewhat contradictory move, by suggesting that they evaluate the player separately from the game.

He had noted that the C3 picked Saxon, not the other way around, and he urged Achilles to judge Saxon on his actions as president alone. "If I were to intentionally shoot a man who was walking across a field, you would call me a murderer and you'd be right." Silver had paused there to dramatically raise a finger, "Unless my country had declared war with his. Then you'd call me a soldier. Perhaps even a patriot.

"Politics is a battle. A high-stakes war. When it comes to what the Executive Branch can and cannot do, the Constitution, Congress and Supreme Court set the rules. I'm not endorsing what politicians do. I'm saying you need to consider the circumstances.

"You, Kyle Achilles, know well that right and wrong are not the simple constructs some people want them to be. The world is a very complicated and nuanced place. The wise educate themselves enough to tackle it with an insider's perspective."

"And the brave change the rules," Achilles had replied, in his head.

But it wasn't the president's transgression that was on Achilles' mind as he climbed the stairs. It was his own.

Saxon was reading a handwritten letter as Achilles and Katya entered his aerial office. Studying it was probably a more accurate description. He set it down a few seconds after they entered. "Katya, Kyle, thank you so much for coming. My apologies for the short notice."

"Our pleasure, Mr. President," they both said.

"Please have a seat. There's chamomile tea in the silver pot and fresh coffee in the carafe."

They sat.

"Nice to see you looking tanned and refreshed. I trust Fiji agreed with you?"

"It was wonderful," Katya said.

Saxon turned to pick up a different document while they filled their cups. A classified report in a Justice Department binder. He set it down before him on the desk and tapped the cover twice. "As I'm sure you heard, Rex Rowe died during your vacation."

Achilles nodded.

"He flew to Vanuatu the day after our last meeting, the one you participated in at Camp David. That's where his body was found.

"Vanuatu was an odd choice, one might think, considering that it's halfway around the world from D.C. It's a beautiful island paradise, to be sure, and the French heritage lends it both a sophistication and a culinary scene that aren't common in the tropics. But I suspect that it had another draw for Rex. Can you guess?"

Achilles could. "No extradition treaty."

Saxon tapped the report again. "Exactly. Vanuatu doesn't have an extradition treaty with the United States. When considering the countries in that category, Vanuatu becomes a much more obvious choice."

Saxon shifted in his seat. "Vanuatu's not far from Fiji, is it?"

Achilles didn't twitch. "They're both in Oceania."

"They tell me Fiji Airways flies there direct. It's just a two-and-a-half-hour ride."

Katya and Achilles said nothing.

Saxon opened the classified report, exposing a gruesome picture. "Rex was found hanging from the ceiling fan of his over-water bungalow. Gave the morning maid quite a shock. There were no signs of struggle in the room, however he did appear to have changed his mind after kicking the chair aside."

"I hear that's not uncommon," Achilles said. "Buyer's remorse, so to speak."

"So they tell me. They also tell me that a large dose of Flunitrazepam was found in his bloodstream. That's the benzodiazepine known in the United States as Rohypnol. The date rape drug.

"Turns out Flunitrazepam is legal in some sixty countries, including Oceania's own Australia, where it's sold as Hypnodorm, and New Zealand, where it's sold as Flunepan." Saxon looked up from the report. "They found a box of Flunepan on Rex's nightstand. Most of the pills were missing."

"I hear it's prescribed for anxiety and insomnia," Achilles said.

"Indeed it is. That's right here in the report. Easy for a person in the know to understand why Rex might need medication for those conditions. Not that you or I would ever permit those reasons to come out, in court or elsewhere," Saxon added, his eyes locked on Achilles. "Anyway, those are the details. The official findings of a case now closed. I thought you'd want to know. As a professional courtesy."

Achilles nodded.

Saxon set the report aside and returned to the handwritten letter he'd been reading when they walked in. His expression changed as he picked it up, softening noticeably. "I have a confession to make. I wanted nothing to do with President Silver when I first moved into the Oval Office. It was arrogance. I can admit that now that I've spent some time behind the big desk.

"He left me a letter, as outgoing presidents do. It was the first thing I read after taking the Oath of Office. The only thing on my new desk.

"Silver's letter was brief, as handwritten documents tend to be. But there were two very wise bits of advice contained therein that I'm now hoping to heed." Silver picked up the pages. "The first comes in the final paragraph of the main letter. 'I wish I'd ignored anyone lobbying for self-serving reasons. The people pushing agendas that benefit others proved to be the few worth heeding. The ones that ultimately made it easier for me to look in the mirror. The rest invariably became dangerous distractions.'"

Saxon set the first page aside. "That sounded like fanciful poppycock the first and only time I read it back then. Now it reads like a lifeline for my soul."

Achilles said nothing.

"The second page of the letter no longer exists in the original. It was a standalone document. A postscript not meant to go into the official record. I crumpled it up and tossed it in the trash. Rex obviously fished it out, read it, absorbed it, and then shredded it. This is a photocopy President Silver was kind enough to provide." Saxon held up the second page, but then set it too aside. "The last line ends, 'when you find yourself needing something important done discreetly, call Kyle Achilles.'"

Saxon folded his arms and frowned. "Knowing what I now know, I can confidently state that President Silver was only half right." He leaned forward. "He should have advised me to call Kyle *and* Katya Achilles."

He smiled.

They smiled.

"What do you say, Katya? Kyle? Can I call on you, from time to time, to assist a grateful president?"

ALSO BY TIM TIGNER

Standalone Novels
Coercion, Betrayal, Flash, Leonardo and Gabriel,
The Price of Time, The Price of Mind

Kyle Achilles Series
Pushing Brilliance, The Lies of Spies,
Chasing Ivan, Falling Stars, Twist and Turn

NOTES ON BOUNDLESS AMBITION

Please find below the web addresses for articles and videos supporting many of the key concepts and elements in BOUNDLESS AMBITION. All these and more are also available on my Pinterest page: www.pinterest.com/authortimtigner/research-for-boundless-ambition-kyle-achilles-5/

- To see where all the world's ships are, click here: www.marinetraffic.com

- The real DelMos Russian-Indian joint venture: en.wikipedia.org/wiki/BrahMos-II

- The Cliff Diving championship Achilles and Katya watched: www.youtube.com/watch?v=cXzNJ1kps9g

- A cargo ship tour: www.youtube.com/watch?v=o2RfyGcRVcI

- Using "+" or "infinite" emails: gizmodo.com/how-to-use-the-infinite-number-of-email-addresses-gmail-1609458192

- Unlocking cars and garages: www.wired.com/2015/08/hackers-tiny-device-unlocks-cars-opens-garages/

- The trillions the United States sinks into foreign wars: watson.brown.edu/costsofwar/files/cow/imce/papers/2019/US Budgetary Costs of Wars November 2019.pdf

- The billions a Defense Contractor earned off a war its former CEO orchestrated: www.businessinsider.com/halliburton-company-got-395billion-iraq-2013-3

- The 22 million "missing" emails related to the Defense Contractor/White House fraud: www.newsweek.com/2016/09/23/george-w-bush-white-house-lost-22-million-emails-497373.html

- My shark dive, 30 meters down in: www.youtube.com/watch?v=dFxYIXBPbzQ&t=13s

The Price of Time

1
One Problem

Palo Alto, California

December 24, 1999

PIERCE DUBOIS bunched his beefy fists, attempting to mask his irritation. He was unaccustomed to discourtesy. Certainly not from people whose paychecks depended on his support. Certainly not after being summoned a thousand miles on Christmas Eve.

What couldn't wait a few weeks until the quarterly meeting? Did the offending executives somehow sense what their angel investor had planned? Had they divined that he wanted to call it quits after seven disappointing years, to enter the new millennium free from past mistakes—and quarterly million-dollar payments? Could this power play be the CEO's last grasp at dignity, at going out on her terms?

Pierce hoped he had it wrong. That they'd found another investor. Someone who'd keep the research progressing toward a possible payout. But as he sat there waiting for the tardy executives to arrive, he wasn't holding his breath.

He shifted his gaze from the three empty chairs to the five faces that had gathered around the Silicon Valley conference room table. A table that, like everything else in the adjacent offices and laboratory, Pierce had paid for. Three bright-eyed scientists, an administrative assistant, and the CFO all sat quietly, studying papers and avoiding their investor's eye.

Despite their cloaked responses and coy behavior, Pierce sensed suppressed energy in the room. Something was up and dammit they knew what it was. But they weren't sharing.

Irritated by the petty game, he picked up his phone and called his driver—who was also his pilot. Pierce hadn't become wealthy by wasting money. "We may be heading home momentarily. Be sure the plane's ready."

"Yes, sir."

Yes, sir. Now that was a proper response. *We don't know where they are, but surely they'll be here shortly sounded infinitely less satisfying.*

Punching off his phone, Pierce decided that he had never really cared for any of the Eos team. Their science, yes. He loved that. Their work ethic, fine. Seven of the eight were married to the job and only the job, so they put in the hours. But the lot of them were more sheep than wolf. Sure, Lisa Perera, the CEO, could show some tooth. And Felix Gentry, the CFO, occasionally displayed a full set of incisors. Neither, however, was a true carnivore. Neither was part of his pack.

Sounds of activity resonated from the outer office as Pierce picked at a pesky splinter in his left forefinger. A remnant of his last wood-chopping workout. The commotion had to be coming from the missing execs. Eos Pharmaceuticals only had eight employees.

All heads turned toward the door as Lisa Perera and David Hume entered the conference room. She wore the confident countenance of the consummate CEO but appeared more shaken than defiant. The Chief Scientific Officer was much less guarded. He wore a dazed stare and strode without his usual spring.

Neither apologized for being late.

Lisa sat at the end of the table opposite Pierce. David settled into one of the two empty chairs to her left. She took a deep breath and said, "We've just come from Kirsten Besanko's house."

All eyes turned toward the sole empty seat while Lisa continued. "She passed away this morning. Her husband found her in the pool when she didn't come in for breakfast after her morning swim."

Gasps erupted around the table.

Allison began sobbing without abandon.

Lisa answered the obvious question. "The paramedics aren't sure what happened. Probably a stroke or heart attack."

"She was only thirty-three," Ries said.

"She was six months pregnant," Allison sobbed, adding, "She didn't want anyone to know."

Pierce saw shock register on a few faces—but not all. To him, the information was anything but surprising. It implied the answer. Pregnancy significantly increased the odds of having a stroke.

He didn't mention the connection. He hadn't flown all the way from northern Montana to talk about Kirsten. Best to move things along. "Why don't we knock out this meeting so you can move on to personal matters? Lisa, you said we had something supremely important to discuss."

The CEO struggled to pull herself together, taking a deep breath while momentarily closing her eyes. It was the first time Pierce had seen her anything but perky and polished.

With a photogenic face and an all-American fencer's quick wits, Lisa Perera was more handsome than pretty. She had shoulder-length brown hair complemented by bright brown eyes and a smile that effectively camouflaged a computer-like brain. Pierce expected her to end up hosting a talk show—once her biotech career bombed.

"Yes, of course," Lisa said, snapping herself back into form with a transformation that was both audible and visible. "Thank you for interrupting your holiday to join us on such short notice."

Pierce decided to set the tone then and there. "You didn't give me much choice on the phone. Or much information."

"As I said, some messages really must be delivered in person. On that note, I'm going to pass the baton to David. He's earned the honor."

David Hume, MD, PhD, and CSO, was the reason Pierce had funded Eos Pharmaceuticals. When he invested, Pierce bet on people. Despite delivering disappointing results for seven consecutive years, the Chief Scientific Officer still struck Pierce as the smartest man he'd ever met.

Unfortunately, intelligence wasn't everything.

David stepped up to the proverbial plate by lifting his head. As he prepared to speak, the fire reignited in his eyes. "It took forty-two more iterations than I would have liked, and nearly twice as many as I predicted when we first took your money, but forty-three proved to be the lucky number."

Pierce felt his heart palpitate. *Did David just say lucky?* "You succeeded?"

"We did," David confirmed, his exuberant expression blasting away all doubt. "Our latest compound keeps telomeres completely intact through thousands of cellular reproductive cycles. There's zero degradation."

Telomeres were like metal tips on the ends of DNA zippers. They kept the long strands from getting fouled up during the unzipping and re-zipping process at the core of cellular reproduction. When telomeres malfunctioned, people got cancer. When they wore down, people aged. By keeping telomeres in pristine condition, Eos—the name of both their product and their company—would act like the elixir of immortality.

At least in theory.

Pierce couldn't believe his ears, even though he had been fantasizing about this moment for seven years. "What are you telling me?"

David's enthusiastic gaze didn't waver. "Without extensive, long-term clinical trials, I can't be definitive. But at this point, and by all indications, we believe we can arrest human aging with two shots of Eos a year."

"What!"

"People won't age a day after their first injection."

Pierce found himself speechless but quickly recovered. This was definitely too good to be true. "How confident are you in your findings?"

"Confident enough to start using it." David gestured around the table. "All of us have."

Pierce felt like they'd just attached jumper cables to his dreams. If David and the others believed in the safety and efficacy of Eos enough to use it on themselves, then they weren't puffing him up as part of a pitch. When it came to science and safety, these were serious people. The leaders in their field. "I was only hoping for a slow-down. The ability to buy a few more years. Maybe a decade. You're telling me you invented immortality?"

David raised a palm, but the other research scientists' microexpressions might as well have been nods. Ries, Eric, and even Allison grew glows of pure pride. "No, far from it. People who take Eos can still die from any number of causes."

"Just not old age," Pierce confirmed.

"That's what all our evidence indicates."

Pierce found himself propelled to his feet by an irrepressible burst of energy. "Well, Merry Christmas! We're about to become the richest people on the planet."

His mind plowed forward as he paced. "If what you say is true, Eos is worth more than all the oil in Saudi Arabia. There's nothing people won't pay, and there's nobody who won't pay it. The big pharmaceutical companies will go nuts at auction. We'll get hundreds of billions for the rights." Pierce ran rough calculations as his lips and legs expelled excess energy. Expected purchase price. Anticipated royalty stream. His percentage ownership. He'd just become the wealthiest man alive—even if nobody knew it.

David raised his other palm, halting Pierce's pacing. "There is one problem. We can't sell it."

ABOUT THE AUTHOR

Tim began his career in Soviet Counterintelligence with the U.S. Army Special Forces, the Green Berets. With the fall of the Berlin Wall, Tim switched from espionage to arbitrage and moved to Moscow in the midst of Perestroika. In Russia, he led prominent multinational medical companies, worked with cosmonauts on the MIR Space Station (from Earth, alas), and chaired the Association of International Pharmaceutical Manufacturers.

Moving to Brussels during the formation of the EU, Tim ran Europe, Middle East, and Africa for a Johnson & Johnson company and traveled like a character in a Robert Ludlum novel. He eventually landed in Silicon Valley, where he launched new medical technologies as a startup CEO.

Tim began writing thrillers in 1996 from an apartment overlooking Moscow's Gorky Park. Twenty years later, he's still writing. His home office now overlooks a vineyard in Northern California, where he lives with his wife Elena and their two daughters.

Tim grew up in the Midwest. He earned a BA in Philosophy and Mathematics from Hanover College, and then an MBA in Finance and a MA in International Studies from the University of Pennsylvania's Wharton School and Lauder Institute.

Made in the USA
Middletown, DE
14 May 2020